Books by B. V. Larson:

STAR FORCE SERIES
Swarm
Extinction
Rebellion
Conquest
Battle Station
Empire
Annihilation
Storm Assault
The Dead Sun
Outcast
Exile
Gauntlet
Demon Star

REBEL FLEET SERIES
Rebel Fleet
Orion Fleet
Alpha Fleet
Earth Fleet

Visit BVLarson.com for more information.

Steel World

(Undying Mercenaries Series #1)
by
B. V. Larson

Undying Mercenaries Series:
Steel World
Dust World
Tech World
Machine World
Death World
Home World
Rogue World
Blood World
Dark World
Storm World
Armor World
Clone World
Glass World
Edge World

Illustration © Tom Edwards
TomEdwardsDesign.com

ISBN-13: 978-1493680559
BISAC: Fiction / Science Fiction / Military

"Only the dead have seen the end of war."
-Plato

-1-

I was with Legion Germanica today, one of the best legions in Earth's history. We'd just dropped onto Cancri-9 for a routine escort mission. During the mission briefing I'd been chewing on a breakfast bar, but I'd gotten the gist of it. Some kind of scaly alien prince needed a color guard to take him through the streets of his planet's largest city. The twist involved the locals, who were in a rebellious mood.

The mission sounded like a cakewalk, but someone must have been worried or they wouldn't have paid for the best protection money could provide: human legionnaires.

"All right, soldiers," my centurion said in my headset. "If we're going to find trouble, it will probably hit in sector eleven. This is what we're paid for. I want to double-up on the troops jogging with the air car. Keep the crowds back—especially those raptor-looking guys. I don't like the way their fangs drip spittle all the time."

The centurion's instincts were legendary, so we followed his instructions without a qualm. I was 2nd squad's leader. I unloaded my team from a ground transport APC, and we hit the streets running.

It was my first outdoor look at Cancri-9. The buildings were randomly shaped like lumps of white clay. The vegetation was a mixture of lush, vibrant green and deep purple. The yellow and red suns in the sky formed two huge, glaring disks that were impossibly bright. Without my helmet and armor, I'd be burnt to a crisp. The local saurian population could take a shocking level of heat and radiation.

My squad moved into position right next to the lizard-prince's car. We couldn't help but question the wisdom of his little sightseeing tour through a hostile city, but such questions were above our pay-grade.

I knew there was no real need to wander around in these narrow, clogged streets. The prince's air car could have flown safely above them, or better yet, avoided the city entirely. But the ruling family wanted to show they weren't afraid of the rebels. They wanted to demonstrate to their people the prince could take a leisurely ride through the city without a care.

It seemed like a dumbass stunt to me, but no one was asking the rank and file—they never did. Besides, the prince had plenty of credits to waste, so here I was. The customer was always right.

When we came into a street that was even more crooked and narrow than usual, the column halted. Everyone swiveled their helmets and adjusted the zoom on their faceplates. They strained to see what was happening up ahead, what had delayed us.

I took a better grip on my rifle. I could feel the stock through my inch-thick gauntlets, due to pressure-relaying technology.

I didn't look off into the distance. Instead, I kept my eyes on the doorways, windows and side-passages that led into this crooked street.

There. On the balcony over our heads an alien theropod stood with something in his stubby fore claws. What did he have? That was the trouble with this kind of mission: we had no way of knowing if this alien was a threat or just taking a picture for his grandkids.

"We've got a dino straight up," I radioed on my squad channel. "Dino" was short for dinosaur, which was a common term legionnaires used for the locals.

Helmets craned up all around me. When the dino realized he'd been spotted, all hell broke loose.

2

The saurian unloaded. It was a suicidal move, but maybe he was in a bad mood today. He opened his mouth to show us about five hundred of his curved fangs and simultaneously fired down a ball of blue light right onto the roof of the air car we were supposed to be protecting. It was a plasma grenade. Even before the falling sphere of energy landed, we'd all shot the attacker, blowing him away.

But it wasn't fast enough. The ball touched down and the air car shook and buzzed. The vehicle's shielding and armor kept it from being taken out. We were pelleted with shrapnel, but we were a squad of heavies, and our armor kept us alive.

I checked the car for damage. There was a scorch mark on the roof, and the shield was glimmering visibly. The brighter the glow, the less stable the shield was. This shield looked like it needed several quiet minutes to recalibrate itself and become a perfect shell of force again.

The air car itself seemed to be having trouble lifting off. I could tell right away the objective of the strike hadn't been to penetrate the shield, but to keep the car from escaping. Standard operating procedure in these situations was straightforward: the cargo, meaning the prince, was to flee the scene and leave us grunts behind to fight the attackers and clean up. But the car couldn't take off. The plasma blast had taken out its flight capacity.

Like the rest of my squaddies, I crouched down, seeking cover—any kind of cover. Fortunately, the streets were crowded with carts and trashcans. Despite their advanced civilization, saurian streets looked like something from an Arabian Nights tale. They weren't paved, and there was dusty junk everywhere. I put my back against a brick wall that was as hot as an oven. On my right was some kind of powered rickshaw, and on my left was a stack of cubic clay urns. I took a moment to fire an extra dozen blazing bolts into the theropod on the balcony, just to make sure he wasn't getting back up.

Nothing happened for about ten seconds, and my squaddies had the gall to think we'd won. My squad weaponeer even laughed and said something about a "waste of time".

3

Then a jugger charged him, coming out from one of the side alleys. Less than a second later he was snapped up like a mouthful of hamburger.

Juggernauts or "juggers" as we called them, were bigger, dumber theropods. They resembled a T. rex from Earth's distant history. They were the workhorses of this civilization; unfortunates who'd been enslaved by their smaller, smarter cousins.

The jugger lifted up my weaponeer in its huge jaws. The legionnaire's heavy armor buzzed as the shield was slowly penetrated by six-inch fangs.

The monster that had him was a green-scaled escaped slave, a big male, with a broken collar around his neck and a wild look in his eye. He stood about fifteen feet high, and I'd wager he weighed in at around four tons.

A force shield is only about an inch thick over a man's armor, and it's designed to stop energy attacks or, less effectively, bullets. Shields don't do much against slow-moving attacks like a bite. If they repelled that kind of motion, we wouldn't be able to pick up our own rifles.

I screamed for backup, and I got it. We poured fire into the jugger. But it wasn't enough. The jaws crushed the weaponeer down, despite the fact that we were pumping bolts of energy into the massive body. The armor could only stop those teeth for a few seconds. The jugger's fangs sank in at the joints and crushed down the chest plate. Blood ran from the weaponeer's dangling boots.

The jugger finally slumped, with my dead weaponeer still in his mouth. I took a moment to look up and down the twisting lane. I swept the scene with my rifle, ready to fire. There were more theropods appearing everywhere, both big and small. They came lunging out of hiding on both flanks. They'd chosen this spot to ambush us, to make their big play.

Something tapped me on the shoulder at that moment, and I flinched at the unwanted contact. I rolled my shoulders and hunkered down, staying immersed.

We destroyed the first charge at range, but another wave of theropods came in before we could reorganize our lines. They found me this time. I was firing, unloading my weapon and shouting for help. Huge jaws opened, and the sky disappeared.

The world suddenly brightened again and shifted dramatically. Fingers dug into my goggles. My helmet was being disconnected. I couldn't breathe, and two juggers had latched onto me, each attempting to remove a limb…

* * *

My mom had pulled my goggles off. A few hairs were plucked out by the rubber strap, making me wince. I blinked as bright, *real* light streamed into my eyes. She'd cracked the autoshades in my bedroom. Thin lines of white glare shone through the silver reflective grid, letting in actual sunshine. I complained with a loud groan.

I leaned back from my simulator and rolled my eyes. Cancri-9, the theropods, my screaming squaddies—they were all on screens inside my goggles. They weren't real, but they were as real as anything was to me. The game was called "Steel World", and in my opinion it was the best of its genre.

"You got me *killed*, mom!"

"The time for gaming is over, James," she said. She had her tablet in her hands and she offered it to me.

I didn't even look at it.

"You understand I lead one of the top clans, right?" I demanded. "I know that doesn't mean anything to you, but it's not cool to waste all my friends' time."

She tried to show me the text on her tablet again, but I wasn't interested.

I turned back to the simulator. It was a first-class rig. I had every component you could buy: the goggles, the pressure-sensitive gauntlets—I even had the full-feedback option on the finger-pads. The primary screen now showed I was down, as were most of my squad mates. The juggers were running wild, eating everyone. In the actual historical battle, Legion Germanica had won the day and saved the scaly prince in the air car. In our team reenactment of the scenario I'd blown it, and the car was already on fire.

5

I reached for the keyboard to talk to my team, who were universally pissed. My mom tapped my shoulder again, insisting on my attention.

I finally looked at her. Her hands were shaking. I sighed and read the words on the tablet she was shoving into my face.

At first, I didn't understand them. I had to read them again, this time trying to focus and catch all the words—to give them full meaning.

The text was an email from Hegemony Financial. Hegemony was the end-all of lenders. They held the lease on our apartment, my education—even the family tram.

As a citizen of North America Sector, I lived under Sector Government, Federal Government, and at the top, Hegemony Government. There was a layer above that, Galactic Government, but they had no direct relationship to any individual earther. We were beneath notice to the aliens who ran the stars in the sky—except when they needed one of our legions.

"Request denied?" I read aloud. I shook my head in incomprehension. "Account delinquent? What's this mean?"

"It means, James, that you're done with gaming…and school, too."

The emotion on her face struck me. This was big. This was real. Her eyes were squinched up, and I thought she might cry, but she didn't.

"But why kick me out of college now? I'm almost finished."

My heart began to pound in my chest. I sat back and looked at my gaming rig. It was a three-screener, with full contact controls, gesture-interpretation and eye-tracking. About a dozen people with handles like "Azzgawd" were sending me tells and chat-invites right now. I ignored them all. I'd spent years living on that machine—but now I could hardly see it.

"Was it my grades?" I asked. "Did I screw it up that bad?"

"You're not getting any scholarships, that's for sure. But that's not the real reason. You're passing. There's something I didn't tell you about."

I looked at her, my mouth hanging open.

Mom gave me a pained smile. "I lost my job," she said.

My eyes slid to the clock. It was three pm. She *should* be at work right now. Thinking back, I realized that she'd been around in the afternoons a lot lately—but I'd never paid attention to such things. Who knew where their parents were supposed to be at any given hour? I was only twenty-two, and it wasn't my problem.

But today, it *was* my problem. Mom explained that Dad was still working, but her job had paid better. They'd been stringing things along for three months, but the bills had mounted up. The short version was that summer was about to end, and I wasn't going back to the university next semester.

I couldn't believe it. All my life, I'd been the one who was screwing around while my parents struggled to cover for me. Now they couldn't do it anymore. I had nothing, and without their co-signatures and good credit, college was unthinkable. Finishing my college degree was going to require at least a million credits, and I was about nine-hundred and ninety-nine thousand short.

A week passed, and things went from bad to worse. The following Thursday, my family was evicted from our housing unit. That day came hard. The new unit we were assigned was a one-bedroom place with peeling paint and cracked concrete floors.

I'm slow sometimes, but I got this message: it was time for me to leave home.

I'd been born on the very last day of 2099. An induced labor on New Year's Eve, I'd been an egg laid early to give my parents a tax break. Growing up, I'd been a typical young male of my generation. I'd always hated school, preferring to chase girls and basketballs with fervor instead. All my life I'd spent most of my time plugged in online, and I had no idea what I was going to do with my future.

That all changed on the day I decided to go to the Mustering Hall. I'd played legion games for years and, like every kid, I thought I was ready for the real thing.

For any earther of legal age, the Mustering Hall was legendary. In my high school years, friends spoke of the Hall with bravado and carelessness. Everyone had been certain they would qualify to join the best of the best. According to any school kid, they could sign with any of the space-going legions they wished—if they bothered to try.

We all bragged we were going to join the Iron Eagles, Germanica or even Victrix. All of these famous organizations would be begging for our contracts.

In the final year of school, the talk had become more serious, less flippant and flamboyant. Most of us still wouldn't admit we didn't have the balls to join any of the legions. Instead, we began to talk-up our planned lives in accountancy, biotech and that vague favorite: an alluring future in *business*. We wouldn't be heading into space because we couldn't be bothered. It wasn't really all that glamorous, and we'd never really wanted to go in the first place.

When high school ended, reality inevitably set in. Most of the youth of the world went home to their childhood bedrooms and realized they were poor and unemployed. Slowly, we found shitty jobs, wandered through college, or occasionally got ourselves kicked out of our parents' houses. The truth was there were very few good jobs around these days. The average high-school graduate entered the world saddled with over a million credits in debt. With bank balances so far in the red, college wasn't for everyone.

I was one of the privileged few who had been able to go to the local university. I hadn't appreciated it, naturally. I viewed it as a sort of dodge, something to keep my parents off my back. I'd received poor grades in high school, but I'd managed to graduate, thanks to parents who never let me sink entirely into the depravity of all-afternoon basketball followed by all-night video games. Their generous discipline continued into college, allowing me to complete my first three years.

I'd been following the path to an IT degree with a less than stellar 2.9 GPA when that unexpected email had found its way to the family account. But that was all history now.

My dad said just one thing to me as I left: "Don't get yourself permed, boy."

Getting "permed" was slang for "perma-death"—the state no soldier ever wanted to reach. Although our medical techniques and reconstructive powers were vastly better than in the past, technical glitches or other extreme cases could leave a man dead for real—permanently.

I sighed and rolled my eyes. "That won't happen. From what I hear, it almost *never* happens."

He gave me a hard look. "Rumors and news reports lie. Just be careful."

"I will," I said and gave them both a final hug. "Don't worry."

I sold my gaming system and gave my family the money for all the shit I'd put them through for the last twenty years. Then I took the sky-train to the big Mustering Hall in Newark.

My parents had told me that Newark wasn't the best city in the northeast when they were young, and from what I could see when I stepped off the sky-train, things hadn't improved. There were tumbleweeds of debris blowing in the streets. Everyone I passed by gave me a flat stare. They seemed to hate me as much as they hated their own lives.

Fortunately, I looked tough enough to make them think twice, and the walk from the station was only six blocks.

The signs directing me toward the Mustering Hall made an unmistakable impression. They were garish and full of half-nude, beckoning men and women. I saw flashing laser carbines, dying monsters, then even more lovely people mixed with thematic shots of stars, nebulae and verdant planets.

I might be young, but I knew when I was being sold. I noticed that the rest of the populace around me knew it, too. They rarely looked up at the huge, glitzy holographic displays.

I took a deep breath, gripped my duffel in both hands, and pressed my palm against the Hall's door pad.

After a moment, my picture came up on the dirty, cracked screen. My basic info flashed up an instant later.

James McGill, sandy hair, blue eyes. I was twenty-two and exactly two meters tall. Unlike most of my friends, I wasn't packing any extra pounds. That was due to good genes and basketball, rather than any lack of overeating on my part.

I didn't read it all. Finally, the door snapped back its bolt and let me in.

I stepped inside the Mustering Hall and the door clanged shut behind me, shooting its bolt home again.

-2-

I felt relieved that I'd at least been allowed into the Hall. If I'd been underage, a criminal, or flagged as a weakling in the medical databases, the doors would have locked me out. That initial screening was for the best, really. No legion would give an unqualified applicant a moment's consideration.

After all the dirt and squalor of the world outside, I was taken aback by the interior of the Hall. First off, it was *huge*—the size of a football stadium at least. The walls soared so high the ceiling was hazy overhead. The roof was glass, and the autoshades far above were set to let in a blaze of cheerful light. The temperature was perfect in here, with none of the summer humidity and heat I'd left behind me.

I walked down the marble steps, and my boots sent echoing reports across the Hall—not that anyone could hear it. The place was incredibly noisy. There had to be a thousand or more people in sight.

The walls were lined with recruitment stations. Over each of these was an emblem or a crest for one legion or another. The testing took place in the center of the great open floor, I knew that much. There were sparring circles, medical booths and countless recruit-wannabes wandering around between them.

"Hey, kid," said a guy in stone-gray coveralls. He had a cap with a globe on it, marking him as a legionnaire. I knew many of the symbols, but I didn't recognize which one he was in.

"Sir?" I answered promptly. I'd decided ahead of time to call everyone sir—if only to get into the habit.

He shook his head. "I'm a tech. You don't 'sir' me."

He slapped his stripes, and I realized he was a specialist and therefore enlisted. I nodded apologetically. Gaming hadn't fully prepared me for this life.

He looked me up and down appreciatively. "You're a tall one, aren't you?"

"Yes, sir—uh, Tech."

"Specialist. You're supposed to call me Specialist Ville. Or Tech Specialist Ville."

I hadn't known his name was Ville, but I saw it now on his nametag. I decided not to say anything, as I felt numbed. I could hardly believe I was really here talking to this guy and trying to join the legions.

Ville took a dime-sized token out of a slot and handed it to me.

"What's this?" I asked.

"Your info. The door made it. Everyone you meet in the Hall will want to see that. Don't lose it, they'll get pissed."

"Okay, thanks."

"Head down to the floor and get tested first. Don't bother the guys in the legion booths until you pass everything. They aren't going to talk to a splat until they know your stats."

A splat? I had no idea what that was but let it pass.

"Right, okay," I said.

"And kid," Ville said, "next time you can take the crosstown connection to the station under the Hall. You don't have to walk the streets. Not everyone out there likes recruits."

"Okay, thanks. I didn't know that."

I walked down more marble steps. I frowned, thinking hard. *Next time?* Was there going to be a next time? I'd been under the impression all my life that getting into the service would be easy. There was always one legion or another recruiting. I was able-bodied and more than half-way through a college degree—honestly, I figured they would count themselves lucky to get me.

11

I started at the medical cubicles. That's where I found the first lines—the longest lines. I wasn't afraid of this part. I'd passed plenty of medical exams to play sports in school.

These guys, however, were thorough. They examined me like a prize pig at the fair. I was poked, prodded, bled and pissed dry. After an hour of that crap, an unsmiling nurse gave me my little chip back.

"How'd I do?" I asked.

"Good enough to get to the next line," she replied.

I eyed her insignia. I could read her rank now, after having paid careful attention. She was another specialist, like the guy at the door. But instead of being a tech, she was a bio—a medic, essentially.

I moved with the flow to the sparring circles. I was given a dummy rifle in the first chamber. I smiled. It felt just like the ones I'd bought to accessorize my gaming rig. I pumped a dozen rounds into a dozen moving targets and was just getting into it when some guy shouted "Time!" and kicked me out.

The next test involved a small arena. I'd caught sight of these guys from the doorway. This was a very different kind of test with archaic weaponry. I didn't feel anywhere near as confident with these things as I had been with the dummy rifle.

I picked up a shaft of bright metal. There was a round, brass-colored knob at the tip, and a guard over the grip. I guess you'd call it a practice sword, but it didn't look like a sword. To me, it looked more like a kitchen utensil than anything else.

I understood then that I was about to be tested for energy-weapon fighting skills. All the legions had to be ready to fight with energy-blades. The heavy troops used them almost as often as they used guns. They were like swords, but made of light and plasma. You never knew what tech level your opponent was going to have and what would work best against them. The Galactics and the Hegemony people decided things like that. Legionnaires just obeyed and fought according to the rules someone else set for them.

Irritable people ushered me into a ring. On the opposite side, I expected to see another dude with an electric sword. Instead, I saw a stick-figure framework of metal and wires and immediately realized I was going to be facing a robot. It

12

reminded me of a skeleton made of steel tubing. I saw that its power source was a cord going from its right foot back to the wall, where it was plugged in.

That's when I noticed the sawdust I was standing in and the hard brown patches in the shavings—were those puddles of blood or dry, hard puke? Or something even worse?

Really, it didn't matter. I wasn't happy to see those stains— whatever they were. But this evidence of past events did serve to sharpen my mind. I figured it hadn't been this electric skeleton that had been bleeding and crapping itself in the sawdust.

No one told me anything. There were no instructions, nothing. They didn't even say "Go!" They just slammed the rattling door behind me, and the robot went into action.

I'd heard about schools that prepped you for this sort of thing. They were supposed to teach a young person all the ins and outs of the legions over a three month term for about forty thousand credits. I hadn't had the money or the time to spare, but right now I wished that I had. I felt like I'd spent my entire education studying for the wrong damned thing.

The robot advanced and began swinging its sword from side to side in slow arcs. My first thought was to run, but I knew the legionnaires were watching. A coward wasn't going to impress anyone.

So I stood my ground and put up my sword to meet the oncoming robot. All I did was put my stick up in front of its stick. It whacked its rod into mine, and there was a bright flash of electricity, a snapping sound, and the alien stink of ozone.

The robot immediately stopped slashing and retreated to its side of the ring. I straightened from the crouch I'd been in and took a deep breath.

"Was that it?" I asked aloud.

Silly me.

The robot reset itself. It came at me again, but this time it was slashing up and down—and its practice sword was moving faster than before.

I'm not a total dummy. I side-stepped and lifted my blade high at a horizontal angle, so it would intercept its up-down slashing.

Another snap and buzz. Again, the robot retreated.

A smile appeared on my face. It was possibly the first smile of my long day. I felt like I was getting the hang of this.

Then it came at me again. This time, it was thrusting at my chest, pumping the sword at me like a piston. I knew by now that the brass knob at the end of its weapon would give me a nasty jolt if it touched me. I guess the legionnaires wanted to give recruits the proper encouragement. From what I'd seen in the sawdust, that jolt wasn't going to be a fun sensation.

My smile was gone. I didn't see how I could stop it this time. The blade was moving faster than ever, stabbing, moving that sword-tip back and forth constantly.

I advanced and tried reaching way out to whack at it. That didn't work; the thing was moving too damned fast. It almost got me with a thrust when I tried to hit its blade with mine.

I retreated until I had a wall behind me. Not knowing what else to do, I was forced to dash to one side. The skeletal robot turned after me, surprising me. I hadn't seen it react to any move I'd made up until that moment. It didn't even have eyes. I wondered if a remote operator was running it, or if there were cameras in the walls of the arena giving it an optical feed.

Finally, a plan formed in my mind. If it was only making lateral thrusts at a predefined height, why not get under it?

I waited until it came in close. At the last moment, I dropped to the floor and slashed up to hit its weapon with mine.

It worked. The buzz, flash and retreating taps of its webbed metal feet were now familiar.

I scrambled up and set myself, legs bent and weapon held ready. I was breathing harder now. How many times was I going to have to outsmart this frigging thing?

The robot transformed as I watched. It now stalked me intelligently, moving like a hunter tracking prey.

I tried stepping to one side and ducking low. Neither move helped. That brass knob at the tip of its weapon followed me with precision. It pointed its weapon directly at my chest at all times and walked toward me. It was no longer restricted to a single form of attack.

This was it, I figured. I made a growling sound and walked toward the thing. I didn't want to be caught up against a wall with nowhere to go.

It came to meet me. I slashed at its sword, missed, then thrust at the robot itself. It made a little swirling motion with its weapon, never touching mine. Then it thrust the point toward me.

I tried to turn my body, to dodge the tip, but it grazed my left shoulder. I heard a snap and experienced a numbing jolt of pain. I felt a little sick.

I was on my knees. The robot lowered its weapon and walked away, returning to its starting position.

Feeling pissed off, I slashed my weapon after it. I didn't go for the legs, or the sword—I hit it on the power cord, which trailed from its right foot.

There was a snap and a wisp of blue smoke. The robot stiffened and stopped moving. Then, slowly at first, it toppled, pitching forward onto its face. I scrambled up and rubbed my shoulder, grinning.

The door behind me rattled open. I saw the tech specialist with clenched teeth standing in the doorway.

"Don't you know you're not supposed to hit the power cord, splat?" he shouted at me.

"Sorry, Specialist Feldman," I said loudly, reading his nametag. "No one gave me any instructions."

"Get the hell out of here!"

Grumbling, he shouldered past me and went to service his robot, which now looked like a tangle of coat hangers. I felt no sympathy for either of them.

Another tech waited outside. She was short, pretty, and had a freckled mouth that was twisted up into a wry grimace. She looked me up and down.

"You're tall," she said, "and crazy."

She offered me my silver disk. I took it and thanked her.

"Don't keep wrecking stuff, splat," she said. "The legions don't like that. No primus wants a man who breaks the equipment."

I nodded, trying to look contrite. I think I failed.

"Why do you guys keep calling me splat?" I asked as she turned to go.

She looked at me in surprise, eyebrows upraised. "Don't you know? No one in your family has served?"

I shook my head.

She smiled, but it wasn't a pleasant smile. "You know you're going to be jumping out of ships, right?"

I nodded. The usual mode of troop deployment was to drop from space onto an enemy world. It was done with pods, tiny capsules that fell from orbit like bombs.

"I've seen the vids," I said.

"Well, what do you think happens to a new recruit who panics on his first jump?"

I thought about it for a long second as she chuckled and walked away.

Then I finally got it...

Splat.

After the medical and physical tests came the psych people. They gave me more tests—the written kind. These were run by specialists as well, bios and techs mixed together. There was one woman among them who was different. She wore insignia I'd never seen before.

I tapped the shoulder of a short, swarthy candidate next to me.

"Who's that?" I asked him.

The guy frowned at me then looked in the direction I indicated. He had thick limbs and a mess of dark, curly hair. I could tell right away he didn't like being tapped.

"Carlos," he said. "My name's Carlos Ortiz."

"Okay, Carlos, who's that lady over there?"

"I don't know. But she's wearing a sunburst—that means she's a primus." He was already back to looking at his screen.

This impressed me. She was a real officer, and not just an adjunct—a *primus*! She was near the top of the command structure of her legion. The only rank higher than primus was that of tribune—the brass who commanded the entire unit.

I squinted, trying to see her legion affiliation. I finally made out a circle with a woven set of lines running over it. There were a lot of people around wearing those.

16

"What kind of legion is that? That globe-looking crest? I don't recognize it."

Carlos looked up from his test again in annoyance. We were both going through an onscreen battery of goofy questions about what we'd do in a given situation, and what we liked and disliked. I was bored already.

"This test is timed, you know. Don't you even want to get selected?"

I shrugged. "There don't seem to be any wrong answers to any of the questions. I'm not worried."

"There's always a wrong answer, trust me."

"Okay, okay. Just tell me what legion that primus is from."

Carlos looked at her again, then laughed. "That's not a legion emblem, dummy. That's Hegemony. Haven't you noticed? Most of these Mustering Hall pukes have those. They aren't from any legion. They're from Earth Forces. Probably retired losers or people connected enough to stay out of space."

I gave him a dark look. I didn't like anything he'd said. I especially didn't like being called a dummy. Couldn't a man not know everything in this place without being sneered at? I was a lot bigger than him, and I considered leaning on him slightly, but the moment passed. I didn't think it would help me to be disrupting the tests.

"Recruits!" barked a female voice suddenly.

I turned, startled. It was the primus, and as she stepped near I saw she looked suspicious.

"Are you two cheating? That's grounds for instant dismissal."

"No, ma'am," I said.

"This guy is some kind of rube from the sticks," Carlos said, pointing at me. "He's clueless, and probably too dumb to cheat."

I gave him a frown but kept quiet. The primus looked me up and down, then stalked away. Over her shoulder, she said. "Shut up and finish your profiles."

"Yes, sir!" Carlos said with false cheer.

I obeyed the primus. The questions weren't difficult—they were absurd, in fact. If I was trapped in a room that was filling with water, but had been ordered to stay there, what would I do? I tapped option C: *Find a way out.*

The next question flashed up. When I stood in line at the supermarket, did I switch lanes when another line looked shorter? I snorted. Option A: *Yes.*

The questions went on. Contrary to Carlos's opinion, I'm not a dummy. I might not apply myself to foolish tests—or to pointless classes in school—but I realized the questions were trying to figure out my personality. I'm naturally a take-charge kind of guy, so I went with it. Maybe they'd give me a squad command, or at least consider me for the job.

When I finished, I stood up. Carlos stood up at the same time, glancing at me in surprise.

"What?" I asked, but I knew what he was thinking already. He'd miscalculated and hadn't realized I was a foot taller than he was. I towered over him.

"Nothing," he said quickly. "I'm just surprised you're done already, after all that chatter."

We moved toward the exit together.

"It was easy," I said. "I figured they must want a man who isn't a coward. I just answered naturally."

He squinted at me, and chuckled. "You made yourself out as a real leader of men, didn't you?"

"Of course. Who else are they going to pick for squad commander?"

Carlos laughed. I realized after a moment he was laughing at me.

"You big retard," he said. "They don't want men who take charge. They want men who follow orders like robots. You'll be lucky to get a contract wielding a power-mop!"

I glared at him, and I swear, I almost took him down right there. The only thing stopping me was the primus. I could see her, watching us. She was watching all the recruits as they left the area. As we happened to be standing at the exit, she was looking right at us.

A moment later, my silver disk dropped out into a tray. I picked it up and pocketed it. Carlos did the same, and we went our separate ways.

I marched straight up the ramps out of the testing pits to the encircling recruitment stations. I saw Victrix was close, and I'd always liked the look of their dragon-head emblem. I stepped up and stared seriously at the attendant.

"I'd like to be considered for recruitment, sir," I said. This time I got it right, as the guy was a centurion. You were supposed to call them "sir".

He didn't say anything. He reached out his hand and made a grabbing gesture. I almost shook his hand—it was a close thing. Then I wised up and put my silver chip into his palm.

He dropped it into a slot and stared into a screen for about five seconds.

"No. Next!"

I was stunned.

"Excuse me, sir?" I asked. "Could you tell me if there's a problem?"

"Yeah," he said. "There's a problem. It's you. Now move along. There's plenty more where you came from."

I headed to Germanica next, then the Iron Eagles. It was much the same. They took one look at my data and passed...rudely.

I walked away in shock. This wasn't going the way I'd expected. Here I was, an able-bodied man with an education, unable to get the time of day from these people.

I figured, okay, so I wasn't the best of the best. I could understand that. There were hundreds—maybe even thousands—of recruits in this hall, and only so many could be given a slot. It was time to leave the picky units behind and look for a less demanding group.

I moved down to the second tier legions. These were good, reputable outfits, but something less than famous.

They didn't want me either.

After a dozen tries, I stopped and stared at the silver disk in my hand. I felt lost. I'd staked everything on this working out. I'd left home, sold all my stuff...

What was on this disk that they didn't like? Was it the man who ran the robot who'd screwed me? Had he given me an "F" for effort? Or was it that psych test? Had that little bastard Carlos been right? Could they really want a mindless killer?

19

I looked up at the big skylight overhead. The sky was orange up there. I knew the sun was setting. I'd been here all day and gotten nothing for my troubles but a swift kick in the pants from everyone.

Disgusted, I made my way back up to the door where I'd entered many hours earlier. I found Specialist Ville still there. He appeared to be very interested in his tapper, a screen imprinted on his forearm. He was tapping at it, but as I approached he pulled up his sleeve and straightened his spine.

He looked me up and down for a second, then I saw a flicker of recognition.

"Washed out, didn't you?" he asked me.

"No luck today," I said, adopting a determined expression.

He held out his hand. "I need your data."

"What for?"

"They get recycled."

My face fell. "But what if I come back tomorrow? Where's all that data stored?"

"They keep the bad stuff on the cloud. But you get a new disk and you get to run all the tests again. I'll warn you right now, though, the odds are bad if you fail on the first day. You'll never erase whatever it was that screwed you."

I thought about what Carlos had said. Could he have been right? Could I have screwed myself by answering questions the wrong way? If I changed all my answers tomorrow, I doubt the test results would instantly become positive. Computers had a way of remembering bad things.

"I am who I am," I said. "If they don't want me, it's their loss."

Ville frowned and nodded. I gave him my chip and he flipped it in his hand. I stepped to the door, and he called after me.

"You walking again?" he asked.

"Looks like it," I said over my shoulder.

"It's gonna be dark soon. You don't want to be out there then, kid."

"I've got nowhere better to go."

I pressed my hand against the door pad. It brought up my data faster this time. I guess it knew me by now.

"Wait a sec," Ville said. "I've got a suggestion for you."

I wasn't in the mood for suggestions. This guy had been as snotty to me as all the rest of them. I was angry and defeated.

The door bolt unlocked itself. I knew if I walked out, that would be it for today. I hesitated.

Finally, I turned around.

"What?" I asked him.

"Go downstairs. Go try the shit outfits—the ones under the main floor. It's worth a shot, anyway."

I blinked at him. I hadn't known there were more legions with booths under the main floor.

"How do I get down there?"

He aimed a finger toward a dark archway. "Take the escalator over there. Here's your disk."

He flipped the silver coin-like object in my direction. I caught it and looked at it. I wasn't really in the mood for more rejections. Especially not from legions so lovingly referred to as "shit outfits".

"What's wrong with the legions down there?" I asked.

Ville chuckled. "The same things that are wrong with you. Nothing and everything."

I nodded. "All right, thanks," I said.

"You might want to hold your thanks even if they do take you. They work the contracts no one else wants."

I peered at him for a second. It wasn't a stellar recommendation. But I really had nowhere else to go and no options. My parents' couch was still open, but that would be humiliating at this point. Jobs? That was a laugh. Even if I landed one, at my age and skill level I wouldn't make enough for rent and food. I'd bet everything on coming here and getting myself signed up for space. If I couldn't even do that…

"I'm going to try it," I said, and I walked away from him.

Behind me, the specialist went back to watching the tiny screen on his arm. I was pretty sure he wasn't supposed to do that while on duty, but his secret was safe with me.

I approached the archway and noticed very few people were moving through it. Those that did weren't the same as the rest of the crowd. They wore uniforms, but they were rumpled and imperfect. The men had stubble on their faces and the

21

women had hair that looked like it had been in a windstorm. Everyone had a scowl on their face.

Great, I thought as I rode the escalator downward. *I get to serve with a unit of losers.*

I tried to perk myself up. I needed to at least *look* like a winner. If I could shine down here, I was sure to get my contract picked up.

I looked around at the legion emblems. There were only six legions recruiting down here and I didn't recognize any of them. With nothing else to go on, I looked for a short line. There was no line at all in front of a legion that went by the name of "Varus". Their emblem was the head of a hungry-looking wolf. I liked the symbol, so I walked up and slapped my disk on the counter.

The man behind the counter was a muscular black guy. He looked me up and down. His manner wasn't sneering, but definitely appraising. He nodded, as if he liked what he saw. He picked up my disk and lifted it up between us.

"You know what this is?" he asked me.

I checked his rank and nametag. I frowned for a second, because I hadn't seen the emblem on his shoulder often. He held the rank of "veteran", a rank that was only given for valor in combat. Veterans were higher on the chart than any specialist, one step below the officer ranks.

"Yes, Veteran Harris," I said.

"What is it?"

I opened my mouth, then closed it again. I took a deep breath. I knew I was being tested, but I didn't really know how to respond. I decided to go with my gut and give him an honest answer.

"It's horseshit, Veteran. Total horseshit."

He laughed roughly and slapped it down on the counter. "That's a damned good answer! Might be the best I've ever heard."

I gave him a slight smile. This place wasn't like the chamber above. These people were different. I wasn't entirely sure if that was good thing or not—but I was certain it was true.

22

"So," he said, eyeing me. "Forget the disk and the tests. What's your name, kid?"

"James McGill."

"Why you down here? You lost?"

"No. The rest of them up there don't want me."

He nodded sagely. I got the impression this might be something he'd heard a thousand times before.

"You know what you're getting yourself into if you join up with Varus?" he asked, looking me in the eye.

"I'm going to see wonders my mind has never imagined," I said, quoting the Mustering Hall ads. "I'll become a man, a babe-magnet, rich and get a tan all at once."

"Ha! Right you are, boy. Sign here."

I looked at the doc tablet. It had a glowing region of the screen, which he'd swiftly spun around and aimed in my direction. My name was there, as was all my data. All I had to do was apply my fingers. We called it "signing", but really it was the storage of my biometric information that would lock me into a contract.

"That's it?" I asked. "No tests, no questions?"

"I looked you up before you made it to the bottom of the escalator. You want to know what your profile says? Why Victrix and all the rest won't touch you?"

I nodded.

"It says you're a troublemaker. A rule-breaker. A man who thinks for himself. They all hate that, you know. But we don't in my legion. Most legions have tribunes that powder their asses before breakfast and think war is a tea-party. Maybe it is for them, with their fancy-pants patrons. But not for Varus. Not for the legions that sit down here huddled around the train station. Any more questions?"

His tone indicated he didn't like questions, but I had one more for him anyway.

"Do you know a tech specialist named Ville?"

Harris frowned for a second, then brightened. "Yeah. He was part of Teutoburg, a couple of doors down. He chickened after they wiped a few years back and went Hegemony. He's all right, I guess."

23

Everything he said made sense to me, except for his use of the term "wiped". I decided it wasn't worth another question.

I looked over the contract briefly. It didn't have any tricky clauses to worry about. These were pretty tightly controlled agreements, regulated by the Hegemony. They all said about the same thing: I was to serve and obey for a period of not less than six years. At that point, I could reenlist if they wanted me.

The trick, of course, was that although the terms of enlistment were all nearly identical, the type of missions each legion took was not. One legion might hire out as bodyguards to an alien prince, for example. That was about as cushy as it got. The food was good, the barracks were plush and keeping your boots shiny was about all there was to it unless there was an assassination attempt or a serious rebellion. Most legions didn't get it that good, of course. They took missions that required actual combat.

Long ago, when the Galactics first met up with Earth, they'd decided we didn't have much going for us. But they'd soon figured out we liked to fight, and that trait turned into a worthwhile trade good: mercenary troops. It was a beneficial deal all the way around. The local alien worlds got us to do their dirty work for them as legions for hire, and humanity was allowed to continue breathing.

"You going to sign it or not?" Veteran Harris roared at me suddenly.

I pressed all five of my fingers onto the glass. I felt my stomach do a little hop in my guts as I did so.

"Excellent!" he said. "Here's your disk back."

He slid the tiny sliver disk across to me, and I pocketed it.

"You keep that handy. That's your ID."

"Okay," I said. "What do I do now?"

"Whatever you want. We don't ship out until morning."

"In the morning?"

"Yeah. That's why Ville sent you to Varus, isn't it? We've got a hot contract, and we're short a few men."

I stared, opened my mouth, then closed it again. This wasn't what I'd been expecting. In movies about joining up with a legion, there was always a lengthy training session on Earth before any new recruit's first mission.

"What should I do until morning?" I managed to ask.

"You got a place to stay tonight?"

"Uh, no."

"Here," he said, slapping a token down on the counter.

I picked it up. "What's this?"

"A sky-train token, yokel," he barked. When I didn't move away, he glared at me. "Well? I'm not going to carry your bags for you!"

There was no handshake, no orientation, nothing. I had a thousand questions in my head, but I didn't want to antagonize a veteran on my first day.

"Thank you," I said evenly. "I have a lot to learn. Is there any kind of brochure or website I can—"

"No. There's no faq, either. You can't access anything like that until you're on the ship. You can sleep on the lifter—we prefer that actually, because you can't be late that way. It will leave for orbit at 0600 hours. You'll get your training en route to our next mission. Use that token by ten pm, the sky-train to the spaceport closes down after that."

I stared at the token for a second.

He glared at me. "Anything else?" he growled, his tone daring me to ask another question.

"Uh, no."

"Then get out of here, McGill!"

I left. I walked to the tracks, but the sky-train was absent. I checked the time and realized I had a few hours before I had to head for the transport.

I felt a little strange. Things had all moved along so quickly in the end. I wondered if I was in some kind of shock. One minute, I'd been wandering around thinking I had no future, and the next I had one—six years of service with a unit I knew nothing about.

An odd feeling grew over me. I thought now that I should have read up on every legion, not just the famous ones. It had simply never occurred to me that something like this was going to happen. I guess every guy assumed he was going to join up with an outfit that was on the nightly news streams doing cool things.

I thought about getting out my tablet and researching Varus, but I didn't quite have the heart. I'd already signed, after all. There was no point in making myself ill with the details now.

Recalling a refreshment stand that sold beer up on the first floor, I changed directions and headed for the escalators. I hadn't touched alcohol since I'd decided to sign up. That sort of thing always showed up in bio tests. But now that I had signed, there was no reason to hold back. And I needed a drink immediately.

On the way up, I came face to face with one of the few people I recognized. It was none other than Carlos, the guy who'd annoyed me since I'd first met him.

He was standing at the top of the escalators, looking downward. He looked worried, like he didn't know if he should go down or not. I released a snort of amusement. I knew in an instant what his story was. No one had wanted his sorry ass any more than they'd wanted mine. I could only imagine what kind of grim analysis the psychs had stamped on his records. The word "asshole" had no doubt been prominent in the write-up.

"Hey! Carlos!" I boomed, greeting him.

He looked startled. I could tell he hadn't even noticed me as I came up the escalator toward him. He stared at me, then his face lit up with recognition.

"Hey look!" he said. "It's tall, dark and stupid! What's up, man?"

I forced a grin and clapped him on the back. He grunted slightly and looked up at me in irritation.

"Having trouble getting adopted, eh?" I said. "Let me guess what they said: 'Not even your own grandma would take a loser like you.'"

"No, that's not—"

"Listen," I said, pointing down the escalator toward the Varus booth. "You want a tip? Varus is hard-up. They're signing right and left."

"For what?"

"They didn't want to say, so it might be some kind of dignitary escort mission. They always keep them quiet for security reasons."

"Those are sweet deals."

"Right. And they're taking me up in a lifter tonight."

Carlos's eyes widened. "You signed?"

I nodded. "On the spot. They're taking me right in and straight up to space. No boot camp. No bullshit."

"All right," he said, straightening his spine and tugging at his collar. "If you can get in, they're sure to take me."

"I bet you're right about that."

He glided downward, and I chuckled all the way to a mug of beer on the main floor. I figured that I might have screwed myself by joining Varus, but at least I'd be bringing along a friend.

-3-

Several hours later, I found myself being shaken awake. An angry Carlos glared at me.

"What's wrong with you, McGill?" he demanded.

"I was sleeping, actually."

We were on the sky-train to the transport lifter. I looked outside, bleary-eyed. It was raining, and huge ships sat hulking in their blast-pans all over the field. I stretched and blinked at them. They were dark, unpainted and ugly.

"Those must be the transports."

"No shit," Carlos said. He seemed agitated. He was standing, despite all the flashing signs telling him to sit down and buckle in.

"I've been researching this Varus outfit. It's a loser. Do you know what? Varus has wiped *twice*."

I didn't want admit I didn't know what wiped meant, so I played it cool. "Yeah, so?"

"You can't be this big of a moron! What's wrong with you? Do you have some kind of death-wish? Maybe you're so tall that you need two brains to drive that body of yours, is that it? Well, please stop talking to me with the hindbrain!"

I was beginning to get mad. I don't get angry quickly, but bad things happen when I finally reach the point of no return.

I unbuckled and stood up, towering over him.

"You know what I want to do right now?" I asked him.

I could see in his eyes that he did.

28

"Yeah, sorry," he said. "I have that effect on a lot of people. Listen—just tell me—did you screw me here? Did you get me to sign with Varus on purpose? That was what I thought when I read that stuff. But then I got here and saw you really *were* here, and you really *did* sign. So now I'm not sure."

"Just tell me what you found out about Varus."

"They've wiped—dead, every one of them, down to the last man. And they've done that more than once."

He'd finally gotten through to me. "Wiped...as in got wiped out."

"Yeah. That's exactly what it means. They were all killed. All of them. Do you get that? No survivors."

"We're not talking about perma-death, right?"

"No, of course not. If they all got permed they would have deleted the legion. But they all died on several occasions and were regenerated from stored data. The point is: they suck. They take losers because no one wants to join. The recruits die *a lot* in this legion."

I shrugged. "It's not like you *really* die," I said. "Not if they can bring you back."

Carlos laughed and sat next to me. Both of us buckled in again.

"Yeah, sure," he said, "they store a copy. They can reconstruct you out of pigsblood or whatever. But that means you still got to enjoy the full experience of death. You know, as in pain, fear—the whole thing. Doesn't that sound great?"

I was beginning to see his point. "Why did they wipe?"

"No one knows. No one knows what kind of work they do, either. They're secretive about it. Once you join Varus, you don't talk about your missions anymore."

I thought about that, and all the possible reasons why that might be the case. None of them sounded good to me.

"Maybe they do illegal contracts," I said. "Maybe we've joined a legion of smuggler guardians."

"Either that, or they're some kind of pirates."

I nodded. "You going to try to skip out?" I asked.

"No, I'd rather risk going off-world than take a tour of prison."

"Why's that?"

"Because they don't revive you if you die behind bars."

I laughed. "I see your point. If I've ever met anyone who's likely to get shanked in prison, it's you."

He twisted his mouth and gave me a sour look. "Thanks."

Just then, the sky-train rattled to a stop. We walked off with about ten other recruits. They looked scared, furtive and suspicious—no one looked happy.

Carlos stayed close behind me. I thought about telling him to shove off, but I didn't for some reason. He was annoying, but I had gotten him into this, and he was the only person in the legion besides Veteran Harris who knew my name.

Outside, we unloaded under the massive shadow of a transport lifter. It blocked out the moon, the stars and even the lights around the field. We stumbled in the dark, but then a shimmering line of yellow LEDs came on. These were embedded in the tarmac like the ones that led you out of a building in an emergency.

Barely talking, we followed the lights until we came to a ramp that dropped down from the transport's belly. It looked as if a massive predator was lowering its jaw to swallow us up. Dutifully, we marched up the ramp and into the ship. At the top, a bored looking tech specialist took our silver disks and checked our identification. She dropped every disk into a container, and we didn't get them back.

On the inside, the lifter was less than dramatic. There were no windows down in the holding pens where we were. Just fold-down seats and harnesses, most of which were empty. A few crewmen walked between the rows, shouting for us to untwist our belt straps, check the buckles twice, and to aim at the crusty drain in the center of each row if we barfed.

Then the ship flew, and it wasn't fun at all. It was wrenching, as if we were riding the fastest elevator in history for about twenty full minutes. There was free-fall at the top, but when you're strapped in and smelling vomit it wasn't as cool as it had looked in online games.

At last, there came a series of tremendous clangs and rasping sounds. The ship shook as if a train was going by.

"We're docking up," Carlos said.

He'd taken the seat next to me. At least he'd managed to hold onto his dinner.

The crew didn't come back. Instead, the ship went silent. Slowly, the recruits began to chatter. There were probably a hundred or more on board all together. We'd taken the last sky-train out to the transport tonight. The rest had come out earlier. A lot of them said they'd been sitting on this rust-bucket for hours.

Everyone looked around expectantly, waiting for something to happen. When something finally did, they groaned aloud.

The lights went out. This unwelcome event was accompanied by a long, drawn-out whirring sound that died at the end. We'd all heard that kind of noise before: It was the sound of failing machinery.

The ship was pitch-black for about ten seconds. Then there were banging sounds as relays were thrown. A dim, reddish glow filled the ship. Emergency lighting, I figured. At the end of each row of seats, a line of status LEDs flashed, turning from green to dull amber one at a time.

"And we almost made it, too," Carlos laughed.

Several more long minutes passed while we waited for them to fix whatever the hell had gone wrong. I kept expecting some crewman or member of the legion to show up and give us instructions, but they never did. They'd all disappeared.

A few troops laughed while others argued and kicked at each other. No one had anything good to say. We were a sorry-looking, disorganized mob.

Finally, something new did happen. A hissing began. I didn't like it from the start. It didn't sound right—in fact it sounded wrong—as in dangerous.

"What the hell...?" asked Carlos beside me.

I leaned forward and stared one way then the other.

"Something's wrong," I said, and began unsnapping my buckles.

"We're supposed to stay in our seats," Carlos said.

"You can do what you want. If this thing is going to depressurize or blow up, I'm going to try to get to an emergency exit."

I was the first recruit to free himself. The last buckle had frozen and wouldn't open. Without hesitating, I pulled a knife out and slashed it. I sawed until the cloth parted and I was free.

I floated away at an angle, going into a spin. I'd kind of forgotten we were in free-fall, as I'd never been in space before. I threw a hand back, grabbing the mangled harness. I pulled myself to it and began climbing upward until I was on top of the row of strapped-in recruits. They gaped up at me.

"Hey man, get back in your seat. If a veteran sees you, he'll toast you alive."

I ignored those who jeered and laughed. But then Carlos called out after me.

"Hey, McGill! Don't leave me here, man!"

I turned and stared. He was struggling with that last buckle. It wouldn't release, the same as mine. I wondered if it was magnetically sealed as some kind of safety precaution. Growling with frustration, I went back hand-over-hand to his seat and cut him loose. Then, with Carlos right behind me, we headed toward the nearest exit.

We'd almost made it when the seal blew. Carlos and I were about ten feet from an emergency pod door when a chunk of rubber gave way somewhere at the back of the chamber. I hadn't been sure what was happening up until then, but I knew the sound of leaking air when I heard it.

What had been a hiss grew into a sucking, roaring sound. The troops that had been laughing and admonishing me a moment before were now screaming and tearing at their harnesses. Many of them got down to that last buckle, and strained with it furiously.

"Cut yourselves loose!" I shouted at them, but I don't think any of them could hear me. There was too much noise and confusion. Besides, most of them didn't appear to have a knife handy.

When we made it to the emergency door, I grabbed the handle and twisted. There was a round portal in the door, but it was black. There were instructions too, but I knew I didn't have time to read them. I was already losing oxygen. The air was thin, and even though I was holding my breath, it felt as if my lungs were going to burst. The depressurizing chamber would soon cause them to rupture. I'd learned that much from video games and movies about space.

I held onto consciousness and tried to lever the door open. It occurred to me the entire thing was futile, we were probably all as good as dead, but I wasn't giving up. I was going to use all the time I had left to open that damned door. The problem was one of leverage. I had a good grip on the handle, but it was built to twist open and unlock. In free-fall, there is very little to push against. Without gravity, getting a good grip on anything is difficult, and I wasn't trained for it.

The sounds of panic in the chamber died slowly. At first, I thought I was losing it. But then I realized the air was thinning and changing the frequency of the sounds. Also, the panicked recruits were beginning to lose consciousness.

Looking back, I saw Carlos had already passed out. He was drifting away from me, his mouth hanging open. I kicked him out of the way and reached back with my long legs. I wrapped them around the nearest seat, which was a good five feet from the door handle.

That worked. I had leverage at last. Using my legs to push, I was able to twist the latch open. The door flew open and a gush of warm air blasted into my face. I tried to suck it in, but it was gone in an instant.

To my surprise, a man stood there in a vac suit. He had a helmet with a red crest on his sleeve, marking him as a centurion. He looked at me and lifted his hand. His thumb stuck up from his fist.

I was losing it, and I didn't quite understand what was happening anymore. I couldn't think.

I passed out at last, and my final thought was one of confusion. I was baffled as to why the centurion had just stood there watching us through that portal, doing nothing to help us.

* * *

Some of the men didn't wake up. A few had expired. But a couple of hours later, as the survivors recovered in the ship's medical unit, we saw the dead return to our group. They'd been revived.

I could only imagine what a revival looked like. Had their bodies twitched and spasmed unnaturally as life returned to them?

We were ordered to gather in a large ready-room with big wall-screens on every side—even the ceiling and the floor had screens. We stared at them, fascinated despite ourselves. Each depicted a different view of the ship we were on or space itself.

The ship was huge, bigger than any ship that had ever crossed Earth's oceans. It was long and sleek in design. There weren't many gunports, as the vessel was primarily designed to deliver troops between star systems, not to fight other ships.

Under the ship was the blue-white marble of Earth, a vast expanse of natural beauty. Sitting in the skies over our homeworld like this made me feel lonely and triumphant at the same time.

Most of the men were just annoyed. They'd died and been revived, and they were sour about it.

The centurion who had greeted me with flinty eyes at the exit of the lifter arrived and stood in our midst. None of the recruits smiled when they saw him, and neither did he.

"Good morning recruits," he said. "I'm Centurion Graves, your commanding officer. Welcome aboard the dreadnaught *Corvus*."

No one said anything. I suspected there were some hard feelings among the troops.

"You almost wiped," he said. "Only a few made it to an exit at all, and only McGill here managed to get one open."

A few eyes drifted to linger on me. I didn't look back. I stared at the centurion instead.

"Normally," he continued, "if this had been a real emergency, McGill's action would have been worth a promotion. But since it was only a training exercise, he'll gain a commending mark on his record instead."

I thought I deserved more, but I wasn't going to complain now. I'd learned something, however: this legion wasn't for the faint of heart. Whatever our missions were, we played for keeps I'd read a bit about training exercises, and I'd never even heard of an outfit killing their recruits wholesale on the first day as part of a routine.

Graves stood easily in the middle of the recruits, as if he didn't know many of us already wanted to kill him. Or maybe he just didn't care.

"Now that you've been properly introduced to Legion Varus," he continued, "I want you to find your assigned bunk and take a break. If you died, you'll find it takes a few hours to feel right again. A veteran can go straight back into combat after a revive, but most recruits can't. I'm giving you all twelve hours leave until we do any more training. Meet me in the exercise rooms after that at 0500."

On the way out, the centurion came by and clapped me on the shoulder. "Good work," he said, without smiling. "I've never seen a man manage to open that door single-handedly. You're supposed to get there and do it with a partner who provides a fulcrum. You happened to be tall and determined enough to do it alone."

I nodded, but I didn't smile at him. He was a prick, I knew that now. He'd made us all suffer in what I thought was a needlessly cruel way. I understood we'd all learned a lesson, and I understood the power of training, but tricking people like that...I wasn't happy.

The centurion eyed me for a moment longer, then nodded as if satisfied. After he left, Carlos came up to me and shook his head.

"The Great James McGill!" he shouted, throwing up his arms in a victory salute. His tone wasn't mocking, however. He didn't sneer; he seemed bemused, like he didn't quite know what to make of me.

"I guess I owe you for coming back to get me," he said.

I shrugged. "It wasn't real."

"Yeah, it was. Plenty of guys *died* for God's sake! The more I think about it, I'm realizing it was worse than it will ever be again. We didn't know that the disks we gave them when we boarded the transport had all our data, enough for a revival. As I passed out, I thought I'd been permed. It will never be that bad again. From now on, whenever I die, I'll know I'm probably coming back."

I nodded thoughtfully. "You're right about that. I figured we were screwed, too."

"What did you see when you opened the door?"

"Centurion Graves. He was just standing there, and he gave me the thumbs-up when I got it open at last."

"What a smug dick," Carlos said, laughing and shaking his head. "So Graves was watching us the whole time? He didn't lift a finger to help? I can't believe he had the gall to just let us all die while he sat in there. You're sure about this?"

"Looked that way."

Carlos' face shifted as he thought about it. He looked more serious than he ever had. "I owe you, buddy. I owe you."

"Owe me what?"

"I don't know. Maybe I'll jump on a grenade for you one day. It will be something cool like that. You'll see."

Somehow, I had my doubts that Carlos would do that when the time came, but I appreciated the thought.

-4-

War in my time was different than in the past. For one thing, it was more regulated. I'd learned in school that the Galactic rulers had decided long ago they couldn't directly govern thousands of worlds with alien populations. While humanity was still squatting in trees, the Galactics had decided it was best to invent a simple set of ground rules for their empire and enforce them vigorously.

The Galactics weren't a single species themselves. They were made up of the original elder peoples, mostly from the galactic center, where stars and planets were very close together. That core group that ran the Empire had battle fleets, but no one on Earth had seen one for more than fifty years. The fleets themselves were reported to be vast, but usually they were only used as a show of force.

They'd come to my planet in 2052, long before I was born, and they'd delivered an ultimatum. It was same choice they'd given to every other species they'd discovered to be experimenting with space flight: humanity must join the Galactic Empire, if we could qualify for membership. In return, we'd be given a wealth of technology and access to interplanetary trade. They made it clear that this was not an annexation—not exactly. We would be allowed to run our own planet pretty much however we wished. Internal matters were none of their affair. From their point of view, we were a primitive wild species that had always been within their sphere of influence. We were akin to an anthill in a wilderness preserve. They couldn't care less who was queen of our anthill, or who had mistreated whom. In their eyes, we'd only just become advanced enough to bother with.

The ultimatum wasn't entirely positive, however. If we refused membership, or could not qualify for it, our species would be erased from Earth and removed from the cosmos forever. As far as the Galactics were concerned, we were squatters on a planet which they owned. In their minds, they were being generous to offer us membership in their vast union.

Not left with much choice, humanity had quickly opted to join. There were only two requirements, and they were fairly simple: first, humanity was not permitted to build starships or any other device capable of leaving our star system. They knew we'd already sent out probes, but that was forbidden in the future. From now on, we could only leave the Solar System by paying for the privilege with Galactic credits.

Their second requirement was harder to meet. We had to have something of value to trade with the rest of the member worlds in order to pay the Galactic government. In other words, we had to demonstrate we could pull our weight and pay our taxes.

At first, the requirement to provide a trade good had been problematic. Our technology was pathetic by Galactic standards. Our foodstuffs and raw resources were, at best, mundane. An alien counselor was appointed to see if something could be worked out before our scheduled demise. This snail-looking official was aloof, but she'd done her job thoroughly. She determined that humanity had been discovered early in our developmental cycle as a species. We didn't even have a world government yet, which made us a throwback amongst the membership. We frequently engaged in bloody wars against one another, and had a long history of conflict, something most worlds had left behind in their histories. She recommended we hire out as mercenaries to other, more civilized planets that lacked professional armies.

Earthers latched onto the idea immediately. Within a month, there were literally millions of volunteers. Joining the legions was the only way to earn Galactic credit or to see the stars.

Many years after our membership in the Empire had been established, I now found myself onboard *Corvus*. She was a dreadnaught, a huge capital ship that was capable of transporting an entire legion from one world to the next. The ship wasn't outfitted for battle in space—that too, was against Galactic Law. But it could provide bombardment to support a landing if a contract called for it.

Despite being a warship, *Corvus* was surprisingly comfortable. Whatever types of missions Legion Varus specialized in, I could tell they'd gathered enough loot to keep their vessel in good condition. *Corvus* was about three miles long, with forward prongs and a spinning central cylinder. The ship displaced something like a billion tons of mass. Most of that tonnage was in the engines and fuel, of course, but our quarters included enough space to make up a small town. There were practice fields that encompassed cubic acres of space. There were centrifugal swimming pools, null-grav rooms— even entertainments, such as a movie house and a small park full of trees.

The ship itself was run by an alien race, the Skrull, who looked like spindly spiders with hard shells and wizened monkey-faces. They didn't interact with the legionnaires much. They kept to their quarters and their strange duties, and we kept to our generous portions of the ship.

The Skrull were another member of the Galactic Empire. Like us, they'd been required to trade something to maintain membership—and thereby continue breathing. They were good at building ships and running them, so that's what they did. Being a peaceful race, they didn't do any fighting—that was our job.

As I understood it, every legion fielded by Earth had a ship like this. *Corvus* was independently operated by the tribune of the Varus Legion under the loose supervision of the Hegemony people back on our Earth. For the most part, we did whatever we wanted. Like every legion, our task was to scrounge up every credit we could to enrich ourselves and our home planet.

Varus Legion, however, did this in their own distinctive way. I hadn't figured out yet what kind of missions we specialized in, but I was sure it was dangerous and well-paid.

I'd met many of my fellow recruits, including some fine-looking female specimens. I noticed that whatever special criteria Varus had for recruiting, it included making sure we were all physically fit. Most of us were young and well-built. There were a few overweight recruits, but the veterans were already picking on them. I had a feeling everyone was going to be in shape before we reached our mission world six months from now.

At 0500 every day I got up and showered. I didn't have much choice in the matter, as the ship's klaxons blew me right out of my bunk. By 0600, we were on the practice fields. Our day was divided up into eating, sleeping and training. Of the three, the training part took the greatest portion of time. Most of it involved physical exercise and basic combat training. I did okay with guns, but like most of the troops I needed a lot of practice with hand-to-hand.

The one of few times we got to socialize was in the mess hall. I'd somehow grown a rep among the recruits, probably due to my early recognition by Centurion Graves. My table was always full, and new people often asked to sit with us. Carlos, who'd never left my side, had appointed himself as bouncer in these situations.

On a Thursday morning in what was the month of May back home, a new person wandered into the mess hall. Everyone stared, but we didn't stop chewing. You didn't have enough time to fill your body with calories if you did that.

The unfamiliar person was a recruit with curly brown hair. She was attractive, tall and muscular. She veered toward my table and approached with her tray in hand.

"Hold on," Carlos said importantly. "State your business, Recruit."

"I'm a transfer from 3rd Cohort," she said.

Carlos frowned. The cohorts rarely interacted and maintained separate quarters. The only time we met up was when we were on the parade grounds under the big star-speckled dome on top of *Corvus*, or when we passed one another as one group left the training grounds and another moved in.

"A transfer?" he asked. "What did you do, piss off an adjunct?"

She smiled quietly. "Something like that. Now, am I sitting here or what?"

I saw Carlos ruffle up. He didn't like anyone who didn't respect his authority, imaginary or not.

I lifted my hand. "Please, take a seat."

Carlos shot me a look of annoyance. I'd stepped on his toes, but that happened all the time, so I didn't worry about it.

"I want to hear what it takes to be transferred out of a cohort."

The recruit sat across from me and introduced herself. Her name was Natasha, and she had a soft-spoken manner, but she seemed very self-confident. Her cheeks were perfectly shaped, and she had eyes that disappeared when she smiled. I found her interesting.

Several other female recruits around me looked disdainful. If anything, they were more annoyed than Carlos was. Sexual activity was pretty common among recruits and wasn't frowned upon by the officers. I'd hooked up with one or two of the women in the unit, and they clearly did not appreciate any new competition.

"I can see this unit isn't much different than the one I left behind," Natasha said.

"How's that?" I asked.

"Full of petty cliques and jealousy. You'd think with more men around than women, the women would feel they had the upper hand."

I smiled. "Maybe they do. But you haven't answered my question."

She addressed her food and didn't meet my eyes as she answered. "I was just like anyone else. I met new people and did what I felt like. Unfortunately, there are some rules involved."

Carlos was suddenly delighted. He leaned forward, face split into a grin. "You screwed your veteran, didn't you?"

41

She shook her head, smiling demurely. She lifted a thumb and aimed it upward. It took us a second to catch on.

"An officer?" asked Carlos excitedly. "What, not Centurion Graves himself, was it?"

Natasha frowned at him. "No. Don't be gross. There was this fine little adjunct. He looked like a kid in his uniform."

Carlos scoffed. "He's probably fifty. If he dies a lot and keeps getting copied, he might have the body of a twenty-five year old. It takes you back to the last time they backed up your data, you know."

"I know that, but he wasn't *old*," Natasha said in irritation.

I marveled at how quickly Carlos could piss people off. It was a gift he had. I'd come to ignore his quirks, but it was always instructive to watch as his personality impacted someone new. Before she took a fork and stabbed him, I decided to intervene.

"All right," I said, "now I know how you got yourself transferred. Thanks for answering me honestly. If you want to, you can become a regular at our table."

"I'd be happy to," Natasha said, reaching across the table and touching the back of my hand lightly.

At that, another recruit named Kivi got up and huffed away. She was a small, olive-skinned girl who moved quickly. She dumped her platter, which was only half-eaten. I avoided her eye.

The warning buzzer sounded. We stopped talking and scrambled to shove food into our mouths. The buzzer indicated there was only three minutes left. I glanced at the tapper imprinted on my forearm. It looked like a tattoo, and the ink changed as the seconds ticked away. The timing seemed off, we should have had another ten minutes or more.

Not knowing what was up, we chewed furiously. Only Carlos attempted to talk and eat at the same time.

"Something's up. Must be a special drill. They never open up the rooms before 0600. This will be big—I know it."

"Shut up and eat," I told him.

For once, he did as I asked. Just as we were finishing up, the second buzzer sounded. This one was longer and louder. We scrambled to our feet as we'd been trained to do over the last several months and rushed out of the mess hall. As we passed the recycling center, we shoved our trays into waiting slots. The automated kitchens behind the walls began the lengthy process of turning whatever we didn't eat from breakfast into lunch.

We charged out in a line, two abreast, and headed down the hallways double-time. Veteran Harris appeared out of nowhere and roared at us, trotting along beside the column. We stared ahead and prepared ourselves mentally for another grueling day on the training fields.

Usually, we began with calisthenics and a long run. Today, however, was very different.

As we marched out onto the fields under the big dome we passed a weapons rack. The veteran screamed at us to grab and check our weapons. Frowning, I grasped a snap-rifle and pulled it off the rack with the rest of my squad.

Snap-rifles fired metal slivers at high velocity. They used magnetics to accelerate the projectiles to amazing speeds with little recoil. For the most part, they operated like old-fashioned chemical gunpowder weapons, but were much quieter. Instead of a bang, they made a relatively soft, snapping sound.

As members of the light infantry, these weapons were preferred. A heavy trooper wore armor shielding and carried an energy weapon. But all those took power and weight. New recruits weren't issued such valuable equipment. We got thin smart-cloth uniforms and snap-rifles.

I cracked open my weapon, checked the magazine, and saw it was full. Another advantage of the snap-rifle was the large capacity for ammo. With no cartridge, each slender bullet took less space and weight.

I heard a distinctive snapping sound a moment later. It was faint and distant—but my head was up and swiveling, seeking the source of fire.

"Incoming!" choked Carlos. "I'm hit!"

He went down beside me. A spot of blood bubbled over his lung, where he'd been shot. I didn't bend down to help him. I dashed away instead.

"Sniper!" I shouted.

Everyone was running now in every direction. Kivi, the girl who'd run out of the mess hall pissed off not fifteen minutes earlier, went down next. Her legs were hit, and she was rolling around and screeching, grabbing her shins. She wasn't dead, but she was in a lot of pain.

This changed my response from fear to anger. I liked Kivi, and, somehow, seeing her shot made things personal for me. I took cover behind one of the practice rocks and aimed my weapon in the direction I thought the fire was coming from. I released what I hoped would be a suppressing spray of fire in that direction. A copse of palms stood in that quadrant. The leaves shivered and made sounds as if they were being hit by hailstones.

The fire kept coming in. I looked around, expecting the veteran who'd led us into this trap to be somewhere, calling out orders. He was nowhere to be found. He had vanished just as fast as he'd appeared.

Often during our training sessions our trainers had surprised us with attacks. Occasionally they'd been deadly. But I hadn't run into a drill that seemed so intentionally cruel since they'd tried to suffocate us all. Sure, we might come out of this situation as better soldiers, but there were already seven recruits down in this ambush. They were bleeding out, with all the pain of death on their faces. I knew they could be revived later, but I didn't think it was a fair test of our skills. What were we supposed to do to avoid this situation? Shoot our veteran instead of following him? That wouldn't have made them happy, I'm certain.

The rest of the team was crouching behind any cover they could find and firing randomly at the trees. I scanned the scene, desperate for any indication as to where the fire was coming from.

On a hunch, I looked back toward the hallway from which we'd entered. There was a shadow there, inside the entrance. The lights in the hall behind the figure had been shut off.

I jumped up and sprinted toward the wall. I threw myself against it and ran along it toward the entrance. I saw two more of my squaddies go down. They were shot in the back. They'd all assumed, as had I, that the fire had been coming from the trees ahead. Instead, the sniper was right behind us.

I came around the corner with my weapon upraised. There was Veteran Harris, crouching and aiming at my squad, half of whom were down and crawling in their own blood.

The veteran glanced up at me in surprise. He chuckled.

"Good work, Recruit. Now—"

I fired six fast rounds into his chest. Several pierced his heart. He slumped forward onto his face in shock. His final moments were spent shivering and pissing himself on the floor, and I didn't feel an ounce of sympathy for him.

-5-

I stood at attention. No less than three veterans and three officers surrounded me. The seventh man, Centurion Graves, was the only one present who wasn't shouting at me. The rest were barking like a pack of dogs.

"You *knew* you were involved in a drill, is that correct, Recruit?"

"Yes, Adjunct. I suspected that was the case."

A tough-eyed woman pressed forward. She was Adjunct Toro, one of Centurion Graves' two supporting officers. Most importantly, she was the officer closest to me in the chain of command. Among all of them, she was possibly the angriest. She was red-faced, and her lips curled away from her teeth as she spoke, as if I'd shot her instead of Harris.

"What you did was unacceptable, McGill. Drill or not, killing a superior on the practice field without cause isn't permitted. I'm formally requesting that you be kicked out of my unit, and preferably the entire legion."

I glanced at her, and then directed my eyes straight ahead again. "May I be permitted to speak, sirs?"

"No!" shouted the adjunct.

"Yes," said Centurion Graves.

Everyone stopped talking. They continued glaring at me but tossed surprised looks at Graves. It was the first time he'd spoken during the grilling.

46

"Thank you, sir," I said. "Veteran Harris was engaged in sniping at my squad mates when I located him. The drill had not ended when I fired my weapon. I believe I took appropriate action."

"That's it?" squawked the adjunct. "That's your answer? He was no longer a threat. He acknowledged you'd located him and therefore had successfully terminated the exercise."

"Excuse me, sirs," I said. "He did not drop his weapon. He did not surrender. He did not announce the exercise was over."

"That's because you shot him before he could speak!"

"That's enough," said Graves, sighing. "Anyone else want to say anything before I announce my disciplinary decision?"

Someone cleared his throat at the back of the room. Everyone turned to look. It was Veteran Harris. He was having difficulty walking, as he'd only just returned from the revival center. I felt my throat constrict at the sight of him.

"I'd like to say something, sir," he said.

"Please do."

"I know Legion Varus is a harsh unit. We train our troops to think for themselves. We kill them now and then to keep them sharp and to make sure they take their training seriously. All that said, I would suggest that this young man has done me a favor."

Centurion Graves' eyebrows raised high in surprise. "And what favor is that?"

"He taught me a lesson today. One I'll not soon forget."

The centurion nodded thoughtfully. "I take it then, that you wish to drop the charges?" he asked.

Veteran Harris coughed and nodded. "Yes, sir."

"Very well. The charges are dropped. Dismissed."

"That's it?" the adjunct asked rudely.

"Do you have something to add?"

"Yes. I don't want a man like this in my group. He'll shoot me in the back one day if he doesn't like how I run things."

"All right. Transfer him to Adjunct Leeson's group."

I couldn't believe the ordeal was over. It had been a grueling day. Before noon, I'd been placed in detention. After hours, the officers and veterans had formed a pack and I'd spent an hour being debriefed, grilled, and just plain yelled at.

A few minutes after Graves had announced his decision I was out in the hallway, breathing a sigh of relief. Harris followed me down the long, echoing tubes toward our quarters.

"Why'd you shoot me, son?" he asked.

"I was pissed off," I said.

He nodded. "That's what I figured. Do you know that I haven't died in three campaigns?"

I looked at him. He did look old. Almost as old as Graves himself. I shook my head. "No, I didn't know that."

"That's why they call me the old man. Do you know how I kept from dying all that time, through three campaigns on three worlds?"

"No, Veteran."

"Because I always killed the other guy first. But this time, you surprised me. No warning, no shouting. You just fired your weapon. You won't surprise me again, Recruit."

"I'm sure you're right, Veteran."

He left me then, moving painfully off toward the non-com sleeping quarters on Deck Eight. I heaved another sigh. I could understand his anger.

A grim thought occurred to me. What if he'd spoken up on my behalf in order to keep me in this unit? Not because he understood my actions, but because he wanted the opportunity to get even—personally.

I'd expected that my actions would make an enemy out of Harris. But now I thought I might have made something far worse: a *committed* enemy.

I crashed on my bunk on Deck Nine, stretching my arms over my head. Lights were already out, and everyone was asleep.

The moment my head hit the pillow, I heard stealthy footsteps. I lurched awake, lifting my hands, reaching for the throat of my attacker—I barely stopped myself in time.

It was Kivi. She smiled at me in the dim light.

"I wanted to thank you for killing the old man."

I laughed softly. "I think you're the only one who's happy about it."

"Are you kidding?" she whispered. "The whole unit is talking about it. No one can believe it. He hasn't died for years, you know. He was the oldest living ground troop in the legion."

"I've heard that. How are your legs?"

"They're good. The bio people worked on them for six hours, pulling out metal and re-growing tissue. Now I'm ready for anything again. That brings me to why I'm here. Have you figured it out, yet?"

Then she opened her shirt as a hint, and I got the idea.

Kivi, like almost everyone in Legion Varus, had a colorful past. She'd been rejected by the name-brand legions just as I had—but for entirely different reasons. I'd heard rumors about her operating questionable websites and services on the public grid during her college years...some people said they were illegal scams. Whatever the case, she was a very expressive and extroverted girl.

What can I say? I'm young, male and as much of an opportunist as the next guy. We made love, despite the fact that I was bone-tired.

* * *

I learned the next day that Kivi had been right about the general mood of the unit. They were secretly pleased by my actions.

"Dude," Carlos said to me before I was even dressed, "that fucker iced me *first*. Not even second, but *first*. He had twenty targets, but he picked me out to shoot in the back."

"Are you really surprised?"

"Yeah, right. Ha-ha, funny guy. Anyway, I'm so very, very glad you took him out. The old man deserved it. You shouldn't feel bad for a second."

"Don't worry," I told him. "I enjoyed it."

He stared at me for a second, then said, "Remind me not to get on your shit list, okay?"

"You're already there," I told him with a grim smile.

We headed back to training and learned that we'd taken a drastic leap forward. We were no longer going to work as independent squads of recruits. For the remaining weeks of in-flight training, we were to be incorporated into our active duty combat units. We trained every day with light troop regulars as well as weaponeers, techs, bios and veterans.

We still held the rank of recruit, however. That could not be changed until we'd gone through at least one campaign. After that, we'd automatically be promoted to full-fledged light troops. If we were lucky, we'd be assigned to a heavy troop unit and be issued armor. Further promotions, however, would be based upon performance and aptitude as noted by our officers in the field.

Varus had a typical legion structure. At the top was a tribune, who was in overall command. The legion was divided into ten cohorts, each of which consisted of six units of roughly one hundred troops. Every cohort was commanded by a primus, while each hundred-man unit in the cohort had a centurion in charge. The cohorts were lightly or heavily equipped. The less experienced troops were always put into the light cohorts.

Our unit was led by Centurion Graves, with two adjuncts serving under him. Each adjunct commanded a group of three squads. The squads were commanded by veterans.

The specialists were next in rank, and we had a lot of those around. Specialists came in several varieties. Each squad had at least two weaponeers, two bios for medical work, and two techs who operated drones and serviced all our complex hardware. Other cohorts were made up largely of heavy troops, people who'd earned the right to wear full armor and shielding in combat.

At the very bottom of the pile were the recruits like me. We wore light armor and carried snap-rifles. We were distinctly unimportant and were offhandedly kicked around by everyone else in the unit.

I'd been assigned to Adjunct Leeson's combat group permanently. In the reshuffle before we reached the target world, Veteran Harris was placed under Leeson as well. The rest of the group, about forty men and women, were made up of various flavors of specialists, light troops and recruits. This was a real fighting unit, not just an assembly of raw recruits doing exercises. The prospect of going into real combat with aliens was thrilling and daunting at the same time.

Several other familiar faces followed me into Leeson's group, the most notable of which were Kivi, Carlos and Natasha. They looked as scared as I was, but they were doing their best to fake confidence.

The experienced light troops were very different from my gaggle of recruits. They didn't think I was cool. They thought I was shit, and they let me know it every chance they got.

We drilled and exercised until our bodies and minds were harder than before. Most of us died in the training sessions during those final weeks, some more than once. I'd managed to avoid the experience so far, but I knew that couldn't last forever.

The training changed me—it changed us all. Our spirits were tougher by the end. I don't think anyone can die, or watch his comrades die around him multiple times, as I did, and still maintain an easy-going personality.

* * *

The big day finally came two months after I'd killed Veteran Harris. Today, we were going into action and landing on our target world at last.

We reached Cancri-9 just after midnight, but the tribune who was running the show up on the bridge didn't let us hang around in our bunks until morning. By 0230, I was suited-up and marching down into the bowels of the ship where the lifters waited. It was from their massive deployment bays the drop-pods would be released.

There hadn't been much in the way of a briefing. I'm sure the officers knew more, but all I'd heard was that we were to drop into a jungle-like landing zone of the planet high in the mountains. Apparently, only the highest lands were wet and green, while the plains were bone dry. There was a large compound that would serve as our LZ, and we were to deploy defensively the moment we were down.

51

What were we defending? As I understood it, there was a large mining complex under us, and it was under threat.

I kept thinking about Cancri-9. I couldn't believe I was actually here. I'd fought online battles on this planet in simulators for years. I was sure it would be very different in person than it had been in the sims, but I felt confident the basics would be familiar. It was definitely going to be hot and full of intelligent, violent reptiles.

In a way, it wasn't that surprising we'd ended up in the Cancri system. Video games had been made about this world for a good reason. The planet was turbulent and full of warring factions. They were, in fact, one of our best customers. They hired Earth's legions regularly to impress one another—I guess they thought alien troops were cool.

I read more about the planet on my tapper and learned details from our briefings. The saurian population was a relatively rich people. The planets in their star system, including their homeworld, were heavy with minerals. Their home planet was a carbide world with an iron-rich core and a high carbon content.

The first carbide planet humanity ever found was 55 Cancri e. In mankind's exploratory days of the twenty-first century, before the intrusion of the Galactics, such planets were found to be odd but not terribly rare.

Cancri, as we called it now, was a binary star system in the constellation of Cancer. Its unusual nature was discovered in 2012. The first planet we noticed was an inhospitable world far too close to its star to support life, but friendlier high-carbon planets were located subsequently. Cancri-9 was one of those worlds, discovered in 2039, about a decade before the Galactics first came to Earth.

As a carbide planet, what made the saurian homeworld unique was its habitability. Most carbide or 'diamond' planets were too toxic or too hot to support life. Cancri-9 provided a rare combination: a warm-water world rich in iron, diamond and many other rare earths, with the added benefit of a breathable atmosphere.

We called them "steel worlds" because they were literally made of iron and carbon, the two primary elements of steel. In places, these two components had formed veins of actual steel, a metal that didn't occur naturally on Earth. The outer crust was sprinkled with organic matter, but this was a mere shell over an inner core of metal and, most abundant of all, carbon.

In short, Cancri-9 possessed a fantastic treasure trove of materials perfect for building ships and other structures. As a result, the saurians had credits to throw around, unlike Earth with her handful of mercenary legions.

After reading several technical articles, I deactivated my tapper and told myself it didn't matter anymore why I was here. The important thing was that I was about to drop onto a burning rock circling a binary star. The drop itself was going to be a terror. We'd practiced drops and null-grav operations many times, but I knew the real thing was bound to feel different.

It was my first drop, my first battle, and my first war. I wanted to crap myself.

"Systems check, legionnaires!" shouted Veteran Harris, marching down my aisle.

I felt the love when his eyes fell on mine. Then he was gone, marching down the row, checking force-buckles and magnetic locks.

We were already packed into the lifter. The plan was simple: the lifters would wallow down from *Corvus*, entering the world's atmosphere. When we were at a sub-orbital altitude, we would be dropped in our pods.

All around me, men and women began tapping at their interfaces and moving their armored limbs. The guy in the jump seat next to me whacked me with his rotating shoulder joint. It didn't hurt too much, but I was wearing only smart-cloth, not an inch of steel. The jarring contact was enough to cause me to flinch away.

"Sorry splat," he said to me in a rough voice. "Didn't mean to scare you."

I glanced at the nametag and rank insignia on his shoulder, which identified him as Sargon, a specialist. Sargon had a cannon emblem over his stripes, indicating he was a weaponeer. I could have figured that out just by looking at his gear. He got up and hauled down a huge collapsed cylinder from the upper racks. It was a weapon nicknamed the "belcher"—a heavy plasma weapon that resembled a rocket tube that needed to go on a diet.

As he retrieved his weapon, he made a point of putting his armored ass into my face. I punched him hard enough to put a bright silver mark on his burnished armor. My knuckles were armored with steel gauntlets, not just smart-cloth.

"Sorry," I said.

Sargon sat down again with the belcher in his arms, and he laughed while I ignored him. I'd been called 'splat' countless times by everyone since leaving Earth. It was something a new recruit had to get used to. The only way to prove them wrong was not to panic on the way down and splatter yourself all over the ground of your first alien world. Apparently, this happened quite often.

I went back to my check-out routines. I tapped at the back of my left wrist with mesh-covered fingers. Lights glimmered green one after another in sequence. Oxygen, power, rifle—they were all good.

Out of nowhere, Veteran Harris appeared again and loomed over me. Like all his kind, he was big, loud and hell-bent on stomping the newest men flat on our first drop.

"Show me your lights, McGill!"

I dutifully rotated my wrist in his direction. He strained to peer down through his faceplate. In full jump-gear it was a difficult trick to read another man's vitals, but he managed it.

My suit wasn't armored, but it wasn't white and papery like the vac equipment of last century's astronauts, either. Instead, it was like wearing thick, stiff cloth covered with aluminum foil. It made me think of a parka made of tough canvas.

The heavy troops around me wore metal shells with spherical rotating joints at the shoulders and elbows. I envied their expensive gear.

"Huh," Veteran Harris grunted after reading my numbers. "You're good to go, splat."

"Thank you for looking after me, Veteran!"

Harris shook his head and chuckled. He clanked away. Both of us knew he hadn't forgotten about taking a half-dozen rounds in the chest from my snap-rifle, and I had a weapon in

54

my hands right now that probably served as an excellent reminder.

The moment he was out of sight around the end of the row of seats, the ship began to shake violently. I saw the weaponeer next to me look around worriedly.

"It's only interceptor fire," I said to him, grinning. "Don't rust your armor. That's legion property."

For some reason, this made him mad. I'd encountered this sort of thing on many occasions. Splats were constantly teased and expected to take it. I did so, but I always took the time to dish a little back whenever I saw the opportunity. This seemed to anger most of my seniors.

"You don't know anything," Sargon told me with conviction. "This is exactly the time to be nervous."

"Why's that?" I asked him.

"Listen up, McGill—what kind of name is that, anyway? What are you, from Scotland?"

"Georgia."

"Whatever. Listen up, you want to live through your first jump?"

"I was planning on it."

"Then get out of this lifter fast. It won't go all the way down, it will toss us out over the target. But that's a good thing. The best and earliest way for any legionnaire to achieve perma-death is right here, right now. This lifter has all your data uploaded. If you want to come back in one piece from this campaign, or get revived, the lifter can't blow up while you're in it."

I frowned. It seemed like someone was giving me actual information for once. But considering the source, I wasn't sure that I should trust it. I wasn't accustomed to such treatment. Maybe it was the reality of what we were about to face in the next few minutes that had prompted the weaponeer to give me survival advice.

"What happens when we reach the surface?" I asked.

"Then everything is automatically downloaded to ground command. At that point, it will be a lot harder to get permed."

Perma-death. That was the one thing we all feared, deep down. Who hadn't, in the vast history of warfare? In my lucky legion, no one seemed to mind the idea of being torn apart in Earth's service. But perma-death was different. No revival, no reconstruction—it was the old-fashioned kind of death, the type that lasted forever.

The ship shook again, and this time there was a new development. A puff of vapor shot out of the curved metal roof over our heads. The puff came inward for a fraction of a moment, showering us with sparks. Then, the vapor vanished, sucked up into the hole that had appeared.

"Depressurization!" shouted the weaponeer next to me. "Seal up, everybody!"

Sargon linked with Veteran Harris and reported the hit. It had to be a chunk of shrapnel. There wasn't any other explanation. I frowned in concern. This shouldn't be happening. Nothing like this was in the briefing.

I looked up at the hole and my computer systems automatically went to work, analyzing and recording it. Our helmets did more than protect our brains. There was a full set of computer displays inside. The heads-up display, or HUD, overlaid whatever we looked at with computerized data concerning the item in question. Our eyes were tracked, and whatever we focused on was analyzed and anything the suit's computer knew about it would be immediately displayed. Viewed externally, the sophisticated helmets were a cross between a biker's protective gear and something a deep sea diver might have worn a century ago. But from the inside, it looked like a flight simulator.

The computer listed "hull breach" as the number one analysis bullet point. There was a small suggestion box at the bottom of my faceplate that recommended patching it immediately. The recommendation wasn't very useful in this instance, as I wasn't qualified, nor did I have any gear for the job. I stayed in my seat.

Veteran Harris came back down the row and stopped at the leak with what looked like a plunger. The silver tip moved like liquid and looked gelatinous, however, as if it was made of flexible metals. It melted into the gap and sealed it.

The old man gave me the finger and walked away. I stared after him, bemused.

"That guy hates me, but he seems to be looking out for me at the same time," I told the weaponeer.

"Just don't get between his guns and the enemy. He'll cut you down if he has to. The same goes for me."

I shrugged, less than encouraged. My job was to snipe and scout. I was expendable and expected to die. New troops in every legion started off that way. To get good gear, you had to earn it. Only experienced survivors who'd proven themselves in combat became regular light troops, or heavy troops with expensive armor and energy weapons. Good gear wasn't produced on Earth, and the legion had to use hard-won Galactic credits to buy it. They didn't like wasting such a precious resource on a loser.

The buzzer finally sounded, and the big light on the ceiling went green. It was go-time. All thoughts of equipment and Cancri-9 vanished from my mind. I wasn't even worried about the saurians I was about to meet on the planet's surface. I was worried about not going *splat* on my first day out.

Properly managing a drop-pod wasn't a trivial task. First off, just loading yourself into one was dangerous. Rather than a calm process where each soldier was strapped into the delivery system by competent techs, the method used was dangerous and tricky.

You began by rushing to a circular hole at the end of the row of jump seats. When the light flashed green, you had to drop within a second down into the hole, careful to place your arms flat at your sides and keep your face looking straight ahead. It was rather like jumping off a diving board feet-first, forming an arrow with the body to fall in the smallest region possible.

Waiting for me below was an automated system. It sensed the falling body, and shot two half-shells from both sides at once. If your form and timing was good, and you were mildly lucky, the mechanism caught you and enclosed you in an instant capsule. The capsule was then shunted at a right angle, loaded into the ejection gun and fired like a bullet out of the bottom of the lifter.

I watched as Veteran Harris went first. He did it like a pro, because he was one. He stepped out over the hole in a smooth hopping motion, pointing his boots downward and keeping his arms stiffly to his sides. He vanished, and the ship shuddered as he was grabbed, encapsulated and fired in about a second. The line then moved forward and the light went green again. A bio specialist took a deep breath and dropped. She did it correctly as well.

At the back of the line, I felt vaguely sick. When I'd first learned how we were expected to deploy, I was shocked. How could such a dangerous, complex system be the best method?

The answer was simple: it did the job as fast as possible.

Ships cost money—a lot more money than any legionnaire was worth. The legion didn't want their ships low over the planet for one second longer than absolutely necessary. The lower a ship was, the more vulnerable it was to defensive fire. That's why they usually didn't land in a hostile environment—they didn't want to get blown up. They didn't want to linger in low-orbit and give us ample time for a safe drop. They wanted to fire us out the aft port like machine gun bullets so their lifters could escape as fast as possible back up into far orbit, where they would be safe.

And if we did screw up, if we did go *splat*—that was no big deal to the officers in charge. They thought in terms of equipment and missions. There was nothing more expendable than our flesh in their equations. They could always reconstruct us from stored data, or just recruit fresh bodies on Earth if we managed to get ourselves permed somehow.

My turn came up surprisingly fast. The troops were marching forward, firing out of the ship at a consistent rate. At the last moment, Sargon the weaponeer spoke to me over his shoulder.

"Just drop straight in the center. Don't try to hold back or put out your hands to protect yourself. Trust the machine. If it screws up, you're meat anyway."

With those words, he took a final stride out over the opening and disappeared into it. I heard the ship clang a shell around him and a split-second later the deck shuddered with the recoil as he was fired down toward the planet.

The light went green again, and I realized numbly it was my turn.

I gripped my snap-rifle tightly against my chest and gave a little forward hop into nothingness.

-6-

I dropped into the black, circular hole in the deck. My heart was pounding and strange, loud clanging noises greeted my ears.

Time seemed to slow down. I was only aware of the scene below the deckplates for a split-second, but I saw a lot. Under the deck, the lifter was wide open. On each side, I could see impossibly bright stars dotting the blackness of deep space. Below me was Cancri-9, a mottled world of brown, patched by green spots and occasional drifting clouds.

Closer at hand, huge robot arms moved with blurring speed. All around me, other legionnaires were dropping obediently into the waiting machinery. Pairs of arms clapped together, enclosing each soldier within capsules. They beat together with such fierce regularity, I thought they resembled a robotic audience giving a standing ovation.

There was a blur of motion as the two closest arms swung toward me. I was caught like a bug, two halves of a capsule slamming together around me. I was instantly cocooned. The noise was deafening, and I felt an instant jolt of claustrophobia. I could see how rookies might well panic and screw up at some point during this procedure. They might have hesitated, messing up the timing. Or, they might drop with their arms out as the slamming hands came together like cymbals performing a crescendo. Any such mistakes would have proven fatal.

The sickening motion didn't stop once I was enclosed. I felt like a ping-pong ball between two desperate opponents. Inside the pitch-black capsule, I was viciously shunted to the right and spun around. My head slammed into my helmet during these maneuvers, and I grunted helplessly in pain. I could tell my feet were now aiming upward and my head was aiming down toward the target world. I knew this intellectually, but I had no way of seeing anything from the interior of my tube-shaped coffin.

The big gun loaded me into the breach. I thought I heard a tiny click, and I would have put my hands to my ears, but I couldn't move my arms, and my ears were buried inside my helmet in any case.

The gun fired, and a surge of crushing pain rushed through me. The acceleration was horrible. It wasn't like a rollercoaster or an elevator. It was more like falling from three stories and slamming your boots into the dirt.

Fortunately, my legs were slightly bent when the jarring impact came. Otherwise, they couldn't have taken the shock, and I might have popped a knee. We'd been warned of this, but I'd forgotten all about it. I'd gotten lucky.

After that, the long fall began. I knew I was rushing down into the atmosphere of an alien world, but, for the moment, I only felt relief. I wasn't dead yet, I hadn't even seriously screwed up, and it would be another minute or two before I had to do anything that required thinking.

One thing began to bother me, however: the HUD in my helmet had yet to light up. It was supposed to automatically connect with the drop-pod and provide a steady stream of data as I fell. Was I trapped in a defective pod? Was I about to be driven into the ground at six thousand miles per hour, without the pod even performing the courtesy of firing a retro? I knew such accidents happened at least once during any legion drop. The delivery systems were workable but far from perfect.

After about ten long seconds, the lights flickered on. I had no idea why they'd waited so long. Maybe Veteran Harris had rigged it as a joke. Maybe this short blackout period was normal, and no one had seen fit to tell me about it. Whatever the case, I could now see that I had about two minutes left before I reached the ground.

The capsule was already reducing its speed. After initial acceleration, most of the journey to the surface was spent braking so the capsule wouldn't plunge into the ground. The trip was further lengthened by the fact that I was coming in at an angle in order to reduce the friction created as the pod encountered the atmosphere. A direct entry would burn up the drop-pod.

Two minutes isn't long, but when you're in a polymer tube rushing to your death, time seems to crawl by. At last, the final warning buzzer sounded, and the pod spun itself around so I would land on my feet, rather than my head. I braced for impact.

The landing itself was surprisingly mild. I was shocked with a jolt, which was mostly absorbed by the pod, but after that the capsule fell over and sort of rolled until it came up against something hard, and stopped. I was shaken but unhurt.

I was down, lying on my back in a polymer tube on an alien world. I had no idea what I would encounter when I exited the pod.

I gritted my teeth and squeezed the stock of my rifle. I took a deep breath and I punched the release button.

This was the moment of truth. I might be at the bottom of a lake, or surrounded by alien troops, or maybe submerged in a pool of lava—a fairly common natural landmark on Cancri-9. There was nothing to do, however, but risk it. Sitting in my cocoon wouldn't save me for long if any of these things were the case.

The capsule fell apart into two halves. I scrambled up and almost pitched forward onto my face. I had to grab hold of a tree to steady myself…A tree?

In all the sims I'd played on Cancri-9, there had never been a tree. But here it was; a tall, lush growth that firmly fit the description. True, the plant was odd-looking. It had fern-like spears firing out at the crown, and nothing else. No branches or leaves. It looked like a palm, but with fronds that were big and feathery, like the largest of soft forest ferns.

I ripped my eyes from the tree and looked around. It wouldn't do to be shot down while admiring the scenery.

I didn't see any of my people in the immediate vicinity, but I did see more capsules coming down. They were falling out of the sky, causing trees to crack and split when they were hit.

It occurred to me that I wasn't out of danger yet. If one of these capsules happened to land on me—well, it would be time for my first revival.

To protect myself as best I could, I hugged the tree my capsule had rolled up against. I waited until several other troops were out and walking around before leaving this position.

Not everyone made it down alive. I met the woman who seemed to be in charge and checked her nametag, which identified her as Bio Specialist Anne Grant. She had severely short dark hair and small features. Her eyes were careworn, but her face was pretty. She had the look of someone who was continually hurried and stressed. I could only imagine what doing revivals all day long must be like.

Grant knelt down to open a capsule that lay inert after it landed. This one looked burned outside. A brown residue coated the exterior, a stain resembling boiled sugar or oil.

The mess turned out to be burnt blood. The recruit inside was female, and part of her head was missing.

"She must have screwed up somehow when she was encapsulated," Specialist Grant said. "There are always a few splats."

She looked at me then, running her eyes up and down once. "You look fit. Get up in that tree you've been hugging like momma and see if you can spot an officer. I'm going to call in this splat. If they can transmit her data now, we can revive her down here and get something useful out of her."

I nodded and climbed my tree. Although they weren't normally front-line combat troops, bio specialists were officially superior in rank to recruits—hell, everyone was. They usually didn't give orders to my kind, but when there wasn't a veteran or an officer around, they served in that capacity. I thought the specialist's orders were a good idea in any case.

63

I shimmied up the same tree I'd landed near, and crouched in the ferny crown. At a height of about thirty feet, I couldn't see much more than I had from the ground. The canopy of fern fronds was thick, and it obscured the immediate vicinity.

What I did see, however, was an imposing range of mountain peaks. The rock cliffs were black and sheer. There were jungle-type growths clinging to the faces of these cliffs. I recalled images I'd seen of volcanic lands back on Earth. The scenery here was similar.

"No enemy in sight—no friendlies, either," I shouted down.

"Great," responded Specialist Grant. "We're probably off-target. What's your unit, Recruit?"

"I'm in the 3rd."

"The 3rd?" she asked, narrowing her pretty eyes. "I'm in the 3rd, and I don't recognize you."

We soon figured out that we were from entirely different cohorts. All in all, there were three different units represented in the immediate vicinity. We'd all been misplaced.

"All right," said the specialist after she'd radioed in our position and requested instructions from the command centers. "I've heard back from HQ. We're to proceed to the base of those cliffs. The mining op we're supposed to be defending is a complex drilled into that black rock mountain. We can meet up and reorganize when we get there."

I climbed down out of the tree and watched the trees around us for any sign of the enemy.

"Specialist Grant?" I asked.

"What is it, Recruit?"

"Why are we so far off target? Is this normal?"

She shrugged. Like me, she didn't have heavy armor. Bios were supposed to patch people up, and usually didn't fight. She did have a large pack on her back, however, which I knew was full of medical gear and supplies.

"Yeah," she said, "sometimes this happens. There's a gust of wind, or incoming fire, or a timing error—whatever. The system will group up all the lost capsules in an area and try to land them close to one another, so no one is left alone."

I counted heads. There were seven of us—plus the splat. There were two light troops, a weaponeer, Anne Grant in command and three recruits, including myself.

Grant looked at me. "Take the point."

A weaponeer laughed behind me, and I tossed him a glance, realizing he was Specialist Sargon from my own unit. I hadn't recognized him in his full kit. All the weaponeers looked alike when they were armored and carrying their heavy equipment.

Sargon walked up to me in his grinding armor and put a heavy gauntlet on my shoulder. "Lucky you," he said.

I shrugged off his hand and turned toward the cliffs. I began walking, rifle ready, eyes wide. I tried to watch everything at once, and to stay in cover whenever I could. That part was easy, because there were a lot of fern-trees handy.

Behind me, the rest of them gathered up and formed a line. They followed me, watching for any sign of the enemy.

We didn't make it all the way to the cliffs before things became interesting. I came around another tree—this one with a very thick trunk. The whole plant was shaped like a giant pineapple.

As I rounded the spiky trunk, I froze. There were three theropods and several empty drop-pods.

The dinos were huge. I'd seen these before, of course. They were juggers, fifteen feet high and covered in brightly colored scales. Two were blue and one was sort of a magenta shade. They all wore steel collars encircled with spikes.

As I watched for a moment in shock, the two blue ones dipped their heads down into the drop pods they were standing over. When the muzzles came back up, they dripped with gore.

"Specialist?" I whispered into the local chat channel. "I've made contact. Three hostiles."

"What are they?" she whispered back.

"Juggers."

That was as far as I got before the magenta jugger swung its huge head in my direction. I saw those eyes zero in on me. *Damn,* I thought, *it must have heard me talking, right through my helmet.* I hadn't realized their hearing was that acute.

65

I didn't waste any more time. I fired a spray of bullets with my snap-rifle. Five or six of them pierced the monster, and it roared in pain but didn't go down.

That was it for me. I turned and ran for my comrades. Behind me, although I couldn't see them due to my helmet, I heard the sounds of thunderous pursuit. I hadn't expected I would be able to outrun these overgrown lizards, and I was right. They were clearly gaining.

"Bringing home three juggers!" I shouted.

I heard the bio specialist curse in response. She ordered our ragtag team to disperse, but I wasn't listening to the details.

There's something special about being chased down by big predators that I can't easily explain. The experience struck a primal chord in my body. Something from my distant ancestors, I suspected. The pack was on my trail, and my feet knew it. I'd never run so fast in all my life.

Dodging between tree trunks and plunging undergrowth, I tried to put obstacles in their path, but it was pretty hopeless. They were native to this land, and they were twice my height. They easily went around trees, hopped over fallen logs and continued to gain on me.

"Hit the dirt, McGill," said a rough voice.

I barely had time to comply. The weaponeer had set up his plasma cannon in the path of the onrushing saurians. A heavy thudding sound rang out, making every frond in the vicinity shake with the vibration.

I flipped over on my back and aimed my rifle toward the enemy. The nearest one was a mass of walking meat. The left side of its body was gone, replaced by a foot-wide smoking hole. The plasma cannon had burned right through it.

As a testament to the fantastic vitality of these creatures, the blue-scaled monster managed to stagger two steps closer, looming over me, before it toppled.

The next one appeared, and everyone there lit it up with fire. I didn't even have time to climb to my feet. I lay there on my back in a pile of rotting vegetation and saurian blood, shooting up at the second blue dino.

In the end, I think it was the pain of our shower of fire that stopped it, rather than the damage we did. Its scales were lashed by bullets, and its flesh appeared to explode with bloody holes. It looked as if its skin was popping with a hundred small eruptions.

It had been intent on biting me, but, when faced with such a withering amount of firepower, it reared up screeching.

It turned to run but fell over and began thrashing instead. I got up and fired with the rest of the team.

That was our collective mistake. I think, looking back on the moment, the older more experienced members of the group should have known better. After all, I'd reported that there were *three* hostiles, not two.

The magenta lizard finally made its appearance. It did not charge in after the two blues, however. This one was smarter. It had spent the last few seconds circling around and now charged us from behind.

Specialist Grant went down first. The creature snapped her head right off, helmet and all. There wasn't time for a scream—she was just gone.

The beast turned its malevolent gaze toward me. As we scattered and fired at the monster in our midst, she picked me out. I think she was still mad about my ambush.

She charged, and she almost got me. I was close enough to see that huge head, full of countless curved fangs. Many were broken, and some had shreds of hanging meat and tendons caught in them. But there were plenty left intact for me, enough to kill a man in a single chomping bite.

Then the monster's head exploded. Sargon had managed to recharge his plasma cannon and bring it to bear again. I was quite happy with him at that moment.

I climbed to my feet again, and gave myself a shake.

"You outlived a specialist, McGill," he said. "That's pretty good."

"I'm very glad you can aim that thing in close quarters," I said, gesturing toward the huge tube he had rested on his shoulder. I knew that the weapon was really intended as light artillery, designed to rain down fire at range upon a distant enemy. But he'd used it like an extremely powerful rifle.

He laughed. "I know my equipment. That's how I became a weaponeer. You don't get that if you can't aim."

Sargon looked around and frowned.

"Ah shit," he said. "I'm in command now. Let's report this. With luck, Grant will be waiting for us at the base camp. But look out, she'll be pissed off."

"Pissed at who?" I asked. "We killed the lizards that got her."

"Oh, no," he said. "We won't get away with that. It will be our fault, somehow. Probably yours, to be specific."

"Why would she make a big deal out of it?"

"This was probably the first time she's been in command in a combat situation. By dying in the field, she's probably blown her chances of advancing to veteran anytime soon. Veterans aren't supposed to get their heads bitten off from behind while the rest of the team survives. It looks bad."

I understood. It was the type of logic the Legion Varus used all the time when considering people for advancement. They didn't believe in luck, and they didn't reward failure.

-7-

When we made it to base camp at the foot of the black cliffs, Anne Grant was there. I found that to be amazing. The technology was so far beyond anything we could do on Earth. The system that grew a new body for the dead was a benefit of Galactic trade. Some planet somewhere made the machines and sold them for credits. Since copying fallen soldiers was extremely useful to a military unit that sees a lot of death, our legions all had at least one.

Varus, I'd learned, had several. One additional unit stayed aboard *Corvus* at all times. The other was deployable and had been brought here by means I didn't understand yet. The light troop regulars weren't interested in talking to me about it, either. I suspected legion officials had shipped the unit to our target world under guard, to be set up by whoever had signed the contract. Once in-system, *Corvus* dropped the troops and downloaded our data. The revival units always had work to do after we'd dropped.

I didn't get to see the machine itself. It remained under heavy guard inside a puff-crete bunker they'd just fabricated and sunk into the ground. I was curious, but no one cared to satisfy the curiosity of a recruit.

The freshly revived bio specialist, on the other hand, *was* interested in us. As soon as Grant came staggering out of that bunker, she wanted us all hung.

When we reached the camp, tired and haggard, she didn't let us reunite with our units and have a shower and something to eat. She pounced immediately. In her wake was Centurion Graves.

While we were still out of earshot, Sargon leaned close and said: "She's not going to let this go easily. She has to blame it on someone—other than herself."

I saw what he meant. The bio was furious. Graves, however, wore his usual stern, impassive expression.

"You two?" the centurion asked, looking at Weaponeer Sargon and myself. "I might have known."

"Is there some kind of problem, Centurion?" Sargon asked innocently.

I decided to keep my mouth shut. In this situation, the weaponeer knew what he was doing better than I did.

"Yes, there is," Grant said. She glared at each of us, but seemed to hold an extra dose of venom for me. "That's the recruit. I sent him out on point, and he led us right into an ambush. He's your man, Centurion. I expect him to be disciplined."

"I discipline all my recruits when it's required," he said. He turned to Sargon and demanded a report.

Sargon stood at attention and gave his recollection of the events that transpired. Grant glared throughout this time, and I suspected her report wasn't matching up with what Sargon was saying. His tale emphasized the use of his big weapon to personally bring down two of the three theropods.

At last, Centurion Graves turned to me. His eyes were dead gray and his face seemed to hold no expression at all.

"Which of these two accounts more closely resembles the truth in your eyes, Recruit?"

I hesitated. I could support Sargon, or I could say I didn't see the details, as I was too busy dodging fifteen-foot tall lizards. I certainly wasn't going to support the bio specialist's story as it had me in the starring role of the village idiot.

I decided to make a dangerous play.

"Everyone sees a combat action through different eyes," I said. "What I saw was three saurians chasing me. One of them was smarter than the others and circled around. She caught the

70

group by surprise while we were dealing with the first two. If you ask me, we were outmaneuvered, that's all."

Nobody looked happy with this statement. Graves didn't react at all. He just stared at me, then nodded. "All right," he said. "You were cut off, you were a straggler group and you encountered the enemy. The team won the fight and returned with only one casualty. I say that sounds about average given the situation. Dismissed."

He turned around and walked away. Grant glared at both of us, but she turned on Sargon, not me.

"You could have covered for me. Why the grandstanding about how big your cannon is?"

Sargon shook his head. "What are you complaining about? No one is in any kind of trouble. Your record will be clean. Next time, just stick to the facts, good or bad, if you're dealing with Graves. He's very businesslike."

She still seemed agitated but less so than she had been. I could tell she was relieved. She'd been expecting to be chewed on, but it hadn't happened.

"Keep your pet recruit. I'm going back to the 3rd," she said, then marched away.

I was glad to see her go.

"Just hope you never need her to call in a revive for you!" Sargon told me, laughing. He wandered off to find the rest of the non-coms. I went to my assigned bunker and joined my fellow recruits in the dimly lit interior.

I could tell right away our post wasn't the best. There were already vermin crawling in from the jungle. I saw mean-looking twelve-legged spiders everywhere. These things were the size of gophers, and they weren't afraid of humans either. Even after we'd smashed a score of them, the rest kept rearing up like angry snakes, hissing and spitting at us.

Other bunkers were equipped with sealed doors, repellants and bug-zappers. The message was clear: we were the lowest of the low. My unit was made up largely of recruits, and it was part of a cohort of light troops, the least respected and most poorly equipped troops in the legion. I felt like we were still in boot camp. No one trusted us with anything important. I would have to see my second planet to earn the privilege of moving up.

We weren't allowed to lounge around in the bunker, either. As this was a defensive mission against indigents, we started by building up barriers around the entrances to the mines. There was a single main entrance tunnel and a few minor ones. The main entrance had thick steel doors. Some air-shafts led out to the cliffs in places high above, but we were told not to worry about those.

We learned over the next day that the enemy was made up of pissed-off dino miners who wanted to raid the mines to recoup unpaid wages. The saurians had a feudal society. The local lord was what we might have historically called a "landed baron" on our world. As the miners had started things by rebelling and eating all their overseers, the baron refused to pay them their wages. He'd decided to call us in to protect the mine instead.

"This could turn out badly," Sargon told me.

This wasn't news to me, but I wanted to know if he had any special insight. "What's so bad about this situation?"

"The saurians on both sides have a reason to be angry. They think they have the right to kill one another or anyone else who stands in their way."

I nodded thoughtfully. "Doesn't that pretty much describe both sides in any conflict?"

"Normally, yes. But saurian minds don't work quite the way ours do. They seem almost like smart beasts, but they have their own cultural norms. In this situation, both sides think they're right, and that means it will be a blood-bath."

Carlos came near and perked up at the term "blood-bath".

"I don't get it," he said. "What's special about this fight?"

"Well, it goes back to saurian psychology," began the weaponeer.

"I take it you've served here before?"

"Yeah. This is Steel World. Here, they hire legions all the time. My second deployment was on this planet."

"I see," said Carlos, standing close to us.

As he so often did, Carlos had joined the conversation without being invited.

72

"I still don't get—" he began.

"If you shut up, I'll tell you!"

I smiled. Carlos had done it again. He was a miracle-worker of irritation, but he did shut up after being yelled at, I'll give him that much.

"A man can't even think with you around," muttered Sargon. "What I was trying to say is that the saurians don't think the way we do. They often pull dirty tricks on one another. They might raid each other's egg-laying nests, or steal mates, or rob their bosses. But in those situations, if they're caught, they'll run. A thieving saurian is a cowardly saurian. He won't risk his life for a quick score."

"So you're saying they will fight harder because they both think they're in the right?"

"Yeah, that's what I'm trying to say. They won't give up. They won't run. The miners know the juggers don't deserve their pay—and the juggers know they haven't been paid."

I joined the talk at this point. "What are the odds both sides will come to their senses before things get ugly?"

"Zero," Sargon said. "Saurians don't come to their senses. They're driven by their emotions. They'll do what their heart tells them is fair—and right now, fair means killing the other side."

"It's a wonder there are so many of them around."

The weaponeer laughed. "Have you seen one of their nesting sites? Females lay thirty eggs a year. Three years later, you have a new crop of full-grown lizards."

"What do they all eat?" Carlos wanted to know.

"The smaller ones—the smart guys who hired us—they're omnivores and eat leaves and meat, mostly. The big theropods eat whatever they can catch. Usually, that's one form of plant-eater or another."

"Wait a minute," said Carlos. "That seems like an inherently dangerous combination. You have big, dumb meat-eaters working for small, smart omnivores? I'm surprised they can get along at all!"

The weaponeer smiled. "Now you know why there's always a fight to be had on Steel World."

73

We might have talked longer, but we were called to the walls at that point to do some "shoring up". At least, that's how it was described to us.

Naturally, the recruits got the worst possible job as we erected our defenses. The puff-crete machines churned and grunted out reams of raw building material. We were given the task of trying to guide the flow and keep it in the desired shape and location.

Puff-crete was an invention of an alien race called Vellusians. They were from a star system that was about two hundred lightyears from Earth, and we rarely had direct dealings with them. But they did have the market cornered when it came to construction. According to all accounts, the Vellusians were very successful and their homeworld was rich. Like all member worlds, they had a monopoly on their single trade good: machines that churned out puff-crete.

Puff-crete was usually bluish in color and was the closest thing to a perfect building material anyone had yet discovered. The goopy stuff was amazing and irritating at the same time. Most of Earth's buildings—anything built after the middle of the twenty-first century—were made primarily of puff-crete. Through a seemingly magical process, squatty metallic machines produced a gout of bluish-gray stuff whenever you turned on the switch. You had to feed in certain raw materials at the other end—water, silicon and a few other elements—but what came out was a thick, paste-like material. When formed into a given shape and allowed to cure for a day, a puff-crete structure was all but indestructible. Harder than concrete or steel, puff-crete buildings were there to stay once you molded and cast them.

"You know," Carlos told me as he slathered and stirred a river of the stuff into a downward sloping trough, "they say that if you measure all the materials you put into one of these puffer units and then weigh all the stuff that comes out, you'll have gained nearly forty percent of mass."

I frowned at him. "How's that possible?"

"I don't know, but if I did, I'd try to run the aliens who made it out of business."

I shook my head. "Wouldn't work. The Galactics would never allow it."

"I can dream, can't I?"

We kept working. We were constructing the basis for a semicircular wall that would protect the front of the mines, allowing only narrow paths to the tunnel entrance.

We used force-shields to hold the puff-crete material together for churning. It was really the most convenient way to do it. All you had to do when the wall was cured was turn off the shields. Unlike wooden molds, the force-shields wouldn't be stuck to the new walls.

One thing struck me as odd as I worked on this project all day and into the night. The force-shields left marks on the walls of puff-crete. I wasn't entirely sure how this happened, but the effect was undeniably visible. Strange swirling patterns were etched forever into those walls we'd hastily built. To me, the patterns looked like ripples on the surface of a slow, muddy river.

Dusk came, and a deep umber twilight fell over the land. Unseen insects and chirping creatures in the underbrush began to sing. Their natural calls were alien but not loud or annoying.

In the break before dinner and my next shift, I stood staring at the details in the walls I'd spent all day building.

Someone came up to me from behind and surprised me. I turned and saw it was Natasha. I smiled down at her.

"The walls are strange, aren't they?" she asked. "I noticed you looking at them. We just snapped the force shields off and all these lovely patterns were revealed."

"Yeah," I said, "I couldn't help but notice."

"They never have these patterns on our buildings back home. But then, we don't use force shields to hold them into place on Earth."

"Why don't we just use force shields permanently?" I asked. "That would save a lot of time. Just align the projectors, switch it on, and snap—you have an instant wall."

"It has to do with power levels," she said with certainty. "We can't move a powerful enough generator down here to make a strong shield. These shields have just enough juice to hold back a gelatinous mass like puff-crete. A bullet or a charging saurian would go right through."

I nodded. It made sense to me. Her knowledge on the topic made me realize something else.

"You're working toward becoming a tech, aren't you?" I asked her.

She smiled. "Does the nerd show through that clearly? Yes, they recruited me for tech work."

I frowned. "But if you have that kind of background…"

"Why didn't a reputable legion pick up my contract? Was that what you were about to ask?"

"Well, I…"

"You're right. There is something wrong with me—with my record. I was caught hacking in school. I took a few parts from the genetics lab—it was only harmless fun, you have to understand. But I built an illegal pet. They found it in my dorm and expelled me."

I nodded in total understanding. She'd been kicked out of college too, and under circumstances that would make a snooty legion turn her down.

"I get it," I said, turning back to the walls again.

"What's your story? I told you mine."

"I killed a guy," I said, keeping my face deadpan.

"What?"

"Yeah, he was trying to steal my wallet, so I beat him to death with a hammer."

She stared at me in shock, but I couldn't keep a straight face. When I started laughing, she punched my shoulder.

"You shouldn't joke about a thing like that!" she complained.

I turned back to the walls again, running my hands over the smooth, swirling patterns on the surface.

"Sorry," I said. "I didn't do anything cool, like build my own freak pet in school. I got kicked out because my family ran out of money. Also, they didn't seem to like my psych evaluation."

"Why's that?"

"Too assertive, too independent. Most of the legions want a bowl of jelly to mold—they could tell I had my own ideas."

She'd stepped away from me when I'd told her I was a killer, but now she came closer. She reached out and ran her fingers over the patterns on the wall.

"They're so perfect, like they were created with careful artistry," she said. "Strange to think they're only the random twists of a force field."

I could feel her presence close beside me. It was nice— almost as if I could feel her body heat.

"It's an odd place for beauty," she continued. "The walls themselves are ugly. I wonder what the saurians will think of us when they see them."

"They'll think we're crazy for making fancy walls of puff-crete. And then they'll try to eat us."

"That sounds pretty accurate," she agreed with a sigh.

-8-

When we finally finished the wall, it looked pretty impressive. Two cohorts of light troops had managed to put up about five hundred meters of puff-crete in a series of one hundred-meter runs. The structure was ten meters high and three meters wide. There was a rampart you could walk the length of, with crenulated battlements all along the top. Unlike fortifications from the past, this wall had a roof. The roof shaded us and provided cover from any type of aerial assault.

At the midpoint of each hundred-meter run of the wall, there was a tower. Four of them stood along the circumference in all. On top of each of these towers, there was a heavy weapon emplacement. These tripod-based plasma guns were manned by weaponeers, naturally. Recruits were only allowed to haul them into place. We couldn't touch the guns after that.

The division of duties was fairly strict in the legion while under non-combat conditions. The weaponeers tended their weapons. The bios tended the wounded and people coming out of the revival unit. The techs did mysterious things with strange-looking devices. I wasn't told, but I assumed they were motion-sensors, radar-arrays and the like.

The most interesting gizmos the tech specialists had were the drones. They hovered, buzzed and zoomed all around the camp. After testing their equipment on us, a few flew over the walls and out into the jungle, but these were quickly retrieved.

We'd all been strictly admonished about the rules of engagement on this mission: no aircraft were allowed. That was in the contract, and we were to adhere to it carefully. The techs were quite disappointed. They'd been ordered to ground all their aerial equipment, including spy-buzzers, sniper platforms and even mechanical ground-support bots. No missiles were allowed either, to the general groaning of the techs. Ground bots were technically admissible, but expensive and deemed unnecessary. The mechanized bots had been left aboard *Corvus* for a future mission against a more technologically advanced enemy. There was no point in having them destroyed by raging juggers.

The only drones we did have were the crawler types that were designed to investigate and detonate explosives. Bored, the techs ran these around the camp and complained to one another about the restrictions.

As I worked, I noticed a pattern. The light troop regulars and the recruits did all the grunt work while the higher ranks complained. The veterans bellowed at us, finding fault in just about everything we did. The officers made frequent inspections, after which the veterans yelled at us with more vigor.

Of the entire legion, I found the group circling the revival unit to be the most intriguing. That special team formed a unit of their own with their own bio centurion. The unit consisted of a mix of bios and techs with orderlies filling out the lowest ranks. They behaved circumspectly as they entered and exited the puff-crete bunker that housed the alien machine. At the entrance, a guard checked everyone who entered. No one without clearance was allowed inside, not even for a peek.

As I'd yet to experience dying, I still didn't know what it was like in there. I wasn't looking forward to my first time, but I was curious about it.

I caught up with Carlos while he was struggling with charging-tubes for a big weapon emplacement atop the northernmost tower. He was cursing, as usual. I lent him a hand, and we soon had a stack of tubes beside the big weapon.

"What are these things, anyway?" he asked me.

"As I understand it, they power this gun."

"Not exactly, Recruit," said a weaponeer. He'd been inspecting his equipment and ignoring us up until now. "Each charging tube holds the energy for multiple discharges, that's true, but they also contain the ammo."

His description didn't sound all that different from what I'd said, but I nodded and didn't say anything. As a fresh recruit, I wasn't about to argue.

I headed down with Carlos to the bottom of the tower. There was a stockpile of charging tubes stored here, but that wasn't good enough for the weaponeer in charge of the tower. He wanted his ammo closer.

Carlos groaned and stretched his back. "This seems like a waste of time," he said. "There hasn't been so much as a sighting for hours. I'm beginning to wonder if the lizards are even going to come to the party."

I took a moment to tell him what I'd run into out in the jungle after my off-target landing. He feigned mild interest.

"I would have shot a few rounds right into the pack of them and kept firing," he said, disparaging my retreat.

"You weren't there," I told him. "And besides, you would have pissed yourself and run without firing a shot."

Just as our argument about possibilities was becoming heated, Veteran Harris showed up and cleared his throat.

"I hope I find you two gentlemen in excellent health today," he said.

"Why, thank you, Veteran," Carlos said. "If you would excuse us, we have work to do."

The veteran looked at him through eyes narrowed to slits.

"You two are goofing off."

"We were just discussing—" Carlos began.

"You're a recruit. Discussing anything is goofing off because you morons don't know enough yet about anything to have a meaningful discussion."

"If you'd like to—" Carlos tried again.

"No," the veteran said, cutting him off. "I don't want to do anything you might be thinking of. See that jungle out there?"

He pointed off out into the forest. It was dark now, and the alien landscape looked forbidding.

"I want you two in the shit tonight," he said. "All the recruits in this unit are heading out as skirmishers. The techs don't have the virtual warning lines worked out yet. You soldiers are going to have to fill in for the missing hardware."

A few minutes later we found ourselves walking around in the jungle with our snap-rifles in our hands. The walls looked positively cozy back behind us.

We spread out, with Harris pacing along at the rear. I could tell this kind of scout work was left to us for good reason. With any luck, if the enemy did arrive, they would only eat a few worthless recruits. Our job was to slow down the charge and maybe take a few down before we were overwhelmed.

"This is bullshit, man, bullshit," Carlos said to me, coming closer than he was supposed to and whispering his complaints in the dark jungle.

"Keep your distance. We're supposed to maintain an even line."

"What kind of plan is this?"

"We're in a skirmish line. Didn't you ever play any legionnaire games?"

"No, I was too busy with my studies."

"Now *that's* bullshit."

Carlos finally shut up and moved off into the trees taking up his position again. We advanced out into the jungle until we were about three hundred meters from the wall.

At this distance, I couldn't see any sign of human presence. The trees blocked all the sights and sounds of the camp behind me. The jungle itself was eerie at night. I found the sounds to be more disturbing than they had seemed in the day. Unseen creatures burbled and screeched occasionally. Each time, I jumped a little. I had no way of knowing if these were natural background noises made by harmless native species or the calls of vicious organized enemies.

When my tapper indicated I'd gone far enough and was supposed to stand guard, I found a wide-spreading fern that looked bright green-white in my night vision goggles. It was emitting heat for some reason; lots of plants did that on Steel World. I decided the heat-emanating plant would cover my own body heat signature. I stopped there and waited quietly.

After a few minutes, I decided to open my faceplate to breathe the local atmosphere. The air was, by all reports, breathable but not pleasant.

When I sucked in my first gulp, I understood what they meant. The air was thick and humid—almost like breathing steam. The mixture of gases wasn't like Earth's atmosphere, either. It had more than enough oxygen, so much that you had to be careful you didn't hyperventilate, but there were other components, too, that left an aftertaste in my sinuses with every breath. It was like breathing the exhaust of some kind of electrical machine.

After a time, I relaxed somewhat and got used to the alien stink of the place. I could certainly hear more clearly with my visor open. I knelt in the midst of my warm fern and slowly scanned the landscape looking for any kind of movement. Since the enemy were native to this world and accomplished hunters, I knew I was at a severe disadvantage. I felt like I was bait, in fact. A sacrificial lamb tied to a tree stump to attract big game.

After an hour, Veteran Harris wandered by. He asked for my report in a whisper. I told him there hadn't been any significant sightings.

"You keep your eyes peeled, boy," he said. "And I'm not just talking about dinos. If anything shows up that looks remotely dangerous, you tell me about it on squad chat."

"I'll be the first, Veteran."

He left, and I felt lonelier than ever. It was about two hours later that something finally happened. It wasn't what I'd expected, however.

Instead of a theropod creeping up on me, or some other jungle predator, I saw a *thing* in a silvery skin. I wasn't sure quite what I was looking at, but I knew it wasn't normal. It had to be an alien of some kind. It had six limbs, and two of them were holding a dark, slim object. A rifle? I wasn't sure.

The alien was moving cautiously, scuttling forward on four of its six appendages. I was reminded of a spider but one that had only six legs—each of which could be used as an arm at will.

From the way it was acting, the creature hadn't seen me in my fern bush. I figured that if the enemy slipped right by me—whatever it was—I could make my getaway then.

Moving quietly, I closed my visor. I engaged my tapper, and it zoomed in on the alien. After a few agonizing seconds of watching a spinning "wait" icon, my suit computer finally made its determination. A blue question mark appeared, and the word "unknown".

I had no idea what I was facing, and neither did my suit. It wasn't a saurian, but it didn't look innocent, either. I figured I couldn't just sit there. I had to report the sighting. I slid my hand up to my chest plate. There, I keyed my alarm signal. Still trying not to make a sound, I lifted my rifle as the signal went out.

The alarm was a silent radio blip on an ultra-high frequency, but the creature picked it up somehow. It responded by swiveling its bulbous head back and forth then zeroed in on my bush. That slim dark rod in its hands came around in my direction.

That was all the warning I needed. I lifted my weapon and sprayed it down with slivers with my weapon set on full-auto. The weapon clattered, and the sound tore apart the stillness of the night. Snap-rifles weren't as loud as gunpowder weapons, but when you really held the trigger down, they made a respectable racket. The snap and whine of projectiles filled the air, and the steel shot ripped through the fern I was crouching in, tearing off big, fuzzy leaves.

The creature was caught by surprise and went down in a tangle of thrashing limbs. I gave it another burst to be sure, and then I snapped an image with my helmet visor. Whatever it was, I was certain command would want to see it.

Nearby, I heard rushing feet. It was Carlos, running to my position.

"What'd you shoot?" he asked.

"I don't know," I told him.

We both stared at the forest, and our chests heaved. We watched the jungle intensely, but the night was silent.

"Come on, what had you so spooked?" Carlos whispered. "You never freak out about anything."

83

I thought about the three juggers I'd run from in this same jungle yesterday but didn't bring them up. Carlos hadn't been there, and it hadn't been my finest hour. I just shook my head and watched for movement.

A channel call came in to us a moment later, and we answered it. Veteran Harris' voice filled our helmets.

"I see you have discharged your weapon, recruits, and Carlos has broken the line. Who gave you orders to maneuver?"

"I'm seeking a new position, Veteran," Carlos said.

True to his word, he found a broken stump and put his back against it. He sighted over the top, scanning for a target.

"Report, dammit!" Harris said.

"Sorry sir," I whispered. "I shot something. I don't know what it was, but I'm sure it was intelligent and armed. It wasn't a saurian."

"Repeat that, please?"

"It was not any kind of life form that is supposed to be on this world. The tapper didn't know what to make of it."

Harris didn't say anything more to that. I wasn't sure what he was thinking. I felt a bit guilty. I had fired without orders, and right now I wanted to run. It was hard to stand a post by yourself in an alien jungle. I couldn't see any sign of the alien from my position, as the grass was too high. I chided myself for not advancing and making sure the alien didn't crawl away.

Even as I berated myself, I heard firing erupt off to my left. Then more shots were fired, very distantly, to the right.

"Contact made, recruits!" Harris shouted into my ear. I could tell he was broadcasting now to the entire squad. "Withdraw slowly, link up and provide covering fire for one another. Those to the rear, take up a secure position. You're on overwatch."

"That's us," I told Carlos. "The rest have moved farther forward."

He nodded and, for once in his life, didn't have anything to say. We both stared into the night wondering what was coming next.

We didn't have long to wait. A squad of raptors showed up chasing a recruit.

I was horrified. The recruit looked to be a female, and she was bleeding. It took me a fraction of a second to realize it was Kivi, then another second to notice her arm was gone and it was in the mouth of the leading pursuer.

Without saying anything, we began applying controlled bursts of fire. The thing carrying the recruit's arm went down first. Seeing us, Kivi ran to our position. I saw her face briefly as she staggered past me. Her eyes were wide and her mouth was hanging open, as if she were in the midst of a long scream. No sounds came out of her, however, other than labored breathing.

We put down two more raptors, and they retreated. I realized with a shock that we weren't fighting the expected enemy: juggers. These were the smaller, smarter variety of saurian.

"Doesn't make sense," I said. "This was supposed to be a jugger rebellion. A bunch of pissed off, unpaid miners."

"Who the hell cares? Let's escort her back to the walls."

I checked Kivi's tapper. There was no pulse.

"She's gone," I said. "I'm not going anywhere. We're on overwatch, and we're staying right here."

Carlos looked at me like I was crazy, but he put his rifle to his cheek and kept scanning for more targets. He was breathing so hard I thought he might hyperventilate.

"They tore her apart," Carlos kept muttering. "I can't believe it."

"Shut up. Kivi will be fine. They're probably reviving her right now back at camp. She'll get to her bunk tonight before we do."

The truth was, I didn't want to think about it. I hadn't been intimate with Kivi lately, but it was hard to keep your mind straight when your ex-girlfriend was dead at your feet. Sure, I knew she'd come back to life soon, but my emotions were running high anyway.

"It just tore her arm right off," he continued. "Running around with it like it was some kind of trophy. Do you suppose that one was saving her arm? To show it off—or to eat?"

"Just shut up, Carlos."

He finally did. His breathing slowed, and for the next minute or two, nothing big happened.

Then we heard stealthy steps behind us. I wheeled and almost fired but managed to stop myself in time.

Carlos didn't manage to control himself so cleanly. He put a single pellet into the chest plate of Veteran Harris.

Harris wasn't hurt, but he wasn't pleased, either. He kicked Carlos in the butt with a steel boot and hissed at him to aim his gun *forward*.

I was surprised that he'd managed to get so close without alerting us. Wearing heavy armor and carrying a beamer, he was slower and louder than any recruit. He stepped beside me and aimed his rifle around the other side of the tree.

He glanced down at Kivi's body.

"Let me guess," he said, "Carlos here blew her arm off, right?"

"Negative, Veteran," I said. "There were six saurians. They charged us and we shot down three, making them retreat. They were chasing this soldier. She died of her injuries."

He glanced at me. "You're telling me you fought off six juggers with two snap-rifles? Show me the bodies."

Rather than arguing, I advanced and showed him the fallen raptors in the underbrush. He came close and stared.

"Regular saurians?" he asked.

"Raptors, sir. The smart kind."

"Where are the juggers?"

"No contact yet, Veteran."

He shook his head in confusion. He took pictures with his helmet and radioed them in. He made a report, but I couldn't hear what he said.

Finally, he came back to us. "All right," he said. "I want you to hold your positions for ten more minutes, then withdraw back to the wall. You did well here tonight."

Then he left us.

About one minute later, Carlos stood up.

"Where are you going?" I demanded.

"Where the hell do you think I'm going?"

"We're holding right here," I told him. "I'm not leaving yet."

He stood indecisively but then crouched down again with a growl of frustration.

"You want a promotion that badly?" he asked.

"I want you to shut up and follow the veteran's orders."

We waited the full ten minutes. The jungle was pretty quiet now. A few more bursts of fire had erupted at the nine-minute mark, followed by what sounded like a scream in the distance. But after that, it was quiet.

"That's it," Carlos said. He'd been pretty much staring at a counter on his tapper.

I lowered my rifle and began walking. We'd done our part. "Let's get the hell out of here," I said.

We took about three steps toward the walls, but that was as far as we got.

I thought later, looking back on it, that the enemy probably hadn't been quite sure how many guns we had, or maybe they weren't certain where we were. Possibly, they'd been getting ready to rush us and thought we were trying to get away.

Whatever the reason, as soon as we stood and tried to retreat, they charged.

Dozens came. There was a line of raptors in the lead, fast and vicious. I couldn't even count them all. Behind them lumbered no less than eight juggers.

I knew it was over. I stood my ground and fired over and over. I held the trigger down until the gun got hot in my hand. Ignoring the pain coming through my gauntlets and my aching shoulder that was taking a hammering from the butt of my weapon, I never stopped shooting them.

I aimed at the raptors, knowing they would be the easiest to take down. I directed my fire at a target until it fell thrashing and screeching, then swung my weapon to the next. I brought down three and was just lining up my fourth when a pair of jaws crunched down on my right arm.

I'd thought I was ready for this, but I don't think anyone ever will be. The shock of it was intense. It wasn't even pain exactly, just a weird, nervous pinching feeling: Like I had a crick in my neck or something.

Using my left hand I tried to line up the rifle again. But long before I managed that, something ate my knee.

One second I had two legs, and then I was down and I saw a creature running off with one of them dangling from its mouth.

I made some hoarse sounds then. They were loud in my helmet.

I looked back, craning my neck. I saw Carlos. There was no point in running, but Carlos was going for it anyway. I could hardly blame him.

At least for him, it was quicker. A jugger ran him down and took his head and shoulders right off, chewing and shaking. He was dead in a second.

I wasn't so lucky. The raptors were all over me, and they didn't make it quick.

I know for certain that no matter how long I live, no matter how many times I die, I'll never forgive those dinos for eating my guts out while I watched.

-9-

I woke up gasping for breath. It had been a dream—it *had* to be—a desperate, horrid dream. A night-terror caused by landing on this strange world.

I looked around like a drunken man. I could barely process what I was seeing.

"Get him up, get him up!" shouted a bio. She was gesturing for an orderly—another lucky recruit.

Arms grabbed mine and hauled me to my feet. I was pushed naked off the hard surface I'd been lying on. I staggered, and almost fell onto my face. I managed to stand, but my feet felt like rubber and my head was swimming.

"Reload, stat!" the bio shouted. She reached up and spread my squinting eyes open one at a time, looking into each for a fraction of a second.

"Forget about him, he's fine," she said.

The orderly let go of me, and I was left to stand on my own. I hadn't even realized the guy had been holding me up. I looked down and all around me. I was still naked, and for a few seconds, I didn't know why. I didn't know what was going on—I barely knew who I was.

I stared at the bio specialist for a second. I thought I knew her... Yes, I did. She was Anne Grant, the specialist who'd led me on my first ill-fated adventure on Steel World.

"I know you," I mumbled. "You hate me, don't you?"

Grant didn't even look at me. She was either too busy to talk or she just didn't care.

"Sorry," the orderly said to me over his shoulder. "We can't afford a bed right now."

Grant was working some kind of device. It didn't look like anything I'd ever seen before. It was like a big furnace, but she was shoving some kind of platter inside of it. Could that be the bed I'd thought I was lying on?

That furnace-like *thing*...it had to be the revival machine. Only, it wasn't exactly a machine. Not in the sense that I understood machines. The inside of it was like a mouth fleshed with pink, brown and gray mottled surfaces that reflected light wetly. It resembled a big, alien mouth.

Or, I thought to myself, *a womb.*

I shuddered. I was sickened and disoriented. It had finally fully dawned on me that I'd died and been returned to life by this strange thing they kept in a bunker. The raptors really *had* eaten me. Somewhere, out in that hellishly hot jungle, they might even be chewing still, fighting over scraps of my meat.

I gaped at the machine that had returned me to life. The surface of it was metal and the exterior had normal-looking controls. Touch screens glowed and indicator lights flickered. But that mouth-like opening showed that the interior was very different. It contained some kind of organic technology I couldn't begin to understand.

"Another one's coming through," said Specialist Grant. "Did you reload the capsule? I want no rejects, we haven't got the time."

"I reloaded everything," the orderly said.

"If this one screws up and comes out with missing organs, Garth, it's your ass."

"It won't, Specialist," said Garth. He turned and saw me, still standing there like a drunk wandering the street. He pointed behind me and then went back to his work.

I turned, following his gesture. There was a pile of uniforms and weaponry in one corner of the room. I took a light trooper suit and began to pull it on clumsily. The suit reformed itself to fit me even as I pressed my limbs into it.

Before I could pick up a weapon, several more bio specialists and a primus rushed into the room. They ignored me and began demanding counts from the operators.

"I'm busy," Grant snapped over her shoulder.

"Not too busy to answer a question or two, I hope?"

Grant glanced back and saw the primus. "Sorry, sir. We've had over a hundred casualties in the last forty minutes. We can't keep up."

"Organization, Specialist. That's the key."

"Yes, Primus."

I grabbed a snap-rifle and checked the magazine. It was fully loaded. I left the revival chamber, walked unsteadily down a long hallway and passed the guards outside. I left the bunker and headed back into the war.

Standing outside, I heard distant rumbling sounds. There were flashes in the sky, and the air smelled of burning things.

I struggled to close my visor. My fingers felt numb and rubbery. They tingled a little as if they'd been asleep. I pushed that thought away.

I didn't want to think about what had just happened to me. The idea of being reconstructed and revived from a data chip had sounded great, but the reality of it was chilling. Was I really *me* anymore? My flesh—the body I'd lived within all my life—that was still out there in the jungle somewhere. Alien theropods were digesting parts of me in their stomachs. What was this clothing of meat I found myself residing in now? This vessel of muscle and bone reconstituted from base chemicals? How could that be *me*?

I closed my eyes for a second and then opened them again, taking deep breaths. A fist socked my shoulder a second later jarring me out of my mood.

"Hey, big buddy," Carlos said, "way to get us eaten out there!"

"Yeah," I said, "sorry about that."

Carlos looked at me in concern. "I don't recall ever hearing an actual apology out of you before. Are you okay?"

"No."

He nodded, staring at me.

"First recycle, right?" he asked. "You're thinking too much. That's what it is. Well, I have the solution for that. Harris wants both of us up on the walls. Right now."

That got me back into the game. I frowned at him. "We're supposed to have a break. Standard operating—"

"That's all out the window. What? Did you think you signed on with a union shop when you thumbed your way into Varus? We're here to do or die—over and over again."

I followed him toward the walls, toward the northern section where our unit was stationed. As I walked, more things were coming at me, as if they'd been shrouded in mist before. My newly reknitted brain wasn't perfect yet. I recalled from the training I'd gotten that a revive often left a soldier in an altered state of mind. Sometimes, a newly revived man even had hallucinations.

There was a battle going on nearby, I was sure of that. I could hear it—and with every passing moment I understood more of what was going on. At first, I'd only been remotely aware of the hammering fire and flashing lights overhead. The smell of smoke and burnt flesh grew, however, until it became a stink in my nostrils. My visor was closed now, but the odor was trapped inside. I was pretty sure it had been there all along, but I hadn't noticed.

The noises intensified as I approached the walls. I wasn't sure if that was because my senses were improving, or if the battle had shifted into high gear. I guess it didn't matter which it was because I was in the middle of this fight again whether I wanted to be or not.

"You two!" shouted Veteran Harris, spotting us. He was standing at the base of the northernmost tower. I remembered when I saw it that we'd spent hours here setting up a weaponeer's gun emplacement at the top.

"Get your asses up the stairs and onto that wall. Stay out of the tower, that's for useful people who don't just wander around getting themselves eaten by overgrown lizards. I want you on the ramparts. If you see something coming out of the trees with scales on it, punch it full of holes."

"Yes, Veteran!" shouted Carlos. He rushed up the steps.

I stared after him. That wasn't like the Carlos I knew. Since I'd met him, he'd been reluctant to fight. Now, there was a new fire in eyes.

Harris watched the two of us, and chuckled. "Bad death, eh?"

"Yeah," I said. "My first."

"Ah… Didn't know you were a virgin! Well, we've given you a second chance. Make Legion Varus proud, boy. Get up there and shoot as many lizards as you can!"

I looked at him for a second. Our eyes met.

"Veteran Harris, I'm sorry I killed you back on the ship. I just lost my temper."

"That's all forgotten," he said. "But I can see now that you know what it means to die. It's not fun, is it?"

"No. And I don't want to do it again."

He came closer and peered into my face. "You haven't gone all soft on me now, have you, McGill? Back on the ship, you were the one with fire in his eyes. Now Carlos looks like more of a man than you do."

"It wasn't his first time," I said, thinking about it.

Harris nodded. "That's right. It wasn't. Now you know why we kill most of the recruits during training. A man like Carlos, he's experienced death. He's not contemplating some metaphysical mind-fuck the way you are right now. He's up on the walls, killing lizards for revenge. That's just where the legion wants him."

I looked up at the walls, and I saw Harris was right. Carlos was in the fight, but I still hadn't moved.

For the first time, I knew something was wrong with me. I was weak right now. They might have called it "shell-shocked" in an earlier time. I suspect my state of mind was even worse than that of men who'd been injured and driven half-mad by combat. I was all those things, but I'd also been forced to consider my place in the universe at the same time.

"Listen, McGill," said Harris, still staring at me with those hard, hard eyes of his. "You've got to shake it off. We're in trouble tonight. There aren't supposed to be so many lizards out there. The big ones and the small ones are working

93

together. That's when they're the most dangerous. They have both brains and power when they fight side by side."

"What about that thing I killed? That alien wasn't from Cancri-9."

"That's an unconfirmed report. But don't worry, I passed it up. Command will take care of it, if there's anything that needs to be done. Now, are you ready to fight or not? I need every man I have up on that wall."

I nodded, and stared back at him. I squeezed my rifle with both hands. "Yeah," I said. "I want to kill lizards. I want to kill all of them."

Harris laughed and thumped his steel-gauntleted hands together. "That's what I want to hear. Get up there with your comrades. Let me see some of the crazy you showed me during training!"

"Will do, Veteran!" I shouted, feeling new purpose.

I turned and rushed up the steps. I might not have been as eager to go as Carlos had been, not yet, but I was into it now. My mind was closer to operating the way it should.

The battle was in a lull when I reached the top. I took a spot next to Carlos and aimed my weapon into the night. I'd decided I was going to get some vengeance tonight.

I thought to myself that I'd probably never had a real goal of substance in my entire life. Something I wanted to do more than anything else—something that would make me growl with satisfaction when it was achieved.

Now, I had two burning desires: The first was to stay alive. The second was to kill these scaly monsters, big and small. I wanted to make a heaping pile of their bodies at the bottom of the wall, to watch them squirming and dying.

"It's quiet right now," Carlos whispered. "But it won't last. They say they've been coming in waves for the last hour."

"How many have you killed?"

"Two or three. It's hard to tell when everyone is shooting at the same saurian. Who got the kill-shot? I'm not always certain."

I nodded. I wanted to get kill-shots. Everyone did.

After ten tense, quiet minutes the smoke had time to clear. I could see with my night vision visor the enemy dead were already piled at the bottom of the wall. Carlos hadn't been kidding about the numbers. It looked like a saurian migration was underway, and we were directly in their path.

The quiet vanished moments later.

"Ready up, people!" Veteran Harris said in my helmet. "Don't spray, *aim*. Finish your target before choosing a new one. If they get to the top of the wall, stand your ground. We'll send reinforcements to your location. Don't let them breach our line and get inside."

These last words made me frown in my helmet. *If they get to the top of the wall?* How were they going to do that?

Then they came at last, a vast rushing mass of bodies, and I soon got my answer.

I fired and fired, reloading and firing some more. The first rank consisted of juggers—big bastards, up to twenty feet tall. When they reached the wall, they leapt and snapped at the men at the top. Now and then they got lucky and managed to pull a screaming legionnaire over the side and down to a quick death.

I aimed for the eyes, as the mouth and the huge bony heads were unaffected by my chattering light gun. It was our heavy troops with their more powerful weapons who saved the day. Their beam weapons slashed and burned the saurians.

As I watched, I learned how to use heavy trooper weaponry against such a massive foe. We'd never been trained with anything better than a snap-rifle, so I found this demonstration of firepower to be instructive.

The beam weapons emitted a lance of force that shimmered and twisted with visible light. Like swords that were twenty feet in length, they reached out and sliced away hunks of flesh from the enemy.

I'd done this sort of thing in games, but it hadn't translated well. In real life that these weapons had to be handled with care. Any touch could tear a hole in a neighboring soldier. Each heavy trooper had to be fluid in motion, almost as if he was fencing with his energy lance.

They stabbed and thrust upward in most cases. This burned a hole in the jugger, then, as they moved their arms up, the monster was eviscerated. Guts poured out in a torrent onto the stacked dead.

"These can't *all* be pissed-off miners!" Carlos shouted into my ear. "What the hell are we into?"

"Just keep firing," I said, "aim for the eyes, it's the only thing we can do that will affect them."

When the juggers were beaten back in a ragged, retreating line, we thought we'd won, but then the next wave hit.

A line of raptors had snuck up behind their massive cousins. These smaller, smarter lizards had been busy while we struggled with the juggers. They were setting up devices of some kind—tripods with cables and coils underneath.

I realized in an instant what was going on.

"Duck!" I shouted.

It wasn't a moment too soon. Gouts of energy burned the air, impacting the walls and any man who was still firing his weapon over the battlements. The heat was so great that the beams caused anything they touched to combust into flames.

Men and women fell, struggling all around me. They curled up and died, shivering and wreathed in flame. Even the walls themselves weren't immune. The puff-crete was tough, but the enemy weapons were powerful. Scorch marks appeared everywhere, and chunks of our walls began popping in a series of miniature explosions.

"Keep down, squad!" I heard in my helmet. It was Veteran Harris. "Those are mobile batteries. I don't know where they got them, but up close like this they'll create such a temperature difference between anything they hit and anything they miss they'll blow it apart."

"You think they can take down our walls?" Carlos asked me, as we hunkered down behind the battlements.

They fired another volley before I could answer the question. The second wave of beams that came at us was narrower in focus. Instead of splashing heat and flame over everything, it punched hard with rays of energy three feet wide. The burning streaks drilled fiery holes in our walls and vaporized screaming troops on the inside. I looked up and saw chunks of smoking puff-crete pop overhead, showering me with rubble.

"If they're allowed to keep firing, I'm sure they will," I said.

"Okay," Veteran Harris said again in my suit radio. "I have new instructions. When the big guns on the towers open up, every recruit is to get up and pepper the enemy gunners with fire. They'll be distracted, don't worry. All right, wait for it…wait for it…"

He didn't have to tell us when the big weapons went into action. We couldn't miss it. Up until now, the heavy weapons in the towers had stayed silent. Perhaps our commanders had decided to hold them in reserve to surprise the enemy when they were needed.

This was the moment, apparently, that they'd been waiting for. Every weaponeer rammed his heavy cannon out a gun port from the tower and unloaded.

All around me, recruits were standing and firing. I joined them. It was nice to be important again. The heavy troops in their armor stayed hunkered down. They weren't armed with the optimal weaponry for distant, soft targets. That was the role of recruits with snap-rifles.

Stricken with withering counter-fire, the enemy gun crews were quickly taken down. Those that survived left their weapons and fled into the forest.

The counter strike was successful, but it was costly. Many of those who participated were burned to death. Their bodies were everywhere, all along the wall tops. Many had fallen to lie in heaps on the ground behind the walls, as well.

But we'd won the day. A ragged cheer went up when the firing stopped. The smoke cleared, and we saw dawn was just touching the sky with pink light.

I looked at Carlos, and he grinned back. We were overjoyed, if only because we were still alive.

"VARUS!" roared a voice. A thousand other throats joined in. I did the same, swept up with emotion.

-10-

Later on, when the battle quieted, I slumped down and fell asleep at my post. This was far from unusual. At least half the troops on the wall were sleeping by midday. We were exhausted. The lizards hadn't come since dawn, but there had been an endless amount of work to be done.

The worst part had been removing our dead. Unlike past armies, we didn't imbue our fallen comrades with special meaning. We didn't bury them with flags and expensive caskets. Those honors were only for perma-dead troops. What would be the point of holding a ceremony and a funeral for a man who stood nearby, hale and healthy?

But we did need the equipment on the bodies. Clearing out the dead, then, became a grisly task. I'd felt like a grave robber in the morning, stripping the dead and dumping them into pits for mass burial. The saurian corpses weren't as bad, as I didn't care much about them. We used power-machines with scoops to scrape them from our walls and roll them into hastily dug graves.

Carlos tried to shake me awake, but I slapped him away. Moments later his hand was replaced by another, sterner grip. I could tell these fingers were steel-wrapped, rather than gloved.

I awoke with a snort and a gasp of breath. Veteran Harris glared at me sternly.

"Up and moving!" he roared, walking away down the line. "Every third man goes on break downstairs. Get a meal and a cot, but don't get too comfy. You're relieved for two hours, no more. Then it's back to the wall. You can sleep all you want when you're dead."

"Lying bastard," mumbled a recruit nearby. I realized in surprise it was Kivi. Her voice was rough and she coughed. "I've died twice today, and I never got more than ten minutes rest."

I wondered about that. Did a person come back feeling refreshed? Was it like sleep? I could hardly recall my own revival. It had been unpleasant, I knew that. The experience was like a dream to me now. I knew I'd remembered everything clearly when I first awakened, but now I'd lost the thread of it.

"You go," Carlos said, looking at me.

"What?"

"You take first break. Take my spot."

I finally figured out what he was talking about. "Do I look that bad?"

"Your face is wet with drool."

I chuckled and heaved myself onto my feet. The truth was, I did feel pretty bad. I could use some food and rest.

"Thanks man," I said. "You're nowhere near as bad as everyone says."

"Oh yeah, I am."

I thanked him again and headed down the steps. I thought to myself that Carlos had changed since I'd first met him. I guess that getting killed and eaten by dinos could change anyone.

When I reached the mess hall I ate with gusto, and when my head touched my pillow, I passed out instantly.

It seemed to be only seconds later when my cot was roughly kicked over. I went sprawling on the floor. I looked up to see Veteran Harris glaring down at me. For some reason, I wasn't surprised.

"Get back out there or I'll feed you to the lizards myself!"

I jumped up, gathered my kit and headed back to the wall. Carlos was still there. He'd been placed on construction duty, patching up the wall with a slurry of blue puff-crete repair formula. His gloves were thick with it.

"Your turn for a break," I said.

"So soon?" he asked sarcastically. "I thought you'd taken a two week vacation on the beach."

"I billed your account."

He flipped me off and staggered away toward the tents. I took over his position, and I had to admit I felt a lot better. The battlefield had been cleaned up by now, and it stank less, too. There was still a steamy haze hanging over the entire fortification, and the light of the binary stars overhead was brutal. In the evenings we could take off our helmets to breathe, but in the heat of day that was unthinkable. We had to have the air conditioning our suits provided to protect us.

About an hour later, I looked up to see a primus named Turov examining me. She wasn't very tall, but she had sharp features and a stocky build. She didn't look more than thirty years old, but I knew she might be older. Dying in combat returned a person's body to their last stored point—essentially making you younger than you had been. The system stored the mind often, but not the body. There was no point in making a dead legionnaire come back older than necessary. Some recruits, I knew, considered dying a perk. They talked as if they'd found a fountain of youth—but I thought repeatedly experiencing death was a grim price to pay just to stay young.

I straightened and threw a salute at the primus, even though I wasn't sure I was really supposed to. She gave me a lazy return salute and narrowed her eyes. Then I noticed Veteran Harris was standing at her side, his arms crossed.

"Come with me, Recruit," Turov said at last.

I followed, not daring to ask what was wrong. When a primus gave an order in Legion Varus, recruits were expected to follow it without question.

I glanced inquiringly to Veteran Harris, but he avoided my eye. A few hundred steps led us to a bunker in the ground. I stared at it for a second then realized it was the bunker that housed the officers' quarters. I stood at attention, having no idea what this was about.

"Now," the primus said, "do you know who I am, McGill?"

"A primus?" I asked, bewildered.

"That's right. Do you know *which* primus?"

I strained to read her nametag just to double-check.

"Uh, Primus Turov?"

She rolled her eyes at me. "At least we know you can read. I'm *your* primus, Recruit."

I nodded. "Sorry, I've never met anyone higher in rank than Centurion Graves."

"Yes, I hear you made quite an impression on him, too," she said. I saw a thin smile on her lips, as if she was enjoying a private joke. "Now, before I send you into the Tribune Drusus' office—"

"Excuse me, Primus," I dared to interrupt. The moment after I did so, I froze. She looked at me in displeasure, but she waited for me to speak.

"What is this about?" I asked.

"It's about making false reports. At least, that's what I hope you did."

I blinked in confusion and looked at Harris for some help.

He sighed in disgust. "He just experienced his first death today," he said, as if that explained everything.

"So what?" snapped the primus. "A lot of people die in Legion Varus. This mission is nothing special. Over five hundred died today alone. We're down to half our protoplasm supplies, and I've had to order more down from the ship."

Five hundred? I thought. I couldn't get that number out of my head.

"I just meant that he might not be one hundred percent—cognitively speaking," Harris explained.

The primus stepped closer to me, peering up into my face. "A tall boy, aren't you? Well? Do you think you're suffering from delusions, McGill?"

"No, sir."

"Good. Go into this bunker, stand at attention in front of the desk and wait. The tribune should come around shortly. Whatever you do, don't embarrass me."

"I wouldn't think of it."

I saw Veteran Harris make a face behind her back. I could tell he believed I was quite capable of embarrassing any officer.

"Well?" she snapped. "You're dismissed. Carry on, man!"

I stepped forward and entered the gloom of the bunker. After the glaring day outside, the dimly lit interior was blindingly dark. I walked down the puff-crete steps as evenly as I could, and when I reached the bottom I stood still until my eyes adjusted.

I was in an underground office. The chamber was quite nicely appointed. I turned my head slowly, trying to take it all in.

On the far wall opposite from where I'd entered, a series of heads were hung. These were alien in the extreme. Not one of them represented a species I was familiar with. There was a centipede-looking thing with pinchers as long as a man's arm. Next to that, a wizened multi-eyed monkey stared at me. Third, and last of the trophies on display, appeared at first to be a bear of some kind—but then I caught sight of the six-inch curved fangs coming down from the upper jaw.

The desk itself was yellow metal and shiny. It appeared to be meticulously polished. There were eagles of the same metal at each of the four post-like corners of the desk. Embedded in the heart of the elaborate-looking piece of furniture was a screen that was smudged with fingerprints.

"Recruit James McGill," said a voice.

I stiffened, stared directly ahead and stood at attention.

"At ease, McGill. I'm Tribune Drusus."

I assumed a more relaxed posture, but it was all a ruse. I'd rarely been addressed directly by a primus or a centurion. To suddenly have the commander of all Legion Varus interested in me was unnerving.

"I see you've noticed my trophies," he said.

"Yes, sir."

"Did you see the flags hanging over the entrance? I'm particularly proud of those."

"No, sir."

"Well, turn around and look at them, man!"

I turned and stared. There were flags draped over the entrance, just as he'd said.

"See this one? With the roman patrician's head? That's an image of Publius Quinctilius Varus. Do you know who he was?"

102

I shook my head.

"No, I suppose not. They don't teach much legion history in Varus. It's a shame, really. He was the commander of three Roman legions, and it is in his dubious honor our legion was named."

I took a second to dart my eyes in the tribune's direction. He was a thin man who looked intelligent and capable. But he didn't look much like a warrior. Sometimes, I told myself, looks could be deceiving.

"Legion Varus," he said thoughtfully. "Our name is a joke, a deception, did you know that?"

I glanced at him again, then away.

"No, Tribune."

"Of course not," he murmured. "Let me tell you the short version of an ancient story. One stormy day in the year 9 A. D., a horde of German barbarians waylaid Varus at the head of three legions. They were strung out and caught in a trackless forest—much like the one we're in now. He and almost all his men were slaughtered. His head was hauled around as a trophy on a pike for weeks afterward. So you see, when they named us Varus, they named us after the biggest loser in Roman history."

"Why would they do that, sir?"

He huffed. "We were assembled to do Earth's dirty work, that's why. To take on the missions no one else wanted, the deadliest of missions."

That part of his little speech jibed with what I knew. Drusus stopped talking for a moment and walked to the opposite wall where his desk stood. He pointed at the heads on display there. I had no idea what he was talking about or why I was here, but I was determined to stay quiet about it. Maybe the answers would come in time.

"These heads are from enemy mercenary companies," he informed me. "They faced Legion Varus in combat and lost. I cut them off and mounted them—just the way the Germans did to old Varus himself."

I frowned.

"I can see you're full of questions," he said, watching me. "Ask them, please."

"Why am I here, sir?"

"Because you saw an alien in the forest. One that can't be here."

I looked at him and he met my gaze evenly. "Am I in trouble for making my report?"

"No. I don't operate that way. I don't *like* your report, naturally. I wish there was video evidence to prove or disprove your claims one way or the other—but there isn't. We have only a single, grainy night shot you took with your suit. We searched the area, you know. There was no body. Only saurian dead."

"You don't believe me, then?"

"I didn't say that. I don't like what this might mean, but I'm not going to shoot the messenger. Not this time."

There was a pause in the conversation. I wasn't sure if I should keep asking questions, but, as he was looking at me expectantly, I continued.

"What do you want from me, sir?" I asked.

"I wanted to meet you, mostly, to take your measure, to decide if you could be trusted to report the truth, or if you were some kind of troublemaker."

"And what's your verdict, sir?"

"You seem like a young, vigorous recruit. A man with a serious mind. Is it true you shot Veteran Harris to death during a training exercise?"

I felt like squirming but controlled the urge. "Yes, sir, I did."

The tribune laughed suddenly. "That was quite a feat, you know. The man almost never dies."

"So I've heard."

"Harris vouched for you. He said that, of all his recruits, he trusted you the most."

I raised my eyebrows in surprise. This was news to me.

"Further, he is convinced that you *did* see what you reported. That it wasn't an accident or some other kind of creature. That's why he brought the issue to my attention."

"What did I see out there?"

"The real enemy, Earth's enemy. A creature that represents a competitor to our way of life."

I frowned in confusion. "I don't understand."

104

"No, but you will. We all will, if I'm right. Let me explain it to you this way: do you know how the Empire works?"

"Only what I learned in school."

He nodded sagely. "That's good enough as a starting point. Each planet that is part of our vast, beloved Galactic Empire has a single commodity to trade. Without it, they're kicked out of the Empire, losing their membership. The beings we call Galactics inhabit the thick clusters of stars at the core of our galaxy. They're ancient and wise beyond our capacity to comprehend. They don't tolerate failures in the fringe members of the Empire. They destroy any race that becomes economically insolvent."

My eyes returned to the trophies. I eyed them wonderingly. What had the tribune called them? The heads of mercenary leaders?

"Sir?" I said. "How can these trophies be taken from enemy mercenary commanders? There aren't supposed to be any."

He lifted a long finger and held it high. "Exactly. You've put your finger on the source of the trouble. Let me tell you part of the story they *didn't* give you in school, McGill: There are other mercenary companies in this galaxy. The truth is that many of the products produced by various planets are duplicated. They have to be. Think of the vast distances. Our ships are fast, but the galaxy is over a hundred thousand lightyears across. There are *billions* of star systems. One planet can't possibly supply every world out there with mercenary troops—or anything else."

I frowned, thinking about it. What he was saying sounded undeniably true. There were only about thirty legions operating on Earth. That wasn't enough to serve more than thirty planets at once, even assuming they were always deployed—which they weren't.

"So," I said, "what was that thing in the forest? What's happening? Why are there so many saurians, both big and small, attacking us? Are there more of those aliens out there? Are they behind these massive attacks?"

"I hope not, but I think there *are* more of them. And I think they are behind the attacks, yes."

He walked to his desk and sat in his chair behind it. His eyes gazed up at his trophies and his flags, but they were unfocused.

"Legion Varus has special duties. We don't get the fame and the fawning publicity from the press. That goes to the better-known legions like Germanica and Victrix. Those legions have much easier paths. We take on jobs that are competitive, jobs which might run us into our real enemies."

I stared at him. "We go against forces that hire alien legions like ours?"

"Yes, exactly. Our competitors have gotten a foothold here on Cancri-9, and we can't let them get away with it. You see, if they beat us here, they will have grounds to appeal their case to the Galactics. If they can demonstrate that their mercenary companies are superior to ours, they will get to serve this world. This planet, one of our best customers, will become their territory. We will no longer be able to supply the saurians—big or small—with legions."

I nodded, beginning to understand. "What happens if we do lose this world? What happens if they win?"

The tribune looked grim. "That is unacceptable. If that were to happen, we would lose a critical account. Our income would be reduced and all of Earth would suffer. In time, we might well lose other repeat customers. Eventually, if we are determined to no longer be a viable trader of mercenaries…well, that would be the end."

"The end? The end of our trade?"

He looked at me steadily. "The end of Earth, the end of humanity, the end of everything."

I swallowed and gazed up at the row of heads on Drusus' wall. He was right. I was beginning to understand.

Our mission was critical to Earth—not just because we brought a few Galactic credits home, either. It was far bigger than that.

Oddly, I felt better knowing this. I hadn't really liked the idea of going through so much pain and death for a few credits. If we were fighting for the lives of everyone back home though…well, that was a different matter entirely.

It dawned on me as I eyed those three alien heads on the wall that my actions were going to have an impact on my own family. They were depending on me to succeed. I took a deep breath, and then I did something I thought I'd never do during my enlistment with Varus: I volunteered.

"Tribune? May I make a suggestion, sir?" I asked.

Drusus was watching me closely. "Yes, I'm waiting."

"I know where the incident took place, sir. Maybe I could go out there—I could take a few bios and some light infantry to back me up. We could take samples, dig up earth and cut the grass, if we have to. The alien must have left blood on the ground—something we could use to identify it."

The tribune looked at me intently. There was a slight smile on his lips. Could it be that he'd been trying to get this sort of response from me? I thought that was likely. He could have ordered me to do it, of course, but instead he'd explained the situation to me and laid it all out to see what I'd do.

I decided I didn't care whether he'd planned this or not. His explanation had brought home to me the importance of this mission. The alien had to be identified—we had to know what we were up against.

"That's an excellent suggestion, Recruit," he said. "That's just the sort of thing that earns a man rank in my legion. I'll arrange everything immediately. But, before you go, I'd like you to look at the heads on the wall. Do any of them appear to be familiar?"

I looked up again. "The centipede thing is the closest, but no. It was definitely not like any of these creatures."

I explained briefly how the creature had appeared: Six legs, all with hands of their own. It was able to scuttle on all of them or lift them up and hold a weapon. I gave him every detail I could remember.

When I was done, the tribune scrawled a few notes but shook his head and frowned. "This is a very consistent report. That's what we got from Harris the first time. I can't say that we've met up with anything like it."

I nodded. It wasn't unusual to meet up with new alien species when the Galactics brought us a new product they thought we might wish to spend our hard-won credits on.

Humanity wasn't allowed to wander around exploring on its own, naturally. That was forbidden. Only the aliens who ran the scout ships did that kind of thing. They were the experts, and the rest of us weren't permitted to compete with them in any way.

There was no empire-wide internet service to inform us about our neighbors, either. Each star system was effectively cut off from all the others and wasn't allowed to interact except for conducting approved trading missions—such as I was on right now.

"I've got to go to a meeting with the owners of this mine," the tribune told me. "I've relayed your request to Primus Turov. She'll organize the details."

I marched up the steps and out again into the blazing heat of Cancri-9. The interior of the tribune's bunker seemed blissfully dim and cool in comparison.

Primus Turov was waiting for me. "Follow me. Veteran Harris, you and Adjunct Leeson will be in charge of the sweep. Take your best troops. I'm sending two bios with you. See they don't die. Everyone else is expendable. The sample must be brought in. Are we clear on that?"

"Uh," said Harris.

I could tell he was far from happy. Accepting hazardous missions into the middle of a forest overrun with aliens couldn't have been his usual operating procedure. He hadn't become famous for staying alive by pulling stunts like this one.

"Yes?" asked the primus, turning and staring at him. It was immediately obvious from her tone and manner he wasn't going to worm his way out of this.

"Nothing, sir," he said, letting a small sigh escape. "It shall be as you command."

She left and Harris gave me a hard reproachful stare. "What the hell did you do in there?"

"We talked. He showed me his trophies and explained what Varus is really doing on this world."

"Yeah? And then what?"

"Then I volunteered to go out and find a trace blood sample, anything that would help us identify this new competitive species."

Harris threw an arm around me and half-dragged me toward our unit's section of the wall.

"Are you nuts?" he demanded, booming the words into my ear. "I should ice you right here, right now. That's got to be the dumbest thing—I never thought you'd come up with that!"

He let go of me, and I straightened myself.

"This is bigger than a recruit's possible death," I said. "I know where it happened, and I think I can locate the exact spot where I shot the thing down. If we just scoop up some of the dirt—"

"I don't give a shit about that!" Harris said. "Haven't I taught you a damned thing? You've got some kind of a death-fantasy going, don't you, boy? You're one of the weird ones, aren't you?"

I frowned at him, not quite sure what he was talking about. Then I caught on: he didn't want any part of a dangerous mission in the bush.

"I know you pride yourself on staying alive, Veteran," I said. "But I honestly thought this situation warranted the risk."

Harris hunched his bulky shoulders and grumbled. "You still have it in for me, don't you? I thought we were squared up after training back on the ship. But here you are, trying to blow my record right out of the water."

I almost laughed, but I caught myself. He wasn't in the right mood to see any humor in the situation.

"Listen up, McGill," he said, halting and facing me. "I'm not going down out there before you do. Remember that. You're not going to be winning any more points with the brass today. If things go bad—you die first."

I didn't know what to say to calm him down, so I let him stomp away. I looked after him wonderingly. The man was vouching for me one minute and then threatening my life in a lowered voice the next. And he thought I was the crazy one.

-11-

Carlos found me soon after my strange encounter with Harris. He listened to my story with his head cocked and his eyes narrowed. First I detailed the mission we were going to be enjoying this evening. Then I told him about Harris' reaction.

"What's wrong with you?" he asked when I was finished.

"What do you mean?" I asked.

He wagged his finger at me. "You sucker. Harris was right. He *should* shoot you. What the hell were you thinking?"

"We have to find that alien," I said firmly. "You were out there. Something big is going on. You should have volunteered, too."

"Are you out of your mind? Did you enjoy that little ride we both took through fifteen hungry lizards' guts? They're still digesting us out there, you know that don't you? Maybe tonight, they'll crap out—"

"I don't care about the dinos," I said. "It has to be done, and you and I are the best two for the job. I need you to back me up on this. If I get nailed, you have to lead them to the spot. Are you in or not?"

He grumbled and cursed for a time but finally he nodded.

"Your special brand of crazy must be rubbing off on me," he complained. "I'm doomed."

Less than half an hour later we were walking quietly through the trees retracing our steps. Carlos was at my side.

"It's a good idea to do this at night," I said, eyeing each landmark and checking my GPS frequently. The device had recorded the position of our firefight when we reported in. "Everything will look the same this way."

"Whatever you say," Carlos muttered.

Behind us were twenty other light infantry and the two bio specialists. Adjunct Leeson was in command, and Veteran Harris was at his side. We hadn't brought any heavy troops or weaponeers. The commanders had wanted us to rush in and rush out, not stand and fight.

Adjunct Leeson pushed his way up to me and looked at my GPS.

"This is it," he said. "This has to be the spot."

"Just a little farther out, sir," I said.

He glared at the GPS. "What's your angle, McGill?" he asked me.

"Sir?"

"If you think the primus is going to love you because you kissed her ass on this one, you're going to be in for a surprise."

I blinked at him. "We're almost there, sir."

"We'd better be."

He fell back ten paces. I marched on, shaking my head slightly.

Carlos slapped my shoulder. "You're always making friends in high places," he said. "I can really pick my buddies, can't I?"

"Shut up," I told him.

I halted suddenly, and everyone in the unit halted a second later. No one spoke.

I looked around at the landscape, frowning. There were so many broken branches and black regions, torn up by the passage of a thousand taloned feet. It did look different—not quite as I remembered.

"This is it, I'm pretty sure," I said.

That was too much for Harris. He charged up behind me and rammed the butt of his heavy weapon into my pack. I staggered and turned to face him.

"You're *pretty sure*? That's it? I'm telling you, kid, we're taking our samples right *here*, and afterward we're running all the damned way back to the wall. And when we get there, your ass is going through the gate dead last!"

"Yes, Veteran," I said. "Don't you think we should get to work?"

The bios scrambled forward when I identified the spot where I thought the enemy had died. They scooped up dirt, leaves and blades of grass.

I watched them work, scanning the area and frowning. "It's a big area. Carlos, what do you think? Is that the right spot? The GPS on the report and the photo were right here, but they could be up to twenty meters off."

"This is your show, McGill. I have no freaking idea. I was too busy shitting myself and being eaten to memorize the scenery."

I walked ten paces back toward the wall, and found a fern bush with a fallen log nearby. "Here! Look here!"

"Shhh!" hissed Harris. "Quiet!"

"Sorry. Carlos, come over here and have a look. You were on your knees behind this log when we fought later. But, first, when I met the weird thing, I was standing in this big fern. I used it to hide myself. The alien came out—right there!"

I walked forward and found a spot I felt far more confident was the correct one. I waved for the bios, who reluctantly got up and came to my new position. They were as nervous as cats. They knelt and scooped frantically.

I knelt with them and grabbed a few leaves and scraped soil into my pockets.

A familiar form hulked over me. "Okay, that's it," Harris said. "We're moving out."

"Just one more minute, please."

"No-go. Move out or be left behind."

I got up reluctantly. The bios were already rushing away toward the distant walls.

I looked at Harris. "Your heart really isn't in this one, is it, Veteran?" I asked.

"Don't you give me that crap. I've been doing this since before you were born."

112

I stared at him, wondering if that could be true. Dying and coming back—if you kept getting new bodies, sometimes rolling back a year or more...

"But Veteran," I said, "what about the aliens? Don't you care if they take Cancri-9 from us?"

"Tomorrow, a thousand of your freaks might show up, and we'll know who they are then. Besides, if they're going to kick us off this world in the end, then this fiasco will probably make no difference."

"But it *might* make a difference."

Harris made a frustrated sound. He walked away, and I followed him. I didn't feel good about it. I wasn't sure I'd found what had to be found. It was harder than I thought it would be to find a particular spot in the woods—even after I'd died there.

It was then that I heard footsteps. Not human steps but those of something larger and heavier.

No one needed to say anything. They'd all heard it. Maybe it was just one scouting lizard, sniffing us out. Maybe he was as scared as we were...but we ran anyway.

We'd been ordered to retreat, after all, not to engage. I was very glad to have that order to fall back on. We ran like the devil himself was chasing us all the way back to the tall, blue-white walls. The gates opened when we got there then clanged behind us the second I made it through.

I bent and put my hands on my knees. My sides heaved. The air was so thick here—it made it hard to run.

I glanced at Harris and saw he was grinning at me.

"I told you you'd be the last one to drag your sorry ass through that gate," he said.

I stared at him, and I realized he was right. He'd made sure I was the last man in line. If the lizard had chased us, I was sure I couldn't have outrun it. The raptor-types were often clocked at better than forty miles an hour. If anyone had died tonight, it would have been me.

I suppressed the urge to shudder. Instead, I straightened up and gave him a tough-guy nod.

He laughed at me. Deciding to ignore him, I followed Adjunct Leeson and the bios back to their lab. It was time to dump dirt out of my pockets and theirs and find out if we'd wasted our time or not.

The bio-lab was interesting. It wasn't like any other bunker or tent in the camp. It was clearly designed to do serious science. There were machines there—things that didn't come from Earth. I'd been in here before when I'd been revived, but I hadn't been in any condition to pay attention to my surroundings then.

"I didn't know we had stuff like this," I said.

"Most people don't," said the bio working the equipment. It was Anne Grant.

Grant turned away from me to work on her equipment. She looked like she was in her mid-twenties—but in Legion Varus, that could have meant almost anything. She had brown eyes, brown hair, and for the first time I noticed her perfect posterior. I kept a quiet eye on that while she worked.

"Hey," I said, "I'm sorry about what happened back when we first landed. It was my first drop, my first real combat action. Maybe I could have done better as the point man."

She sighed. "I wish you hadn't brought that up."

"Painful memory? I mean—of course it is. No one likes to die in the mouth of a dino."

"It's not that. You did fine given the circumstances. I was at fault. I was in command, and you were a splat. I should have put a more experienced man on point."

"Well, I just wanted to say—"

"Forget about it, okay?"

"Right," I said, happy to do so.

There was a brief, awkward silence.

"What's that one do?" I asked, pointing out the main machine she was working with.

"It compares known genetic strands to anything you give it. We've got a lot of samples to run through this baby."

"Will it know about our alien friend?"

Grant shrugged. "Possibly. This isn't a first class scanner. The best ones are hooked up to the Galactic databases, cataloging everything known galaxy-wide."

"Why don't we have the best?"

She laughed. "This is Legion Varus, and believe it or not, we get one of the biggest budgets from Hegemony that any legion gets for specialized equipment. But a forensics device like that just costs too much."

I asked if I could stick around while the machine ran the tests, and she said I could. We chatted for quite a while. I found that I liked her, and she seemed to have gotten over her rage at having died during the dino rush when we first landed. Having died myself recently, I now better understood how such an experience could leave one in a bad mood.

When the tests were finished, she read the results carefully. She let out a sigh.

"The tests are inconclusive," she told me.

I tried to hide my disappointment.

"What's that mean? Are we out of options?"

"It means that the unit isn't sure. There is biotic material in the samples—lots of it."

"Including blood?"

"Yes. But most of that is from known sources. The few unknowns might be alien to this world, or they might be from a species this device can't identify. The point is, nothing definite showed up that we can say for sure should not be on this world."

"What's next?"

"I'll send the readings up to *Corvus*, and on to Earth. That will take a while. But you know, there is one element we've identified with certainty."

I nodded encouragingly. "Tell me."

"We found your blood, James."

I stared at her, uncertain how to take this news. She looked happy about finding my DNA in the jungle dirt.

"Actually," Grant said, "that's a good thing. It means you did find the right spot. There are samples we haven't identified yet—there's still hope. The problem is we don't have data on every species indigenous to this world. We're a combat unit, not a scientific exploration team."

I nodded, understanding. "Thanks," I said, and I turned to go.

Grant called me back. "Look, McGill... For what it's worth, I don't agree with Harris and Leeson. It was a good mission, it went well, and it needed to be done."

I gave her a smile, but I had to wonder if she'd be talking like this if a pack of lizards had eaten her for a second time.

Next, I headed back to my squad's quarters where people weren't as happy with me. Kivi was the first one to declare this without any soft-pedaling.

"Hey," she said, coming up to me and sitting on my bunk. "I hear you've been brown-nosing the brass."

I looked at her in surprise. "I thought you knew me better than that."

Kivi gave me a hard stare. "The gang has decided collectively that we don't like special missions. We could have wiped out there hunting for your bug or whatever it was you thought you saw. I'm here to ask you not to do anything like that again—ever."

I felt an angry heat rising up in me. It usually took a while, but I could get pissed off eventually. "If this kind of situation comes up again, I'll do the same damn thing. You can bet on that."

She stood up beside my bunk and ripped open her shirt. The smart-cloth struggled in her hands, trying to close again, but she held the two leaves open and flashed her chest at me. I couldn't help but stare. After a few seconds, she covered herself quickly.

Kivi leaned close and whispered in my ear harshly. "Then you can just forget about getting anything from me when the lights go off around here."

"All right," I said. "If that's how it has to be."

She stormed away angrily.

I realized we'd just broken up. I told myself I didn't care—but I did. During training, we'd hooked-up occasionally, when we both felt like it. Every time had been memorable. Now, that was history.

I flopped down on my bunk and stared at the one directly above me. I boiled inside thinking of a hundred rude things to say.

A head popped over the side of the bunk above mine.

"You screwed that up pretty bad," Carlos observed in a whisper. "I could have kept that going, you know. You went straight-up against her. Never do that with a woman, buddy, especially with a woman who is that hot."

He turned his head looking after Kivi, then looked back down at me. "In fact, with your permission, I'm going to—"

"Shut up," I said. "She's never been interested in you."

"Okay, okay. I'll tell you what: I'm gonna cry a special tear for you and Kivi tonight, big guy. One big tear."

I kicked the bottom of his bunk and he retreated.

"Asshole," I muttered.

I tried to fall asleep, but it didn't come easily. When I finally did drift away, I dreamt of Kivi, saurians and multi-legged aliens gripping me with all six of their freaky hands.

* * *

"Ha!" shouted Veteran Harris the next day when the DNA test results were released to the unit. "A big, friggin' zero. That's what I suspected all along. At least no one died for your little fantasy, McGill."

He stomped away, shaking his head and mumbling.

Pretty much everyone gave me the evil eye after that. Carlos looked like he was going to eat sitting next to someone else for a minute—then he sighed and plopped himself down next to me.

"You're killing my mojo, McGill," he said. "I'm never going to get laid again if I keep hanging out with you."

"That's quite a sacrifice for friendship," I told him. "Thanks man."

He shook his head and we ate quietly. After a few minutes, Natasha came and sat down with us. We both looked at her inquisitively.

"Don't stare," she said. "This is just me being friendly, not a marriage proposal or anything."

Carlos immediately began chatting her up. I could see this flattered and amused Natasha, so I didn't interrupt. I kept thinking about the alien I'd met—and about Kivi.

Before we could finish lunch, the aliens made their next move. We jumped up, shoving food into our faces as the alarms went off. We rushed out and got our kits together. The bunker rang with the sound of a hundred pairs of stomping boots.

"The bastards couldn't let us finish a meal?" Carlos complained.

"Why do they keep coming when we beat them every time?" Natasha asked. "You think they'll hit the walls again?"

"Ever seen a lizard in your backyard?" Carlos asked in return. "They never looked like geniuses to me."

"Yeah, but they just keep dying..."

I lost track of the conversation as we reached the surface. The heat of day made us slam our visors closed the second we exited the bunker. It was intolerable outside. Troops were scrambling for cover everywhere. It took me a second to realize they were being shot at, and at first, I couldn't figure out where the fire was coming from. But then I looked up and over my shoulder.

They had come at our fortress from behind, this time. Somehow, a few hundred snipers had scaled the mountain at our backs and crawled out on top of the cliffs. There were no juggers in the group, only saurian regulars. They peppered our exposed positions from above. Two dozen troops were nailed down to the ground before they could scramble to cover.

I ran and took cover with Carlos at our section of the wall. More troops came out of bunkers behind us, confused and looking around. By the time they realized what was happening, they were being cut down. They scrambled for cover too, but many didn't make it far. I watched them die, shot over and over again by the snipers. There was nothing I could do—I wanted to run out and drag them to my safe position, but the veterans were screaming for us to hold our positions on the covered wall.

"Let them die," Harris said, walking the line, bent at the waist. "There's nothing you can do for them. They'll be popping back out of the oven in less than an hour."

I wasn't sure how we were going to meet this new threat, but the counterattack plan was quickly deployed by my commanders. Earth's legions were nothing if not experienced and versatile.

While we hunkered down and endured the crack and whine of fire from above, quartermasters ran down the line and issued us new equipment: scopes and extended barrels for our snap-rifles.

It quickly became a game of cat and mouse. We nosed our way out of cover, eyeing the cliffs. Sometimes, an enemy sniper sighted us before we did him. In that case, our man went down with a new hole in his skull.

Almost as often, one of our light infantry spotted an enemy sniper lifting his scaly snout over the top of the cliff. When that happened, we painted the target with an infrared beam and everyone leaned out and blew the lizard away.

It was difficult, as the range and angle weren't the best, and it's always easier to have the high ground, but we took them all out in time. There were just too many of us: A thousand light-infantry gunners against two hundred or so saurians. They didn't really have a chance.

After twenty minutes, they stopped sniping at us. They'd either withdrawn or they were all dead.

"Did you get any hits?" Carlos asked me excitedly.

I nodded. "One."

"Kill-shot?"

"I think so."

"Lucky frigger. I shot two, but they were both already sliding down the side of the mountain."

"Too bad."

When the all-clear was sounded, we headed back toward our bunker. A familiar voice behind us called us back.

"Not you guys, not today," Harris said. "All my light infantry are to report to the mine entrance."

We did a collective U-turn and headed for the base of the cliffs. There, sealed portals were located. We found our units and lined up, rifles held to chests, visors shut.

We were met there by none other than Centurion Graves himself.

"All right," he said. "This is real, people. We've just had snipers appear on the roof, coming out of those air shafts.

119

We've got reports of more enemy intrusions in the lower regions of the mine itself. It's our belief they tunneled in from the far side of this mountain."

We looked at each other in alarm. I could read everyone's thoughts: *some worker's rebellion this was turning out to be.*

"We're going in, squad by squad. Inside there are lots of twisty tunnels. Most of them lead downward. But there are shafts, too. Avoid those. They go straight down with sheer sides to the bottom. When I say the bottom, I mean two or three miles deep."

"This already sounds like bullshit," Carlos told me. "You better give the bio running the revival unit a tip. She's going to be earning it today."

I took a breath and hoped he was wrong.

"When you get into the tunnels, spread out into fire teams of five. A weaponeer or a veteran will be leading every team. Our mission is to locate the enemy. Due to a high content of metals, the tunnels are immune to our sensors. If you make contact, withdraw and report in person. Do not attempt to repel the enemy alone. Do I make myself clear?"

There was a general shout of: "Sir, yes, sir!"

Graves was walking along the line, eyeing each of us in turn. He stopped when he got to me.

"One last thing, recruits," he said. "There are a lot of goodies down there: Uranium, gold, diamonds—every mineral worth stealing that you've ever heard of and plenty that you haven't. But we aren't going to take anything. Do you know why?"

He was looking straight into my eyes as he said this. I felt like he was asking me personally, but at the same time I was pretty sure he was talking to the entire unit. The fact that he was shouting every word reinforced this impression.

I stared straight ahead, deciding to play dumb. After a few seconds, he walked away to stare down another recruit.

Carlos chose this moment to pipe up with an answer to the Centurion's last question, which I was pretty sure was rhetorical.

"Because we aren't thieves, sir?"

Graves whirled around on him and marched back. Since Carlos had planted himself at my side, as he usually did, this made for an uncomfortable proximity between me and the officer.

Just in case some form of discipline was required, Veteran Harris rushed close as well. He glared at Carlos from under bushy eyebrows.

"Would you care to elaborate, Recruit?" Graves asked.

"We shouldn't take anything. The saurians hired us, and we're here to protect the mine, not steal from it."

I could tell Carlos was stressed. He just couldn't keep his mouth shut.

The centurion stared at him for a moment longer, then walked away slowly.

"That's a good answer, Recruit," he said.

Carlos was visibly relieved.

"But it's wrong," the officer finished. He nodded to Veteran Harris. "Veteran, could you explain it to them, please?"

"I'd be glad to, sir."

As the Centurion walked away, Veteran Harris walked the line like a tiger pacing in his cage, a pissed-off, hungry tiger.

"Let me clue you morons into some realities," he shouted. "The reason why none of you will steal so much as a hairpin of metal from this planet is right above us."

He pointed his finger up dramatically into the sky. We all glanced up, seeing nothing but hazy clouds. We quickly returned our eyes to the front and center.

"I'm talking about that big ship up there in the sky. The *Corvus* is a *troop* transport, people. It is licensed and contracted to do one thing: carry an Earth legion. That's it, nothing else. If we're caught smuggling local goods off-world—especially the very materials that the good fork-tongued residents of Cancri-9 sell to the Galactics—we'll be found in violation of every treaty Earth ever signed."

He paused for a moment while he let that sink in. I understood the problem immediately. Cancri-9 was called Steel World because it was extremely mineral-rich. That's what they provided to other worlds—minerals. If we took a sample, we would be violating not just local law but Galactic Law.

"And do you lazy, thieving, good-for-nothing, sorry sacks of excrement know what the penalty for breaking any Galactic Law is?"

That one was easy. We answered in unison, as we had to our teachers in every grade since kindergarten.

"Death, sir!"

He nodded. "That's right. If any of you are caught, you'll be executed. And you will not be revived, not even to hang you a few more times for fun. Do I make myself clear?"

"Yes, Veteran!"

"That's good."

He looked back to Centurion Graves, who nodded. We were quickly broken up into fire teams and sent into the mines.

For some reason, my team didn't get deployed until last. Veteran Harris was the only leader left standing with us— except for Centurion Graves himself. Carlos and I exchanged alarmed glances. We'd been rewarded with the gracious presence of Harris again?

The truth, when we realized it fully, was worse than that.

Centurion Graves suited up in combat armor and marched into the portal, with Harris trailing him. He looked over his shoulder at Carlos and me. His face instantly darkened.

"What are you two dogs waiting for? Get your butts over here and open the door for the Centurion!"

We rushed forward, unable to believe our good fortune. We were to be personally led into the tunnels by Graves *and* Harris. It was the best of everything.

-12-

The interior was dark and forbidding. When they'd said this world was high in metals, they hadn't been kidding around. The upper crust was silicate matter—rocks and sand—but down here it was mostly metal and carbon mixed with rock. Graphite and melted iron was everywhere, fused into the walls in silvery-gray lines.

The portal itself was insanely thick and apparently solid steel. When the portal shut with a tremendous clang, at least a meter of metal stood between us and the hot surface of the world.

"You know what that is, McGill?" Carlos asked me. "The sound of doom."

"Shut up, Carlos," I said, without looking at him.

"Keep in mind," Graves was saying, addressing everyone on the team, "we're now cut off from radio contact. Once you go underground anywhere on Steel World, there's very little radio range. The metals interfere too much."

There were about ten of us circled together just inside the portal. Graves was the only one who didn't look nervous.

We formed up, and I tried to get close to Natasha. I liked her company and was already planning pleasant things to say to her.

Veteran Harris squashed my plans by waving me forward. I moved up the column and took a position on the right flank. He smiled and waved harder.

I knew what that meant: I was taking point. It was a thing between the veteran and me, I realized that now. He liked putting me into danger. He wanted to see me die a few extra times. Not having any other way to deal with it, I'd decided to pretend I didn't care. So far, that hadn't been working.

"Pair them up," Centurion Graves said.

Harris ran his eyes over the rest of us. They came to rest on Carlos, and his smile turned into a grin.

"Let's see if you can keep quiet in enemy territory. Partner up with McGill."

Moments later, Carlos and I found ourselves ahead of our little patrol team. Since we were the last team to enter, I could see the flashing lights and hear the tapping feet of the other teams ahead. I started to relax. If there was going to be trouble, surely they would run into it before we did.

My relief was short-lived.

"We're going to spread out," Centurion Graves announced to the team. "Each team is to cover a different level. In case you're wondering, we're covering the bottom level—the one labeled 'incomplete' on your tappers."

We all checked our tappers, making sure they were in working order. When you had your suit on, the normal screen embedded just under the skin was naturally covered up. But Legion Varus had an easy work around for that. The smart-cloth immediately over the tapper relayed the glowing data onto the surface of the fabric. The system worked pretty well, but occasionally you had to peck at it two or three times to get a tap to register when your sleeve wasn't perfectly smooth.

I crouched and brought up my mapping screen on my arm. I tapped at a little red down-arrow until I was at a level of the map that displayed "incomplete" and I frowned. There were tunnels down there but nothing like the higher levels. They trailed off, and many of them had dashed lines. I turned back to Harris.

"Veteran? What do the dashed lines mean?"

"Those are flooded zones, cave-ins," he shrugged. "Areas that are full of rubble. Incomplete means not finished yet."

"How do we get down there?" Carlos asked, looking this way and that down the long, echoing tunnels.

"Elevators are dead ahead. But we're not going that way. They shut them down because no one wanted to give the enemy an easy way to move around. We'll take the tubes. They're over there."

I followed his pointing finger with my eyes. I saw the mouth of the tubes, which resembled two black holes like eye sockets in a skull. They were cut into the wall of the tunnel we were in, and they appeared to go down into nothingness.

We found junk everywhere as we moved forward. Broken tools and machines with power-meters registering zero lined the dusty walls. There was a small pile of helmets shaped like a saurian's head and a few scattered bullets rolled around under our boots.

I moved forward, my eyes behind my rifle. I aimed my rifle down the shaft and looked around, using the night vision scope. I could see movement.

"Someone's down there," I reported, "but they look friendly."

"Should be," Harris said in my ear. "Most of the teams are using the shafts to reach their assigned levels."

I looked back at Harris. "Do we rappel down, or…?"

"Just jump in there. You'll float down."

I almost did it, but hesitated. Carlos frowned and glared back at Harris. "You trying to kill us right off, Veteran?"

"Oh, sorry!" Harris said, coming forward. "You're supposed to take this and put it under your feet, first."

He reached over and grabbed a pair of disk-like things out of a barrel. He handed one to each of us.

"Careful not to flip over," he said, giving us a little grin.

Centurion Graves shouldered forward. He appeared to be annoyed with Harris and at us for causing a delay.

"Here, put them on like this," he said impatiently, demonstrating. "They're built for saurians, but they'll hold a human if you balance right. You boys ever ride a skateboard?"

We shook our heads.

He cursed in disgust and told us it was just like surfing or skiing. I didn't have the heart to tell him I hadn't done a lot of either in the hills of Georgia, and I could tell Carlos, who was from the Chicago mega-habs, didn't know what to make of it either.

As recruits, it was our job to obey rather than to complain—at least when our superiors were listening. We put the damned hubcap-looking things on our feet and stepped off into the shaft.

At the last minute, Harris gave me a little shove.

"You're taking too long!" he said.

I cursed and wobbled, but soon achieved balance and found myself falling at a moderate rate. Carlos came down after me.

"The water's fine, sirs!" I called up to them. "Come on down."

"We will. Get down there and secure the LZ. We're going all the way to the bottom."

I heard them fooling with their gear up above us. The sounds of scraping metal and gritty crunching noises faded as we fell farther and farther.

We passed openings in the shaft as we dropped. Sometimes, we saw lights and heard troops talking. Our men had spread out all over the mine.

"Why don't we exit the shaft and have a look below first?" Carlos asked me.

"You heard the man," I told him. "All the way to the bottom."

We kept falling. At about the seventh or eighth level, I saw a bright stabbing beam of light coming at us from the side shaft. We aimed our weapons in that direction, but I wasn't sure how we could defend ourselves while riding these hubcap things. I figured they'd probably tip over from the recoil if we fired. But we aimed them all the same.

"Hold on! Friendly!" shouted a female voice. We drifted down and the owner of the voice peeked out at us.

"Hi, Inga!" Carlos said.

I didn't recognize the girl, but she waved at us as we drifted down.

"Don't go down too far," she said. "I hear it's bad down there."

"Thanks for the tip," Carlos said unhappily.

126

We kept dropping. Once, we heard the chatter of snap-rifle fire in the distance. Twice, I could have sworn someone screamed or at least shouted in pain.

There wasn't much we could do. We had our orders. Eventually, we crunched down onto a surface of rough grit. It wasn't quite sand; it was more like a mixture of ground-up granite and metal shavings.

I struggled and ended up sitting on my ass while I tried to pry the dish off my foot. Carlos came over and flipped a tiny sliding switch on the rim of the hubcap. Instantly, it sprang off my foot.

"Magnets, I guess," he said.

I nodded and climbed to my feet. He waited for me and let me exit the shaft first.

It was dark down here. Up on higher levels there had always been light. Now there was nothing but a dim bluish glow. The light seemed to come from strips on the roof of the tunnels. I supposed it was some lizard's idea of emergency lighting.

"Let's turn off our suit lights and go with night vision," I suggested.

"Let's sit in this shaft until the rest of the team gets down here," Carlos said, voicing a reasonable counter proposal.

I shook my head. "Orders were to secure the LZ."

"Yeah, right, but they aren't going to know what we did or didn't do."

I frowned at him. Carlos was never going to be Legion Varus' poster-boy.

"Fine, I'll take a look around by myself."

I nosed out of the shaft and aimed my rifle in a slow sweep, while looking through the scope. I didn't see any movement, but I did see a lot of gravel and half-clogged tunnels.

"It looks like they've had some cave-ins or something."

"Naturally," Carlos said. He was right behind me aiming his weapon the other way down the shaft.

I glanced at him. I'd noticed that he never wanted to do anything adventurous, but if I did it first, he couldn't hang back. He had to come and look at whatever I was up to. I smiled to myself. Carlos hated to think he was being left out of anything. I guess there were worse traits in a soldier.

The shaft opened into a tunnel that led to the right and left. We checked out the immediate vicinity, going no more than twenty paces in either direction.

Carlos flipped on a penlight and splashed it on the walls. After a few seconds, he knelt and fished something out of the rubble. It was a fist-sized lump of reddish, translucent material. It looked like melted glass.

"You know what this is?" he asked me in a whisper.

"Junk?"

"No. My HUD computer says it's pure ruby. About a thousand carats worth. Would be even better if it was a red diamond. Those are the rarest kind, you know. A raw diamond this size is worth millions."

I aimed my snap-rifle in his direction. I indicated he should toss the jewel down with the barrel of my weapon.

"What's your problem?" he asked me.

"I don't have a problem. You're the one looking at perma-death for violating Galactic export laws."

He made a face and tossed the jewel aside.

"You're no fun," he said.

We found nothing else of interest so we flipped off our lights again and returned to the shaft.

When we got there, we heard the rest of the team landing. The second we came around the corner, a half-dozen rifles aimed into our faces. They had their lights on, and we didn't. They'd been making more noise than we were, and we'd come out of the dark quietly.

"Report, recruits!" Harris demanded, lowering his weapon.

"Nothing much. The tunnel runs at least a hundred meters in both directions. It appears to be damaged or unfinished. No contacts, nothing."

"All right," said the Centurion. "We'll move out—to the north. According to the map, that area is smaller. If we can clear it in an hour, we'll mark it safe and go south."

"Excuse me, sir?" Carlos asked. "What exactly are we looking for? Besides lizards, I mean."

"You're looking for signs of a break-in. The miners reported seeing intruders in the middle levels of the mine. I personally find it unlikely they'd come in this far down, but we just don't know.

"A break-in, sir?"

"As in a tunnel that has been recently dug to merge with these."

"One last thing, sir," Carlos said. "Have any of the other teams met up with the enemy yet?"

"Negative. There have been some reports of sightings, but they haven't panned out. People are shooting at phantoms up there."

I wasn't sure I believed him. Communications were far from perfect down here. Maybe some other group had run into something and been wiped out. But I decided not to argue about that. Instead, I lifted a hand.

The Centurion nodded to me.

"Are we going to divide up in to two-man teams, sir?" I asked, bringing up his initial plan.

The Centurion directed his light out into the dark, forbidding tunnels. He shook his head.

"I don't think so. We'll stay tight. It will take longer, but since the enemy hasn't been found yet, and we're the last ones to get started—we're going to keep all our firepower together. Now team, if you do see a definite enemy down here, you have my leave to fire. We're going in hot. There is no legit reason why an innocent lizard would be down here at this point."

I was relieved to hear this. I checked my magazine, made sure there were no jams, and flipped off the safety.

Without asking, Carlos and I headed into the tunnel and swung left. We both knew we were going to be on point until Harris had his share of our blood on his hands. There was no sense in pretending otherwise.

As we moved forward, I couldn't help but notice Harris had taken up his position at the rear of the team. I shook my head. I guess he figured that the dinos would have to eat all of us first to get to him.

We left the group behind again, and I realized Carlos and I weren't talking anymore. This place was creepy, and we both

129

felt a bad vibe about it. I think it was the quiet. Our boots were the loudest thing down here. We crunched on grit and heard water dripping somewhere. Everything echoed.

We reached an area that was crisscrossed with tunnels that ran with wet, dripping walls. We began moving from intersection to intersection, staying in cover as much as possible. Carlos and I were leapfrogging from one corner to the next, walking with knees bent on high alert. Puddles of water sent up wisps of steam when our boots splashed into them.

Carlos signaled me, and I rushed forward across an open side tunnel. As I passed by, I took a glance down that dank, rubble-filled tunnel.

There was something there, something inhuman. It was crouched over a lump on the ground, and appeared to be digging at it.

I made it to the far side and threw my back against the tunnel wall. I signaled Carlos, indicating enemy contact.

He followed our orders, withdrawing to the rest of the team who were about thirty meters behind us. That left me alone with an alien rooting around in the tunnel next to me.

Quiet fell after Carlos was gone. It was *too* quiet, I decided. The enemy should have been making some noise doing whatever it had been doing.

I nosed around the corner to have another look.

To my surprise, the alien was right there. It must have heard me as well, and had been stalking forward to investigate.

I could see it clearly now, and knew it was a saurian regular. They looked a lot like the juggers, but smaller, sleeker and faster.

What happened next surprised me: the saurian lifted a round object. It had to be a weapon. Most of the enemies I'd dealt with on this campaign had relied on their teeth. A few had possessed advanced weapons, but most hadn't.

I fired at him and missed. He'd ducked behind a spur of glittering rock. A flash of blue-white energy lit up the tunnel then. I saw the source clearly: he had a plasma grenade in his claws.

All this happened in about half a second. I didn't bother to shoot at him again because there wasn't time. The grenade was already flying in my direction. I threw myself backward instead, and around the corner from him. I landed on my back, rolled over onto my front, then began crawling away. Blue light built up behind me in a silent flare of energy. I kept crawling. Water splashed up and I could feel the heat of it through my gloves. I reached up and ripped away my night vision goggles.

Then the grenade went off.

Light filled the chamber. It was a quiet explosion, like a flashbulb as bright as a blue star rising behind me. The glare of it seemed to burn right through the back of my skull.

I was lifted up and tossed forward. I felt as if a giant had kicked me right in the ass. A thousand slivers shot into my skin through the smart-cloth suit, stinging and making me hiss in pain. I knew what that was, I'd learned about it in training. Plasma grenades were weird. Instead of being an explosive wrapped in metal which turned into fragmentation, they picked up whatever was around them and shot it out in every direction.

In this case, I was feeling bits of grit and probably even slivers of water from the puddles I'd been scrambling through. They'd been turned into tiny weapons, some of which had punctured my thin suit.

Half-blinded and in agony, I rolled back over and tried to get to my feet. I knew that the saurian would be backing up its grenade-toss by rushing in close.

I made it up into a sitting position before the thing was on me. Its claws scrabbled as it eagerly charged and rounded the corner to face me. It scrambled close, making a grunting sound. Behind it, my team had their lights on. They were coming, but not fast enough.

I knew I was going to die again. I can't explain how horrible that feeling is. It was worse this time than it had been the last. The first time you face death, you can deny it. You can pretend it really isn't happening.

But not the second time around. I knew all too well what being savaged by a half-mad saurian felt like. Their teeth were curved and sharp and numbered in the hundreds.

I managed to get off a burst of slivers, but that was only enough to get the rifle slammed out of my hands. The thing's muzzle was lunging forward, dipping down. The jaws opened.

A rattling cascade of fire came to my ears. I saw the saurian shiver and lurch to one side. It fell heavily and struggled to get up. But before it could, the rest of my team closed in, pumping rounds into it. The tunnels rang with the snap and whistle of our rifles as we shot it again and again.

I slumped down on my back in pain. Carlos' face loomed over me.

"You're alive?" he asked as if surprised.

"You're ugly," I said.

They laughed and hauled me up. I found I couldn't stand. Sitting down was a problem, too.

Centurion Graves came to me and squatted nearby. He coldly assessed my status. "Can you walk?"

"Maybe in a minute, sir."

"Why are you lying on your side like that?"

"Because my butt is full of needles, sir."

That brought a chuckle from some of the others.

"Right, plasma grenade. I bet it picked up this grit. Perfect terrain for that kind of weapon. You're a lucky man, McGill."

"People keep telling me that, sir."

I didn't add that I didn't *feel* lucky right now. It was probably obvious anyway.

"All right, McGill will have to be hauled back to the surface. He's no good to us down here. Veteran Harris? Go back up the shaft and alert the rest of the unit. Tell them we've had a confirmed contact, and we have an injured man. I want three more full squads down here in ten minutes. Pull them from the upper levels."

"Right, sir," Harris said. Without missing a beat, he turned to Carlos. "You heard the centurion. Get up that shaft—"

"Negative, Veteran!" barked Graves.

"Sir?"

"You heard me. You, *personally*, are going to sound the alarm. I doubt these recruits even know how to operate the disks well enough to travel up the shafts again. Get moving."

I thought I heard Harris mutter something unpleasant, but I could have been mistaken. He turned and ran double-time for the shafts.

Carlos tried to help me up, and Graves grabbed my other arm and hauled with him. I was placed on my feet, where I swayed slightly. I could stand, but walking wasn't in the cards, not yet. Just standing was painful.

Then the chattering of gunfire came from down the tunnel. We all turned and lifted our rifles.

It was Harris. He was running back toward us, howling. Behind him thundered a jugger. The thing was racing down the tunnels after him, slapping its fat tail against the walls. Chunks of grit and shale showered the floor with every sweeping step it took.

-13-

Harris was aiming his gun behind him and firing blindly as he ran. Orange sparks splattered the walls. I saw that most of his rounds were missing, but a few caused red spots to sprout up on the charging jugger's chest. Rather than stopping the monster, these injuries only served to piss it off. It ran faster, gaining on Harris.

"Ready your weapons, but hold your fire," Centurion Graves ordered calmly.

We spread out and leveled our rifles. Harris was in the way, or we would have fired. I thought about doing it anyway, but Centurion Graves had given the order to hold, so I held.

It was a close thing, but Harris didn't make it. The jugger caught up with him and snatched off his right arm, the one with the rifle in it. Along with the weapon, he lost most of his shoulder and the side of his face.

It was the strangest thing I'd ever seen. One minute, Harris was running for all he was worth, and the next a big portion of his upper body was—just gone. The jugger paused in its charge to toss back the morsel and gulp it down.

What remained of Harris took one more weird half-step then flopped down into the blood-soaked grit.

I fired. All of us did. We didn't wait for Graves to give the order. He was firing too, so I was sure he didn't mind.

We tore the monster apart. It took about ten seconds to bring it down. After about ten more seconds of thrashing, it finally lay still.

Graves walked forward and picked up Harris' weapon. "Grab his ammo. Split the load. He'll need it when he's back in action."

So calm, so nonchalant! How many deaths had this man witnessed firsthand? I couldn't even guess. He'd sounded more concerned about my injuries than he did Harris' death.

"I made a mistake," he said. "I didn't realize we were being stalked. Recruit, check out that lump in the tunnel down there."

He pointed, and I realized he was pointing at Natasha, not me. That made sense, as I was injured.

It took Natasha by surprise. She was standing next to me, and she looked shocked. I don't think she'd ever been sent out to scout alone before.

"What lump, sir?" she asked.

Graves gestured impatiently. "Whatever McGill saw the saurian messing with. It's down that tunnel. Recon and report."

Natasha was breathing hard. She had a wild look in her eye. She stared at Harris' mangled body. I could tell she didn't want to go down any of these tunnels for any reason.

Graves understood the situation instantly. He walked up to Natasha and smoothly placed his rifle under the woman's chin.

I had to admit, upon seeing that, I was unnerved. I instinctively took a firmer grip on my weapon. I felt a protective surge.

"The penalty for directly disobeying orders is perma-death," Graves told her. "But I'm a lenient man. If you like, I'll put you out right here, right now. You can revive later and apologize."

"That won't be necessary, Centurion!" Natasha said. She turned and trotted down the tunnel into the dark. I watched her go, not knowing what to think.

I eyed Graves sidelong. The look on his face reminded me of the first time I'd met him aboard the transport that carried me up to *Corvus*. He'd been in the emergency compartment dispassionately watching us all suffocate. That same steely eyed gaze was on his face now. He really didn't care if Natasha lived or died.

As if he was aware of my scrutiny, Graves turned to look at me.

"You don't approve, Recruit?"

"I didn't say anything, sir."

"No, you didn't. Keep it that way. You're here to learn, and you've already learned a lot. Never forget what the tribune told you, McGill: Legion Varus is playing for keeps on this planet. If you don't like it, you can get out in five more years."

Natasha reached the lump in the tunnel and examined it for about three seconds with her suit light. Then she raced back toward us as if her butt was on fire. I didn't blame her. Every shadow looked dangerous to us now.

"It's another saurian, sir," she reported. "It appears to be a miner, and it looks as if it's half-eaten."

Graves nodded. "Dinos aren't averse to cannibalism," he said, as if he was describing some kind of strength. "There does appear to be a rebellion among the miners here, but it's much bigger than a few unpaid juggers. The enemy includes both large and small lizards, and one example of something else, if McGill is to be believed. Puzzling."

He gave me a cold glance. I got the feeling he didn't entirely believe my account of the alien I'd met in the forest.

I shrugged. I didn't care what he believed, because I'd seen it with my own eyes. Hell, I'd shot it to death.

Graves turned and signaled two fresh recruits to take point. I was relieved. Natasha came to my side and helped me walk.

We proceeded as a tight group back up the tunnel.

There were no more mishaps until we reached the shafts themselves. I stared in disbelief when we got there. The shafts were full of rubble.

"Looks like a cave-in," Graves said.

He didn't even sound upset. The rest of us were horrified.

"How are we going to get out, sir?" Carlos asked.

Graves gave him a wintry smile. "We could just shoot ourselves. We'd be revived in a day or two based on our last backups whenever they figure it out. You wouldn't remember much, but maybe that's a good thing, eh?"

Everyone looked at him in wide-eyed horror, unsure if his suggestion that we commit mass suicide was meant in earnest. Then he laughed.

"Can't take a joke?" he asked. "Recruits never can. I would never order that—not now, anyway. We've got a mission to perform. These lizards aren't going to win so easily."

We weren't quite sure how we should feel. By staying alive, we were stuck down here. I could hardly walk, Harris was dead, and we had no idea how many more lizards were stalking us right now.

"What could have filled the shaft, sir?" I asked.

Graves shrugged. "A lizard, probably. Maybe one with another plasma grenade. They're pretty quiet when they go off. We might have missed the noise and the burst of light. We were far away and distracted. The more interesting question is *why* they blocked the shaft."

I thought about it. "To keep us from warning the others, sir?" I suggested.

He looked at me and pointed a finger at my chest.

"I agree, McGill. Your file said you were a college dropout, but I'm beginning to think there were extenuating circumstances."

I stiffened. I had no idea he'd been nosing in my files. "My mother lost her job, and I lost my funding."

Graves nodded. "That fits. Well, we've met up with three lizards down here including the dead one, and there are bound to be more. Back to our original duty, team. Except this time, we aren't going to recon these tunnels. The mission has changed. We're going into search-and-destroy mode from here on out."

We proceeded to carefully search the tunnels for the better part of an hour before we made any fresh contacts. I began to realize just how big this mine was. This planet was riddled with mines like this one, and the mineral deposits were amazing.

There were clusters of garnets, diamonds, rubies and hard metals everywhere. We called Cancri-9 "Steel World", but it was much more than that. It was a treasure house of rare elements. The basic components of steel were more common than granite on Earth, but there were plenty of other valuable minerals as well.

The difference between this place and Earth was the core mix of elements. This world had a lot more iron and less silicon. In practice, that meant it was more metal than it was dirt and rock. Instead of veins of ore embedded in stone, there were veins of stone embedded in walls of pure metal.

Just about when we were all starting to think we'd met up with every saurian that was in this place, big or small—they jumped us.

They'd chosen their ground carefully. We came to an intersection that led in five directions—north, east, west, up and down. None of these tunnels had a long run before they twisted or turned. Centurion Graves called a halt as we entered from the eastern tunnel.

"I don't like it. They could be anywhere. We'll all take the tunnel downward together. That tunnel looks freshly drilled."

There were indeed shavings of steel littering the floor of the place, and the tunnel that led downward had sharp, flanged edges. I stared at these as we passed them.

"Centurion?" I asked.

"What is it, McGill?"

"I think someone just drilled this tunnel up from below. I don't see the boring machine, but it must be around somewhere."

"Let's keep moving. We don't have time to sightsee or indulge our engineering curiosity."

"But sir?" I called, running my gloved fingers over the blade-like edges of the tunnel mouth.

He turned back in irritation. "What?"

"This tunnel that comes up and joins the primary run—look at the drill marks. They must have drilled *from* that tunnel *into* this one."

He stared at me for a second, then Carlos came near and ran his fingers over the walls.

"He's right," he said. "They drilled from the outside inward."

Centurion Graves got it then. He examined the walls with squinting eyes. "I think you're right, Recruit. Very observant.

The striations are curved in the opposite direction. This tunnel is probably the route the enemy used to enter the complex. They bored their way in right here…"

We heard footsteps and rasping sounds. Everyone unslung their weapons and aimed them in every direction. It wasn't immediately obvious from which way the threat was coming, but one thing was for sure: they were coming. I wasn't sure if they'd finally grown tired of waiting for us to choose a path, or if they'd just all reached their set positions. But, I was sure it was a planned ambush because they came at us from five different directions at once.

It was chaos from the beginning. Ten of us could not possibly cover all five avenues of attack evenly. Centurion Graves roared for us to move forward, into the low tunnel. We did so, and found ourselves in a gloomy hole which was crudely cut and had no lighting installed.

I was more convinced than ever that this was the way the enemy had entered the complex. Everywhere else in the mine there were lights installed and often rails in the floor which served for powered carts to carry minerals to the surface. This tunnel had none of those amenities. It looked like an animal's burrow—but one made of dull gray metals.

By pulling us deeper into the low tunnel, Graves made sure there were only two directions we had to aim our guns. I had to admit, as the saurians began their attack, I was glad Graves was in charge. He never panicked or froze up. He smoothly ordered us to respond to the situation and made the right move the first time.

"Front rank get low," he ordered, "I want two men on their bellies in front, two men firing over their heads, and the rest of you in the center. Wait until they break either line to commit yourselves."

There were only nine of us, and the tunnel was only about three meters wide. I found myself on my belly facing back the way we'd come. The saurians rushed us, and we were immediately surprised by what they had: snap-rifles.

Fortunately, they weren't very good with them. It was immediately obvious they barely knew how to use their weapons. They sprayed ahead, sweeping the tunnel with clattering rounds.

We gritted our teeth and returned fire. Our aim was dramatically better, and the first line of saurians went down in a thrashing heap. Fresh troops bounded right over them, snatched up the dropped guns and kept coming.

"They're using our own weapons on us!" shouted Carlos beside me over the din of fire. Inside the tight confines of the metallic tunnel walls, the noise rebounded painfully from every direction.

I saw that he was right. The snap-rifles weren't just any weapons, they were our weapons. They even had the Legion Varus wolf's head stamped on the side.

I realized they must have taken them from other light troops. How long had this fight been going on? We certainly weren't their first victims—but were we the last survivors in this mine?

Pushing aside such thoughts, I kept up a steady hail of fire. Natasha, who'd been standing behind me, fell. She was from the second rank, the standing rank. I guess I was lucky to be on my belly as I made a smaller target. I took a fraction of a second to glance back, and I knew instantly that I couldn't help her. She was dead, eyes staring, mouth open. There was blood on her cheek.

I didn't bother to look back at her again, I could feel her weight draped over me as I fought on. It was horrible, but I didn't have time to care for her, or even to push her off my back. I just kept firing into the charging line of angry lizards.

We sent a hail of steel in their direction, but it wasn't enough. They reached our line and overran us. The whole firefight so far had only taken thirty seconds, but lizards move fast. They were all over us.

"Gunners, hold your positions!" Graves roared. "Keep firing. Center people repel the enemy. Knives out!"

I heard clicking sounds and blood splashed over my faceplate. I had to wipe it away so I could see. I wasn't sure whose blood it was—enemy or human. The saurian blood was about the same color as ours, just a little darker and thicker. In the dimly lit tunnel, I couldn't tell the difference.

Trusting my struggling comrades, who were literally battling over my head, I kept putting bullets into the saurians that were charging in. So many! I didn't see how we could—

Something clamped down on my leg. The back of my right calf was in the jaws of a saurian, and the teeth went right through the tough smart fabric of my uniform. I hissed and howled, rolling over to face my attacker. I slashed up at it, opening up the leathery belly with my combat knife.

The razor-sharp edge spilled lizard guts all over the floor. This made the saurian release me and it raised its head in pain but wasn't finished yet. It made another attempt to bite me, the head darting down toward my other leg.

I jerked away and the jaws snapped shut on nothing. Carlos and I managed to nail it with a burst of shots each, and it fell as dead as a stone.

The saurians stopped coming after that. A few of them ran off into the dark. We chased them with bursts from our snap-rifles. They slid in their own blood and screeched. The sound of their pain did my heart good.

By this time, I'd had enough of laying on my stomach, so I got to my knees painfully and tried to stand. By the time I was on my feet, the next wave came. I'd dared to hope we'd seen the last of them, but there were more.

The final wave was comprised of six juggers. They weren't the biggest I'd seen, but they were knocking their heads against the rough roof of the tunnel. All of them had red scales, with bellies of silvery-white—almost a pearly color. I might have thought the look of these beasts to be entrancing on a travel brochure but not when they were hell-bent on eating me.

Carlos and I glanced at one another. We were both covered in sweat and blood. Our sides were heaving from exhaustion and fear. This was too much. We couldn't bring them down with small arms. There was no way we were going to live.

But I knelt and began to fire steadily into the lead monster. Carlos did the same.

"Aim at the throat!" I said, remembering the tactic from my past. I'd read about and simulated legion engagements on Cancri-9 since I was a kid. Juggers were hard to kill with tiny bullets, but if you could do enough damage to vital arteries…

We peppered the face and neck of the leader with red sprouting wounds. But it seemed to catch on and ducked its head low, putting the crown of its thick-skulled head into our stream of fire. There was no way we could penetrate into its brain with these weapons.

"Good try, recruits!" Centurion Graves boomed. "It was an honor to serve."

I marveled at the evenness of his voice. He sounded like he wasn't even sweating.

"You too, sir," Carlos shouted.

I looked up, bewildered, and Graves' eyes met mine. "You're in charge," he said.

Then the Centurion did something unexpected.

"Ceasefire!" he shouted. "Put your heads down!"

Then he sprinted forward, rushing directly into the charging mass of juggers. The leader didn't see him until he darted by. Confused, it faltered in its lumbering charge and turned.

I watched with my mouth sagging open. What the hell was he doing? Did he think he could make it past them all and leave us behind as a sacrificial dinner?

Then I saw the glaring blue light, and I knew what was happening. He'd pulled out a plasma grenade, and he was standing in the middle of the juggers.

Fortunately, juggers were not geniuses. They whirled on him and lunged with snapping jaws. When the explosive went off, I doubt Graves had a limb left on him—but he was past caring by that time.

We followed his final orders and ducked low. The whole tunnel rippled with the force of the blast. Magnified by the closeness of the metal walls, the concussion reverberated painfully.

That did it for the enemy. However many of them were left, they'd had enough. They pulled back and licked their wounds leaving their dead behind them.

We weren't in much better shape. I did a headcount and came up with seven survivors. We'd lost half our original number, and we weren't out of these tunnels yet.

-14-

The rest of the mission was a sweaty haze. I kept thinking of Natasha, and how she'd died on my back. There'd been nothing I could do—it was galling. I tried to push those thoughts away. Lots of people had died. It was no big deal. If we could get out of here, we could all cry about it later.

We huddled in the tunnel for the next hour treating our wounded and talking about what we should do. We were down to seven recruits, and all of us were as raw and inexperienced as they came.

"Graves put McGill in charge," Carlos said to the rest. "Yeah, I know, it's crazy, but I heard it. Granted, he was probably certifiable by that point... One second later, he ran into the middle of a pack of juggers and offered up his juicy parts."

"It was a noble sacrifice," I said.

Carlos scoffed. "Yeah, right. He knew he would be back in camp sipping coffee in a few hours while we're still stuck in this rat-hole."

"I didn't see you doing it."

Carlos snorted, but he did finally shut up. The peace that fell over the group once he stopped yapping was blissful. No one else felt much like talking. We were all thinking too much about the grim fate that probably awaited us when the next charge came.

Plasma grenades weren't cheap. We couldn't make them on Earth, and they cost Galactic credits—real money—to buy. For that reason only a few troops had them, weaponeers and officers who requisitioned a charge for their own personal use. Graves' grenade was the only one we'd brought down here with us.

So we were left with snap-rifles, a few extra magazines and our combat knifes. The dead were all around us to remind us what might happen any minute. The group was in a depressed mood.

I took a deep breath and struggled to my feet. I pushed away Carlos' hand and took a few painful steps on stiff legs.

"Maybe dying would do you some good," Carlos observed. "Fastest way to heal up."

I frowned at him. "Enough with the quitter routine. Graves put me in charge. Get up, everyone. We're moving out of this damned tunnel."

"Where?" demanded Kivi. She was the last living woman on the team. Her eyes were big, blue and a little crazy.

Carlos jumped in before I could answer. He pointed down the tunnel. "Back to the shafts. If there is going to be a rescue, it has to come from that direction."

I slapped his hand down and pointed in the opposite direction. "We're going to see where this shaft leads."

They all looked at me like I was mad. I had to admit they could be right, but I didn't care. I wanted to complete our mission. I wanted to know where the enemy was coming from.

"Look," I said to them. "We're screwed anyway. We might as well find out how they got into the mine."

"We'll all die for sure," Kivi said. "What's the point of that?"

"If we find the end point, we'll have completed the mission. When they revive any one of us who's been down here, we'll report then."

Carlos stepped forward and put a hand on my arm. "Hey, McGill," he said, "I don't want to rain on your parade, but your idea could get us permed."

I frowned at him until he pulled his hand away. "What are you talking about?"

144

"That's one of the ways it happens. It's against Galactic Law to copy anyone who's not confirmed dead. If we wander down into the bowels of this shit planet and get burned to ash by lava or something, they won't be able to ID our bodies. No ID, no reconstruction. Perma-death."

I paused, having not considered that possibility. Throughout our battles so far, we'd been on the surface and easily located by sensor equipment. Down here, however, it was a different story. We were cut off by the planet's metallic soil. No one back at HQ knew if we were alive or dead. Probably, they hadn't revived any of the team members yet. Not even Harris. They wouldn't do it until they had some kind of confirmation—which I doubt they had yet.

I shook my head. "Doesn't matter," I said. "I'm not talking about walking ten miles or jumping into any lava chambers. I'm talking about exploring this tunnel. What's the difference if we're a few hundred meters farther away from the shaft when they get down here?"

"It's a risk."

"One which I'm willing to take," I said, and I began walking.

They grumbled, but they were used to following unreasonable orders, so they fell into line. I headed down the tunnel in the lead, not having the heart to order anyone else to take point. This was my idea, after all. The least I could do was get myself eaten first.

As we progressed, it did seem that the level of heat in the tunnel was increasing. I didn't know what to make of that. All Carlos' talk of lava chambers might have had me spooked—or it might be real.

"Check the external temp," I said, halting.

Carlos frowned and did as I suggested. "No change," he said. He looked toward Kivi, who was next in line.

She shook her head, looking up from her tapper. "Nothing."

I frowned and examined my systems. I found a fault within seconds. "It's me," I said. "My suit must have been damaged during that last fight. Really, I'm not surprised."

"You've got a leak?"

"Maybe…either that, or my air conditioner is dying."

"Bad way to go. This planet runs a fever of forty degrees Celsius, even underground."

I shrugged. "I'll be hot, but I'll survive. The tunnels won't broil me the way the open land would."

I kept going. We'd gone far more than a hundred meters. We'd gone at least a thousand, but as my troops weren't complaining, I didn't stop.

After nearly three kilometers had passed, however, Carlos tapped me on the shoulder.

"McGill? This is crazy, man. This tunnel might run forty kilometers for all we know. And the rescue party might be behind us, baffled as to where we went."

I leaned against the wall of the tunnel and sipped water. My suit's reservoir was running low.

"All right," I said at last. "Let's give it ten more minutes. We march that much farther, then turn around."

They groaned, but they followed. I had to admit that even I was giving up hope.

Fifteen minutes later, we rounded a slight bend in the tunnel and saw daylight only a hundred meters ahead. That was a stunner.

We crouched, stared and zoomed with our optics. We spoke in whispers despite the fact we couldn't see any lizards.

"I can't believe it," Carlos said. He was working on his tapper, bringing up data. "My GPS doesn't work down here— no surprise. But the computer counts every step you take. I reset the counter when we started. We marched over four frigging kilometers. Ten minutes...you're such a liar, McGill. I hate you."

"I found the way out, didn't I?" I said, smiling. "Okay, what we're going to do is poke our noses out. Take off your safeties and be ready for anything."

I took a half-step, but Carlos' hand fell on my wrist. I pulled it away and almost shoved him. He'd never dare try that crap if I had real rank on him.

"McGill? James?" he asked, shaking his head in disbelief. "It's *over* man! You found what you wanted. Let's get the hell out of here."

"That's what I intend to do. I'm going to march out of this tunnel and radio our report in. They can come pick us up. That will be much faster than walking back."

"But they don't have any airpower. That wasn't in the contract. We'd have to wait for the ship to send down a lander or walk all the way back through the forest."

I thought hard for a second. The rest of them looked scared. We all knew that going out onto the surface was dangerous. Walking through that forest was going to be close to suicide, and my suit's AC was already failing.

But I wanted to see where this tunnel went. The answer was so close I couldn't give up now. I came up with an angle that I thought would give them a good reason to follow me.

"Listen," I said, "this is all about avoiding perma-death at this point. If we walk out there and get wiped—well, at least the finish will be recorded by our GPS systems. We'll be back in camp within an hour, healthy and fresh. If we stay down here in this hole, anything could happen. We're all taking the risk of being permed if we stay in the tunnels."

In the end, their fear of getting permed outweighed their fear of being overrun by hungry lizards. They complained and gave me frustrated groans, but at last they pulled it together and followed me to the mouth of the tunnel.

We crept up to the glaring entrance. The mouth was overgrown and half-filled with sifting mud. It was raining outside and relatively cool. The green canopy of the jungle softened the glaring sky, and as our eyes adjusted, it no longer seemed brilliantly bright.

We sat just inside the entrance for several minutes, listening to the rain and talking in whispers.

"Do you see anything?" Carlos asked me.

"Trees—that's about it."

"No lizards?"

I looked at him in disgust. "Don't you think I would have mentioned that?"

I was closest to the entrance. The rest of the team hung back, with their rifles aimed at the opening. They looked extremely nervous. I tried to see them through the confident eyes of Graves. He'd never have let his troops see him worried—especially if he *was* worried.

I straightened my back and stared out into the jungle. "You still can't get anything?" I asked Carlos.

"Nothing. Not from inside. Damn these metals walls."

Without further discussion, I moved out of the tunnel.

I had to crawl to get past the debris-choked entrance. Mud had slid down into the hole, and I thought it must have been a tight squeeze for a jugger even when it was freshly dug.

I walked outside in a crouch, trying to look everywhere at once. A flock of flying reptiles screeched at me, and took wing. Their flapping, leathery wings made snapping noises in the air, and they showered me with dark gray guano.

"What's going on?" Carlos hissed.

I looked around for a second longer then returned to the tunnel entrance. "Not much. Looks clear, come on up."

They did so, reluctantly. They were all working their tappers soon, but they didn't operate.

"I can't connect," Kivi complained. "It's just saying: 'synching with network' and keeps spinning."

Everyone had the same problem.

"Maybe we're too far out from base."

Carlos shook his head. "No, no way. These things can reach ten miles or more."

"Can they get a signal from *Corvus*?" asked Kivi.

We glanced at her then tried it. But it was no good.

"Our basic tappers aren't strong enough. I bet an officer could do it."

"The techs can. I've seen them do it."

Carlos made a pin-wheeling gesture of exasperation with his arms. "Well, that's just great. They give recruits the best of everything, don't they? Shit guns, shit suits, and shit com equipment. The trouble is, we're the only ones left alive! If I'd known, I would have stripped Graves and left him naked for the dinos."

I was working my tapper, ignoring him. I was deep in the confusing options screens. I'd spent some time poking around in there but hadn't figured out what every screen did. Now, there was a serious reason to do so.

148

"Let's set up a local network, so we can at least talk to one another."

"What the hell for?"

I gave him an irritated glance. Before I could answer, Kivi spoke up.

"That's a great idea!" she said. "We'll set up our own little net then make it discoverable. Anyone else with a system more powerful than ours might detect it. They could receive our weak signals and if they did a little work, link up with us."

I nodded, as if that had been my idea. In truth, I'd just figured we could communicate if we were separated.

Carlos came near looking over my shoulder to stare at my options screens.

"Well, look at the big brain on you," he said. "I guess you learned something in school before you dropped out."

I considered punching him, and I almost did it. But it would be counterproductive at this point, so I saved it for later.

"Well, I have a fix via the GPS on our location at least. Camp is that way."

I didn't get an argument after that. They followed me toward camp.

We hadn't gone a hundred steps before we found digging equipment, and a big pile of loose shale. It shone with metallic spiraling strips of metal.

"They bored in, and took pains to hide the evidence," I said.

"They knew we'd be watching from *Corvus*."

I nodded, and we pressed on. What we came to next startled us. It was a lizard camp, with sleeping nests and campfires. The surprising thing was the massive size of it. The camp stretched for over a mile.

"There must have been thousands of them here," Kivi said.

"Yeah, but where did they all go?" I asked. I walked into the deserted camp, and for nearly a minute, no one followed me.

They hung back at the edge of the jungle.

I looked back and laughed at them.

"What? Do you think you're safe standing there behind trees? If they aren't gone, we're all dead anyway. Come on."

They followed me at last.

As we walked, we all took video with our suit cameras and tappers. If they wanted detailed data, that would give it to them.

"Isn't this weird?" Carlos asked me as we passed the massive camp. "I mean, we would always leave behind a few troops in a camp this big."

"Yeah, they aren't us. They don't have non-combatants in their armies. They all fight. Every one of them."

"We shouldn't walk straight to our base from here. If they are hitting it and retreat, we'll run right into them."

I stopped, frowning. The rest pulled up behind us, nervously watching every tree.

"You're right. Let's veer off at a ninety degree angle for a kilometer or so. We should be out of their path then."

We turned and walked away from the alien camp and our own base for a time. The jungle became deeper and the suns began going down. In truth, that was a blessing. I was overheating in daylight. My suit's AC was operating, but only barely. I could feel every outlet of cool air trickling down inside my suit, drying sweat as it went. It was barely enough to keep me from getting heatstroke.

About two kilometers later, I called a halt. Everyone worked their tappers. We still couldn't connect with the base network.

"Something's wrong," Carlos complained. "This can't be right. We are only two or three kilometers out. I know our signals should reach this far."

I privately agreed with him, but didn't want to make a big deal out of it.

"Let's keep marching," I said, doing my best to sound like Graves. "It will sort itself out soon enough."

Kivi wouldn't let it go. "Yeah, Carlos is right. This is all wrong. There are too many repeaters. They can't *all* be down."

"Look," I said, "maybe their power is down. I don't know."

"That doesn't make any sense. In order for—"

"Kivi," I said, interrupting her. "There's nothing we can do about it. Let's keep moving, not talking. We're easy meals out here."

Talk of being eaten got them all moving again. After nearly an hour, it finally was dark and we came within sight of the walls.

They didn't look good. Using our night vision equipment, we could see they were damaged, and the entire area was filled with a pall of smoke.

"They're dead," Carlos whispered with sudden, panicked certainty. "They're *all* dead. That's the only answer."

"They can't all be dead," I told him.

"We're screwed," he said, not even looking at me. "Look at those walls. There's no one up there. Big holes punched right through. No network. We're screwed. Totally screwed."

We were hugging a bushy area about two hundred meters from camp. It looked quiet—too quiet.

"If we die now, they won't even be able to revive us," Kivi said. She had the same panicky tone Carlos had. It was becoming infectious. "Everyone who's died—they're already permed."

"We'll be fine," I said with a certainty I didn't feel.

"James, our data is here—on the planet," Kivi said. "Even if they did transfer it up, they have no way of knowing if we're alive or not. They can't produce a copy of any of us without being certain."

"Oh, God," Carlos said. "Varus did it again. My first damned time out."

"Did what?" Kivi asked.

"What are you? An idiot? They wiped. You know what I'm talking about, McGill. Just like I told you back on Earth. The legion is gone!"

I stared at the walls quietly. Kivi stared with me in mute horror.

I had to admit it—he could be right.

-15-

We crept into the camp, passing one at a time through a smoldering hole in the puff-crete walls. The rim of the hole was still smoking, and I crushed hot embers with my boots as I slipped inside.

We'd expected to find piles of dead inside, and we did—but they were mostly lizards. Our own dead were stripped of equipment and left to rot—every last one of them.

"Where are they?" Carlos asked loudly, spinning around and lifting his arms into the air. "There aren't more than a thousand of our dead here."

"Quiet!" I ordered. "Someone stripped these bodies. The only question is: who did it?"

He snorted at me and dropped his rifle. "What's the difference? There's no one here. Don't you get it? They pulled out. They check-marked us as lost underground, and after getting hit hard, they pulled out. We're totally screwed."

"A minute ago you were certain they'd wiped."

"Yeah, well—this is probably worse. I can't believe it. They just ditched us. I mean, a few recruits I can understand. But Harris and Graves? They were loyal Varus troops, you know? Graves even cashed in his chips to give us a chance to march out."

"Maybe," Kivi said. "Or maybe he knew what was going on, and he bailed out on us. He knew they would revive him so he ditched us down there."

We all looked at her. I frowned. This rumor-mill was in high gear.

"That doesn't make any sense," I told her. "You're all panicking like a bunch of splats." I turned back to Carlos. "Pick up your rifle, Recruit."

Carlos laughed. "Make me!"

I aimed my rifle at him. "Graves left me in charge. If you don't want me to test our revival equipment today, you'd better start listening. Pick up your damned weapon."

Carlos grumbled, but he picked up his rifle.

"Let's go to the tech bunkers," I suggested. "Maybe they left some equipment behind."

They followed me to the tech bunkers, but they were pretty much stripped bare. We spent the next hour searching the place. The humans were gone. It was clear they'd suffered a massive attack and then pulled out.

"Here are the skid marks," Carlos said, indicating deep furrows in the land.

I looked at them. They did indeed look like the footprints of a lander.

"You believe me now, McGill?"

"Yeah," I said, nodding. "Anyone find any com equipment? Anything powerful enough to reach space?"

"No way," Carlos said bitterly. "That stuff costs money. They would never leave *that* behind. Fortunately, recruits are almost free."

I had to admit, I was beginning to buy into Carlos' doom-and-gloom bullshit. I didn't want to, but I couldn't deny how things looked. We'd been written off.

"All right, did anyone find anything useful?" I asked.

"I found two crates of food."

"I've got a few uniforms—but they're ripped."

I moved immediately to check on the damaged uniforms. I grinned. "AC units look good. We'll use these for spare parts."

Carlos hooted at me and shook his head while I dismantled my pack and plugged a new one into place.

"The batteries will be dead in a few days, you know."

I closed my eyes and sighed in pleasure as the cool air slipped into my suit, blowing it up like a wet balloon.

"I don't care," I said. "At least I won't die bathed in sweat."

We gathered water next and drank a lot of it. We found a few medical odds and ends. I unzipped at around midnight and let my teammates work on my back and legs. There were plenty of other injuries in the group as well. We had to rub them down with antibiotic salves and skin-growth creams. They tingled after that. I could feel the freshly growing skin. It was rubbery and numb.

"This is worse than a revival," Carlos complained.

For once, I agreed with him. When you were reborn, at least you didn't have to go through the pain of healing wounds.

It was about two hours later that our sentry shook me awake. I got up, grabbed my rifle, and crept out of the bunker we were hiding in.

The rest of the team were awakening and following me. There were some murmured complaints, but everyone shushed one another. We used hand-signals and our tappers to communicate.

There was something outside, something big. It was a machine of some kind.

I eyed it, and it took me a moment to realize it was an air car. Cruising at an altitude of about fifty meters, it glided slowly over the camp. All the running lights were switched off.

"What are they doing?" Carlos whispered nearby. "Who are they?"

"How the hell should I know?"

He shut up for a second, and we all stared. The air car came lower, and we could hear a soft thrumming sound. It was remarkably quiet for a machine of its kind.

"That thing cost some money," Carlos said. "That isn't standard tech. Someone had to buy that from Galactic with hard credits."

He was right. I knew what air cars normally sounded like, and this one wasn't a noisy, buzzing machine. They usually used fans and turbo jets that roared loudly enough to be heard a mile away.

I frowned at the machine. I was under the impression it was sneaking around, observing. I didn't like it. I pulled out my rifle and sighted on the exhaust system.

"You can't be serious," Carlos said. "You don't even know who's in there. It could be our own tribune reviewing the damage. If you bring him down, Varus will fry you."

"You want to walk out there and signal them first?" I asked.

"Um...no."

"Right. If we shoot that thing down, our team will know we're alive."

"What if it's an enemy?"

"All the more reason."

"And what if it is legion equipment, and you kill the occupants?"

I shrugged. "That's what revival units are for. Besides, no aerial units are allowed on this mission, it's part of the contract, remember?"

"Oh, yeah."

"All right team," I said, "take aim. Concentrated fire, aft portion of the ship. Let's bring it down. At the very least, we might get a radio aboard big enough to communicate with *Corvus*."

There was no more hesitation from my team members. They were desperate and scared.

"Mark...Fire!"

We all opened up. We only had light snap-rifles, but the air car wasn't armored. There was a shield, but aiming at the exhaust ports bypassed that in many vehicles. The exhaust had to have a way to exit the vehicle, so the shield didn't cover the vulnerable area. The bullets splattered the vehicle creating a shower of orange sparks in the night.

All in all, I'd say we were lucky to get a critical hit before it could rotate the exhaust section away from us. The aft fan cut out almost immediately. The craft wobbled, and the nose tipped up. I could hear it revving, showing the pilot was trying to get away, but it was hopeless. The air car slid downward at an angle, and went into a spin.

We got up, whooping, and charged after it.

155

The car crashed down into one of the puff-crete walls. I think the pilot had been trying to make it over the wall and out into the jungle—but he didn't make it.

We swarmed the smoking car, standing on the hood and slanting windshield. The shields sparked and buzzed around our boots. Everyone had a gun trained on the passenger compartment, but the windows were dark.

"Open up!" I shouted. "Or we'll shoot our way in."

The window on the passenger side buzzed open. It was dark inside. We all peered in, trying to get a look at whoever was in there.

"Come out," I said. "You're trespassing in a combat zone."

I heard series of clicks, and then the artificial voice of a translator spoke: "You have made a grave error."

"This is a combat zone. All non-friendly vehicles can and will be treated as hostile. Who are you?"

Carlos was on the roof of the car, and I was standing at the door. Slowly, a figure unloaded itself. I could tell right away it was some kind of alien by the way it moved. I snapped on a light and was startled.

I'd seen this kind of thing before. It was an alien with six hands—or six feet, depending on how you looked at it. The limbs were long and spindly and between them hung a heavy, bloated thorax. In a way, it reminded me of a black widow spider.

The hands gripped the edge of the car door and it hauled its body out of the seat. It moved slowly, almost painfully. I wasn't sure if it was injured or just being cautious. Then again, maybe it moved at a sedate pace naturally, like a sloth.

It was bigger than a human, but not absurdly so. If I had to guess, I'd say it weighed about three hundred pounds—and two hundred of that was probably located in that central, dragging belly.

Carlos made a little gasping sound when it emerged. The rest of the team stepped back a pace and gripped their rifles tightly. Unlike them, Carlos squatted on the roof over its head.

"What an ugly mother!" he said, his voice full of disgust.

The translator clicked again. "How dare you direct a weapon toward my person?"

I realized the alien must be talking to me. One of its hands extended toward me—toward my upraised weapon.

Thud! Carlos slammed the butt of his rifle onto its head-section. At least, it looked like a head. It was smaller than a human skull, but it seemed to contain a cluster of sensory organs.

The alien froze for a second then sank down. Its limbs folded underneath it.

"That doesn't look good," Carlos said.

"You killed it!" I hissed at him. "You idiot, we didn't even get to ask it any questions."

"It was reaching for your weapon. You saw it, didn't you, Kivi?"

"Just keep me out of this," she said, coming forward warily to investigate.

"Are there any more of them in there?" asked Carlos, poking his nose into the interior.

I pushed him away. "You've done enough. The creature was alone and unarmed."

"Huh," he said, prodding it with his toe.

I gave him a shove and he staggered backward.

"Just trying to see if it's still alive," he said, glaring.

As he said this, the creature stirred weakly. It didn't speak, and fluids were running from its head section.

"Kivi," I said, "get into the car on the other side. See if you can find a com system."

Fortunately, except for the interface which had to be specialized for various species, Galactic com systems were fairly universal in their appearance and operation. Kivi found a unit and quickly connected with *Corvus*.

"They want to know what we're doing down here," she told me.

I looked at the alien, who was no longer moving.

"Tell them we're engaged in diplomatic negotiations."

Carlos laughed at that. He soon had another hatch door open and was rummaging in the car.

"Hey, you know what?" he called out to me. "I think this guy is an alien—I mean one of *your* aliens, James. This proves you weren't just crazy-drunk the other night."

"Who said I was?"

"Everyone."

"Hey, McGill," Kivi called out to me. "They want to talk to you."

I tried to swallow, but my throat was dry. I wasn't sure if I was a hero or a villain, but I was certain I had some explaining to do.

Kivi patched the com channel to my helmet.

"Recruit James McGill online, sir."

"You're a recruit?" asked a female voice. I thought I might recognize it, but I wasn't sure. "This is Primus Turov. I asked to talk to the team leader."

I had it now. Primus Turov was my primus, Centurion Graves' direct superior.

"I'm sorry sir, but I'm all that's left. We lost our veteran and the unit centurion."

"Pathetic. All right McGill, report."

I hesitated. How much should I confess over this transmission? Were there more of these aliens gliding around the camp, ready to invade? For all I knew, this one had already transmitted for help to its saurian friends.

"We're in trouble. We were trapped and ambushed at the lowest level of the mine by about twenty saurians, both raptors and juggers. We retreated and fought for hours. We finally found the tunnel they used to enter the mining complex and escaped through it."

"We've pinpointed your position. You're in the middle of the base camp."

"That's right sir, and we've just brought down an air car that was apparently spying on us."

"An air car? You brought it down? Who gave you orders to do so?"

"I acted on my own initiative. We were left here, cut off, with no—"

"What's the condition of the air car? Are there survivors?"

"We found one alien. It appears to be the same species that I encountered earlier on patrol. Identification should be much easier now that we have—"

"Listen to me, Recruit: *is that alien alive?*"

158

"Uh…I'm not certain, Primus. It has suffered injuries."

"You had best pray that it is unharmed. Guard that alien with your life. I'm sending down a lifter. Standby."

I stood there dumbfounded as the connection broke. Carlos came to me and clapped me on the shoulder.

"I listened in," he said. "Looks like you screwed up, big-time."

I threw his hand off and cocked back my fist to punch him.

"You fool!" I shouted. "I didn't tell you to attack that alien. *You* are responsible for this!"

"Hold on! We all know who's in command here, don't we, people?" He swiveled his head and examined the crew.

They all looked uncertain. Finally Kivi spoke up. "No. You did it without orders."

"Oh yeah, sure," he said. "Right. I can see how it is. Why don't you all just fill me with metal right now? That would be a better alibi, wouldn't it? I went nuts, you shot me down, and then—"

I put the muzzle of my snap-rifle against his head. He froze.

"Don't tempt me any further," I said.

"Okay, whatever."

The lifter came down to pick us up—or rather, to pick the alien up. They virtually ignored us, shoving us out of the way. A team of bio specialists ran in with some anti-grav gurney and carefully transferred the injured alien onto it. Then they rushed away. We followed, walking, but when we saw the ramp was already going up, we ran to it and hustled up into the ship.

I found a porthole and looked down at Cancri-9, which was all mist and darkness in the night. I wondered if I'd ever see this alien world again. I had to admit, I wasn't missing it yet.

An hour later, I found myself facing Adjunct Leeson and Primus Turov. Neither of them was happy. The worst part was, I wasn't entirely sure what I'd done wrong.

As I stood at attention, I reminded myself that I'd been in this position before, being shouted at by a group of officers. I kept my eyes straight, my face neutral, and I did my best not to react to the abuse my superiors were heaping upon me.

To be sure, it seemed grossly unfair. By my accounting, I was a hero. I'd led my team out of the mines, and after Centurion Graves' sacrifice, there hadn't been a single casualty added to the list on my watch.

We went over the story again from the top. Same questions, same order, same answers.

"Who told you to exit the mine through the shaft, Recruit?" Primus Turov demanded.

"No one, sir," I said. "I did it on my own initiative."

"And when you reached base camp, who ordered you to shoot down the air car?"

"No one, sir."

"May I ask you again, who put you in charge?"

"We were surrounded by hostiles. Centurion Graves decided to use our only plasma grenade on the enemy, and he delivered it by running into their midst. It was a brave moment of self-sacrifice."

Turov uncrossed her arms just long enough to motion impatiently for me to get on with my story.

"As he left us, he told everyone I was in charge. From that point on, I was in command of the team."

She leaned forward, and her butt lifted from the desk she'd been sitting on. She came close enough so that I could feel her body heat. I wanted to look down at her, but I didn't. I kept staring ahead and remained at attention.

"Do you know who was aboard that air car?"

This was a new question. One she hadn't posed five times previously.

"An alien, sir. Alien to Earth, alien to Cancri-9. Origins unknown the last I'd heard from our bio techs. It was the same type of alien I'd encountered before in the forest on patrol."

"And that previous alien, you also killed him, am I correct?"

"Yes, sir."

"Had either of these aliens at any time attacked you? Did they fire upon you? Did they perform some other overtly hostile act?"

I paused. "No. The first one was in a forest full of enemy combatants, however. The second was on the scene of what

160

appeared to be a wiped out camp with no living legionnaires in sight. I took action based on the situation I was in."

Turov chuckled and shook her head. She turned to Adjunct Leeson. "He's screwed us good. No excuse. Nothing."

I glanced after her and frowned. When she looked back, I flicked my eyes to the forward bulkhead again.

"Do you have something to add, Recruit?"

"I—I just don't understand, sir. Have we identified the alien that I encountered?"

"Indeed we have. That's the core of the problem. Do you want to know the scope of the damage you've done?"

I was beginning to sweat. Having acted without authority was one thing, but she seemed to be indicating this matter had exploded into some kind of diplomatic incident.

"I can only assume that the aliens were innocent, and that we acted without full knowledge of the situation."

"No," she said dryly, heaving a sigh. "The alien was far from innocent. None of his kind are."

I turned my head and looked at her. "Who are *they*, if I may ask, Primus?"

She stared back at me. "We weren't sure at first. But now we are. We sent the data off-planet for identification, and all hell broke loose. You see, we don't have their blood samples on hand for obvious reasons."

The reasons weren't obvious to me, but I waited patiently, hoping everything would be made clear to me.

Turov opened her mouth to speak further, but the door chimed. "Come in!" she shouted irritably.

The portal opened and a familiar face met mine. It was none other than Veteran Harris. He looked sick. He leaned on the doorframe with one hand and took a shuffling step forward.

"Veteran Harris?" Leeson asked. "What are you doing here? You should be in recovery, man. How long has it been since you came out of the revival machine?"

"A few minutes," he said. His eyes were only half-open. He had his uniform on, but it looked like he'd pulled it over wet skin and it hung on his frame unevenly.

"Get back to the infirmary."

"If I might ask to be present, sir..." he said.

161

Leeson looked at Turov.

Turov sighed.

"All right," she said. "He's your man. There should be a witness from his unit, anyway. I think there's a regulation to that effect. But if you pass out on this deck, I'm throwing you out into the passageway until this is over."

I watched this interchange with growing bewilderment. *A witness from his unit?* What did that mean? And why had Harris worked so hard to drag himself out of medical to this scolding, anyway?

Turov turned back to me. She stared at me for several seconds, looking me up and down.

"It's a shame, really," she said quietly. "We value recruits like you, McGill. Did you know that? Men who show initiative and leadership. Natural-born killers who shoot first and sort the enemy out later are useful. Under different circumstances, I'd call you a hero and give you a commendation. I've handed out promotions for less, in fact."

I opened my mouth to speak but closed it again. As long as an officer is heaping praise on you, it's best to stay quiet.

She turned to Adjunct Leeson. "Is the inspector able to join us yet?"

Leeson checked his tapper. "He's coming down the hall now."

The door chimed again, and everyone stiffened. Even the primus looked nervous. They opened the door and a now-familiar alien stepped into the room. It was none other than the six-handed creature I'd had run-ins with on two occasions.

"James McGill," the Primus said, "let me introduce you to Inspector Xlur. He honors all of us with his presence."

I looked from one of them to the next. I didn't really understand what was going on.

"An honor to meet you, Inspector," I said.

The alien didn't look at me. It looked instead at the primus. A click sounded, and the translator scratched out words: "It still lives. Why has this matter not been attended to?"

"We thought you might wish to witness the event so that there could be no doubt."

"Get on with it, then."

Primus Turov turned to me and straightened her body. "Recruit James McGill of Legion Varus, I hereby sentence you to perma-death. The sentence is to be carried out immediately."

Turov then took a step backwards and nodded to Leeson, who lifted his weapon.

I was in shock. I'd been surprised by the alien, but I had no idea I was going to be executed. Reflexively, I reached for my sidearm—but of course, it wasn't there. I'd been ordered to leave it behind when I came to this "briefing".

"I don't understand," I said loudly. "Who is this alien? How can I be executed for a crime I don't even comprehend?"

"James," said the primus, staring at me. "Inspector Xlur is a Galactic. One of the many species from the core of the galaxy. He is here to observe—and you should recognize him. You killed him twice within the span of a few days."

I opened my mouth, but no sound came out. I was stunned. We'd never seen the Galactics on Earth. Naturally, there were plenty of vids of their ships. They had a vast armada that had once visited our backwater world and threatened to blow it up. But they never socialized with us directly.

Like most earthers, I'd always thought the Galactics looked like the mollusk race that had come to negotiate with us. But now I realized that species was just another member of the empire. Perhaps they traded services, such as their diplomatic expertise.

So here, standing before me on its six hands, was a true Galactic: A spider-like creature with warm, dark blood. At least I knew they could bleed like we could.

Leeson worked his weapon, ratcheting the muzzle. It wouldn't do if the hull was pierced by a stray bullet. I watched him—watched his hands moving—as if in a dream. I was trying to think of a way out of this, but I didn't see one. I thought about physically attacking them—that was my first instinct, I admit.

I didn't feel guilty, I felt angry. What I did next came a surprise to everyone, including me. I stepped toward Inspector Xlur, baring my teeth like an animal. I wanted to dig my thumbs into those soft sensory organs of his. If their skulls were as thin as I suspected they were, maybe I could kill him a third time with my bare hands.

A gun muzzle touched my chest. I heard the chamber rattle. Six times—or maybe it was seven. It's hard to count bullets as they're slamming into your body.

I fell to my knees, and looked up. Veteran Harris looked back. It was his gun that had unloaded into my chest.

I didn't feel pain. Not exactly. It was more like being dizzy, sick and weak. I fell forward onto my face, and I had time to roll onto my back.

"Vicious creatures," the Inspector said. "They should put you all down."

Harris looked at me, and I stared back. My eyes slowly dimmed.

The Veteran bent down, putting his hands on his knees.

"And now kid," he said. "You and I are even."

-16-

The first thought that impinged on my brain as I awakened an unknowable time later was that I *shouldn't* be awakening at all. That was the entire point of perma-death—you didn't come back.

But I was alive—barely. I was naked, cold and coughing. I gasped and coughed up thick liquids, choking. I rolled away from the attendants, who pushed me back down. I flopped onto an unforgiving slab and struggled weakly.

"He's fibrillating. Defib—*defib*, dammit!"

The bios grabbed me and held me down. At the last instant, they all pulled their hands away and they shocked me. A wrenching pain bit my chest, my face—every inch of my skin.

"Again!"

Another ice-cold touch was followed by a sharp jolt. I squirmed weakly, no longer able to cough. My mouth opened but no breath was drawn.

"He's going. We're gonna to have to reroll."

"Don't do it. We're not allowed."

"He's a bad grow."

"I don't give a shit. Hit him again."

They zapped me a third time. Fortunately, I lost consciousness...

When I came back to the world of pain and bright lights, which was how I now thought of my universe, I did so with trepidation. I took each breath cautiously, experimentally.

165

No one grabbed me or shocked me this time around.

I opened my eyes and stared. There was a brilliant glare, but nothing else—was I still dead?

Slowly, I became more aware. I was on a slab of cold metal. There was no sheet over me, nothing. The room was cold, and I shivered in random twitches.

I heard footsteps.

"You made it. Congratulations."

I forced my head to roll toward the voice. It was female and stern, but not without a hint of kindness.

I stared at her without recognition for a few seconds. Then it came to me.

"I know you," I croaked.

"Speech?" she asked, tapping at her arm. "A good sign. This might not have been a total waste of time. The pool was fifty-fifty betting you'd come out brain-dead."

"You're from Cancri-9," I said hazily. "You were running the revival unit at the base."

I remembered her now, in a flood. She was Anne Grant, the woman who'd been killed after sending me out on point: The woman who'd done my first revival. It all seemed so clear...but the current situation was fuzzy.

In fact, the moment of my first rebirth now seemed clearer to me than what I'd been doing more recently in the mines. It was strange how memories worked after they rebuilt a person. They didn't come back with quite the same priority structure in the brain. It was very much like waking up and being uncertain if one was dreaming or fully awake.

"Yes," Bio Specialist Grant said, her voice softening. "I know you, McGill."

She put a hand on my wrist, took my pulse, then leaned over me and checked my eyes, spreading them open and looking into them. She had a light on her forehead, one that made me wince with the bright, probing glare it shot into my pupils. "I was on Cancri-9, and I ran the unit non-stop. Did you die down there?"

"Yeah...just once. The second time was aboard this ship."

She withdrew her hands and worked on her tapper. "As soon as you can stand, you're good to go."

I couldn't stop staring at Grant. She still had her short dark hair and narrow, careworn eyes. But her face was pretty. I remembered that part. I almost asked her to turn around—but stopped myself in time. I was a little out of it.

Specialist Grant turned away and made as if to leave. I reached out to her and caught the hem of her lab coat with rubbery fingers.

"Explain a few things to me," I croaked. "Please, Anne."

The bio turned back. She frowned, looking troubled. "I really shouldn't," she said quietly.

"Just tell me if I'm going to be normal. I heard you guys saying it went wrong."

"You'll be fine—I think. You're recovering."

"What could go bad? What should I look for?"

"Toxemia, necrolysis—there are a few other side-effects."

I shook my head. "What went wrong?"

"Nothing, really. Nothing unexpected, anyway. Sometimes, when we revive someone with poor quality base materials, it doesn't go right and we have to redo it. In your case, that wasn't possible."

I tried to lick my lips. They felt as dry as sandpaper. I frowned, trying to think.

"Bad materials? Why would you use—?"

She leaned forward and adjusted a pillow under my neck. Then she pretended to examine my head. This put her mouth quite near my ear.

"Do you recall the circumstances of your death?" she asked quietly.

"Yeah, I was supposedly permed. Executed by—"

Anne winced as I said that. "I don't want to hear anything else about that, you understand? Don't talk to *anyone* about that! Just pretend you don't remember a thing."

I thought that might be difficult to pull off, but I nodded. I needed whatever information she could give me.

"Why did you revive me?" I asked. "I didn't think you liked me."

"Saving lives is what I do," she said.

"You know," I said, my mind wandering a bit, "when I was first coming awake, I thought maybe the execution hadn't been

167

done according to regulations. I thought maybe they'd revived me to do it again."

Grant looked at me with real concern. I thought it might be the first time I'd seen pity in a superior's eyes during my tenure with Legion Varus.

"No, that wasn't it," she said. "Listen, I don't know what you did, and I don't want to know. I *never* want to hear that story, okay? All I know is they asked me to do an untraceable regrow. So that's what I did."

I frowned. "Untraceable?"

"The Galactics keep tight tabs on the use of key equipment like revival units."

"Why?"

"The technology would be easy to abuse, don't you think? What if a madman bought one on the black market and proceeded to copy himself a million times?"

"Oh," I said, having never thought about that before. "Is that possible?"

"No. They keep tight controls over how often it is used and for what purpose. Your regrowth wasn't sanctioned, so I had to pretend it was a test. We do that sometimes, as part of maintenance. We grow a random biotic construct with expired protoplasm. Then we destroy the mess that issues."

I thought about that, and I was beginning to catch on. "So, no one knows I was killed and regrown?"

"That's right, and I'm getting the hell out of here before anyone figures out what I've done. When you feel capable of leaving—which had better be very soon now—you should get the hell out and head back to your bunk. We're in the middle of your shift's rest period. Go to bed, and in the morning, give random, nonsensical explanations that no one can comprehend concerning your disappearance from the unit."

I wanted to ask her more questions, but I felt tired and closed my eyes for a second. When I opened them again, Anne Grant had vanished. I sucked in deep breaths for about three more minutes before I painfully heaved myself up and stood on unsteady legs.

At first, I thought maybe the regrow hadn't worked properly on my knees, but with a little time and patience, they held me up. I was just weak and sick. I found a generic smart-cloth suit in the room and I put it on. The suit resized itself to my body automatically. It wasn't a combat suit, but it would have to do. I knew I had a spare uniform in my locker I could change into when I got back.

I staggered out into the hallway. Two orderlies passed me, running their eyes up and down my body with strange expressions.

I didn't have a ready lie to tell them yet, so I decided to bluff it through. I nodded to them and did my best to walk with steady, confident steps. I didn't even know which way to go, but I just wanted to get past them.

Fortunately, they seemed to be busy, so they let me pass without questions. I found the nearest exit from the medical section and left what we called "Blue Deck" behind.

A few minutes later I managed to find my quarters. I fell into my bunk and heaved a great sigh. I wasn't sure if it was the cheap regrow or not, but I was exhausted.

Someone's butt landed on my bed a moment later. I opened one eye, fully expecting it to be Carlos, but it wasn't. It was Natasha.

I smiled at her with half of my face.

"Hi," I said.

She stared at me. "What the hell happened to you? What did you tell the brass? They've been sweating all of us since you disappeared."

"What did *you* tell them?"

"I died in the caves, but as I understand the story from the others, you played hero and led them out. That's about it. I don't know what they wanted."

"What about the alien in the air car? What did you tell them about that?"

Natasha shook her head. "I heard about that, but I wasn't there, remember? Carlos had some story about the alien attacking us. They didn't seem to buy that. I'm sure they'd already pulled the vids from people's suits. Our own helmets spy on us, you know."

I frowned. I hadn't known that—or at least, I hadn't thought of it that way. Natasha was studying to be a tech, so I

169

didn't doubt her on this point. It did make sense that our superiors would have access to any vid we made with legion equipment at any time.

"Natasha," I said. "What everyone should do is forget about Cancri-9. Or at least, forget about the mine and the air car—all that. Spread the word: pretend it never happened."

"Easy for me, but what about the people who made it to the end? How are they supposed to forget everything?"

"Just tell them to do it. All of us have to if we want to keep breathing, okay?"

Natasha stared at me for a few seconds. Her eyes darted from one of my eyes to the next, then back again.

"You're serious, aren't you?" she asked. Then she began running her hands over me, checking my pulse and temperature. "You're not okay. I'm getting yellow readings on my tapper. You have a fever."

"It's all right," I said. "Just forget everything that happened on Cancri-9. Everything you saw and everything you heard about. For your own sake."

She stared at me again, looking more worried than ever. She put her face close to mine.

"What did they do to you?" she whispered.

I managed a weak smile. "Nothing. I'm just tired. I need a little sleep, okay?"

Suddenly, a head dipped down over the side of the bunk above us.

"Are you two going to get it on or go to sleep? Do one or the other, *please!* The suspense is killing me."

It was Carlos, naturally. I gave him the finger, and he withdrew his round face, grumbling.

Natasha kissed me, then gave me a worried smile and left. I felt the burning tingle of her kiss as it evaporated on my cheek.

I fell asleep the moment she was gone.

The next day I felt crappy. It was like having the flu or just getting over it. I was running a fever, and my face was slightly flushed. When I got up, I vomited in the bathroom. This gathered me no sympathy. Recruits live pretty close to one another aboard ship. They towel-snapped my ass as I bent over the commode.

170

"What'd you do, man? Steal a bottle from Graves' office?"

"Something like that," I said.

They laughed and left me alone. I crawled to my feet and Carlos came to my rescue—sort of.

"Nothing to see here, folks," Carlos said, waving the others away. "I know a few of you have had a beer or two in the past. Give the man some air!"

"Thanks, man," I said.

"Come on, get your butt off the can," he muttered harshly into my ear. "We have to get our stories straight."

His shadow left me, and I was able to get to my feet again a minute or so later. I showered and felt better. I tried very hard to avoid thinking about why I was feeling low. I didn't like to believe I'd been reconstructed with spoiled meat. I told myself it was nothing more than a hangover. I was alive and getting better, and that was the only thing that mattered.

When I made it out to roll call, I was the last man to find his spot. They called my name twice before I answered. Neither Veteran Harris or Adjunct Leeson said anything to me.

After breakfast, which didn't go well for me, they trotted us out to the field. I was already sweating. I was relieved when Harris pulled me out of the line.

Looking at him was hard to do. I was glaring and sick. I couldn't help but think of myself pulling the trigger and killing him again. I think he knew it, but it didn't seem to bother him much.

"McGill, Graves wants to see you upstairs."

I glanced up toward the observation tower. In the center of the exercise area was a tower with tinted, bulletproof glass. I turned and began trotting toward it.

"And McGill," he shouted after me. "Try to keep your head on straight. This could be big."

I had no idea what he was talking about, but I was certain he didn't want to turn his back to me while on the training field today. It was one thing to kill a man during training. But to tell a man he was being executed without trial, judge or jury—then pulling the trigger with glee on your face—to me, that crossed the line.

171

I might be alive now, but I'd experienced what I thought was my final, one-and-only permanent death. That hadn't been fun, that soulless, hopeless moment alone. To know the lights are going out for the very last time…

-17-

I shuddered and found myself at the base of the observation tower. I opened it and discovered a spiraling staircase inside. I was huffing by the time I reached the top, which wasn't normal for me.

The top of the tower was air conditioned and possessed its own snack and drink counter. There were five comfortable chairs circling the room. Graves was in one of them, and he and I were alone in the room.

He didn't look at me when I entered. He was staring outside at the training field watching the squads as they broke up and began to spar with one another. There would be no live-fire exercises today. It was all light exercise and hand-to-hand. Even the officers knew when the troops were tired of dying and needed a break.

"Mind if I help myself to a glass, sir?" I asked him.

He waved his hand over his shoulder at me. I took this as approval. I poured myself something fizzy and sweet. It eased my sweating body when I drank it.

"You feeling all right, McGill?" he asked finally.

"Never better."

He chuckled. "You're a tough bastard. I like that. I really do."

"You've got a funny way of showing your love, if you don't mind me saying, Centurion."

He spun around in his chair which swiveled without a squeak. "You want to know why you're up here?"

"So I don't fall on my face on the field and give it all away?"

His smile faltered. "You're angry? I'm surprised, but I guess I shouldn't be. Gratitude is a rare component in most people's personalities."

I blinked at him, then frowned. "You want a big thanks for having me executed?"

"You weren't executed—at least not permanently."

"It felt real enough, sir."

"I think you need to keep things in perspective, Recruit. I didn't have to bring you back. I took a major risk in doing so. I'll have you know that Primus Turov was against it."

That bitch, I thought to myself. But I nodded. "Sorry if I don't feel like kissing anyone's ring today. They told me when I came out it was a bad grow."

Graves frowned. "A bad grow? Why didn't they recycle and do it right?"

I wanted to shiver at the idea of being *recycled.* Right then, for the first time, I wondered how often that happened. How often did a man miraculously return to life, only to be killed again instantly and brought back yet again? I bet they threw those little slices of our memories away by not copying our minds when such dark events occurred.

I sipped my fizzy sugar water and stared out at the practice field. "They didn't want to risk a regrow. The bio said I should be all right in a few days."

He nodded. "Well enough, then. With any luck, the Galactics will never bring it up again. You were executed promptly with one of their own as a witness. Fortunately, they can't tell us apart nor do they track individual IDs for us. To them, we're like fish thrashing in a vast pond or rabbits nibbling in an endless field. There are billions of us, and we don't matter as individuals."

I looked at him seriously. "Why did you bring me back, sir? It was less of a risk to leave well enough alone."

174

"Because it wouldn't have been right," he said. "You did your job well. You led your team out of an impossible situation."

I almost believed him. But I waited quietly, staring, just in case.

Graves returned my gaze evenly then he shrugged after a moment. "That's not the only thing, naturally."

Naturally, I thought to myself.

He turned back to the practice fields. The teams were being issued combat knives—sharp ones. They flashed with edges like white lines in the bright sunlight that streamed in from the dome overhead. I winced as one recruit opened up another's arm. There would be plenty of nu-skin sprayed over open wounds tonight.

"The real reason was that Harris and I owe our lives to you."

I looked at him in surprise.

"How's that, sir?"

"We were at the bottom of the mine and cut off. Several teams never made it out of that mine, McGill. Yours did. When you made your report—that changed everything."

I began to put it together. I nodded.

"When I made my report they had confirmation of your death, right?" I asked. "At that point, they authorized your revival. So, they were holding off on doing it until you came out or were confirmed dead?"

He nodded slowly. "That's right. And with the legion leaving Cancri-9, that would have been it for all of us if you hadn't made it out. They'd keep the data, but never make our copies. Perma-death for all."

I understood now why he was impressed by my efforts to survive and why he'd felt the urge to go the extra mile to keep me breathing. If I hadn't made it out, we'd all have been done for.

"Sir?" I asked. "What will the Galactics do if they find out I'm still alive?"

"They won't."

"I know that sir. But, hypothetically?"

175

"Hypothetically? I don't know. I don't know how connected that inspector is or how pissed off he might be. I would guess we'd all be permed officially. Possibly the entire legion would be unloaded on a rock and nuked. Hell, I don't know."

I stared at him. "That wouldn't be right. I remember Galactic Law from school. It's quite egalitarian. The Galactics are no more—"

By this time, Graves was laughing. "You read their laws? Their treaties? The deals they signed with Earth? That's grand. You should read a little more of history, son. Those who rule don't take insults lightly. They bend the rules now and then, and when they do, they always bend them in their favor. It's a natural part of life, I think."

I shut up because I realized I didn't know what I was talking about. Graves had been out here in space for decades. Who was I to lecture him on the way the universe was supposed to work?

"Well then," I said. "I thank you for reviving me. Am I free to go, sir?"

"Sadly, no. I have to have your word that you won't speak of this incident to anyone. You won't bring up Galactics or being executed—none of it. If you do, your data will be lost, and your next revive will never happen. Do I make myself clear, McGill?"

"Like starlight, sir."

"Good. Now, head to Blue Deck. You look like shit. Get yourself some chemical help. We'll be redeploying tomorrow, and I need every man in fighting shape."

I paused, stunned.

"Redeploying? Where, sir?"

He frowned. "I'm not accustomed to being questioned by recruits, McGill. Don't take our little conversation as some kind of comradery. We're not best friends."

"Of course not. But I thought we were leaving Cancri-9. I thought we'd given up on this mission."

Graves laughed at me. The laugh was an unpleasant one.

"Given up? No, Recruit. This war has just begun. Legion Varus always triumphs. It does not give up when Earth's territory is threatened. We were tricked into this contract but aren't done yet. The Galactics are observing—as you know intimately. Before this is over, we'll have proven to them yet again who the best fighters are."

I was confused. I had no real idea what he was talking about. I knew that Legion Varus often fought other mercenary companies to demonstrate we were the best, but so far, I hadn't seen any evidence of this occurring on Cancri-9. All we'd fought were packs of angry natives.

"One last question, sir," I said. "If you don't mind."

"I do mind. But ask it anyway."

"Who are the enemy? What mercenary company are we fighting against?"

He looked at me in surprise. "Really, McGill? I thought you might have figured that out by now. Maybe that regrow did scramble your brains."

"But sir, we've fought nothing but saurians since we got here. Endless waves of lizards. The only other alien we encountered was the Galactic inspector himself."

"Endless waves of lizards…" he said, smiling tightly. "You should be a poet, McGill."

I thought about that for a second. "Are you saying that saurians themselves are the enemy? That they want to challenge us for supremacy in this region of space? Are they trying to form their own legions?"

"I doubt they'll call them that. They tend to fight in hordes. More numbers, more meat, less armament—but you have to admit, they are pretty effective."

"But why, sir? They have their steel, their minerals to sell. Isn't that easier for them?"

He shrugged. "How the hell should I know why they've decided to try this takeover? Maybe the market on steel has crashed. Maybe they've lost a number of accounts and are hurting for credits. Whatever the case, I think they've been working toward this for a long time. Otherwise, why are they our very best clients? Why so many missions? To observe and learn, that's my guess."

I didn't know what to say. "They are warlike, primitive by alien standards. They don't even have a worldwide

177

government. Maybe mercenary work would suit them. Do you really think they can beat us? We slaughtered them out there."

Graves lifted an admonishing finger. "Never underestimate an opponent, McGill. If they had all their credits dumped into weaponry the way we do…just think of it. What if the saurian waves you faced had been as well-equipped as we were? What would have happened?"

"I don't know. They may have wiped us."

He nodded slowly. "Exactly. That was their plan from the start. They gave us a phony contract and we signed on. Then they cheated by fielding, as you so eloquently put it, 'endless waves of lizards'. Now, they're claiming victory with the Galactics. Worse, you personally managed to kill the chief Inspector, the very individual that will decide the outcome of this territorial struggle, *twice.*"

I stared at him. My eyes were squinched up and my teeth were bared in a grimace. I felt slightly sick, and I didn't think it was due to the bad regrow this time.

"Yes," Graves said, smiling at me grimly. "I can see now that you fully grasp the situation and your part in it. Now, kindly get the hell out of my tower. I'm already regretting letting them revive you at all."

I headed for the door, and I didn't look back.

Fortunately, I was excused from the knife-fighting exercises for the day. I wasn't really up to it. I was feeling better by dinner, and by the next day, as the ship began lurching and firing maneuvering jets, my stomach was operating fully again.

But I wasn't happy. I knew, possibly more than any other recruit in the legion, what was really going on. We weren't here to guard some mining complex. We were here to prove we could outfight an equivalent number of lizards—and from what I'd seen, the enemy was more than willing to cheat in this regard throwing at us ten times our weight in lizards. I had no idea how many dinos we'd killed thus far, but it had to be more than ten thousand all together. Maybe the number was twice that high.

The problem was the enemy had the resources of an entire planet to draw upon. They had *millions* of lives to spend. We had a finite number of men and guns. Our only advantages were in equipment and know-how. We had professional, well-armed troops—troops that could come back to life and fight again, over and over. It was a grim thought, and I felt that a grim battle was surely coming.

Our first advantage, which our tribune was hastily employing, was maneuverability. Using *Corvus*, we could come down wherever we wanted and face the enemy on our own terms. I was sure the saurians below us were watching closely wondering what our next move was going to be. Aboard ship speculation was rampant.

"What the holy hell do you think old Drusus is up to, McGill?" Carlos asked me loudly.

Everyone looked at me. They'd seen my special trip to the observation tower, my day off from exercises and my trips to the blue level. They knew something odd was going on with me, but they didn't know what it was. In particular, Carlos was going mad with curiosity.

"Carlos is right," said Kivi, jumping into the pack. She'd taken every opportunity to snipe at me since our break-up. She wasn't too fond of Natasha, either. "You know something. I want to hear it. We've got a right to know."

"No," I told them both, shaking my head, "you're in Varus, remember? None of us have rights of any kind. But it doesn't matter because I don't know where we're going. Even if I did, I wouldn't be at liberty to say."

"You're such a kiss-up all of a sudden," Carlos complained. "You were such a tough-guy down in the steel tunnels. What did they do to you? Do you feel bad inside now?"

I actually did feel rather off-balance, but I wasn't going to admit it to him. I knew that Carlos and the rest were half-joking and half-serious trying to browbeat information out of me. I struggled not to get angry with them.

"I'm fine," I said. "But it's time for you to shut up unless you want a fresh lesson in hand-to-hand."

I'd started off untrained, but over the last six months I'd become known as one of the best with primitive weapons. Right now I didn't feel good, but they didn't know that. No one wanted to challenge me after a grueling day on the field. They broke up their circle and wandered off grumbling.

All of them, that was, except for Natasha. She lingered and stared at me with narrowed eyes.

"What? Are you suspecting the worst, too?" I asked her.

"You know something," she said. "I can tell that. We all can. You really don't want to tell me?"

I wanted to all of a sudden. "What's in it for me?" I asked.

She smirked and gave me a small kiss. I reached for more, and she pushed me back.

"I'm not Kivi," she said.

I laughed. "Okay, sorry. I can't tell you anything, but I suspect we'll all find out very soon."

We left it at that and headed for our bunks. I'd been asleep for less than an hour when a whooping alarm went off. It was the emergency klaxons. Bewildered and half asleep, I tumbled out onto the steel deck, scrambling with my kit.

All around me, recruits were doing the same.

"Is the ship under attack?" Kivi asked.

"No, dummy," Carlos snapped. "The evasion jets aren't even firing."

Kivi apparently didn't like being called a dummy any more than the rest of us. She kicked him in the butt, and he caught her foot. He tried to twist it, but she snapped it back and threw a punch.

"Hey, hey," I said. "Let's get our gear on. This is for real."

"Oh yeah?" Carlos asked. "You knew, right? Let me guess: the date marked on your calendar? Or did Graves text you personally?"

"You know what, Carlos?" I said. "You're an even bigger asshole in the middle of the night."

Everyone laughed and loudly agreed. Carlos grumbled, but he shut up and put his gear together.

Five minutes later, we were jogging down the passages to the tubes. We shot down, one at a time. The arrows were lit yellow on the floor and walls—even the ceiling. Our squad number was easy to follow.

I knew long before we got there where we were headed. The team chit-chatted around me as we moved quickly toward the lower decks.

"It's not another drop?"

"Can't be."

"This is yellow-level...that could only mean we're boarding a lifter."

"At least we don't have to get fired out of the cannons again."

In general, the group was happy it wasn't going to be a hot drop. If the LZ was clean enough to allow a lifter to land, it had to be relatively safe.

We were herded aboard a lifter and clamped into place. Rows of troops faced one another, but few of us made eye-contact. Not even Carlos was up for any new jokes. We were tired and worried.

The troops had been elated when they'd pulled the legion off Cancri-9. My team had been left behind, of course, but most had seen it as a narrow escape. The assignment had been rough, and no one wanted to stick around to see just how many lizards they would throw at us the next day.

Now, however, that feeling of relief was over. We weren't going home. We weren't even going to another planet, another assignment. We were going back down onto a planet that had turned utterly hostile.

I leaned back and closed my eyes. The lifter shook, rattled and squeaked. I smelled hot metal and strange chemicals. Cold air and hot vapors chased over us as different parts of the ship vented and adjusted themselves. It was nothing like the luxury ride a passenger ship provided back home.

My head lolled, and I nearly fell asleep. Off and on, my chin touched my chest and woke me up.

Suddenly, an elbow jabbed my belly. I lurched awake, angry. I grabbed Carlos' hand and twisted one of his fingers up away from the rest.

His grin faded away. "Sorry man, I know you feel like shit. Now, please don't break my finger. I need that one. I kinda need them all."

The truth was, I had been planning to break his finger. In my mind, I could hear the snapping sound it would make, and I knew that for an instant it would feel very good to have done it.

I sighed and let him go. Sometimes Carlos and his rude joking around could drive a man crazy. At least he was smart enough to know when he'd crossed the line.

I closed my eyes again, and my chin touched my chest. I dreamt for a few minutes that I was back in the revival room, and I'd just experienced another bad grow. My legs were missing—I saw that first. But then I lifted my hands to my face—and they were gone, too.

I lurched awake. The lifter had landed with a final, rattling crash. Everyone winced. The shocks on these things were huge but old and creaky.

None of that mattered now, though, because we were down.

"Welcome back to Cancri-9, people!" Carlos shouted.

People shouted back unkind things. There were a few ragged cheers, but most of the troops were groaning.

My eyes were locked on the ramp. It slowly unclamped itself and began to lower. A line of bright sunlight struck us in the face. Everyone squinted, but we couldn't look away.

Where on this heartless world of steel were we now?

-18-

The ramp went down with a loud whirring sound. The orange line of sunlight grew and grew until we had to dial our faceplates to their darkest setting. With black, shiny visors hiding our faces, we felt the clamps disengage. We were free of our seats.

We slapped the buckles and they fell away. Veteran Harris appeared as if on cue and walked up and down the line. I knew that every squad on this ship had its own veteran, who was doing the same thing with his allotment of troops.

"All right, on your feet!" he shouted. "We've lucked out, recruits, as I'm sure you've figured out by now. The brass figured we were homesick and missed our pet lizards. They, in their infinite wisdom, have redeployed us to a new location."

"Where's that, Veteran?" Carlos asked.

We all watched, wondering if Harris was going to thump him. He didn't.

"I don't know, people. But I do know what we're supposed to do. We're getting our butts off this ship and down that ramp. There will be arrows leading us to our first destination."

"What the hell?" Carlos asked. "What kind of briefing is that? Does anyone know why we're here?"

Harris' hand reached out and clamped onto Carlos. He pulled him close and squeezed him until he choked.

"Now, didn't I just say that I didn't know?"

"Yes, Veteran," he gasped.

"Ortiz, don't you ever know when you should shut up and follow orders?"

"I have trouble with that."

Harris propelled him toward the ramp. Carlos rammed into me, but I was ready for that. I took the shove with my pack, having set my feet against the movement. Carlos grunted unhappily.

A minute later, we were trotting off the ship, carrying our gear. Everyone on the lifter appeared to be a light trooper, with only a few weaponeers mixed in. All I saw were snap-rifles and unarmored suits.

I had a bad thought then: what if they'd only sent us down here? What if the heavies were being held in reserve? It was a horrible idea, and I tried to abandon it, but I couldn't. After all, they'd sent just the light troops down into those lizard-infested mines. Didn't we deserve a break?

We followed the flashing lines onto miles of wide open tarmac. They led us away from the ship. In a long line, two abreast, we trotted toward what looked like a massive building.

I turned this way and that, looking at everything I could. We were clearly at a spaceport. It was big—at least as big as the one on the east coast of North America Sector back home.

"Hey, check it out," Carlos said, pointing off to the right. "That's a Nairb ship, or I'm Irish."

We all looked the way he'd pointed. Even Veteran Harris swiveled his head.

"A Nairb ship?" asked Natasha. "There's no way that's local shipping."

I thought about it, and suddenly, things began making sense. The Nairb were an odd race. They were our Galactic bureaucrats. They hired out as accountants and customs inspectors, ensuring that every world was following their trade restrictions and meeting their obligations. In fact, they had a monopoly on the service—an official monopoly on hiring out as officials.

"McGill is right," Kivi said, almost stumbling as she tried to run and look at the Nairb ship at the same time. "I recognize those lines. They always put those shark-fin-looking things on top."

184

"This must be their Galactic spaceport," I said. "The *real* one."

I received a number of faceless stares from their visors. Every planet had one spaceport that was authorized to engage in interstellar trade. The Nairbs, working as agents of the Galactics, liked to keep a close eye on ships from other systems, making sure they traded only what they were allowed to. Their presence indicated this spaceport handled interstellar trade.

"But what the hell are we doing here?" Carlos asked. We were all thinking it, but he was the only one that voiced the thought. "If we mess with their interstellar port, won't the Galactics get pissed off?"

"That's enough chatter," Veteran Harris shouted. "Save it for the run. We're not done yet. We're running up those steps. Look!"

We turned away from the Nairb ship and paid attention to where we were going again.

"We're climbing the outer walls?" Carlos asked in disbelief.

"That's what it looks like," I said.

We watched as the leading elements of the cohort reached the walls surrounding the main complex, which had to be the terminal and warehouses. Such areas had strong security. There were saurian guards there, posted on those walls. They were watching us, and we watched them.

"They must be wondering what the hell is going on," I said.

"Yeah, they're probably radioing their headquarters, reporting this invasion firsthand."

It wasn't until elements of the first squad reached the top of the walls that things turned ugly. The saurian guards were all raptor-types, and they were well-armed. They had armor on, which glinted in the overly bright sunlight.

For the record, I was slightly proud to see we didn't fire the first shot. Maybe that was what the tribune had planned all along. Maybe Drusus had decided to just send us charging at the walls in vast numbers, looking scary, to force the dinos to act.

185

The guards soon figured out we weren't tourists. They began closing the gates as we reached them, but a hundred or so troops made it through before they clanged together. When the light troops mounted the steps inside, the guards finally opened fire.

This was an expansion of the war, a breaking of the rules. Normally, events at the spaceport were very civilized. We'd brought warfare and mayhem to our enemy, on ground of our own choosing. I could imagine that the saurians had been communicating with their leaders, surprised and uncertain as to how to proceed.

When they did get the order to fire on us, we were shocked by their powerful weaponry. Each saurian guard had a long tube which rode on his shoulder. I didn't recognize the weapon type, but I knew it wasn't going to be snap-rifles versus teeth this time.

Violet gouts of energy leapt off the walls, quickly burning down the men who'd made it inside. There were at least thirty heavily armed and armored guards up there now, and more were showing up all the time. They directed their beams down onto the tarmac like men with fire hoses, nailing those of us who were locked outside the compound. The beams incinerated whatever they touched. Men fell burning like a field of dry grass.

I felt glad as I watched that we weren't the first to reach those walls. As there was no way through, our orders changed.

"That's it!" screamed Harris into our headsets. "Break ranks, squad, follow me!"

He veered to the right, and we followed him in a knot.

"Spread out! Spread out! Run for that truck!"

We were running all out now. The only cover nearby was a refueling truck. We'd almost reached it when another squad beat us to it. They huddled close, and began peppering the enemy on the walls with their snap-rifles.

We slowed down and Harris lifted his arm, directing us toward another, more distant scrap of cover. This time it was a communications tower of some kind.

We never heard his order to move on, however. Suddenly, the refueling truck a group of our troops were hugging up to was taken out. It flared cherry-red—then transformed into a white explosion.

My entire squad was thrown off their feet. Some of us had burning uniforms. The squad that had been taking cover behind the truck had vanished. There were only a few smoking boots and broken bits of gear left.

"Head for the tower," Harris said. "From there, we'll spread out and charge the wall."

It was insane, but we had no other choice. There were landing pits for ships here and there, but nothing that wasn't over a mile off. The walls of the terminal building were closer than that.

From all around us, groups of troops began firing. They were exposed, but we outnumbered the enemy fifty to one. Things changed when some of our weaponeers got their big projectors set up and raked the top of the wall. The enemy was forced to duck, and I saw some of them get knocked right off their perches.

I'd had some hopes that the early assaulters would win through and take the wall for us, saving those of us still out in the open. But despite their surprise tactics, they were burned away, swept right off the puff-crete stairways by the heavy energy weapons. Unarmored, light troops couldn't take any kind of hit from such powerful guns.

"I hit one with my rifle," Carlos complained. "I swear I did. No penetration, zero."

"How the hell are we going to get up those walls?" Kivi asked. There was a touch of panic in her voice.

Veteran Harris didn't answer right away. We'd reached the tower, and were hiding behind it. They couldn't take this structure down as easily as a truck full of fuel—it was a solid building.

That didn't stop them from trying. As soon as they noticed we were hiding back there and taking potshots from cover, they swept the base of the tower with their energy weapons.

Only one of us got hit. Kivi was too slow to pull back—either that, or she never saw it coming. She was there one second, screwing on her scope and barrel-extension to turn her snap-rifle into a sniper's weapon, and the next—she was gone. There wasn't much left. At least it was quick.

"Damn," I whispered.

Harris came to me and banged his hand on my shoulder. "McGill, I need a volunteer."

I nodded. It was my fate to be the perpetual volunteer.

Harris seemed to divine my thoughts. "This isn't bullshit to get you killed. We have to get into this battle. We're pinned down and taking heavy losses."

I nodded again. He pointed to a small car sitting behind the tower. I stared at it, hoping he wasn't serious.

"Take that thing to the wall."

"Sir, I could run faster."

His big hand lifted from my shoulder and slammed the back of my helmet.

"Maybe," he said, "but you can't fly."

I looked at the unit again, and I understood. It was an air car. The smallest, sorriest, golf-cart-looking air car I'd ever seen.

"Take a man with you to fly shotgun," he said.

I looked at Carlos, and I grinned.

"Just because I woke you up on the transport?" he demanded.

"No, because you snapped my ass with a towel while I was puking."

"Oh yeah, that."

We climbed in and had it working twenty seconds later. Air cars were part of the tech the Galactics handed out to every world. They weren't special enough to warrant shipping from one planet to the next, but they were cool.

Fortunately, the controls were virtually identical on worlds with humanoid populations. Saurians were a stretch, but they did have the same number of limbs and were about the same dimensions. The tail-holes in the seats made you feel like you were going to slide out backward into the air and fall, however.

I poured on the vertical lift, and we sailed higher and higher. I suspected at that moment that the saurians had refused to pay for air power in the contract so we couldn't do things exactly like this. They'd wanted us to stay trapped on the ground with them, stacking the deck in any way they could.

When we passed over the tower, I veered off and flew at an angle. I already had a plan. From my vantage point in the air, I saw another lifter had landed and I was going to park behind it and hide, looking for a moment to charge in and land in the compound. If we could get behind the saurians, they would have to worry about us. They'd have a much harder time killing all our attacking troops on the tarmac.

The second lifter, I realized after a moment's surprise, was one of ours. As I watched, troops gushed out of it. I was disappointed to see it was another cohort of lightly armed recruits.

These guys never had a chance. The saurians weren't about to be taken by surprise from another flank again. They unloaded on them the moment they ran down the ramp.

A hundred died in the first minute. They never even knew what hit them. The survivors were in shock, rolling under the ramp itself, trying to climb back up onto the ship—the saurians were giving them hell.

They made sure not to damage the ship itself, of course. There were rules to this game of war. We could kill saurians and destroy their equipment. They could do the same to us. But any neutral aliens—or especially Galactics, as I'd found out— were strictly off limits. *Corvus* and all her lifters were owned by the Skrull. Unless they attacked directly, they were non-combatants.

"Fly around to the other side—fly low and fast," Carlos shouted.

I didn't have any good ideas at the moment, and I was sickened by the waste of good troops coming off the second lifter. Against my better judgment, I did as he suggested. We dove around behind the lifter and skimmed low. We dashed in a spiraling circle after that, moving around the walls of the terminal.

"They're all focusing on the second lifter, trying to kill every troop that comes down the ramp. While they're occupied, we'll swoop in from the other side."

It was worth a try, so I did it. The move almost worked, to Carlos' credit. We were within about two hundred meters of the wall and zooming toward it when the enemy finally noticed us—or at least one of them did.

He must have been posted on the far side of the complex by someone with a brain. Instead of joining the feeding-frenzy of his comrades on the side of the wall where all the action was, he stood his post on our side, looking bored.

Even so, he had his head cranked around to watch the interesting stuff going on behind him. When he finally spotted us it was almost too late.

He raised his heavy tube and directed it toward our tiny craft. One of us began screeching in fear—I'm pretty sure it was Carlos.

I pulled back on the steering controls, which was essentially a tube of metal with a v-shaped head on it. My action caused the craft to buck upward, and we rose rapidly into the air.

The dino's first shot burned the air under us. We saw the blinding glare of colored plasma, like a flame-thrower, gush past below. Not satisfied with a miss, he levered it upward to track us. I thought I knew how a bug felt when a spray of deadly gas came out of a gardener's can.

I heaved to the right, away from the plasma. This threw us into a corkscrew spin. We went over the walls and crashed on a roof inside the compound.

Carlos rolled out on top of me. I thought my leg was broken for a few seconds, but I forced it to work and the pain subsided. I rolled Carlos off me and got out my weapon. I expected at any instant the saurian that had spotted us was going to burn us both to ash.

The next gush of energy roared over our heads, however. I realized that the roof we were on was higher than the wall that ringed the compound. He couldn't hit us from his position. We were safe for the moment.

I groaned and struggled to get back into the game.

"My ribs are broken," Carlos said, wheezing.

"Get up anyway."

On our hands and knees, we crept to the edge of the roof.

I couldn't believe it—but we'd made it inside the compound.

-19-

The first thing we did was try to find a way down into the building. I figured if we could get inside, we'd be safe, because the building was full of Nairbs. As non-combatant aliens, no one was allowed to fight in their presence and risk injuring them—that was against Galactic Law.

Unfortunately, we ran into a problem immediately: there was no way into the building from the roof.

"Any human would have put at least a hatch on this roof!" complained Carlos.

I had to agree with him. I'd had more than my fill of cultural differences for the day.

"We have to find a way down or we'll be pinned up here, and they'll come kill us eventually."

In the end, it took some risky behavior to find the way down. Instead of ladders, or internal stairways, the saurians had built an external set of steep stairs that went down one side of the structure. The stairs were exposed and there wasn't even a guardrail.

Carlos and I looked at one another. I knew what we were both thinking: did we run down those stairs, risking annihilation, or did we lay on the rooftop and hope our side won the battle?

"I guess we have to do what we can sniping from up here," Carlos said.

I shook my head. "Sniping isn't enough. We can't get through their armor without focused fire."

"What do you suggest?" he asked suspiciously.

"People are dying down there."

"Yeah? And we're probably going to die up here, too."

"We have to go for it," I told him.

I got up and set myself like a runner prepping for a sprint. My side hurt, my head hurt and even my eyes seemed to ache in my skull.

Groaning, Carlos heaved himself into a crouch at my side.

"This is crazy, we don't even know if there is a way in at the bottom of the stairs. I mean, don't you think they probably locked all the doors by now?"

"I don't know," I said, "but I'm not sunbathing up here while these lizards kill two cohorts of light troops."

"Why not?"

That was the last thing either of us said. Our conversation was interrupted by a singing sound. We didn't even have time to throw ourselves flat.

An energy-charged mortar shell came down on the top of the building. Some of the weaponeers supporting our light troops must have gotten into position.

The building shook under us.

"They're crazy!" shouted Carlos. "If they kill one of the Nairbs, we'll all be in trouble."

Another singing sound came, and the building shook again.

"Look!" Carlos said, pointing across the expanse of the roof.

We saw the shell had punched a burning hole through the roof. Without another word, we got up and ran to it, jumping blindly into the black, smoking hole. Anything was better than waiting around on the roof or charging down the exposed stairway.

We came down on a dusty floor lined with offices. It appeared to be deserted. There were pod-like desks and seats that looked like blobs of paint. I landed on one of these and my boots punctured it. I learned that the formless blob was indeed full of colored liquid. I guess that was a comfortable seat for a Nairb.

193

The important thing was, we didn't see any enemies. We looked, but there weren't any stairways on this level either.

"Are we going outside to run down, or are we going to dig through the floor?" Carlos asked me.

"There has to be something," I said.

I found it pretty fast. A trap door that led down to the next level. We dropped through, and found another trap door. Carlos followed me, complaining every step of the way.

When we reached the bottom floor, we found the bureaucrats who'd abandoned their desks in panic. Startled-looking Nairbs huddled down here, and as one they turned to look at us in surprise. I'd seen pictures, but had never met up with them personally. They had bulbous faces the color and consistency of thick green pea soup inside of a water balloon. To me, the aliens resembled their chairs: they looked like beached seals.

They all began squawking at once in their own language when they realized who we were. I'm sure if I could have understood them, I'd feel insulted. As it was, I ignored them and pushed through the mass of their bodies to the doors.

The doors weren't your typical affair from Earth. There was no automatic swishing sound, or obvious pad to put your hand on. Instead, I was confronted with a bank of large rods in various positions. I figured they were switches of some kind, as they could be moved up and down in various directions. But which way to move them?

Carlos followed me, bumping through the crowd of angry Nairbs.

"Do these guys bite?" he asked.

"Only your bank account. Come here and help me get this open."

"You're nuts, you know that? Why do you want to open the doors? The saurian guards will murder us."

"I'm not trying to open the door. I'm trying to open the big gates outside. I want to let our troops inside the walls."

All the while we talked, I worked various levers experimentally. I tried them one at a time. Most seemed to do nothing, while a few caused the sounds of grinding machinery to start up, then stop.

Carlos ignored me. He walked over to a box on one of the Nairbs desk. He adjusted it, and suddenly sound poured forth. The sound turned into an incomprehensible babble of angry voices.

"It's a translator unit," he said. "I'm trying to dial it for earthers."

Seeing what he was doing, a small Nairb with a band around its neck waddled forward and nosed the device. Large yellow teeth snapped at Carlos' hands, and he pulled them away quickly. The Nairb worked at the device, making careful choices.

"Do you understand this, barbarian?" the box asked.

"Ah, yes!" Carlos said. "It works!"

"Excellent. You have accrued seven criminal charges since you entered my awareness. I order you to perform self-execution."

That made us look up. The Nairb had our full attention. Nairbs didn't make idle threats or demands. They were as unpleasant in personality as they were in appearance, but they followed rules to the letter. This concerned me, because as far as I could tell, we hadn't done anything yet to warrant execution.

"Self-execution? On what grounds?" I asked the blob.

"Your attack upon this facility was monitored—as was everything you've done since arriving here on Cancri-9. Damaging this property is not in your contract. You have violated Galactic Law through willful breach of contract."

I looked at Carlos, and he looked back at me. Our visors were clear now that we were inside and the blinding light of Cancri's suns wasn't burning overhead. I could see that Carlos was as worried as I was. Trade contracts were more important than any other element of Galactic Law. They took it very seriously, as the entire fabric of their empire was based upon it.

"We're not aware of any violation," I said angrily.

Carlos lifted his hand and waved urgently for me to stop talking. I fell quiet, wondering if he knew how to handle these beings.

I noticed the Nairbs had shut up, too. They were no longer a pack of barking seals. Instead, they were a quiet, vengeful group that stared in eager anticipation.

"You have not performed as ordered," said the Nairb. "Refusal to comply is an additional crime. Penalties may be elevated if you continue to resist."

I wasn't too worried about elevated penalties, as I was already up for self-execution. How were things going to get any worse?

But then I reminded myself that things *could* get worse. Our unit, our legion, our ship—even our race could be penalized if the crime was big enough.

"What violation has been performed?" Carlos asked. His usual joking tone was absent.

"Do you refuse to comply?"

"No," he said firmly. "I do not refuse to comply. I'm requesting clarification."

"That is permissible to a point," said the Nairb. "Your contract strictly forbids the use of aircraft during this campaign. That stipulation has been violated."

"Aircraft?" I asked, interrupting. "Are you talking about the air car we used to come here? That isn't Earth equipment. It doesn't count."

Again, Carlos waved for me to be quiet.

"High Justice," Carlos said. "I'm sorry if there has been a misunderstanding. But no aircraft have been brought from our world to this world."

"That is not germane to the violation. Aircraft were used in this conflict."

"What proof do you have of this?"

"Your presence in this compound proves the violation. I don't see why you are bothering to evade my edict. It is valid, and delaying the order to self-execute will only worsen the violation."

I didn't see what the hurry was, but then, I'm not a Nairb.

"Not if the violation is in error," Carlos said confidently. "I'm attempting to determine whether or not the order is valid before it is followed."

This made the Nairb ruffle. "I'm the prefect of this world. There is no higher authority on contracts. You offend me personally with your statements."

"I apologize, but as the accused, I am within my rights. If we understood the violation and agreed with it, we would of course self-execute immediately."

"Ah," said the Nairb, its ocular organs changing shape and retracting somewhat. "I understand the nature of your delays now. You believe your bodies will be copied. Perhaps, you're awaiting a signal from your fellow criminals that indicates this process is prepared. I will take steps."

The Nairb turned to its fellows and barked out orders in its own language and they squawked back. The translator burbled as it tried to translate multiple inputs, and nothing intelligible came out of it for a few seconds.

"Carlos," I said, "what are they doing?"

"Turning off our revival machines."

"They can do that?"

"Yeah. My dad worked at the spaceport on Earth—the big one. The Nairbs have to have power to enforce their decisions. They can turn off any Galactic tech we bought from someone else—even our guns."

I was stunned. I hadn't known about that. Perhaps Carlos had learned a few things in life I hadn't. At least he had a better understanding of the Nairbs than I did.

"Prefect," Carlos said, trying to politely gain the creature's attention again. "Prefect, if I could just—"

"It is done," said the alien, turning back to us triumphantly. "There will be no more of your kind avoiding the reward you all so richly deserve."

"What you have done is a violation," I said, unable to keep quiet. I ignored Carlos, who tried to shush me again.

"We do not violate any rules. It is not in our nature."

"You have made a mistake. We did not use combat aircraft to land on this building. We did not kill any Nairbs. We are in conflict with the saurians only, and we apologize for any inconvenience we might have—"

"Ha! It is far too late for apologies."

"Fine, let's focus on facts and realities, then."

"That is always our way."

"You have accused us of a contract violation," I said, trying to control my temper. "We have declared our belief you've made an error. There must be some kind of arbitration."

The Nairbs quieted. "Arbitration? You claim the right of arbitration?"

"I do," I said quickly.

There was a fresh round of grumbling from the assembled aliens. I could tell they didn't like what I was saying.

"Very well, a stay must be granted in that case."

The Nairb turned and spoke to its fellows, who seemed disappointed.

"Have you reversed your disconnection of our systems?" I asked sternly.

"We have."

"I demand confirmation. Prove you have done what you say."

The Nairb ruffled anew. "You suggest we are lying? Your insinuation is insulting."

"I am within my rights."

"Your sensory organs can't read our incoming data. How can we prove our case?"

"Easily enough," said Carlos suddenly. He was smiling, and I could tell that he was finally catching on to my plan. "All you have to do is open the front gates so we can see for ourselves."

Grumbling and no doubt cursing our names, the Nairb went to the collection of switches. He organized them into a precise pattern, and the front gates rolled slowly open.

-20-

The battle outside had been one-sided up until this point. Our fellow legionnaires had been driven back to their lifters and were scattered around the spaceport, huddling behind any cover they could find.

It had been a while since Carlos and I had been able to observe events firsthand. Apparently, Tribune Drusus had decided the light cohorts weren't going to be able to do the job alone. He'd ordered a cohort of heavy troops to head down to the planet.

I'd gathered by this time the plan had been for the light forces to race from the blast-pans to the central terminal and take it by surprise. By using our fastest ground forces, the saurian guards were supposed to fall without much of a fight.

Things hadn't worked out that way. Our lightning strike had reached the enemy, but they had been prepared. The battle had turned into a costly grind, and the legion had been forced to commit more forces to the attack. At the same time, the saurians in the city nearby were mobilizing their own defenders.

We learned all this as the gates opened and we were able to reestablish our network with local troops. The puff-crete walls, the distance and the heat of action had prevented us from surveying current events up until now.

"This is great," Carlos said, looking outside. "They don't even know we are right here behind their lines."

"Maybe they do know, but they don't want to come in here and get blamed for any Nairb casualties."

Carlos shrugged. "Could be. Well, in any case, we've done our part. We can just observe through these viewports until—"

"I don't think so," I said. "When our troops come in hard, I'm going out there."

Carlos looked at me like I was crazy. I guess he had a point.

"Why?"

I pointed. He followed my finger and sighed.

Two of the saurian troops were dead at the base of the wall on the inside. They'd been hit by heavy weapons fire, by look of it. But what I was pointing at wasn't the broken, ragdoll-like corpses. I was pointing out their weapons, one of which looked undamaged.

"I'll go out there," I said, "grab that plasma weapon, and hose them down from behind. They don't have a lot of defending troops left. If we can nail them when their attention is diverted, we'll save a lot of our people."

"James," Carlos said, staring at the thick tubular weapon, "that thing looks heavy."

I smiled at him. "That's why I need a wingman to help me operate it."

"I knew you were going to say that."

We bided our time. The incoming fire on the walls intensified suddenly, and I knew the attack had to be underway. The saurians returned fire sporadically, but for the most part they just hunkered down, clearly planning on nailing our troops when they got in close.

One of them finally noticed that the gates were open, and that we were there behind them, watching.

All my plans went out the window in that moment. I turned to the Nairb Prefect, who had lost interest in the battle and was riffling through contracts on his computer system. I'm pretty sure he was reading up on ours to screw us somehow later on.

"Prefect!" I called. "If you want to avoid the death of everyone in this room, including yours, set that translator to let us speak with the saurians."

"Why would I wish to help you?"

"So you don't die," I said. "The saurians are coming in here, and there's going to be a fight if you don't—"

"Too dangerous! Not a violation, but a warning to the offending parties will be issued immediately if—"

"Yeah, I know. Just turn on the translator so I can talk to him."

The Nairb hesitated, but then a saurian in armor loomed at the windows. He peered inside. The Nairb humped his body like a racing seal and managed to reset the device before the saurian forced his way in.

"Soldier!" I shouted, hearing the translator hiss and rasp. "No energy weapons, it's Galactic Law!"

The trooper had a heavy beam unit aimed at my chest, but I'd made sure to stand directly in front of the massed Nairbs, who were now squawking behind me. I had no doubt they were bitterly complaining about my conduct.

The saurian lowered his gun, but he did not retreat as I'd hoped. Instead, he extended a hand-to-hand weapon from each of his metal-covered fore claws.

I'd heard about these weapons. *Scizores*, some called them. They were like artificial claws of hardened steel. They resembled the killing claws of the saurians' distant ancestors, and had been used in the past and present to gut an enemy in close combat.

Without a word, he charged us. I'm sure he felt confident. He was stronger and larger than us, and wearing heavy armor.

Carlos and I dropped our snap-rifles. They wouldn't be much use in this fight and a ricochet that killed a Nairb would only seal our doom. I pulled out my combat knife, as did Carlos.

Fighting an alien biped in hand-to-hand was a new experience for me. Up until now, everything had been about energy weapons or ballistic weapons. Now, it was all about strength, skill and tactics. Armor counted, too.

As there were two of us, the alien took the simplest course: he ignored Carlos and charged me. I guess it made some sense. I had been the one with the balls to talk to him via the translator. Perhaps that had angered or insulted him in some way.

I fought defensively. All around me, Nairbs humped away desperately. Desks were smashed and chopped as the saurian slashed with his two heavy claws. I knew I couldn't cut through his armor easily, so I retreated, watching for an opening.

Carlos trailed behind the saurian and soon made his play. He lunged in and stabbed the saurian in the back.

Our combat knives aren't formed from normal steel. They're modified and hardened with advanced techniques. The blade didn't just bounce and spark from the armor, it gouged it, leaving a scratch a half-inch deep.

Without missing a beat, the saurian tried to backhand Carlos. It swept back with one claw, slashing the air where he'd been a moment before. But Carlos must have suspected something like this. He'd darted in, struck, and danced back out of the way again. He wasn't waiting around.

The saurian turned in his direction, perhaps frustrated he hadn't made an easy kill.

I dashed in and stabbed, as Carlos had, going for his closest, uplifted fore claw.

His counterattack was even faster against me. He almost caught me, whirling back and cutting the air with two vicious strokes. Fortunately, his heavy armor seemed to be slowing him down. He couldn't move as quickly as we could.

"This isn't working, McGill," Carlos complained.

"Maybe we can hit him low at the same time, taking his legs out from under him."

"He'll plant those blades in our spines if we try it. And he's got a tail, too, don't forget. That's like third leg for balancing on these scaly bastards."

The saurian was intent on me again, marching forward slowly, making powerful slashing motions. Equipment was destroyed as he went.

"Hold on," I said. "Carlos, do you think you can get that translator flipped back to its default setting? I want the saurians to be able to talk to the Nairbs."

"Maybe."

"Do it. I'll keep retreating."

"Why?"

"Just trust me for once."

"Why?"

"You *owe* me, that's why!"

With a sound of exasperation, he went over and fooled with the settings on the translator. Around us, the Nairbs sounded like a pack of angry, squawking seals.

I kept my distance, and was sure not to damage any equipment if I could help it. My plan was simple: all I had to do was get the saurian to screw up and damage some critical piece of hardware. With any luck, the Nairbs would order him to self-execute.

"I got it!" Carlos shouted. "All I had to do was turn it off and on again."

"Fine, now—"

The alien finally caught me. I simply ran out of stuff to hide behind. Backing and retreating can only work for so long in a cluttered environment. My footing slipped, and one of his blades came flashing in to gut me.

I dropped my knife and latched onto his armored arm with both hands. It was like wrestling with a foot-thick snake. The lizard was *strong*.

The other arm was coming up, ready to kill me, but Carlos tackled him from behind.

The saurian almost went down but not quite. Using two thick legs and a tail, it held its feet. But the point of its free claw did stab downward—directly into the flesh of a particularly bulbous Nairb.

As I thought back on the scene later, I believe that the Nairb had been trying to get itself injured. Maybe it had had enough of this nonsense and had gotten the same idea I had—or maybe it was trying to save a file at its workstation and screwed up—I was never certain.

Whatever the case, blood like green-black paint spilled over the floor. The Nairb began keening, even though it was only a flesh wound in a single flipper.

The effect on the rest of them was immediate. They all began barking. I could tell the saurian understood them.

I don't know what they told him, but it must have been pretty bad. He lifted up the claw that had damaged a Nairb's flipper and thrust it into a slot in his neck armor. I'd never noticed it before, but it was obviously a weak point in his armor that he knew about and we didn't.

Whatever the case, the saurian dropped dead at our feet.

Carlos and I stared. We couldn't believe it.

"He did it," Carlos said. "He really executed himself."

"As it should be," said the prefect. He was back at the translator and had switched it to allow us to speak. "Any honorable soldier of the Galactic would follow the Law to its final endpoint. I sense you humans are not fully civilized. You're new to the empire and still half-wild. Do you at least have a sense of shame when faced by a true soldier?"

"Ha!" said Carlos. "He's dead, and I'm not. I'm not impressed."

I looked at him, and so did the prefect.

"Disgusting…" said the Nairb.

I saw something the alien couldn't, however. The Nairb couldn't read our facial expressions. Carlos' eyes lingered on the fallen saurian, who we'd been struggling with so closely moments before. He *was* impressed. I could tell.

I could understand that. The dedication the act took…there was no revival system to back him up, nothing.

Oddly, I thought that the revival units had made us less willing to die in most situations. Sure, if we were being burned to death or something, we'd rather a quick death and a revival. But we didn't relish the idea of giving our all for a concept. Repeated painful deaths quickly relieved a man of such lofty ideas.

Still, I could not help but stare at the dead saurian who'd fought so powerfully and well. Really, he would have beaten both of us, but for his rigid belief in the legal system.

I knew that saurians weren't like us in many ways. Their lifespans burned shorter—and, I think, hotter—than ours did. People said they weren't that smart, not even the smaller raptor types, like this one. But I'd been impressed by their capabilities. They'd had superior arms, and a relative handful of them had held us off at the spaceport for a long time today.

The time came quickly for us to make our next move. We watched the walls, and we saw the first flash of silvery metal from a snap-rifle.

The front line of charging light troops were just reaching the compound walls and entering the open gates. We could see, from our vantage point, what was waiting for them.

The saurian heavy guardsmen had hunkered down, no longer taking shots from the walls. They'd opted to focus their weapons from covered positions, encircling the open gateway. The light troops that stormed in leading the charge were burned to ash in seconds from concentrated firepower.

It had been hard to wait this long to act, very hard. But we'd both felt it was necessary. If we engaged the saurians before that point, they would know they were in a two-front firefight and would adjust their positions. Our biggest advantage—that of surprise—would be lost.

So we let them burn down the first squad that charged triumphantly into the breach. I wondered if those troops believed the enemy had all been killed or had retreated. Why else had the gates finally opened? But instead of an easy victory, they were ambushed and killed to the last man.

"*Now*, it has to be *now*," I said, tapping at the wall. The door swept open. Even through my air-conditioned reflective suit, I could feel the heat of the two glaring stars overhead.

I grabbed up the heavy weapon the saurian had discarded. That was easier than going out to take a weapon from a fallen enemy, which had been our original plan. It also gave us time to figure out how to operate the captured weapon.

I ran with it, essentially balancing the tube on my right shoulder. I was the taller and the stronger man. Carlos followed. He was going to be my gunner.

I stepped out into the courtyard behind the ring of saurians, who were all staring ahead at the light troops trying to get into the gate. The first wave had gone down, but the next was aiming their snap-rifles around the walls and firing. This did nothing to the saurians, who burned away gloved human hands and snap-rifle barrels with eagerly probing beams of energy.

"They seem to be enjoying themselves," Carlos said. "Let's do this."

205

I went to my knees, balancing the heavy tube. It felt like I had an I-beam on my shoulder.

Carlos swiveled to the right first, depressed the firing stud, and sent a blinding surge of energy into the saurians on that flank.

The effect was dramatic. Three of them were devoured within seconds. Their armor melted to slag, and their flesh merged with orange, bubbling steel.

"Sweep it!" I shouted. "They're turning!"

"They aren't going to fire," Carlos said confidently.

I could not help but think that part of his confidence stemmed from the fact he stood behind me. I would shield him from the first blast at least.

But most of his reasoning came from the fact we'd propped open the terminal door behind us. The Nairbs were visible inside, directly behind our position. It didn't take a genius lizard to realize that if he fired upon us, the odds were very high indeed he'd hit a neutral alien, and thus violate Galactic Law.

So Carlos swept the beam over another knot of enemy and annihilated them. An officer rose up from their ranks and shouted orders. From his gestures alone, we could see what he was planning.

"They'll pull back a squad and hit us from the side," Carlos said, "while the rest keep firing at the troops coming in the front gates."

"I think your next target has marked himself," I said.

Carlos swiveled the cannon. I grunted with the shifting weight, trying to keep it steady. He unleashed another beam, and I was impressed by his accuracy. The officer was swept off his feet and turned into a sparkling mass of slag within seconds.

Still, the damage had been done. The enemy was maneuvering in response to our attacks. They were moving to flank us.

"Turn, turn!" screamed Carlos. "They're going left!"

The big tube banged into my helmet. I saw what he wanted: six of the enemy had jumped up and were racing away from their entrenched positions. They were going to take a safe firing position behind a heavy crawler with treads three meters high. From there, due to the angle, they could safely kill us without risking hitting the Nairbs.

I struggled to swivel the heavy gun without dropping it or losing my balance. I was on my knees, having taken that position to provide a good gunnery mount to Carlos. It's hard to quickly rotate while on your knees with a huge weight crushing your shoulder. I already knew that there was going to be a bruised indentation over my right clavicle for a week— given that I survived this battle, which seemed unlikely.

I pitched forward under the weight of the tube and threw out one long arm to stop my fall. The other was curled around the tube, keeping it on my back.

"Just fire from there!"

I hadn't needed to give Carlos any encouragement. He pulled the trigger the second the tube was lined up with the saurians.

He came as close to killing me then as he ever had. I was pretty much down on all fours, and part of my helmet had gotten itself between the muzzle of the weapon and the enemy. The side of my helmet was on fire.

A roaring sound rang in my ears. I thought I was hit—and in a way, I was right.

"Shit! Sorry man!" Carlos said.

I did my best to drop my head and get it out of the way.

"Keep firing!" I shouted.

The gun sang and trembled on my back. It felt strange, like getting a low-level electric shock.

I could smell heat, burning plastic and even cooked flesh now. There must be a hole in my helmet, letting it all in. I held my breath in case it was a toxic brew. It wouldn't do to pass out at this point.

Carlos was a good gunner. He did better than I could have, I think. He killed three of the lizards that were trying to flank us and one more the second he came around the crawler to engage us.

The battle sort of disintegrated after that. With their officer gone, and rattled by having been hit from behind, the enemy didn't know what to do. They didn't keep enough fire on the front gates, and our people outside got smarter. They threw in plasma grenades and blue flashes first outlined, then devoured, the enemy.

Another charging group of light troops came into the smoking ruins of the barricades that had been protecting defending saurian troops a minute ago. I got to watch as my comrades swept over the last of them, got in close, and pulled them down with sheer weight of numbers.

To their credit, the saurians never called a retreat. These were dedicated foes. They fought until the last of them was pulled down and killed. I could see that our veterans were trying to get them to run or surrender—but these weren't wild naked juggers running around in the jungle. They were heavily armed and trained regulars.

They didn't run. They fought to the very last.

-21-

"My men improvised and broke the enemy defenses," Centurion Graves told Primus Turov calmly. "I apologize on behalf of my entire unit if heroic actions don't meet with the approval of Legion Varus."

The Primus glared at him with narrowed eyes. Her mouth was a thin, lipless line of disapproval.

"We're not discussing the Legion, nor are we discussing the battle," she said.

I could tell she was struggling to keep her cool. Her voice was even, but her face revealed the depths of her anger.

"That's unfortunate," said Centurion Graves, "because I have some questions about the tactics we employed during this operation."

"Take your questions and suggestions directly to the Tribune. I'm sure he'll be interested in your sage advice."

My eyes slid from Graves to Turov, then back again. That was all I dared before returning them to stare at the wall in front of me. I stood in a line with the rest of my squad—all those who'd survived, or who'd made it back from the revival units by this time. I'd heard the systems were backed up for hours and were going to have to run at full capacity all night long to get every lost member of the legion back on their feet again. I'm sure the bios were working hard and hating their career decisions about now.

Although this was technically a dressing-down by a superior, I wasn't feeling overly stressed. This time it wasn't *my* posterior that was in the spotlight. Somehow, when the report had gone upstream from Graves concerning my squad's actions, he hadn't specified my personal involvement. I suspected it was to hide the fact I was at the heart of the problem—again. After all, he'd just gone to great lengths to un-execute me, after duping a certain Galactic Inspector. He didn't want me to be a screw-up because that would reflect badly upon him.

I'd already determined that if Turov did get around to questioning me personally, I was going to be as evasive and vague as humanly possible. I figured it was the least I could do for Graves. I'd learned my lesson the last time: there were situations where a member of Varus had to apply some good, old-fashioned stone-walling.

I glanced over to Carlos, who was standing at attention to my left. He didn't return my gaze. Veteran Harris did, however, and he gave me a stern frown. I flicked my eyes back to the center-locked position.

I'd told Carlos to shut up before the debriefing, but I was still worried about him. He'd been always a weak link when it came to keeping his mouth closed.

Graves and Turov were still making hate eyes at one another. That was nothing unusual, however. From what I could tell, the primus was always pissed off at someone.

"I'm considering disciplinary action for your entire unit," Turov said.

"Really? We'd been hoping for a commendation."

"Absurd. Yes, you took the spaceport. But your men violated Galactic Law while doing so—*again*."

"That is a false allegation," Graves said calmly. "It will be thrown out by the arbiters in the end."

Turov walked to Graves and snarled up at him. "Oh, really? Has it occurred to you that the ones performing the arbitration are none other than the offended parties? How do you think the Nairbs will rule when they're the ones who originally brought the charges?"

210

I had to admit, Turov had a pretty good point there. Graves didn't have a quick answer and stood silently.

I watched as she forced herself to calm down and began to pace with her hands clasped behind her back. Her pacing caused my eyes to wander. She was a trim, small woman. Her body was pushing thirty—her real age probably being much older—but even so, she caught my eye. I'd never really noticed before, but I found her legs and rear to be worth a second glance—even a third—especially when she was strutting angrily in front of our lined-up squad.

A moment later my pleasant reverie was rudely interrupted by a jolt of pain. Harris' boot had caught me in the shinbone. I grunted and looked at him in surprise, but he was already back to standing at attention. How had he done it? He was two men down the line and had to be at least five feet away. He ignored my shocked look, which for me was solid proof it had been him.

I knew the reason he'd given me a kick, of course—he'd caught me ogling the primus' rear. I did my best not to react to the throbbing pain in my shin. Harris really knew how to hurt a man, quietly or loudly.

Turov stopped in front of me, surprising me with her sudden attention.

"What are you doing here?" she demanded.

"I was not killed in the battle, sir, I—"

"I don't mean that," she snapped. "You were recently executed in my presence. Clearly, it didn't take the first time."

I opened my mouth then closed it again. Was this some kind of threat? Or was she just in a vindictive mood? Maybe she was eager to start a witch hunt, and I was her first witch.

The Primus strode back to Graves, and I was no longer interested in staring at her ass.

"Your trickery with McGill will come out during the inquiry, you know," she told Graves. "*Everything* will come out. The Nairbs are obsessively thorough. They don't care about right or wrong or circumstance. They care about the letter of the law. They will apply it with the power of the Galactic Battle Fleet if they have to. They would happily erase our species on a technicality. In the course of a single week, you've given them several."

"Primus," Graves said, his voice surprisingly steady, "the light troops were deployed to take the spaceport. We did as we were ordered. Upon *your* orders, there were no briefings given to the troops. These are raw recruits. They had no idea they weren't supposed to use an air car or endanger the Nairbs. They did an amazing job given the fact they faced the enemy alone."

"They were not alone. Heavy troops were deployed—"

"I was there on the field. The heavy troops hung back. The weaponeers did shower the walls with suppressing fire, which was helpful, but it was the light troops that stormed the walls again and again, eventually taking out the entrenched enemy due to the brave improvising done by my unit."

"What's your point, Centurion?" she asked.

"*You* are in charge of this cohort, Primus. The very cohort that took the spaceport, and the first one deployed. I have it on good authority that it was your idea to do this operation with light troops alone. It was also your idea not to brief the recruits."

"Are you suggesting that I was attempting to hog glory?" she asked. "Because I don't feel I've had my fill of it today."

"I'm simply stating the facts as I know them."

"What has any of this got to do with anything?" she demanded.

"Just this: according to Galactic Law, the ultimate party responsible for the actions of any soldier who is following orders is the commander who gave him those orders."

Turov stared at him for a few seconds. "Is this some kind of threat?"

"Negative. It is only a statement of fact. Everything, as you say, will come out in the inquiry. The Nairbs are very thorough, and I'm sure their final arbitration will be a fair one."

She stood motionless for several seconds, glaring at him. Then she drew in a full breath and shouted: "Unit, dismissed!"

We all fled as quickly as we could.

Natasha found me in the hallway and looked me over nervously. "You were executed? That's what happened? You didn't even tell me."

"Sorry," I said. "It was a secret at the time."

"It's all right. Hey, do you want to go to the park?"

I glanced at her. The park was what we called our small zone of greenery under a starlit dome on green deck. In the day hours, it served as a training ground. But at night, soldiers could go there to relax and pretend they were on an Earth-like world, rather than orbiting an alien globe or hurtling through space at relativistic speeds.

"Yeah, sure," I said, smiling.

Before we even reached green deck, we were holding hands. Soldiers since time immemorial have had to move fast in the romance department. The recruits of Legion Varus interacted with even more speed than usual, I suspected. We never knew when we might die—literally.

I walked under the canopy of pine needles and leaves with Natasha beside me. I couldn't help but wonder how this little date was going to end. Would I get lucky tonight? That was the unofficial reason why people went to wander around in the trees on green deck. They kept the lights low, I suspected for just this reason. There were other couples nearby, but we managed to find a spot to sit on a low hill and lie on our backs, watching the stars.

Natasha had probably already decided how this was going to end, how far she was going to let me go, but I knew she wasn't going to tell me. Fortunately, I wasn't dumb enough to blow it by asking. I played it cool and watched for cues.

We stared up at the heavens, and we tried to figure out where Earth was. This was a natural pastime for all human star travelers, and we were no exception to the rule. We pointed and reasoned, but in the end we weren't sure. I was certain, however, that looking at all those overly bright alien stars was making me homesick.

"You know," I said, "I'm feeling lost right now. It's funny, because I've been flying out here and fighting on an alien world for months. In all this time, I didn't really miss Earth. I guess I was too busy to think about it."

"I know what you mean," Natasha said softly. "I'm feeling it too. Cancri isn't a very bright star, but you can see it from Earth. But from here, Sol is just a dim smudge. We're so far from home—we can't even pick out where our star is."

I worked my way up to kissing her, and she let me. But I quickly got the message from her body language that she didn't want more than that. Maybe she was concerned about Kivi, or maybe she just didn't like to move that fast. Whatever the case, I wasn't bothered. I stretched out on my back again and stared at the stars.

"When you're down there on the planet fighting," I said, "you don't have time to pine away for home."

"We're in luck, then," she said.

"Why's that?"

"Haven't you heard? We're going back down in the morning. We're to help garrison the walls with the heavies."

"The walls of the spaceport?" I asked in shock.

"Yeah."

I sat up and frowned at her, not sure at first if she was serious. I could tell at a glance that she was. I groaned and flopped onto my back again.

"This is bullshit," I said. "The deal was simple: the recruits went in and took the place. After that, we withdrew into reserve on the ship and the heavies set up to guard the walls."

"That was the original deal. But the enemy is fielding a large force. They mean to retake their university, their government buildings and the spaceport. They intend to kick us off into space again. The brass wants us to guard the spaceport, as it's the least important target."

"They didn't think it was unimportant a few days ago."

"I know. But they have their grand strategy, I guess. They want to embarrass the lizards—which is forcing them to attack."

I thought about that, and the more I thought the less I liked the situation. I'd really hoped to be moved to the university. The word was the fighting there was very light. The saurians didn't seem to want to blow up their hallowed hive-like learning structures. But that damned spaceport—it was a deathtrap.

214

"What about those damned Nairbs?" I demanded. "Are they still there, cluttering up the place? It sucks to fight with them underfoot. You can't fire a weapon without worrying about getting permed for hurting one of those nasty seals."

Natasha laughed. "I don't think I've ever heard such bitter words out of you, James."

"I've had a rough month."

She laughed again. Then she seemed to have a sudden thought, and she propped herself up on her elbow.

"James?" she asked in a near whisper. "What's it like to be executed—to know...or at least *think* you know, that you've been permed?"

I looked at her and shrugged. "You probably know already. You died in training, didn't you?"

"Yeah. Most of us did. But that was different. It hurt and I was scared, but in the back of my mind I knew it wasn't permanent. I knew I'd live again."

"How about back in our very first exercise? When we were on the lifter, and they let the air leak out? Did you die then?"

She shook her head. "I was scared, but I survived. I sat in my chair and conserved my oxygen. I remember holding my breath and watching you spin that damned locked door open. I could tell you were doing everything you could—it looked like you'd tear the door apart if you had to."

I chuckled, remembering the day. "I didn't realize you were on that lifter with me back then."

Natasha smiled. "I've been thinking of you since that day. It's hard not to remember a moment like that."

I'm not an expert with women, but I am an opportunist. I made another grab for her. She let me kiss her, but stopped my reaching hands short of any further goals.

"You haven't told me how it felt yet," she said.

"You really want to know?"

"Yes."

"It felt like the end of the world. In the end, I—I got really mad. That was my reaction. I wanted to kill someone, to take someone down with me."

Her eyes widened and she studied me in the dark. "Did you try?"

"Yeah," I said. "I went for the alien. I wanted to kill him a third time. If I was going down for the final count, I wanted him to feel a little more pain first."

"Wow. What did he do?"

"He called me a barbarian. He said something about putting us all down, that we were wild dogs…I don't know."

"All of us?"

"All of humanity," I said. "I'm sure that's what he meant."

Natasha pulled away and studied the stars with me. We were both quiet, and I could sense any kind of romantic mood we'd had going was gone now. I chided myself for having told the truth. I should have told her I wanted to smell a flower in my grandma's garden one last time, or something like that. Damn.

"Thanks for telling me the truth, James," she said.

"Sure. Are you glad you asked?"

She hesitated. "Not really."

"What about tomorrow? Are you ready?"

"No. I don't want to go back there ever again. I doubt I'll even sleep tonight. I was killed, you know."

"No shame in that. Nearly a thousand died with you."

"But I was burned alive. The saurians didn't hit me dead-on, they hit a fuel source I was near. It lit up, and I was engulfed in flame. My suit kept me alive for a minute or two, but the heat was too much for it after a while. I cooked inside like a piece of meat in foil, trying to find a way out of a pool of burning liquid."

It was my turn to sit up and stare. "Ouch. Try not to think about that. It happened to a different version of Natasha—not to you. For you, it's only a dream."

"Yeah. I'll try to do that. But I don't want to go down again. These saurians are fighting hard."

It occurred to me that Natasha wasn't the typical woman I'd met in Legion Varus. Maybe that's why I liked her more than the rest. She was a bit sweeter than most of them. Not so rough around the edges.

"Why are you in this legion, Natasha?" I asked her, breaking an uncomfortable silence.

"I screwed up," she said. "Isn't that why we're all here?"

216

"I guess so. The top-level legions didn't want me. I still don't know what those psych tests told them. Maybe they didn't want a scene like the one we watched today between the Primus and Graves to play out in their outfits."

"That's not so bad," she said.

"What about you? I remember you said you built some kind of illegal pet, right?"

"Well...that's not *exactly* how I screwed up," she said. "I didn't want to tell you before—but I came in with a worse mark on my record they found during recruitment."

"What'd you do?"

"I robbed a place. The place where I worked."

"Yeah?" I said, perking up. "Was it a bank, or something?"

I sat up. This story sounded fairly exciting. I could see how an ex-con could be a perfect fit for Varus. What would they have stamp on her files that would want them to take her? Something like: *a resourceful self-starter.*

"No," she said, "not a bank. I worked for a pharmacy."

"You were a druggie?"

She made an irritated clicking noise with her tongue. "Let me just explain. My family had a little trouble paying the bills."

"Who doesn't?"

"We had particular trouble with our medical bills," she said. "There wasn't enough in our medical time-share account last year. They pool it for each family, you know, and that works all right if only one person gets sick at a time. But both my parents started needing drugs—expensive ones."

"Oh, *that* kind of drug," I said, somewhat disappointed.

"What? Were you envisioning masks, guns and wild parties?"

"Something like that."

Natasha laughed again, and I found I was beginning to like the sound.

"I stole medicines," she explained. "Expensive ones."

"Isn't stuff like that tracked?"

"Of course it is. You can't just lift a bottle off the shelf. You have to skim. A few pills from one bottle, just one from

217

the next. Who notices if they have twenty nine caps in the bottle or thirty?"

"Well, sounds like someone did."

"Yeah. They traced it back to us, but couldn't pin it on me enough to convict. Still, the charge went on my record. That's a sector-level crime. I couldn't get another job after that, so I tried to join the legions. Only Varus was interested."

I nodded slowly. I'd learned over time that many recruits had a story like that behind their decision to join up.

"We'll be fine tomorrow," I said. "Stop worrying about it."

"You're a bad liar. You'd do better just keeping quiet."

I did as she suggested, shutting up and holding her hand instead of talking. Then I kissed her fingers, one at a time. After a while, we were kissing more passionately than before. Maybe she'd needed to tell me a few things first.

Before the date was over, I managed to get a little farther with Natasha—but not as far as I wanted.

-22-

The next morning, we were on the lifter heading down again. The mood aboard the transport was grim. No one wanted to return to Steel World—especially not to the spaceport.

We'd learned more about the invasion over the last twenty-four hours. Apparently, things were going pretty well for the legion in general. Our plans had been secret until they went into action—as a recruit, I was the last one to be told anything.

"It's unbelievable, really," Weaponeer Sargon told me. He had been assigned to our unit, along with a few techs and bios. "The tribune has some serious gonads. He blitzed the lizards—all around their own capital city. We now hold their university—which looks like some kind of beehive—and their government buildings and the spaceport."

I was glad to get the info, even if it came from the dubious source known as Sargon. I decided to play along and pretend I believed he knew everything that going on. For all I knew, he did.

"Why didn't we just grab their military headquarters or the royal palace?"

Sargon shook his head. "I don't know. I bet because the tribune looked at it and decided those targets were too well-guarded. Besides, we aren't here to conquer the planet. That would be illegal. We could help a saurian faction take power, but Earth forces can't take invade and take over another sovereign member world of the Empire. No, the whole point of this op is to embarrass the saurian military, to show the Galactics that we are better fighters than they are. If we can invade and hold vital spots, they'll have to concede we're superior."

It made a certain kind of sense. At the same time, this kind of limited, rules-filled warfare felt a little crazy. Even more crazy was attempting to do this with such a small force. How could we fight an entire populated planet? I asked Sargon that question, and he nodded sagely.

"Good point. I don't think we can. The legion has only around ten thousand fighting troops when we're all deployed. But we don't have to take on the entire planet to win this. Tribune Drusus has been in fights like this before—we're here to show that we can take our weight in lizards and more, that's all."

"What's to stop them from bombing us into the dust?"

"They can't do that. Air power and drones were not part of the deal. No heavy artillery, either. They made that rule to screw us originally, but I think it's screwing them now."

"Well, they have to have a million troops they could muster up and throw at us. Why not try that?"

"They might, but I think it would be embarrassing to them. What does it prove if we get overrun by overwhelming forces? We might kill three times our number before we go down, and that will just make our case for us."

I thought about it, and it did seem to be a strange situation. The lizards had to beat us, but they had to do it with a similar level of force. If they used too big of a hammer, they would lose in the end—even if we all had to go through the revival machines several times.

The part about expecting to die a lot is what had led to the grim faces I now saw on most of the lightly armed recruits around me. Sargon, the weaponeer, hadn't fought in this spaceport battle yet. He was ready to get into this, but the rest of us had had our tails handed to us at the spaceport already, and we weren't so eager.

"Seems to me the lizards should cheat just enough to win," I said. "That's what I would do if I were them."

Sargon looked at me, frowning. "What do you mean?"

"I mean, make it look like an honorable fight, but throw in every dirty trick possible."

He shrugged. "War is war. The worst you can do is die a few times. I'm game."

That's because you didn't charge that wall manned by heavy lizard troops, I thought. But I kept those words in my head. Why should I demoralize my fellow legionnaire?

"The spaceport fight was rough," I said. "If anything, they embarrassed *us* on those walls. They showed they were better fighters by slaughtering us."

"But we did win in the end. I'd say we are even now, they threw lots of troops at us at the mining complex, and we threw more at them here. We're down to the third round."

"How long do you think we have to hold out?" I asked. "I've been inside the spaceport—at least, inside the office buildings—staying there for weeks or months will be torture."

"Our people will time it," Sargon said. "The tribune is good at this. You watch. He'll wait until we look really good, then he'll retreat to the ship and claim victory."

"Do you think they'll hit the spaceport again? There are plenty of other targets."

"Who knows? But with the Nairbs and the Galactics around, this has to be the most embarrassing facility to have lost."

Sargon looked at me suddenly, as if having a new thought.

"Oh yeah," he said, eyeing me curiously, "I heard you played a big part in the first battle for the spaceport—a bigger part than Graves or Harris wants to talk about."

It was my turn to shrug. "I got inside and helped open the gates, that's all. Carlos was with me. We didn't do the hard fighting and dying like the people outside did. I would say the real heroes were the guys who charged into that gate after we opened it. They'd already watched a lot of people die ahead of them."

Sargon nodded slowly. "Still, I think you did good. If you don't piss off too many people, I bet they'll fast-track you to specialist."

I didn't tell him that Graves had already hinted as much. It wasn't time to brag, I figured. But I *was* happy he wasn't calling me "splat" any longer.

"I don't know about that," I said. "I have a gift for pissing people off, especially brass."

Sargon gave me a loud, hitching laugh and thumped me on the shoulder. I gave him a pasted-on smile.

We didn't have long to wait before reaching the spaceport. This was technically a combat jump, even if no one was shooting at us. Apparently, that had something to do with the rules, too. If they fired anti-air flak and missiles at us, we had the right to bomb them. Neither side wanted to escalate in that direction.

I recall reading of complex rules of engagement back on Earth in the past. They were pretty common in history. In the Napoleonic days, troops would line up neatly and spray lead at one another. Just the simple expedient of hugging the ground and seeking cover was considered dastardly.

There were always rules to war between nations, and my time was no different in that regard. The Empire had added the twist of applying a penalty for breaking those rules. We had the Galactics sitting on the sidelines, observing.

We didn't know which Galactics were watching, or what they thought. Most people didn't even know what one looked like. We knew they weren't all from the same species, but that's all we knew.

We could do whatever the hell we wanted on our own worlds—as long as we didn't break their rules. But when it came to invading other worlds, things became tricky.

The lights changed and buzzers sounded. The lifter went almost dark, filled with red light at first. Then the ramp dropped, and there was a sliver of gray radiance coming from it.

Night had fallen outside. I couldn't see any stars yet, but I knew they were out there. I gripped my snap-rifle and checked the magazine for the hundredth time.

This was it. My guts squeezed up, and I felt like I could use a trip to the head—but I knew that wasn't going to happen now.

222

Veteran Harris came through the rows, climbing over legs with his boots banging into our knees. He whacked men and women on the helmet as he passed by, marking who was going out the door first. I wasn't surprised when he passed Sargon by and thumped my helmet. The light troops usually were sent in first. We were faster on our feet and infinitely more expendable.

I slapped my belt buckles off, got up and envied Sargon with his big black tube he had to lug around. It kept him at the rear of the line.

Less than a minute later, I was running over the tarmac again. I could hear the thumping tread of a thousand boots around me. There were whispered prayers and hitching sobs. Some recruits were having trouble with this. I didn't blame them. This place held nothing but terrible memories for most.

The last hundred meters, we broke into a sprint. No one told us to—we just did it, like a herd crashing for the safety of the tall grass. Our leaders didn't complain, they were running, too. No one wanted to be last guy to reach the gates.

There were figures all along the wall-top, I could see them now. Shadowy hunched forms that blotted out the starry sky. Those had to be the heavies that had been assigned here. There were a lot of them, and for that, I was glad.

Somehow, out of the crowd, Carlos managed to find me as we rushed through the gates. "Just like old times, eh, McGill?" he shouted.

"Yeah, I'm feeling real homey about now."

We were directed by veterans with screaming voices and wild hand gestures. We poured into the compound and separated by unit and squad. Soon, I found myself standing with my team, looking around at the high walls around us. Every inch was pock-marked and scorched.

"What about the Nairbs?" I asked. "I don't see them."

"Didn't someone tell our famous hero?" Carlos asked loudly. "The man who single-handedly took this spaceport? The guy who stands ten feet tall, and—"

"Cut the crap, Carlos. Do you know where the aliens went or not?"

He shrugged. "I heard they left. They probably didn't like the stink of so many primitive humans around. I bet we made them nervous. For them, it was like sitting in a monkey house full of heavily armed gorillas, wondering when we were going to go crazy."

"Well, without the Nairbs, is this still a strategic objective worth holding?"

"That's not our problem," he said. "But I think it definitely is worth holding. Think about the symbolism of it—it's embarrassing. People who protest right in the middle of your town always get noticed. Remember those clowns who chained themselves to the last living trees in Central Park a few years ago? They were on the news every night."

I frowned at him. "You're not much for causes, are you?"

He stuck out his thumb and jabbed himself in the chest. "I'm always down for one cause…the only one that matters."

I nodded, unsurprised. My eyes wandered up to the walls, where the dark shapes of the heavies were moving now. "Hey, are they coming down from their posts?"

"Yeah, didn't you listen to the reports?"

"Maybe I was too busy…" I said, thinking of my long night pawing Natasha.

"That's what we're here for, big guy. We're relieving the heavies. These walls are strong, and they gave us back a few of our weaponeers. We're supposed to hold here until someone else is assigned to relieve the cohort."

I watched in alarm as the heavies made their way to the front gates and clanked away. They could only walk or trot, such was the weight of their armor. I knew that without a helping exoskeleton, they would barely be able to move.

Feeling left behind, I watched as the heavies marched away back toward the lifter we'd come down on. Wherever they were going, they seemed like they were in a hurry to get out of here. I couldn't blame them. Without Nairbs to keep the combat in check, the lizards could do just about whatever they wanted to take this fortress back.

-23-

"You two are coming with me," Veteran Harris said. He seemed happy, and that was almost always a bad sign.

We followed him down a long passageway that ended in a steep saurian stairway. We'd learned the lizards usually got down low on stairs. With their long, powerful hind legs they could take big steps and didn't need handrails. The other reason their stairs were big was because both juggers and raptor types had to use them. They had to fit both types of lizard.

In practice, this meant we had to hop from step-to-step going downward. We followed Harris. Carlos, Natasha, and I, as well as a half dozen others, hopped and cursed steadily.

I could tell none of us wanted to be here. It was dark, and the walls ran with moisture. They were arched and uneven— tunnels cut through steel, rather than smooth concrete walls. The lights weren't really lights, either. They were glowing patches along the walls.

When we reached the bottom of the tunnel, I managed to get close enough to Natasha to talk to her.

"I guess the lizards like it this way," I said. "This is kind of like the mines we had the joy of exploring. Must seem natural to them."

She gave me a worried look. "Do you think this place is safe?"

"You mean from collapsing, or from lizard-invasion?"

"Either."

"No," I said.

Veteran Harris finally called us to a halt.

"This is it," he said, tapping with his snap-rifle on the door.

This is what? My mind asked. I'm sure everyone was thinking it—but no one else said anything.

After a minute or two, a code pattern came up on the door. It shone with red letters and numbers. Harris typed something into the keypad and the door chimed and opened.

"Red?" Natasha asked. "Isn't that the color the lizards can't see?"

I nodded. They were supposedly colorblind in some parts of the spectrum. Troops joked that the twin Cancri suns had burned their retinas out over the years.

"Now here, see this lock?" Harris asked, pointing. "That's a special anti-alien job. How it works is by presenting a series of symbols that are familiar to humans. The pattern is random. You must memorize it, then type the same pattern into the keypad within five seconds."

"What happens if you screw up?" Natasha asked. "Does it fry you or something?"

"Fry you?" Carlos echoed. "She's kidding…right, Veteran?"

"For you, Carlos, the door will make an exception," Harris said. "It will strike you as dead as a cooked hamburger if you're one second late." He laughed then, and it was a rough, unpleasant sound. "You just have to try again," he explained at last, "but it will warn the occupants and after three tries, if you keep screwing up, it will shut down for a few minutes, alerting security to come investigate."

"What's inside, Veteran?" I asked.

He smiled at me. "Nothing, right now. But later on this vault will have our most prized possession."

We all looked at him quizzically.

"If you haven't guessed by now, this is where the revival unit is being deployed."

"What?" Carlos demanded. "Are you telling me that there isn't one on site yet?"

Veteran Harris frowned at him. "Yeah, that's exactly what I just told you, Recruit. The unit the heavies had went up with them. Yours is an older model. It will be sent down soon."

Older model...those words rolled around in my head and seemed to echo. Could that be why they had trouble and "bad grows"? They gave light troops the worst of everything.

I raised my hand, and Harris jabbed his finger at me. "What?"

"Why are we here now, Veteran? Ahead of the machine?"

"Because you're going to help carry and deploy it," he said. "It weighs about a thousand pounds—and it's a little gross when you have to move it."

Everyone turned and craned their necks, looking back up the tunnel and the long, steep stairway.

"This just keeps getting better and better," Carlos muttered.

"Gag yourself, Ortiz, before I do it for you."

I could see Carlos had a rude retort in his mind, but he held it back with difficulty. Harris was known for cuffing recruits who mouthed off too much, and Carlos was one of the supreme mouths in the unit.

"What do we do in the meantime?" Natasha asked.

"Wait here, or look around. Guard and secure. It shouldn't be long. The lifter that brought you brought all your gear, too. I'll call you back together when they're ready to slide the machine down that stairway."

He left, and we all looked at one another in disgust.

"Typical," Carlos said. "Absolutely typical. Nobody gives a shit about recruits in Legion Varus. We climb walls, fall over cliffs and die like lemmings for the cause, you would think—"

"Shut up, Carlos," Kivi said, kicking him in the rump.

The two jostled for a moment, and I lost interest. I walked to the door with the lock on it. I could see it had been cut very recently. The door was old, but the lock and bolt were new. I tugged, then had to heave. The door was very heavy and creaked the way only thick steel can when I opened it.

A few of the others nosed close behind me. Natasha was first in line. I wasn't surprised by this. She was kicking around to become a tech, which took special training and legion investment. She had to display an interest in anything the real techs and bios did. In her case, however, I figured the curiosity was real.

"Look at that stuff on the floor!"

Our suit lights played around the chamber as we walked in. It was obvious the heavy cohort had kept their revival unit down here. The walls were stained with colorful gore. The floor was—puddled.

"Is that blood?" Carlos asked from the back.

"Not just blood," Natasha said, "looks like lymph and other stuff. Gross."

They'd pulled out in a hurry. I had to wonder what kind of special horrors this room had seen over the last few days. There had been deaths among the heavies, but not too many of them.

"I would guess that they revived some of the light troops down here, after they set up. They died assaulting the walls, and our own units were overwhelmed. They had to use every revival machine in the legion to get us all back on our feet."

"Yeah," said Kivi, looking around. "I came back to life in here."

We looked at her, and she shuddered, remembering. "I didn't remember it until just now. Seeing this place—it's like finding something you thought only existed in a dream. A bad dream."

Besides the biotic waste, there was a pair of large generators and a few barrels of raw materials. Protoplasm, tanks of pre-grown skin and the like.

The call came in from Harris a few minutes later, and we all jumped. The buzzing in our helmets startled everyone.

"Get up here, team. We're at the top of the stairs."

We were glad to rush out of the place—but we shouldn't have been. I recalled watching an ancient comedy about two men taking a piano up a steep staircase, and I soon commiserated with them.

The machine was huge. It barely fit in the tunnel. Carlos, as usual, was the first to complain.

"Vet?" he called. "How the hell are we getting this thing through the doorway?"

"It disassembles, mouth," he said. "Now, I want all of you grunts down under it on the stairway. You're here to break this

228

thing's rapid descent. Let it crush your bones before you let it slide to the bottom. You hear me? We can replace you—but not this monster."

"If it disassembles, why don't we—"

"Shut up and start braking the fall!" Harris roared.

We jockeyed into position, but Harris didn't join us. It was soon clear what his job was: he was going to be up on top, pushing.

The revival unit was big, about as big as a pickup truck. It was covered in metal, but I knew from experience that it was fleshy inside. When it began rolling down toward us, I honestly calculated that it had to weigh more than a pickup. It had wheels, but they were small steel circles with a rubber coating. They reminded me of larger versions of the wheels on a shopping cart. They were inadequate when it came to traversing a steep stairway.

The worst part was the bounce the thing took every time it dipped over one of those big, wide steps. Each time, I thought we were going to lose it and be crushed.

We roared, heaved and sweated. Up on top, Harris laughed at our cursing and carrying on.

At last, the steps ended and we were allowed the relative luxury of rolling the monster down the steel tunnel.

"Fifty-six," Carlos said, panting.

"What?" Kivi asked him.

"Fifty-six steps. I counted them."

"Why?"

"Because I figured at least one of us was going to die under it, so I thought the dead guy might want to know how far down they made it."

"That makes a lot of sense, Carlos," she said, shaking her head.

"I know, huh?"

We rolled it to the end of the hall and found the doors locked. I frowned.

"Veteran? Are these doors supposed to be locked? Cause, we didn't close them."

"Are you sure?" he called from the far side of the machine. We couldn't even see him back there.

"Yeah, pretty sure."

"I heard the tunnels were haunted. Now you've gone and proved it!" he guffawed, but no one found him funny.

"Vet, I don't think—"

"Just open the damned thing, you idiots!" he roared suddenly. "They're frigging security doors. If you leave them open too long they shut themselves."

Everyone looked at me, but I shook my head. I pointed to Natasha. "She's the smart one," I said.

This seemed to please Natasha, who gave me a little smile. Kivi, however, rolled her eyes and put her hands on her hips. "I'll do it," she said.

She walked up and pressed the start button. Letters and numbers flashed quickly. She hesitated afterward.

"Come on, come on!" Carlos said. "You only have like five seconds."

She started tapping. I thought she had it right, but it beeped at her. The screen went blank again.

Kivi cursed and kicked the door.

"If you clowns can't open the door, so help me..." began Harris, his voice muffled by the hulking machine between us.

"Natasha?" I asked.

"You do it," she said. "I don't want to get security down here on my first shot."

I wasn't sure if I should urge her to try again, or what. Then Carlos made a sound of disgust and approached the machine. Everyone reached out and pulled him back.

"What? All of you think I'm some kind of moron, is that it? Uncool."

I sighed and put my hands on the pad. The trick, I thought, was to concentrate. It was only seven symbols. Just like memorizing a license plate. Somehow, that simple task seemed harder when everyone was staring at your back and you were sweating at the bottom of a slimy alien cellar. I couldn't stop thinking about how bad it smelled in there.

"Press the damned button, McGill!"

I slapped my palm on the button, and the sequence flashed. I thought I had it. I began typing. I nearly panicked on the sixth symbol. *V for Varus,* I remembered. After that, it was easy to finish.

People immediately began second guessing me.

"Nothing's happening."

"It took a second before."

"You forgot one. There were eight."

"No there weren't."

Then there was a click, and the door popped open. I smiled. Everyone seemed happy, except for Carlos.

"No one likes a show-off, McGill," he said. "Nobody."

Next, we found out how the machine "disassembled". Essentially, it came apart in two halves, the lower and the upper. This was not good, as it revealed some of the meaty parts in between.

"What kind of sick alien dreamed this up?" Carlos asked.

For once, I agreed with him. The machine was grotesque inside. It was like the inside of a giant stomach, or a toothless mouth. When we slid apart the two halves, we had to tip them onto their sides. No one wanted to touch the flesh parts, so we all tried to grip metal with our gloves.

"What the—" Harris began when he saw what we were doing. "Get over here, Recruit!" Saying this, he grabbed and shoved an unfortunate into the middle of the fleshy section.

The recruit looked back at us in horror. "There's nothing to grab onto here."

"Yeah, there is. It has bones and ridges, kinda like shells. Stick your hands in there and find something hard. Don't worry, you won't damage it with your bare hands. It's strong."

Looking like he was going to puke, the guy did as he was told. "I feel something."

"Don't let it bite!" Harris said suddenly.

The recruit jerked his hands out, and they came away slick with semi-clear liquids that dripped to the floor.

Harris cuffed him, thumping a hand on the back of his helmet. "I was kidding…the teeth are in the other half."

He burst out laughing again, and we grumbled. Once we all had a firm grip, we heaved and dragged. The outer steel shell of the machine scraped and screeched on the floor. Sparks flew up in bright orange lines from the two metals rasping on one another.

Finally, we had the bottom half in the room. The top half seemed to go more easily. I think it was the lighter of the two. Getting them both back together was a problem. They didn't seem to want to match up.

As we heaved, shouted, pinched fingers and sweated, two bio specialists showed up at the entrance. I turned and was surprised to recognize one of them: Anne Grant. I nodded to her, but she just stared for a second, then looked away.

I decided not to make anything of it. She probably didn't want anyone to know she'd helped fool the Galactics. A wise choice on her part, all things considered.

But still, I couldn't help but feel slightly put out. I liked her. She was pretty, experienced, tough—and she'd risked her life to help me.

The two specialists began working on the revival units. They tsked and called us morons. We'd done everything wrong. Carlos pointed out they hadn't been around to give us direction, and they were lucky it wasn't upside down.

This earned him some dark looks, but they stopped complaining and got to work fixing the monstrosity.

Really, in the end, it fixed itself. They connected thick cords to the generators, and it began to make slapping sounds inside—almost like it was chewing something. They flipped some switches, and the two shell-like halves—the top and bottom jaws, they called them—rolled and shivered until they'd aligned themselves.

I couldn't help thinking that the machine resembled a person adjusting and stretching after a long sleep. The "jaws" yawned slightly at times, and the joints rasped and clicked like cracking bones. We all took a step back, except for the bios. The machine stopped clicking and began to make more of those odd, slapping sounds.

How the hell did this thing work? How did you plug flesh into electrical current and get it to come alive?

I began to wonder what the aliens who dreamt it up looked like. I imagined freaks of dripping slime. I figured I probably didn't want to meet them.

-24-

Veteran Harris got a call from Leeson, and he raced out the door. We looked after him and shrugged. Having no orders was just fine for any recruit. We all looked for a wall to put their backs against and took a break.

We removed our helmets despite the stink, and I found the room sweaty and close.

The bios specialists were still working on their machine, cursing and speaking in their own technical lingo. I took the time to watch Specialist Grant. Kivi was the first to notice this.

"Quit staring, no girl likes that," she told me in a loud whisper.

I looked at her in surprise and gave her a half-smile. "Didn't know you still cared."

She twisted her lips. "You're pathetic," she said and left me.

I shook my head and looked back at Anne. She was working hard and frowning. Her forehead had a sheen of sweat already. I could tell the machine wasn't in working order yet, and they were worried about it. That brought a frown to my face. What did the specialists know that I didn't? I thought it was all quiet outside.

I pushed off the wall I'd been leaning against and walked closer to the two bio specialists. The second one was a tall guy named Specialist Matis, who I didn't know.

"Can we help?" I asked Anne.

233

Her eyes flicked up to meet mine, then she looked down again, as if flustered.

"It's okay," she said. "You recruits would just get in the way. You need a lot of training to work on one of these. This model is an old one—thousands of regrows on the gauge."

I looked and saw the gauge she was talking about. Strangely, it wasn't digital. Instead, it had an analog look to it. Rather than a dial or a numeric readout, it had an instrument that looked more like a vertical temperature gauge. Shaped like an elongated racetrack, the instrument was dark at the bottom and white at the top. The dark part was larger than the light section.

"Looks like you've got a quarter tank left, Specialist," I said.

She glanced at me again. "Yeah. Enough for a few thousand regrows, if we're lucky."

"What happens after that?"

She shrugged and began wiping her hands. They were sticky, and I saw she'd pulled them out of the machine. A drop of goo clung to each fingertip. The stuff was pinkish and looked like thick honey. I was certain, however, that it didn't taste good.

"I don't know," she said. "These machines vary. After the gauge is full, you run on borrowed time. Kind of like using an engine with barely any oil in it. Or a printer that says it's out of ink, but keeps printing those last few pages."

I nodded thoughtfully. "I wouldn't want to be the last guy out of this box. You might come out missing a limb or something."

"It happens," she said. "How are you holding up?"

I glanced at her, but saw she wasn't looking at me. She was squatting and had her face up to the aperture in the front, where the two halves met. I squatted next to her and peered inside.

"I'm okay," I said. "No noticeable side effects after the first few days."

"Good," she said. "But I wouldn't plan on living forever on this grow if I were you."

I laughed. "I can't fix it. My body is my body. What might go wrong?"

"Deafness, blindness, bone cancer. Lots of things…I'd give you two to five years."

I frowned. This wasn't what I'd been expecting to hear. In fact, it gave me a sick feeling in the pit of my stomach. I stopped talking and stood up again.

"What's the matter?" she asked, sensing my mood change immediately.

"Uh…nothing. It's cool. I'm not dead, and I guess that's good enough for now."

"What's the big deal? Just fix it."

"How?"

She stood up and took a look around, then came close, whispering her next words: "Just get yourself killed at some point doing during the next month or two. It's no big deal. Should be pretty easy to do as a recruit. It will probably happen without you having to do anything, in fact. Dying will get you a fresh grow—problem solved."

She bent down again and returned to working on her alien contraption. A spill of dark liquid ran from the mouth section, and when she saw it she shoved her hands in there, cursing.

I stood there for a second, staring at her and the machine in turns. The bios had such a strange way of thinking about life and death. *Don't like your body? Well, just throw it away and get a new copy…problem solved.*

"Well," said a voice at my side. "I see you're helping out the specialists. Can I join in, or is this a private party?"

I looked down and saw it was Natasha. I felt a jolt of concern. I'd kind of forgotten about her. I know a few things about women, and one was that they hated to be ignored after a date.

Worse, I could see how she'd probably been watching my conversation with Anne and figured I was hitting on her—or worse, that we were already involved. I hadn't been helping out, after all, just talking. And from her angle, it had probably looked like I'd been studying Anne's figure—which was looking good in her jumpsuit.

"No, no," I said. "You can help."

"No she can't," Anne said over her shoulder. "Neither one of you know a damned thing. Now, could you back up a bit? I have to get under this manifold."

As she spoke, she went flat on her back and slid underneath the machine. Natasha and I both curled our lips. It didn't look too sparkly clean under there. The machine dripped unidentified liquids all the time.

"Sorry to intrude," said Natasha, turning around and walking away.

I followed her lamely. "Natasha? What's wrong?"

"Nothing at all."

"Come on."

Kivi huffed in disgust and moved away from us.

"I should have known," Natasha said, when we were standing in a quiet corner.

"What?"

"I always get involved with guys who chase everything they see like dogs."

"I'm not—"

"It's all right," she said. "You're just immature, that's all. I shouldn't have expected anything else in Varus."

"It's not like that."

"Sure it is. I didn't let you do what you wanted last night in the park, so you lost interest. It's okay, really."

I heaved a long sigh.

Natasha patted me on the arm and slid away. "It's cool. Don't worry about it."

I thought fast and came up with a solid half-truth to stand behind. As a habitually late, second-class student, half-truths were on my skill-list.

"Let me explain," I began.

"There's nothing to explain. I'm not pregnant. I told you, it's cool. Go in there and chat her up. You might get lucky."

Just then, over her shoulder, I caught sight of the big, round, grinning face of Carlos. He was eavesdropping and delighted with what he was hearing.

"Look, I had a bad regrow," I told her.

"A what?"

"I—well, remember the morning I was sick?"

236

She frowned and nodded suspiciously. It made me feel a bit guilty, but I sternly reminded myself that I hadn't done anything wrong—other than a little staring—and I couldn't tell her the full truth.

"I had what they call a bad grow. It happens sometimes. This machine isn't perfect. Sometimes it rebuilds you out of raw meat and ends up making mistakes."

Natasha looked alarmed. "You're saying you're messed up inside?"

"A little. That's what I was talking to Anne—uh, Specialist Grant—about. She was giving me medical advice."

Natasha glanced into the chamber and knitted her face into a frown. "What's wrong with you...exactly?"

"I'm not going to last. She talked about blindness, deafness, cancer. Lots of things could go wrong. I'm living on borrowed time."

"That's horrible."

"It's cool. She said they can fix it eventually. But not right now."

Natasha looked relieved. "Well...that's good. Are you feeling sick now?"

"No, no. I'm fine. I'll eventually have serious health problems, though."

She brightened suddenly. "Hey, I have an idea. Why don't you just get yourself killed? New body, no more problems."

I forced a smile. "Great idea," I said. Internally, I had to wonder why everyone wanted me to off myself.

I noticed then that every member of our team was standing up and adjusting their kits. Carlos lifted his helmet, clicked it into place over his head, and handed me mine.

"You're supposed to keep this close. You didn't even hear the alarm."

I put my helmet on and saw the digital readouts that floated in a ghostly fashion over my vision. It identified Natasha as Recruit Elkin. I used my tapper to join the squad channel. Down here, the signal was iffy and it had disconnected with some kind of timeout.

"...Elkin, Cooper and Moore! Move inside, now!" shouted a voice I recognized instantly. Veteran Harris was never far from our ears.

Natasha rushed past me with several other recruits. "Ortiz and McGill, you two will stand guard outside the door, the rest will stay in. Lock the door!"

"What's going on?" I asked Carlos when Harris stopped shouting orders into my earpiece.

"Nobody tells us crap," he said. "Some kind of assault is going on upstairs, I'd say. It's about time the lizards made another play."

"Maybe they saw us pull the heavies out and back up to orbit and they decided it was time to strike."

"Yeah," Carlos said, "you might be right, there. The timing is suspicious. Everybody knows light recruits are easy."

He leered at me when he said that, and I thought he might be making some kind of rude remark regarding my problems with women. I ignored him and unslung my rifle. I shortened the barrel, as any combat in this hallway was going to be fought in close-quarters.

"You two," shouted Specialist Grant behind me. "If anyone comes down here they have to use the human-lock to get in. Understood?"

We looked at her and nodded.

Grant looked at the rest of them. "I don't need everyone crowding me. I'll keep you, you and you inside," she said, pointing to Natasha, Kivi and one other recruit. "You can serve as orderlies for now until trained people show up. The rest of you go back to your Veteran topside. Matis, go find me some trained people."

Specialist Matis left with the rest of them. They climbed the stairs, taking the huge steps one at a time

Kivi caught our eye from inside the vault and waved goodbye to Carlos. Then she gave me the finger.

I laughed.

The vault door slammed in our faces a moment later, and Carlos and I were alone in the dank corridor.

"No worries," Carlos said. "This sure beats manning that wall up top. When they start running the machine and pouring fresh bodies out through this door, then we'll know the fight is on. Until then, I'm taking a break."

I didn't share his relaxed state of mind. Sure, this should be an easy duty. All we had to do was keep the door safe, and in the meantime the battle would play out above us. Still, I didn't like being stuck down here. Something about this dank hole made me feel trapped.

"There's nowhere to run from here," I said.

"Yeah, well…don't worry about it. If they get this far past our lines, we're all dead anyway."

I had to agree with him.

-25-

A series of thuds began. They were quiet at first—like the tread of distant feet. But then they became louder, and we saw the ceiling tremble. Droplets of condensation from the roof of the tunnel showered down with each rhythmic beat, and we stared around with open mouths.

"Could that be a herd of charging juggers?" I asked.

"If it is, the boys on the walls are in it pretty deep," Carlos replied. "Those juggers must be the size of lifters. But no, I don't buy that. The lizards aren't big enough to shake these steel walls. I bet it's artillery."

I figured he was right. The sound was getting louder as if the enemy were isolating the target and homing in on us.

We put our backs to the door, and I tried to reach the team inside. "You guys okay in there?"

Nothing came back but static.

"The door must be too thick," I said. "It's metal and slag like everything else around here."

"Maybe you should tap in the door code and check on them," Carlos said.

"Why? Nothing can get through. We'll stand our posts and do as ordered."

Carlos shrugged. We both knew why we wanted to stick our noses into the room. The sounds of the attack were unnerving. Just to see more human faces and voices—any contact would be better than standing here listening to doom slamming down on the base outside.

The sound of explosions continued unabated. In fact, they grew louder.

"So *loud!*" I shouted, giving my head a shake.

"What?"

"It's super loud. Must be the acoustics in this metal tunnel. It's carrying the sound."

Carlos nodded, but I wasn't sure he even knew what I was saying.

After about five more minutes, during which we hunkered down aiming our weapons in different directions down the hallways, an officer appeared on the stairway. He came down at a run, almost falling as he had to hop from one giant step to the next. Many were slick with a fine sheen of condensed water that reminded me of sweat.

"Where are the revivals?" he shouted at me.

I knew he was an officer from his kit, which included a sidearm, rather than a snap-rifle. When he got closer, I recognized Adjunct Leeson. He trotted up to us, removing his helmet and looking around wildly.

"They should be coming out now," he said. "How many have they processed?"

Carlos and I looked at the door and shrugged.

"No clue, sir," I said. "Radio doesn't go through the security door."

He frowned and hammered on the door. It was like hammering on a boulder.

"Open it," he said.

"There's a code, sir," Carlos said.

"Then type it in, Recruit!" he snapped.

Carlos went for it first. A series of symbols appeared on the screen, and he began pecking at the lock.

Leeson groaned when he saw what Carlos was doing. "Not one of those damned things. Human-locks only keep out humans."

I thought it might have been one of the smartest things he'd ever said, but I kept quiet. Carlos failed to open it, and Leeson began cursing.

"I'm sorry, sir," Carlos said. "I thought I had it, my fingers in these gloves—I might have touched the contact once."

"Get the hell out of the way!" Leeson roared and pulled Carlos away.

"What's wrong, sir?" I said. "I know we've been hit, but it takes a while to get the revival unit operating."

He looked at me, his eyes wild. "Centurion Graves was taken out with the first salvo. We need him back on the line as soon as possible."

I realized that with Graves down Leeson was in charge of the unit. He didn't seem happy with that situation.

"So, it is artillery?" Carlos asked him.

"Yeah. Overkill, if you ask me. I think the Saurians are mad, they—dammit!"

He broke off. It was his second try, and the door still wouldn't open.

He stepped back and glared. "Something's wrong with it," he said.

"Let McGill have a go," Carlos suggested. "He's the only one who got it to work earlier."

"All right," Leeson said, waving me forward. "Nothing works down here. We have a direct wire to this room, but no one can talk to the revival room bios. We should never have put it down here."

I glanced back at him, then finished the sequence. I straightened, absolutely sure I'd done it right.

Nothing happened. The door blinked, but then flipped from green to red again.

"I thought it was open," Carlos said. "I saw it go green."

"Try it again!" growled Leeson.

"Okay," I said, stepping up to the door again. This time I put my ear to the door latch as I worked, looking at the symbols sidelong.

Carlos started talking again, but both Leeson and I shushed him. I could tell the Adjunct knew what I was doing.

I tapped and the door went green and clicked—then the indicators flashed red again.

"I heard it," I said. "It opened, but now it's closed."

242

Leeson was clawing at his tapper, bringing up his com link. He tapped but it didn't work, either.

"These tunnel walls," Carlos said.

"Get that door open," Leeson ordered, jabbing his finger at it with every word. "I'll go get reinforcements."

Carlos took his rifle and hammered on the door. I worked the lock again and tried to ignore the noise he was making. For once, I thought he was justifiably loud.

The third time around, the results were the same. The door was opening, but the lock wasn't working for some reason.

"Here," I said, "maybe it's just jammed. Get your knife out and hammer the tip into the crack. The next time I open the lock, we'll try to pry it open. If we can get it to open just a crack, before the thing faults and locks again, we might be able to get in."

Carlos did as I said, and it finally worked. I heard tramping feet on the stairs and in the passage behind me.

But I didn't really hear the others coming. Leeson had brought reinforcements, but I knew it wasn't going to matter.

Everyone in the chamber was lying on the floor. Specialist Grant, Kivi, Natasha—all of them. They were all dead or badly injured. Grant was *beyond* dead—she'd been torn apart.

The worst part was the revival unit was missing. There was only a hole in the wall behind the unit or where it used to be. The hole was ragged as if it had been cut with heat. Beyond it, a tunnel opened. I couldn't see much as it was full of smoke and steam and was pitch-black.

"What the hell happened here?" Leeson screamed at my side. He reached out, grabbed my shoulder and spun me around. "You were guarding this equipment, soldier! Report!"

"It had to be the lizards, sir. We never left our post. They came through the back wall. They might have had help—or there was a preexisting tunnel back there. I can't believe they drilled it that fast, and that quietly."

Leeson looked up, we all did. The bombardment had stopped.

"Cover," he said. "The artillery was cover. They hit us hard for a few minutes, long enough to get into the chamber and take our machine." He shook his head. "We have to seal this up."

Leeson turned to a trio of weaponeers he'd brought down with him. I recognized Sargon among them. I knew right away his plan must have been to burn the door down if we couldn't get it open. Risky, but as it turned out, it could have been the right move.

"We have to seal this up. We can't have them getting in behind us."

Three bio specialists pushed past me and began checking the fallen. They gave up quickly on everyone except Kivi.

"Is she going to make it?" I asked them.

"Maybe," they said noncommittally. They carried Kivi up the stairs as I watched. I felt shocked and little sick to see them all taken out like this.

"But sir," I said, following Adjunct Leeson, "what about the dead? We can't revive them now…are they going up to the ship?"

He shook his head slowly. "I would guess not. Their data was here, and we only had the one copy. They've been permed. There's nothing we can do."

I stared with my mouth hanging open. I looked at the bodies all over again as if really seeing them for the first time. Natasha and Specialist Grant had been *permed*? That couldn't be… We all died now and then, sure, but we always came back.

"Sir?" I called, catching his eye while the weaponeers set up tripods and calibrated their weapons. At this short range, they had to be careful or they'd be consumed by the back-blast.

He glanced at me but turned away.

"Sir? Adjunct Leeson?"

"Recruit, it happens. Only one machine has your data at a given time. That's the rule. If the machine is wiped out before a copy can be transferred—so are you."

"What about the rest of them? The people who got hit during the bombardment?"

"The moment the com link was cut with the revival unit, the command post reported that to the ship. It's all automated.

244

We can die down here safely now, and just about everyone who died in the bombardment should be in the clear."

"Did we lose the data or something?" I asked. "Why don't we have backups?"

"To prevent illegal duplication. Only one unit is assigned to be a legitimate revival point per file. Once we lost contact, we could legally transfer the duty up to *Corvus*. They're probably reviving right now aboard ship."

I thought about that. It was something of a relief to know I wasn't in line to be permed next. But I thought of my friends in there again, who'd all just been eviscerated. I couldn't leave them like that. Not if there was a chance.

"Sir, I volunteer to go after the lizards," I said. "If I can get the data chip back from that revival unit, we can make the transfer and these people will live again."

Adjunct Leeson said a few more words to the weaponeers, then turned, sucked in a big breath and put a hand on my shoulder. "You have to let them go, son," he said. "I know it's hard. I've done it before."

"They can't have gone far, sir. That machine is a bastard to move. I should know."

"It's not just about that," he said. "I have a unit to command now."

I stared at him. "What about Graves?" I asked. "He was hit early. He was permed too, wasn't he?"

This seemed to startle him. I realized as I said it that he hadn't thought of that detail. He'd only considered the people in the room at the time of the attack. But they weren't the only ones who'd been erased today.

Leeson didn't answer me right away. He looked like he was thinking hard.

"The bombardment began before the com link to the chamber went down, didn't it?" I asked quietly. "You said Graves was dead in the first salvo. His data didn't transfer. He's gone."

Adjunct Leeson's eyes slid up to meet mine. I saw real worry there. I could tell he didn't think he was ready to fill Centurion Graves' shoes. I had to admit, I didn't think he was either. Graves really knew what he was doing.

"You really want to go into that hole?" he asked me. "They'll be commandos, you know. Real fighters. Not a pack of naked hunters like we met out in the jungle."

I nodded. I knew what he meant.

"I fought a real lizard regular right here in this building. That alien knew how to fight—and how to die."

"All right," he said. "I can't fault a man for wanting to save his commander. In fact, I'm impressed, McGill. Maybe you aren't the screw-up I thought you were. Graves always thought you were something special, but I didn't see his point until now."

He pointed into the hole, which was smoking less but still pitch-black inside. "Go get them, boys."

"Boys?" asked Carlos. He'd been watching and listening quietly all this time. "Oh sure, I get it. Make a big attempt to talk McGill out of it, but Carlos—forget it. Hell, you can throw Carlos off a cliff if you want to. The whole unit would be better off."

"Shut up and get going. They could be gone already. I'm giving you one hour then I'm sealing this hole with hot steel. They won't even be able to drill through."

I stepped toward the hole, and Carlos followed, complaining all the way.

Then another figure loomed up behind us. It was none other than Weaponeer Sargon. I grinned when I saw him.

"Did Leeson order you onto this death-hunt?" Carlos asked. "That prick. One day you should miss with that big cannon of yours and nail him."

"No, fool," Sargon said. "I wanted to come. I didn't like the idea of McGill getting all the glory."

We stepped through the ragged hole one at a time, with me leading and Sargon bringing up the rear.

"Glory?" I asked.

"Yeah," he said. "I used to be known as the craziest guy in this unit. Now, I'm like some kind of accountant or something. 'No one tries harder to get himself permed than James McGill'—that's what I hear all the time now. The worst part is: it's true."

"Permed?" Carlos asked. "Who said anything about getting permed? I thought our data was transferred up to the *Corvus*."

Sargon laughed roughly. "Yeah, sure. But without a confirmed death, they can't legally revive any of us. You know that."

Carlos cursed quietly for a long time as we made our way down into the tunnel. Behind us, the big door to the vault clanged shut. I knew they'd wait to burn the mouth of the tunnel closed—but only for an hour.

-26-

"Do you even frigging know what the data component looks like on a revival unit?" Carlos demanded.

It was the second or third time he'd asked, so I figured I might as well answer. He wasn't going to shut up no matter what I did.

"No, I don't, but it should be in the main panel. If we can get the copy back, then they can reconstruct everyone whose signature is on it."

"Yeah, sure, that's how this is going to work. Do you even have a computer at home? I mean, if you ripped part of it out, it may or may not be readable. Damaged data means a damaged grow, and it's all over."

"What's all over?" Sargon said.

"They are. The people we are risking our necks to save. My point is, we don't know if this mission can be completed even if we do everything right."

"Yeah, yeah," Sargon said. "You want to go back and hide in the complex, don't you? Let me tell you, those walls won't be any fun in an hour or two. The lizards are deploying all around us. They're going to march right in and take us out, down to the last man."

"If they do that, they won't win the contract," I said. "Using a million troops against a few thousand doesn't prove anything."

"I don't even think they care about that anymore," Sargon said. "They haven't used air yet, but they are pouring it on otherwise. This is about pride and honor now. We've embarrassed them, and they have to save face."

I had to admit he had a point.

"Wait a minute," Carlos said, halting.

Sargon bumped into him and made a sound of disgust.

We were pretty far down the tunnel now but hadn't found anything—not even a fork in the road. The tunnel gently twisted and curved but didn't seem to lead anywhere in particular. I'd begun to think they'd dug it recently, after all: maybe when we'd started the attack on the terminal. It might have been drilled originally as an escape tunnel, but after we'd taken the building, they'd decided to use it as a secret method of attack instead.

"Wait just one minute," Carlos said, as if getting an idea he didn't like.

"What now?" I asked.

"The data might be stored organically. Did you think of that? We don't know squat about this machine. Absolute zero. But we do know it is alien and organic. If the data is stored inside some kind of ten-pound hind-brain, we are righteously screwed. We'll never retrieve it, and we'll never be able to read it if we do."

"Carlos," I said, "you're right. This might not work, but I think it's worth a try. We're talking about Natasha, the bio, Graves and maybe Kivi, too. You like Kivi, don't you?"

"Oh, hell yeah. Every guy in the unit does."

"Well, then, I'll lie and tell her that you demanded we go in and save her—just her."

Carlos brightened. "You'd do that?"

"Yes, I sure would."

A heavy hand reached down from the shadows and slapped Carlos' helmet.

"I'll back up that lie," Sargon said, "if you'll shut the hell up."

"You've got it, friend! I know when I've said enough. No one has to tell me twice. I'll—"

I heard a thud and grunt. Carlos fell silent. I wasn't sure what Weaponeer Sargon had done to him, but I was grinning anyway.

We finally heard sounds in front of us. They were baffling at first—then I realized what they must be: sounds of metal scraping against metal.

I whispered into my helmet, which was linked to the others. No one could hear us beyond our small team as these walls wouldn't let anything through.

"They're ahead of us," I said.

Sargon immediately took command. I didn't argue. He had the rank and the experience. He moved quietly for such a big man. In a crouch, he edged up next to me. We all squatted and peered around the next bend in the tunnel. We had our visors dialed for infrared, but we couldn't see anything—not yet.

"I'd love to take them all out with my cannon," he said, hefting the tube on his shoulder, "but I can't risk hitting the machine. Why the hell are they dragging it down here, anyway? They can't use it, it's calibrated for humans."

I'd thought about that myself. "Maybe they think we'll die without it. Maybe that was their big plan."

"Yeah," Sargon agreed. "They probably don't know we can just transmit our data up to *Corvus*."

"How do they do that?" Carlos asked.

I expected Sargon to bonk him again, but he didn't. He turned and said: "The data in your cells is really pretty short, you know. The body is easy. It's the mind that takes a lot of storage to get all the synapses right."

I decided I'd take his word for it. In truth, I didn't like thinking about medical processes much—especially not when the process involved me dying first.

"Uh..." I said. "Aren't we going to attack, or something?"

"Not yet."

"What are we waiting for, Specialist?"

"A big, loud noise. I think they're stuck right now, but they'll get the machine moving again soon. It's too quiet right now."

I glanced at him and nodded. I thought I knew what he was thinking.

"What are we going to do when they make this loud noise?" Carlos asked.

"We're gonna charge in close and wipe them out—or die trying."

"Subtle," Carlos remarked, "but it just might work."

Sargon turned to look at him quietly. I thought maybe Carlos had earned himself another kick. But Sargon turned back again to watch the tunnel ahead and to listen to the lizards.

We listened for several minutes. Finally, we heard them moving again. The scratching sound of the machine being dragged over the roughly drilled floor of the tunnel was loud and painful to the ears. It squeaked, groaned and clanged.

"Okay, we move on three," said Sargon.

We all rose up into a crouch. I'd been expecting some kind of complex battle plan, but I could tell I wasn't going to get one. We were going to race up from behind them and kill them any way we could.

"One," said Sargon, hunching his shoulders and straightening his legs.

At least, I thought, *he's not asking me to go first.*

"Two."

We were all up. I flexed my muscles, which had cramped slightly from crouching low for so long.

"Three—GO!"

Just like that, he was racing up the tunnel. I rushed after him, with Carlos bringing up the rear. We tried to run quietly, but that wasn't really possible. We were wearing heavy boots and running over a rough floor with corkscrew-like gouges in it. I found it hard not to stumble. I had to look down often just to keep my footing.

We almost reached them before they sensed us. Almost.

At the last second, some alert saurian craned his long neck around and saw our charge. We didn't have our lights on, but we could see their body heat. There was very little illumination. Saurians have excellent night vision, and they don't need special gear to see in dark tunnels.

The saurian made a raspy, croaking sound, and it was the last sound he ever made. Sargon stopped, leveled his tube and fired. I barely had time to throw myself against the wall of the tunnel.

There was a flare of green light inside my helmet. Fortunately, the visor was built to automatically dampen extremely bright illumination so as not to blind me with the amplified input. Still, I winced from hitting the sharp tunnel walls and from the assault on my eyes.

The saurian in armor fared much worse. He was taken out, blown apart by a direct hit. Sargon's aim was excellent, but taking the shot wasn't the best move I'd ever seen a weaponeer make. The plasma bolt tore through the saurian and caromed off the ceiling—bouncing down again right into the machine we were supposedly rescuing.

"I can't believe it," Carlos said. "He frigging killed it!"

"We don't know that. Move up!" I shouted.

"What's the point? Let's get out of here."

I didn't listen to him. Maybe the data unit was still intact. I pressed forward, hammering my snap-rifle on full auto into the surprised lizards.

We were lucky in one regard: the saurians were working hard to drag the machine, just as we had been a few hours ago. It was insanely heavy, bulky and unforgiving.

They weren't wearing helmets—maybe it was too hot for them—so I aimed for their heads. It wasn't as hard as it sounds. When surprised, the dinos had a well-known behavioral tendency: they all perked up, lifting their heads high and twisting their long necks rather than their bodies. As a result, they were all arching and staring at us for a moment, trying to figure out what they were facing.

Sargon was the first one to close with them. He rushed up, put his tube to his shoulder and took out a second lizard, this time one that was pretty far from the machine.

My snap-rifle jumped in my hands, chattering. I could hear sliver-like bullets spraying out, ricocheting and sparking from the metal roof of the tunnel. I knew I had to be hitting them—right in the face—but they weren't going down.

The few seconds of surprise passed, and the lizards responded to our attack with deadly effectiveness. As Sargon was the closest, they turned on him like a pack of hungry wolves. They leapt, hind-claws leading, their tails making curved lines behind them.

He never had a chance. He dropped his tube, got out his combat knife, and managed to sink it into the chest of the first saurian who reached him. But then the weight of those hind legs hit him, sending him sprawling. The saurian he'd knifed staggered, but the rest closed in, biting and tearing. I heard a screech that was probably human, and I saw a reptilian head lift up with a bloody trophy. I wasn't even sure it was a limb—it could have been a ripped-loose strip of skin and flesh.

"Don't worry about hitting Sargon," I said, "he's gone."

"Concentrate on the closest one!" Carlos said, breathing over the microphone in his helmet in what sounded like panicky gasps. "He's permed. I can't believe it, we're all going to be permed right here in this hole."

"Shut up, and keep firing."

We laid fire into the leader until he went down. The one Sargon had gutted was down as well. With the two he'd shot earlier, that left four of them out of the fight.

The last two got smart and retreated behind the smoking hulk of the revival unit.

"Are they running or getting guns?" Carlos asked.

"It hardly matters which. We can't break off. They'll come after us, and they run a lot faster than we do. Let's charge."

"Okay. You left, me right."

"Go!"

We'd been hugging the ragged walls of the tunnel, but now we fully exposed ourselves and rushed forward. We ran to the machine, stumbling over dead bodies and uneven spiraling cuts in the steel floor. We each came around the sides of the tunnel—and met up with two armed lizards.

They were picking up gear from a sled of sorts they had on the ground. I could tell right away it was some kind of air sled, a machine built to help carry heavy loads. I'd used them before, guiding them with tugs and nudges.

One of the two was looking right at me when I came around the machine. He opened his mouth at me, but I didn't hear him make any sound, not even a hiss. I don't know if his yawning action was a challenge, a greeting or a laugh.

253

We both fired at the same time, but Carlos slammed into the dino, spoiling his aim.

I was stunned for a split-second. Carlos had not stopped his charge—he'd plowed right into the lizard that was going to shoot me. The other one hadn't gotten his rifle up yet. Maybe he was loading it or configuring it—I had no idea.

Two bullets found me in the crossfire. They bit into my right shoulder, punching through the fabric of my uniform like I was wearing a windbreaker instead of light infantry armor.

My right arm didn't work quite right anymore, but I shot the lizard in the skull with a burst that caused visible damage. Even with the strange glare of night vision, I could tell most of his snout was missing.

I turned my barrel in the direction of the second lizard, who was still working on his gun. Maybe it was jammed, I don't know, but he never fired it. I killed him before he could get it into action.

Then, I moved to Carlos and pulled him away from the dead saurian. The two were entangled. I saw a curved blade and a lot of blood. Carlos had been gutted.

"You going to make it?" Carlos asked me with a strange, rattling voice.

"Yeah. I'm good."

I was lying. My shoulder was on fire. I could feel the blood trickling down into my suit, dribbling with cooling runnels all the way to the tips of my gloves and the soles of my feet. The air conditioners chilled the blood as it ran over my skin, making a sticky, cold mess that was worse than sweat.

"How about you?" I asked him.

"No way," he gasped. "I'm dead. But if you get the hell out of here now, Sargon and I—we won't be permed. You can tell them."

"Is that why you did it?" I asked. "Is that why you hugged this lizard and got yourself killed?"

"Partly, yeah," he said. "But no matter what, I don't owe you anything now, McGill. We're even."

It took me a second to understand what he was talking about.

"You're still hung up on that first training exercise? Where Graves suffocated us—is that what you're talking about?"

"You know damn well—" he broke off to cough wetly. I didn't have to look to know that the mess he was coughing up was dark with clotted blood. "You know what I'm saying. You came back for me, so I threw myself on a lizard for you."

"Okay," I said. "We're even, but we're not finished yet. I'll see you around after some hot bio revives you."

He laughed and coughed. His head was moving, but the rest of him was deadly still. It was strange, almost as if he was paralyzed—which he wasn't, as far as I could tell. His body was in shock, I guess: Already dead, but still functioning for a few minutes more.

We talked a bit longer, quietly, until he died. It didn't take more than two minutes. When I was sure, I let him down carefully, took pictures of the fallen in case there was any argument from the bios, and went to the machine.

If I ran out right now, I knew I'd make it. Carlos, Sargon and I would live. But that wasn't why I'd come down here. I'd come to save Graves, Natasha, Anne—all of them.

I flipped on my suit lights and climbed all over the machine. I found the front panel and dug around on it. I didn't see any obvious data ports or removable storage devices.

I heaved a sigh. This was a lot of work for nothing. My shoulder was stinging and getting stiffer every minute. Soon, it would be hard to defend myself without a regrow.

I got out my tapper and searched it, but there was precious little on alien tech. It was against Galactic Law to study and reverse-engineer an alien device like this. If you couldn't do it on your own, you had to let the original builders keep their monopoly.

As a last ditch effort, I engaged my helmet computer. It identified items I looked at—but most of us found that distracting. When you looked down at your gun, it told you all about the snap-rifle in your hands. If you lifted a fork, it told you *fork* in glowing letters with a command section that would honest-to-God look up the word fork and give the dictionary definition. Because these systems were annoying, we usually

255

kept them flipped off. But right now, I needed all the help I could get.

I turned it on and carefully eyed the machine. It needed time to recognize each component—if it could. That meant staring fixedly at each item for about ten seconds before the computer popped up its best guess at what the hell I was looking at.

A few times, the results were hilarious. I wasn't in any mood to laugh, but I had to when it saw the stiff, dead upraised claws of a saurian corpse and identified them as *fingers*.

"Moron machine," I said. "Scales, claws, wrong dimensions and shape. Hell, they don't even have the same number of joints that we do."

The computer ignored me and went right on happily identifying things. Sometimes, the identifications shifted as my point of view and angle shifted. To get a full scan, I tried looking down on an object, then staring at it head on, and finally looking at it from below.

During the last of these three steps, while I was looking at a keyboard-like device on the front panel, the identification system spit out an interesting classification on my screen: data slot.

I frowned, because I didn't see anything like a slot. I flipped on my lights, then got all the way down on my knees and crawled under there.

Data slot, it said again.

"Are you sure?" I asked.

As it wasn't voice-activated, it didn't react to my query. I tapped at my arm. The test was run again, and the answer came back the same: *data slot*.

I opened my helmet and peered at it up close. The only thing it could be talking about was a rectangular section of metal in the surface of the machine under the control panel. Experimentally, I pushed my finger up to it and applied pressure.

The metal folded inward, and allowed my finger to push inside. I pulled it back, and it snapped shut.

"That's got to be it," I said aloud. "But how can I get anything out of it? I don't have a data stick—certainly not one that will fit that slot. And I don't—"

Growling in frustration, I realized I was talking to myself. Was that a sign of shock or insanity? A little of both, I suspected.

I got back to my feet and began disassembling the panel. If the data slot was there, it had to lead somewhere in the guts of this machine—quite literally, in the case of a revival unit.

I'd been trained on data systems of every variety in college. But we'd never been allowed to fool with alien tech. That was something most professionals rarely saw unless they worked for a very rich company or Hegemony itself.

Fortunately, our suits came with a small toolkit. I disassembled the outer housing and pulled the front panel right off.

I was immediately disgusted. My lips curled away from my teeth slowly and stayed there.

It was a hybrid. I could tell right away these "machines" didn't come to Earth with a nice metal casing over them. Inside the box was a blob of flesh. It looked like a fatty ham, skinless and pink. Embedded in this wall of meat were numerous probes. These probes were connected with wires to the front panel.

I ripped them out by the handful. I was horrified to see the flesh shiver as I did this. Could it be alive? Could it *feel* what I was doing, somehow?

I tried not to think about it. I tried not to think about anything. I took the housing off completely and ripped it loose from every connection, ignoring the disturbing, shuddering reactions.

Finally, I had it off. It was big, about the size of a refrigerator door torn off its hinges. I put it on my back, but my right arm protested.

I thought of the air sled the saurian had been using earlier. I tried it, but it was dead. It looked undamaged, but possibly it wouldn't work for a human. I cursed and gave it a kick.

It was time to do things the hard way. Cursing steadily, I took a strap from Carlos' rifle, attached it to the panel and began to drag it behind me.

I looked at my watch. Adjunct Leeson had said he'd give us an hour, and I had eighteen minutes to go.

I began trotting with the panel sparking and banging behind me. If there were any other lizards around in these tunnels, they sure as hell weren't going to have to work hard to track me.

-27-

In the end, I made it out of the tunnel with about four minutes to spare. We'd marched into that hole carefully, looking around every corner. On the way out, I'd been running for my life, despite my heavy, bumping burden..

When I came out of the tunnel mouth, they almost blew me away. There were six weaponeers and a full squad of light troops aiming at me. I must have looked like I had scales to these people because every finger was on a trigger, and they looked like they were sweating and itching to pull them.

"Friendly!" I shouted breathlessly. "Hold your fire! It's me, Recruit McGill. No pursuit is inbound."

Leeson himself stalked forward. I saw Veteran Harris behind him, waving down the upraised guns. The squadron let their muzzles drift down to aim at the steel floors disappointedly.

"I can't believe I gave you clowns an hour," Leeson said. "About one minute after you left, I regretted it. If you only—"

He broke off as I emerged and removed my helmet. He'd noticed the burden I was dragging behind me through the tunnels and now stared down at it with a heavy frown.

"What the hell is that, Recruit?" he demanded.

"That, sir, is the front panel of a revival unit. It will probably look more recognizable if I flip it over."

I got down on my knees and strained. "Could you help, sir? I'm injured."

"Are you shitting me? What did you *do?* You've damaged it—you've torn it apart. That's a very expensive piece of equipment, McGill. Do you realize that?"

I looked up at him. "Sir, did you really think we were going to be able to go down there and haul back the entire system intact in one hour? That would have required a full squadron and a lifter."

"I didn't expect you to tear it apart!"

"Well, sir, this is the section of the machine that contains the data slot."

"What are all those meat-thermometer-looking things dangling from it?"

"As far as I can determine, those couplings connect our human-tech computers with the organic alien components inside revival units."

"That will be enough," said a new, loud voice.

We both looked up. A stern, pissed-looking bio named Thompson stood with her hands on her hips. She was a centurion, which surprised me. Most bios weren't officers.

"I'll take that piece of scrap, Adjunct," she told Leeson.

"Can you do anything with it?" he asked.

"I can remove it from your possession. Those are my orders. This mission you sent the recruit on was ill-advised, Adjunct. Authority levels have been superseded."

Adjunct Leeson chewed his lower lip for a second. "Sir, I know the revival units are sacred cows for you bios, but we are talking about permed legionnaires, here."

Centurion Thompson glared at him. "Please release the component into my custody immediately. I have an air sled with me."

Leeson stepped out of the way and waved them forward. I watched as two orderlies helped her load the broken panel onto an air sled. I would have liked to have had one of those handy earlier today. It was too small to have carried the entire machine, but it would have helped a lot in getting this piece out of the tunnels.

The centurion threw a rattling plastic tarp over the scrap of metal when she had it loaded and then carefully pushed the air sled away. She refused all help from the grunts around her and only allowed her orderlies to touch the wreckage. She handled the air sled personally and attentively. She guided it away as if it was carrying an injured infant.

Leeson stared after her with an unpleasant expression. "Sanctimonious bios," he growled. "They're all like that, you know. More worried about their machines and their protocols than they are about the people they're supposed to be caring for. They think they're some kind of lab coat-wearing priesthood."

I thought about Anne, and I had to disagree with him in her case. She was very caring, if a little touchy, and she seemed to want to break with her fellow bios to be a dedicated healer. But I didn't see any reason to tell Leeson this. As long as he wasn't yelling at me, there was no need to give him a fresh cause.

His distraction didn't last long. He wheeled on me and regarded me with a growing frown.

"Where's Sargon and that other irritant—what's his name?"

"They didn't make it, sir. But I have the vids to prove they're both dead. We can revive them immediately on *Corvus*."

"Right, sure. They get a nice vacation, eh? While they leave us down here in the shit?"

"That's a painful way to get a vacation, sir," I said.

He tossed me an acid glance and then waved to the weaponeers. "All right, people. You're finally going to get to use those toys of yours. Light this tunnel up and melt it to slag. I want no more lizards coming through from that direction ever again."

We left the chamber, and they began beaming. The chamber became white-hot and I, for one, wasn't unhappy to see it destroyed.

Veteran Harris approached me when we were on the steps going up to the main building.

"You've been missing the party, McGill," he said.

"I've been having one of my own underground, Veteran."

He chuckled. "So I heard, so I heard. Did you really volunteer for that?"

"Yes, Veteran."

"Crazy mother," he muttered. He hesitated for a second before continuing. "Why don't you go to the infirmary and get that arm patched up?"

I stopped climbing the stairs and looked at him to see if he was serious. I could tell by his eyes that he was. With a major attack inbound, I'd thought for sure he was going to have me man the walls until I dropped.

"Thank you, Veteran."

"Never thank me for anything, Recruit. That isn't good for morale."

"Why not?"

"Because when or if I have to gut you later, we'll both feel bad."

I nodded but didn't entirely understand his meaning. Now that training was over, when was he going to have to kill me?

"I'll be going," I said.

I left and sensed him watching me as I walked away. I didn't bother to look back and check, though. I was tired and needed to get my arm fixed.

Legion medical was pretty good. We had more fancy gadgets than just the revival units. Often, troops were injured but not killed and needed repairs—that's what they called the process: repairs. You didn't heal the sick in Legion Varus. You repaired a broken soldier. We were like cars or robots. I guess, in a way, it was an accurate definition. Since they could stamp out new replacement troops, were we really all that different from any other piece of equipment?

I shook my head. It was best to leave thoughts like that in storage rather than letting them carom around in your mind and possibly bounce out of your mouth later on. They were damaging, difficult ideas—what officers in Legion Varus called "bad thoughts".

Outside, it was eerily quiet. People spoke in whispers as if they thought making noise would attract the enemy. Apparently, the lizards had yet to make their attack. They'd pounded out a few holes in the walls and scorched much of the roof, but they hadn't charged in yet. I wondered what they were waiting around for.

262

I crossed the compound to a small, squatty building. I could tell the legionaries had been busy. They'd domed many of the structures with a quick layer of puff-crete to reinforce them.

Medical was inside one of these igloo-like buildings. I went inside and felt a cool blast of air wash over my face as I removed my helmet. A bio met me and ran a critical eye over me.

"You don't look good," he said.

I showed him my shoulder.

"Shrapnel?"

I shook my head. "Bullets. Snap-rifle slivers, to be exact."

He gave me an odd look. "This isn't blue-on-blue, is it?"

"No, Specialist. The lizards have them too."

He nodded and made a note on his tapper. "Good. Loads more screens to fill out if its friendly fire. Let's get you onto a gurney."

I let myself flop onto a floating surface as soon as it was brought near enough. It was really an air sled with a pad on it and a white sheet over that. It wasn't overly comfortable, but right now it felt good.

They scooted me into a back room and left. I sighed and peeled my uniform away from my injuries. They didn't look good. At the very least, they were infected. The skin was an angry red all around the puncture wounds. I wondered if the lizards had dirtied up their bullets on purpose, or if it was just the natural microbes of Steel World that were eating my flesh and poisoning my blood.

The wait went on for several minutes. I reflected that every medical establishment I'd ever been in seemed to automatically place you in a room and forget about you for a while. At least the air was cool and dry in here. I tried to focus on that and enjoy it, letting my suit open at every vent point to allow my sweat to dry.

Finally, another bio entered. Her nose wrinkled in disgust immediately. I guessed I wasn't the freshest-smelling recruit she'd ever met.

She didn't say anything to me. Two orderlies came in behind her and stood with arms crossed. They were muscular guys, and their cold stares had me worried. Was this going to hurt more than I thought it was? They had the look of men who were thinking about how to hold me down.

The bio looked up again, and for the first time I saw her rank insignia: she was a centurion. I finally recognized her. She was Centurion Thompson, the same woman who I'd met when I came out of the saurian tunnel. I sat up on my elbows, wincing in pain as I did so.

"Sir?" I called out to her.

"What is it, Recruit?"

"Did you get the revival data out of that unit?" I asked. "The one I hauled out of the tunnels?"

She gave me a sidelong glance. "It's best you don't ask about that."

"Why not?"

"Why not, 'Centurion Thompson'," she corrected.

"Sorry, sir. Why not, Centurion Thompson?"

She sucked in a breath and let it out. "You're forcing my hand. Don't they teach recruits how to keep to their own tech?"

I stared at her, unsure how to answer that one.

Thompson waved forward the two orderlies. I didn't like the look in their eyes. Hard hands gripped my arms, one man on each arm. I thought about kicking them, but I'd been surprised.

"What the hell do you think you're doing?" I demanded.

They had restraints out now. I hadn't seen them before. I guess these guys were good at hiding them.

Alarmed, I struggled. I managed to get a knee into one man's gut, but he didn't let go. They were strong, and I was injured.

I saw the bio readying a needle.

"This is bullshit, Centurion," I shouted. "My commander will hear about this!"

"No he won't," she said in the sweet voice her kind used on screaming children who didn't want their shots. "Now listen, James, it's best for everyone if you calm down. There's no need to make this unpleasant."

My hands were lashed together and my ankles too. I was tied to the same air sled gurney I'd been enjoying a minute before.

264

I looked across the room to the regrowth equipment. They had a flesh-printer right there. All she had to do was pull the metal out of me, shoot in some antibiotics and run the printer over my wounds. They would spray out fresh cells, and the wound would seal over almost immediately. What was the delay?

"Do you really think all this is necessary to pull a few slivers out of my shoulder?" I asked her.

"All your injuries will be taken care of," she said. "Don't worry."

I had no idea what she was up to, but she waved away the orderlies. She held her syringe up, and a single droplet of amber liquid ran down the needle.

The orderlies left, and Thompson and I were alone. I glared at her while she gave me a reassuring smile in return.

"I'm going to ask you some questions before I inject you with this," she said in a very professional-sounding voice.

"What is it?"

"Nothing important."

I eyed the needle, then her face. Her eyes were fixed upon mine. She was still smiling.

"Ask," I said.

"Have you ever been revived illegally?"

I hesitated and immediately cursed myself for that. So that's what this was about. I should have suspected I couldn't stay below the radar forever. Even if the Galactics were in the dark about it, not everyone else would be.

"I don't know what you're talking about," I said, trying to be as convincing as possible. "I've been killed multiple times if that's what you're asking: In combat and in training."

"Negative," she said, examining her tapper. "You never died in training. You were killed in combat twice, and you were revived twice. There is one other entry, however: Treatment for toxemia. The toxins found were quite unusual. That sort of treatment isn't given without us knowing about it, James. Healthy people only get these blood-gas numbers from being revived with bad materials. If it had happened on the battlefield, they would have done a regrow immediately."

"Are you going to do your job and fix my arm, or what?"

She smiled calmly. "Yes, of course. But not in the manner you're expecting. In answer to your other, earlier question: yes, we did get the data from the components you salvaged. And yes, most of the people stored there were revived."

I was glad to hear the people I'd meant to save had survived. Graves, Natasha, Kivi—all of them. But right now, I had other concerns. I had no idea what this crazy centurion was up to, but it didn't look good.

Clearly, the bios knew something was up, and they wanted to know what it was. I couldn't tell them I'd been executed and illegally revived. That wasn't going to help anyone. Specialist Grant and I would both be in trouble then. I couldn't do that to her after she'd taken big chances to save me.

"Centurion," I said, "you seem quite upset about something. I hope it's nothing I've done."

Thompson laughed. "I'm not upset at all, James."

"So that's why you're going to murder me?"

"This isn't *murder*, Recruit! Think about it as the correction of an unfortunate error. You're not supposed to be dismantling our revival units. You're also operating on a bad grow—another error. Lastly, you aren't being truthful with me. I'm going to correct all these problems by recycling you now. This injection will solve further problems. Mentally, you'll be taken back in time. You won't remember anything about our equipment. Really, you should be thanking me. You'll be back on *Corvus* in no time."

I was breathing hard. Part of me could see what she was saying—but I didn't want to die. Every instinct in my body fought against it.

"Don't you people take an oath to protect life and heal the sick?" I asked. "What kind of a loser were you in school?"

I'd been trying to provoke a response with this attack, and I got a bigger one than I'd expected. She stepped quickly to my side and put the needle in my face. Her eyes flared with anger. I realized I'd overdone it. Her calm, caring façade had vaporized.

"You know what this is?" she demanded. "When I stick you with this, you'll be dead in thirty seconds. Now, if you tell me how you got to keep a bad grow—how you got revived without proper authorization or records, I'll let them revive you on *Corvus*—but not if you piss me off too much. If that happens, this can be a one-way trip—"

That was as far as I let her get with her little speech. I'd been sawing away at the straps that held my left wrist, using the same knife I always carried. I'd last used it to cut away locked seatbelts on the lifter my first day after joining Legion Varus, and here I was doing it again.

I reached up with my left arm—my good arm, and grabbed the syringe she had in my face. I twisted her wrist and pressed the needle against the skin of her neck.

"Freeze," I said. "Or I'll kill you right now."

The needle was automatic, as they all were these days. The second it sensed it was inside human flesh, it would pump the contents into the recipient's bloodstream under power. I could see the sac at the end was already trembling, ready to compress itself.

The look on her face was indescribable. I grinned at her.

"Yeah," I said. "I'm full of surprises."

"How did you...?"

"My dad bought a knife for me on my eighteenth birthday, and it's still as sharp as the day I'd unwrapped the package. It's a quality blade, but I never knew when I got it that it would be this useful."

"Recruit," she said sternly, staring down at me. "I order you to release me."

"We're both way over the line today," I said, summoning a confident air that I didn't feel.

"I'm sorry," she said quietly, her voice calm and professional again. "I've overstepped the bounds of civilized behavior. But I am your superior officer, and—"

I wiggled the needle, and she shut up.

"I'm sorry sir," I told her, "but I can't let you kill me right now. If you'll kindly undo my straps, without attempting to withdraw from the needle, I'll be on my way."

"What about your injuries?"

"I'll fix them myself."

Thompson made a mistake then. Her hand had been drifting down toward her belt. She had a com-link there. At the last second, she moved fast, reaching for the button, fumbling blindly with it.

I jabbed the needle into her neck and the syringe began to pump automatically. The little bulb at the end pulsated. It was like watching a bee's poison sac contract when it's rammed home in your flesh.

I grimaced sympathetically as she made a strangled sound. I hadn't wanted to hurt her, but she might have been going for a weapon. I'd killed her on reflex.

Her hands flew up to her throat, and her face purpled.

I sat up, sawing at more straps with my small knife. I talked to her as she died.

"Sorry about that," I told her. "You shouldn't have made that sudden move. Try to look on the bright side: you're out of this hellhole. I'm sure they'll revive you on *Corvus*. Good luck."

Centurion Thompson sank to her knees. She tried to talk, but couldn't. I figured I was happy about that. She probably wasn't trying to say anything I wanted to hear.

"Listen," I said as she lay on the floor, gasping for breath. Her eyes were glazing over. "If you keep quiet about this, I'll do the same. It will be an accident, nothing more. I'll stay away from your tech. I'll leave the bios alone. I hope you'll do the same for me."

I don't know if she even heard the last of it. By the time I'd stopped talking, she was stone dead.

-28-

I took a few minutes to barricade the door with a chair tilted under the door handle. It wasn't much, but I knew she'd told the orderlies to leave us alone. Hopefully, this would give me the time I needed.

Scrambling and dropping things on the floor, I found a pack of syringes labeled with something that ended in "mycin". That had to be an antibiotic, so I shot myself with two of them, right into my shoulder. The injections burned and my flesh crawled. I hoped I hadn't just poisoned myself somehow.

Then I removed the skin-printer from the wall. Really, it was just a wand with a wide nozzle. I ran it over my injured flesh—the bullets inside would have to wait. If it was at least clean and sealed, that would do for now. I'd bother a field medic in my own unit about it later on—if I lived long enough to get fancy.

The dead woman on the floor did nothing to keep my mind on the task at hand. It was strange standing there, sweating and nervous, while trying to heal myself with a flesh-spraying device. Wet, pinkish material went everywhere looking like juices from a raw steak.

I told myself I hadn't really killed her—at least not permanently. She was already queued up on *Corvus* waiting for her turn to come out of an alien oven. I wondered if she'd blab about how she got there—I suspected she wouldn't. She'd held me illegally and tried to murder me.

After about a minute with the wand, I decided I'd done what I could. My arm felt a lot better, but it didn't look much better. The flesh was growing in and around the damaged tissue, healing over what would have taken months to do naturally.

When I pulled my suit over the mess the new skin tore in places. I winced, even though it caused no pain. There were no nerve endings in there yet, just raw skin cells. I should have dressed it more carefully, but I didn't have the time or the training.

Hoping for the best, I stripped to the waist, laid gauze over my shoulder, taped it as best I could, then suited up again. I removed the chair from under the door and walked out like I owned the place.

This was going to be the hard part. I'd decided there was only one way to handle it: by brazenly heading for the exit at a steady walk. I didn't run, I didn't even rush. I just walked.

As I passed through three longish corridors, I earned several looks and a few frowns. I ignored every duty-nurse, orderly and bio. They all seemed to have something to do. As far as they knew, I was just a grunt heading down to the lab for a test or looking for the bathroom.

Once, I saw one of the orderlies who had brought me in. He gave me a glance, then did a double-take. But someone tapped him on the shoulder, demanding his attention. Bios didn't like it when orderlies ignored them. Before he could investigate, I turned a corner and did my best to vanish.

The only problem came when I reached the front door. We were in a bunker, after all, and there was security. Fortunately, the protocol seemed to involve the automated door checking people's IDs as they entered. I waited just inside until a group passed by on the way out, then fell into step behind them. The guards didn't give any of us a second glance.

When I was outside, I took a deep breath. The night was dark and quiet. The air of Steel World was hot, as usual, but not oppressively so. I'd left my helmet behind, and as I walked to my bunker I let the sweat dry off me.

Twenty minutes ago I'd been certain I was going to take another trip through the revival machines. I dared to smile.

That bio was going to wake up pissed-off if she did remember all this. I wasn't sure which one of us had broken more regulations during our encounter, but I sincerely hoped I wouldn't need her help again.

By the time I reached my own bunk and sank into it, I had a jug of water in my hand. I drained most of it then poured more on my head. I sighed and stretched out.

I half-expected Carlos' face to come over the top of my bunk like a full moon. I could almost hear his big mouth smarting off at me—but then I realized he was dead. They all were dead. I was almost alone in my unit on Steel World. Most of my squadron had died over the last few hours and were now up on *Corvus*—if they hadn't been permed.

I found a snap-rifle and planned to fall asleep with it across my chest. I closed my eyes and tried to rest. I was tired and felt beaten down. I knew I shouldn't sleep right now, but I had to get rest whenever I could.

I awoke a few hours later to a terrible grinding sound. I felt sure for several confused seconds that the orderlies had me again. I came up into a sitting position in my bunk, feeling feverish. My snap-rifle was aimed into the dark with the safety flipped off.

No one was there but a few fellow recruits. They groaned and rolled out of their beds to their feet.

"What's going on?" I demanded.

"How the hell should I know?" came an answer from a female voice in the dark. I recognized the voice: it was Kivi.

"Hey!" I called out. "I thought you died a while back."

She got out of her bunk and came down the row to sit on mine. We regarded each other in the dark room, waiting for orders.

"It was close," she said, "but while you were chasing dinos in that tunnel, the bio people patched me up in their bunker. They can do more than just revive us if they want to."

"Yeah, I've just come from there. I'm sore, but functioning."

"Maybe the people who died are the lucky ones," she said. "But only because you risked everything to keep them from getting permed. That was cool, James."

271

I smiled. "Not everyone thinks so." I was about to tell her the story of the bio centurion who'd decided I'd seen too much and needed recycling, when the lights flipped on and the arrows on the floor lit up. They were red this time—emergency colors.

We pulled on our gear quickly and rushed out together. There were plenty of spare helmets with so many people missing, so I took one and put it on. More people from our unit gathered, but there were no veterans or officers. Not knowing what was happening, we aimed our weapons at everyone else who joined us in the main hallways.

"Have you heard anything over the unit channel?" I asked Kivi.

"Nothing," she said, "but something's up. I bet someone got hit."

We followed our ant-trail of arrows to the exits and stepped outside. I half-expected to see an incoming bombardment or even an invasion force at the gates. But there was nothing there.

"Look at HQ!" shouted Kivi at my side.

The command post was a puff-crete bunker they'd set up behind the terminal building. It was—gone. Or at least half of it was. There was a small cloud of dust with a flickering orange light inside.

"Fire," Kivi said. "It's on fire!"

"It's more than on fire," I said, "it's been taken out. That's why we haven't gotten any orders."

"Can you get through to Harris or Leeson?"

I tried—all the troops coming out of the bunker did. Our tappers had locating units on them. The tappers worked, but they weren't telling us anything because we were disconnected from the network.

More and more people were coming out of their barracks, and some were streaming down from the walls where guards had been posted. As a group, we decided to head toward the HQ to see if we could render assistance. There was a lot of confusion about what to do with our command post knocked out.

"That's a crater," a tech specialist said next to me as we trotted closer. He was a small guy with small eyes and an angry red face. He'd come over from the non-com barracks following his own set of emergency arrows. "That means the lizards must have used air power."

"I don't hear any planes," I said. "It's been quiet except for that single grinding sound followed by some kind of explosion."

"Well then, what did this?" the tech asked me petulantly.

"I don't know," I said. "But someone purposefully knocked out the HQ. That means we have no networking, or officers on duty."

The tech was nodding. "That explains the emergency arrows. The systems only know how to lead people to their gathering points when something really goes wrong."

When we reached the HQ, I was relieved to find Harris directing traffic and Leeson giving orders.

"About time you recruits showed up," Leeson said to us. "Form a perimeter. I have enough people looking for survivors already."

We spread out with Harris bullying us into good firing positions. There wasn't much cover, but we took what we could find and watched the night around us.

The next event took everyone by surprise. I think it was more startling because we all saw it with our own eyes.

The blue Medical center—the same building where I'd been abused just hours earlier—suddenly turned into a plume of dust. I saw dust shooting up into the air in a dark cloud. When it cleared, the Medical bunker was gone.

"We need to get the men out of there, sir!" shouted Harris.

Leeson looked at him and nodded. "I'm in contact with the surviving officers. We're evacuating every structure."

I stared at the missing building and thought for a moment.

"I heard something, sir," I said. "A grinding sound. Right before it went down."

"Yeah? What the hell does that mean?"

"I think—sir, I think they're tunneling under us. Weakening the supports and sinking our bunkers."

Leeson, Harris and the red-faced tech guy all looked at me like I was crazy for a second, but then Leeson nodded.

"It does make sense. I've been wondering why they were taking so damned long to hit us after the initial bombardment. If anyone should know what drilling through the metallic soil on this planet sounds like, it would be you. Okay, I'm relaying that up the chain of command."

What happened next surprised us all again. Although, in retrospect, maybe it shouldn't have. The saurians were playing this game their own way. As it turned out, they liked to tunnel.

Like every world, the reptilian inhabitants of Cancri-9 only had so many credits to spend on imported alien tech. On Earth, we spent that cash on interstellar invasion ships, weaponry and special devices like our revival machines. We put our Galactic credits into tech that would help return more credits—anything that helped us fight was an investment to us.

The saurians had done a similar economic calculus. If there was one thing they had the very best of, it was drilling equipment. Steel World was a mining planet, and to mine right through hard metals, you needed amazing drills.

Plasma-burning drills just such pieces of equipment. When the first rig surfaced, it looked like a plasma grenade on overload. It was blue, and ran with sizzling force fields.

Unlike standard military screens, the fields enveloping the drilling machines weren't set to repel incoming ordnance. The screens moved and churned like invisible blades of force that spun around the central machine like knives of energy.

Steel, puff-crete, soldiers and vehicles were sliced away to nothing when they touched those spinning fields. We all hunkered down and stared as the ground vomited up one, two, three—six of them. They weren't terribly large, but the troops that rushed out of the back end when they stopped spinning looked big to me.

Armored and carrying heavy weapons, saurians charged out to fire on anyone in sight. We returned fire, but our weaponry wasn't penetrating their armor.

"Harris, gather all your light troops and attack," Leeson shouted.

I looked at him like he was crazy. We all did.

"You heard the man," Harris said grimly. "Stay low. Flank them while staying under cover. Spray fire at them from the sides."

We deployed and did as we were ordered. Unsurprisingly, it was a slaughter. Every time they got a bead on one of us, we were splattered. Our chattering snap-rifles raked them, but did no damage.

"With all due respect, Veteran," I shouted when he hunkered down nearby. "We can't get through to those troops. Why are we doing this?"

We were taking shelter behind a broken wall that was about three feet high. The top was black with soot and smoldering.

Harris reloaded his gun methodically. I couldn't help but notice that he had kept his head down and only taken a few pot shots at the enemy now and again.

"We're here to engage and distract, McGill," he said. "That's the real purpose of light infantry in any serious fight. You should know that by now. Don't worry, the revival machine on *Corvus* is operating just fine."

"I understand we're cannon fodder, Veteran. I just don't understand why we're throwing away troops."

He shook his head and chuckled. "We aren't. Leeson is organizing the weaponeers. They're the only ones who can take out these saurian heavies. We have to give him the time he needs to get them into position."

I thought of Sargon back in the tunnels. I wished I had him with me now. Even if I only had his plasma tube, it would be an improvement.

"I understand, Veteran," I said.

I got up from my hiding spot and sighted on the nearest saurian.

The alien looked resplendent at night. Such fine armor! He had a full body-shell with a sheen of powered force-shielding over it. In the dim light, the surface of his fields reflected like rippling water. I heard my gun chatter, and saw sparks light up his shield with a score of hits. Staggered a step, he turned and swept his weapon toward me. It looked like a fire hose of gushing orange light.

I stumbled and went down. I thought I'd lost a leg—but then I looked and saw Harris had his hand on my ankle. He'd pulled me down at the last moment.

"You're eager to die, aren't you?" he asked.

"Only if it's for a good cause," I replied.

He snorted and slammed my bad shoulder. I winced and gritted my teeth. I worked hard to give him a smile.

We both heard heavy movement then. The pile of broken rubble we were hiding behind was no longer lighting up with plasma. Harris and I looked at one another with wide eyes. We both knew the saurian was marching over here in his heavy suit to finish us off. Like two trapped rodents, our heads swiveled looking for an escape route.

"He's onto us, Veteran," I said.

"No shit."

"Have you got a grenade?"

He nodded and pulled it off his belt, staring at it. "After this, I'm out. They don't issue a lot of these beauties."

It was a strange situation. We both knew there was nowhere to run. The second we stepped out of cover the alien soldier would burn us down. But we weren't panicking, not really. When you know death will be quick and temporary, it's more of a feeling of personal defeat and honor than it is a matter of terror and desperation. At the same time, I found I still didn't want to die.

Harris lifted the grenade and put his finger on the timer. I saw him reduce it to zero. My eyes widened.

"Going to wait until he's right on top of us?"

He nodded. "You and I are going to Hell together tonight, McGill."

The impossibly heavy tread grew louder and closer. I felt my guts tighten and churn. My throat burned as my stomach tossed acid up into it. Despite my intellectual certainty that I would live again, my body was beginning to get worried. I guess you can't erase a million years of instinct with a few months of training.

Harris got up into a squatting position with one hand on the grenade. His thumb was hovering, and the shell of the device was already leaking power. In order to build enough of a charge for an instantaneous reaction, I knew the grenade had to cycle up before you triggered the ignition.

"Want me to stand and distract?"

"Go for it, Recruit!"

I waited until the last possible second. I stood up and there was a shout in my helmet from other nearby troops. Then, a blinding flash went off in my face. My only thought was one of regret: I hadn't even gotten to shoot the dino in defiance.

For some reason, I had enough time for a follow-up thought: *Why am I not dead yet?*

I was standing there, blinded, but I could still feel my rifle so I pulled the trigger and held onto it. I fired at where the saurian had been—where he had to be.

Something kicked my calves. There it was. I'd finally been hit, I figured. I probably had no legs by now.

I went down, and a hand shook me. I was shouting hoarsely.

"McGill! Shut up, you idiot. He's gone."

I stopped struggling. I could feel my breath hitting my faceplate inside my helmet and bouncing back, warming my face with steamy puffs.

"What?" I asked. "Who's gone?"

"The saurian. The weaponeers blew him away. Pull yourself together, man."

I tried, I really did, but it took a few minutes. My vision slowly returned during this time, and I figured out what had happened.

When the saurian had walked up to us preparing to burn us down to slag, the weaponeers Leeson had been organizing had burned him instead. The blinding flash hadn't been his weapon burning me, it had been their heavy tubes hitting his force field. The resulting energies that had been released had caused a blinding flash of radiance.

When I could think and see again, with purple and green splotches occluding much of my vision, I saw Harris. He was leaning against the slag heap, toying with his last plasma grenade.

As I watched, he thumbed the timer back up to five seconds again and put it back onto his belt.

-29-

The latest phase of the battle was soon over. They'd hit us hard and hurt us—but they hadn't taken us out. The saurians had sent up six drilling machines, each loaded with a team of heavily armed lizards. Altogether, they must have killed hundreds of us, but our weaponeers had killed all of them.

I was in a ruined bunker with Leeson, Harris and a dozen other fighters. None of us had eaten or bathed today. Our survivors were scattered around the compound in small groups, waiting for the saurians to start a new attack.

"I'd expected a big, organized battle," I told Harris. "This is anything but. Why don't they hit us with everything they have and finish this one way or another? They have the numbers."

Harris chuckled and shrugged. It was Leeson who answered me.

"I wish they would just charge in here and finish this too, Recruit," he said, "but they won't play it that way. They're trying to win everything right here, and it's making things all the more painful for us."

"Sir?" I asked, confused. "Win what?"

"The planet, the contract—the whole thing. This is it. That's what the brass up on the ship suspects, and I'm pretty sure they're right."

I shook my head, still confused. I looked around at the devastation. Around us, the spaceport was in shambles. There

278

were no more lifters coming and going. There were no troops in sight other than our reduced forces. A lot of dark holes yawned in the puff-crete walls.

Leeson looked at Harris wearily. "Should I bother to explain it to him?"

"Suit yourself, sir," he said. He had his helmet off and had made a hat out of his smart-cloth shirt. He tipped his makeshift hat over his eyes and made himself comfortable on a pile of rubble.

"You see, troops," Leeson said, addressing others who were listening in, "Legion Varus cheats—all of Earth's legions do. How do you think we've won so many battles? Our weapons are good, our tactics are superb—but really, it comes down to not taking permanent losses. Our troops return to the fight, sometimes before the battle is over. That's how we win so often. Tech at the level of our revival units is rare in our quadrant of the galaxy. As far as I know, only the Galactics and Earth forces have it."

"Are the revival machines that expensive?" I asked.

"Yes, insanely expensive. But it's more than that. Every world in the Empire only gets so many credits to spend from their trading. Each government must choose very wisely what to purchase with them—spending on frivolities is an easy way to doom your race to low status in the empire, so most of the credits are reinvested. We bought this tech—revival machines—because it made our method of gaining credits more secure. Our soldiers come back to life when they die, surviving to become superior fighters. We might lose battle after battle, but we always win the war in the end. We never run out of troops, and that makes us the best."

I wasn't sure I got the message. I looked around at the rest of the recruits, and they looked as baffled as I was. Kivi was among them. She raised her eyebrows at me questioningly. I shook my head in return. I didn't really get it, either.

"It's about body count, that's all," Harris chimed in. "That's what the Adjunct is getting at. That's all the Galactics understand, anyway. They're accountants at heart. If your troops are still standing when the dust settles and you took fewer losses, you won."

279

"Carry on, Harris," Leeson said. "I'm going to check on our firing positions."

He got to his feet and left.

"Are you saying the Galactics are watching us and scoring this battle?" I asked Harris.

"Exactly," Harris said.

"And they're just trying to see how many each side can kill?"

"Right."

I thought about that. Without revival units, we couldn't win in the end. The saurians outnumbered us and they would just keep coming.

"So this is to the last man, sir?" I asked.

Harris finally removed his hat and looked at me with bloodshot eyes. "You've finally got it, kid."

"But how can anyone tell if the Galactics are watching right now? Isn't that just guesswork—unless you run into one the way I did? They've been watching several battles from what I could see."

He nodded slowly. "Normally, that would be true. But things aren't going normally. First off, you—and I do mean *you* here, McGill—have killed a Galactic. Twice."

I shifted on my haunches uncomfortably. "I didn't know what it was."

"You think they care about that?"

"But how does that change the situation?"

He shook his head at me as if I was being slow. Maybe I was.

"The Galactics have it in for us. They have since the beginning. I tell you, the fix is in. They're scoring *this* fight, the one where we don't have the revival machines. So this time, we can't make one troop come back to life over and over. We can't make it look like he never died. We'll have to confess our real losses."

I thought about that. "Body count... You're telling me we really do cheat to keep our position? We get contracts because it looks like we always win...because our troops are still alive when it's over?"

"Yeah, that's about right. It's not that way on every world, but this is a tough one, with a tough local competitor. They've studied our methods for years. All those crazy contracts, asking us to protect every snot-nosed heir and mining complex... The saurians have rigged this game. We fell into it face first, too. We even pissed off the judges: the Galactics, the Nairbs—everyone. Now, when this mess is over, the Nairb accountants will come out here and count bodies, living and dead. We won't be around to hide the evidence. The results will be clear. The saurians will have won with fewer losses."

"But what about tech and firepower?" asked Kivi, suddenly. "Why doesn't the tribune send down his heavies to relieve us?"

"He might, but I bet he won't," answered Harris. "He's doing the calculus, too. He knows that the level of armament counts. The number we start with counts against us, as well. He could have sent the heavy units right away—but didn't. If he relieved us now that would make the battle bigger and erase any claim we could make that we were outgunned. I'm sure he's playing it the best he can, from his point of view. But no matter what, I think we're screwed."

I thought about the revival units in a new light after that conversation. They weren't just insurance policies for the unfortunate few. Our commanders thought of them as vital equipment. Our legions never ran out of troops. It was like having magic magazines that never ran out of ammo—a huge advantage. This was especially true when it came to scoring who won battles and who was the most effective fighter. In order to stay on top, we had to prove we were the best over and over.

This time, however, we were going to lose.

The next attack came in daylight when the sun was at its worst. The two hot suns of Cancri were fully revealed overhead with no cloud-cover to provide merciful relief. Inside our suits, our air-conditioners whispered and whirred with fans that struggled to keep up.

In the early afternoon, I was dozing underground in a crater covered with slabs of leaning puff-crete. Harris came by, tapped my helmet and I jumped awake.

He gestured with a thumb jabbing upward. I knew what that meant. It was my turn to do a twenty-minute shift on the surface, watching for the enemy.

Like a gopher poking his head out of a hole, I warily crept up to the top of the rubble-heap we inhabited and looked around my position in a slow circle. Seeing nothing other than a few other gophers posted here and there around the compound, I got out my snap-rifle and gazed through the scope, increasing my range of vision.

The scope automatically adjusted for the glaring light of the suns overhead. But still, it wasn't enough to make the light pouring through into my eye socket completely comfortable. Squinting, I did my best to scan the area farther out, looking through the gaps in our walls and the mounds of metal shavings piled up around the entry holes their drillers had used the last time.

Some of the guys in my unit were grumbling that only the recruits had to play gopher and do surface duty. I didn't feel that way. Sure, we were at greater risk and felt more discomfort, but the others—the weaponeers, officers and our last few techs and bios—they needed to be protected. They were not as expendable as we were. In a siege, everyone was decidedly unequal.

I didn't like guard duty, especially around the fifteen minute mark when my air conditioner began to hiccup and the air in my helmet turned warm. But I understood that I wasn't here to have a good time. If the enemy decided to hit us with their heavy troops again, only the weaponeers with their thick black tubes could kill them. Only the bios could repair the wounded, perhaps keeping our body count low. And the techs—well, they kept our suits, communications systems and other critical equipment functioning. Even now, they were underneath my position in the tunnels connecting our bunkers underground, so we could move between them without exposing ourselves. If the walls were penetrated by the enemy again, we now had vital cool spots for soldiers to rest and recuperate.

What was I? Only a guy with a rifle. A lightly trained, lightly armed recruit who was on his first campaign. I could hardly demand nor expect special treatment.

So I sat sweating and trying to adjust the cooling tubes in the fabric of my suit every minute or two. It was an impossible task, of course. Spots on the upper surfaces of my arms and helmet grew burning hot frequently. I tried to crouch in the shade of an overhang, but there was only partial cover. Overly exposed to the radiation of Cancri, it was all I could do to sweat, mutter curses, and constantly check my tapper to see if my stint was up yet.

When they finally hit us, I didn't believe it at first, thinking that the shadows I saw moving through holes punched in the walls of the compound must be something else—anything other than what I knew they had to be.

Then, the first jugger dipped its massive head into the hole and dripped saliva on the rubble. I froze for a fraction of a second. This was *real*, I told myself. I was facing a monster, and its spittle was steaming to vapor the instant it touched the hot stones.

They'd told us the monsters wouldn't come until evening. It was too hot out—even for them. They were native to this world, but in the warm season, even native animals kept to the cool green forests and the shade of their stark buildings. Most of the planet's wildlife was nocturnal for very good reasons.

But none of those assurances applied today. I was so hot, I wasn't even sure I wasn't hallucinating, but I wasn't going to sit on my can, anyway. I swung my snap-rifle up, sighted on the left eye, and hammered out a burst of ten pellets.

With one eye destroyed, the jugger reared up, roaring. Its great head struck the top of the hole it had leaned through, but a moment later it managed to pull back and disappeared.

I opened a com-channel and tried to report the sighting, but it was unnecessary and nearly impossible. Everyone was chattering, giving orders, asking for confirmation—they'd all heard the firing and the roar. They knew it was time to scramble into our defensive positions.

Harris came up behind me, looming close. His body blocked out the yellow sun. The red one was behind a building, and for that I was grateful. I stayed with my rifle sighted on the hole, but so far the jugger hadn't reappeared.

"Was that you firing, McGill?"

"Yes, Veteran."

"Did you hit it?"

"Took out an eye."

"Well done—did you know your AC is dead, kid?"

I looked up at him for a moment. I had to admit, I did feel even hotter than I had a minute ago.

"I thought I was just getting overexcited," I said.

He huffed at me. "Get below before you fry, you moron. I need every troop I have, even you. Take it to the techs, and have a bio check you for heatstroke."

"But, they're about to hit us."

"Yeah," he said. "I know. Hurry."

I slithered from my position downward. Harris assumed my spot and I could hear him muttering curses about exposure and heat. That brought half a smile to my face. I rather liked hearing him suffer up there on the hot seat.

I was staggering when I reached the central tunnels. A tech grabbed my arm and began working my tapper before I could speak.

"Exhausted fuel cell," she said. "Your generator isn't recharging your cells."

"Can I get a new generator, please?"

"No," she said. "They're on reserve for emergencies."

I nodded, but I was thinking that, as far as I was concerned, AC failure in a hundred fifty degrees *was* an emergency. But what did I know? I wasn't a tech.

Before I could say much else, she opened my back panel and rammed two new cells into place.

"Without a generator you'll have to switch these out every two hours—less, if you go out onto the surface."

I mumbled a thank you and went in search of water. Harris had said something about bios, but right now, I needed a drink.

The bios might be territorial about their equipment and a little nuts when it came to protecting secrets—but when they saw me weaving and wandering down the tunnel toward their station, they rushed out to help.

Matis reached me first. He was tall and thin, with dark, serious eyes surrounded by deep worry-lines. He looked me over quickly and professionally.

I'd first met Specialist Matis when the raptors had stolen the revival machine—he'd been one of the lucky people who'd escaped slaughter in that underground vault.

"Where are you hit, Recruit?" he asked.

"What?"

"I don't see any punctures," said an orderly, talking over my head as if I wasn't there. "But he seems disoriented."

"I really need a drink," I said.

"Get that helmet off him," Matis ordered.

Both the techs and the bios, I'd found, were extremely effective when it came to spotting trouble that they could fix. I didn't struggle. I let them do their work.

I sank down on the floor of the tunnel. Hands gripped my helmet and opened it. Cool air washed in a moment later. I sighed in relief. I hadn't realized that it was cooler in the tunnel than it was inside my suit.

"That's better," I said.

Bio Specialist Matis was crouching over me, looking into my eyes, tapping on my tapper. He looked concerned. I marveled at how specialists thought nothing of taking over when they had you in their grasp.

"Your blood levels are off," he said. "I'm seeing toxins that shouldn't be here. Have you been poisoned?"

"I don't think so. My suit AC shut down and I had my cells replaced."

"Is there a leak? Turn him over."

I felt hands grab me and flip me over. I felt like a kid, and I resisted slightly, then let them do it. I wasn't too trusting of bios lately, but these people seemed to be trying to help.

"No rupture in the cells," Matis said.

I finally opened my eyes and stared into his. He was frowning suspiciously.

"You're not telling me something, Recruit," he said.

At first, I was baffled. But then I thought I understood what he must be reading in my blood tests, which my suit monitored constantly.

"I had a bad grow a while back," I said.

"A bad grow?" he asked, looking surprised. "Are you saying they didn't recycle? Why not?"

I shrugged. "I'm not a bio."

Feigning ignorance as a recruit was usually effective, but not this time. He stared at me, his expression changing into a frown. He pulled back, taking his hands off me, as if I was some kind of plague victim—or maybe a rabid dog.

"Orderly, get this man some water."

"I already did. It's in his hand, and he's drinking it."

Matis gave him an acid glance. The orderly wasn't dumb, because he nodded and stood up.

"I'll go look for some in the back of the station," he said.

The orderly vanished. Specialist Matis watched him leave, then turned back to me. He leaned close—then froze.

We both heard a metallic click. It was the sound of my snap-rifle. I'd pulled the bolt back and planted the muzzle against his chest.

The bio glanced down at it, then met my eye.

"So it's you," he said. "Recruit McGill is the fugitive. They didn't give us a name. They say you're crazy, soldier. Did you know that?"

"Why, exactly?"

He looked a little confused by that one.

"Because you murdered Centurion Thompson, and you're holding onto a bad grow."

"Murdered?" I asked, smiling faintly. "How can you murder someone if they're already back to life? Isn't she up on *Corvus*, complaining about me?"

"No. She doesn't remember what happened, but she may in time. There were two orderlies who reported you. They found her body. They said you were crazy and a bad grow. That you had to be recycled."

Recycled. Every time I heard that word, I found I liked it even less.

"Recycling me *would* be murder," I said. "That's just the kind of excuse they need to have me 'accidentally' permed."

"What do you mean?"

"I've pissed off my primus and Centurion Thompson."

"I think you need to let us do what we must. Don't you want a new body that operates properly?"

"This one has done pretty well," I said.

But in truth, I *was* feeling sick. I wasn't sure if that was due to heat stroke or a bad grow, but I knew it was true.

I decided it didn't matter. I couldn't take the risk of being permed by some overzealous bio on *Corvus* who had an accident with my data.

"Are you going to shoot me or let me work on you?" the bio asked. He stared at me as if he didn't care which it was.

Maybe he really didn't care. If I shot him, at least he'd be out of this hellhole. I knew that a few of the guys had quietly offed themselves already. They figured a regrow back on *Corvus* was better than waiting here to be eaten by angry lizards. The officers would lean on them for that, of course. It was bad for morale.

I lowered my rifle. I took a deep breath and another swallow of water. The bio, for all his bravado, looked relieved. He sat down next to me.

"You said you don't think they'll revive you on *Corvus* if you die down here? What's so bad they'd perm you?"

I looked at him, wondering which crime I should confess. Shooting Galactics, messing with revival units—which was worse? After a moment of thinking, I decided to confess to more recent crimes. They made more sense, and I knew that not every bio agreed that secrets were worth the violation of their oath to heal the injured.

"I was ordered to retrieve the data storage of a stolen revival unit. I did so. Without it, many troops would have been permed. That list could have included you, I might add, if you'd stayed in that chamber and been slaughtered with the others."

Matis frowned. I could tell he didn't like what I was telling him. After a moment, he motioned for me to keep talking.

"I did as I was ordered," I said, leaving out the part about volunteering for the job. "When I got back and delivered the unit, Thompson was upset. I'd partially dismantled the unit, and she thought I'd seen too much of her specialized tech, I guess. She tried to take me out. I resisted—successfully."

He nodded slowly.

"Thompson has always been a little on the overzealous side," he said. "All of the people who operate the revival units are like that. Those machines—they're more valuable than everything else this legion has combined. Did you know that?"

"Yeah," I said. "I'm sure that we're all expendable in comparison. We should all be permed as far as Thompson is concerned."

"It's not that. I'm sure she was upset that the unit was lost and not retrieved intact. You were involved as a guard, right? That would make you partially at fault."

I nodded, seeing the logic in that. Thompson *had* wanted to kill me. Maybe she'd been blaming me for the loss of our greatest piece of tech.

Matis worked his tapper thoughtfully. "I think I can help. She doesn't remember anything about what happened. Maybe the next time you meet, you can make a better impression on her."

I thought about that. With water in my hand and cool air blowing in my face, I found I was able to get my mind working again. Whatever had come over me seemed to be fading.

"Okay, I'll try," I said. "What about the orderlies that are accusing me of murder?"

He got up and touched my shoulder. "Just let me talk to them. I have a good relationship—better than most. They see lots of strange things on the job. They know when to clam up for the good of the team."

He left me then, and I wished him luck in my head. I thought about what he'd said. Yes, I could imagine the orderlies saw *lots* of strange things in Legion Varus.

I got up, swayed for a moment, then picked up my helmet and snap-rifle. I began slowly walking up to the surface. I could hear the distinctive sounds of battle now. I had to get back to my unit.

I had high hopes that Specialist Matis would convince the orderlies to drop the whole thing. But I had the feeling that wasn't going to fix all my problems. I'd burned too many bridges with too many people.

And many of them, it seemed, were out to burn me in return.

-30-

Once the juggers started coming, it seemed they would never stop. They came in waves of about forty beasts each time. I wasn't up top for the first wave, which was easily repelled. But by the second wave, they seemed to be getting smarter. They came in every opening in the walls at once, not just randomly without coordination.

It took a lot of firepower to take even a single jugger down. By concentrating from our entrenched positions, we were able to do it easily when they came through one at a time. By the third wave, they were charging in every breach at the same time, running full speed. The first one or two monsters went down in a hail of fire, but the next ones scrambled over the dead and rushed forward. The piling bodies even seemed to help them, providing more cover for the next group.

I was there for the third wave—the one that reached our lines. It was strange to watch our positions being overrun. They were right on top of us, blotting out the twin suns for a moment of lavender shade. Up close, my snap-rifle wasn't much good. I could put out an eye, or hammer away until I destroyed a monster's gullet so thoroughly it couldn't breathe and died from catastrophic blood-loss, but really, it was the weaponeers that did most of the killing.

A weaponeer name Lund was nearby, protected by a fire team of five recruits, including Kivi and me. We were there to distract as much as anything else. When the juggers overran us, dipping down their massive jaws to snatch up and chew, I tried to get a big golden-scaled monster's attention, but failed.

Kivi hammered rounds into the thing's face, tearing apart a huge flaring nostril that fountained blood. She was next to me one second—and then she was gone. She'd been eaten while I'd survived.

I fought harder for a while after that. For some reason, every time they killed a friend I became a little crazy for a few minutes. Even though I knew the dead would live again, I was still angry.

Then the next snapping set of jaws came down. I was lying on my back now, staring up at four juggers with alien, pitiless eyes. Their tails lashed excitedly and their jaws dripped gore. They'd torn apart the recruit they'd managed to snatch up out of the demolished building we were sheltering in and were now returning to the spot, eager for more.

When the jaws came down for me, I was firing, of course, but the chattering rifle didn't seem to be having much effect. At the last moment I thrust my rifle up into the beast's mouth. I didn't know what else to do. It wasn't designed to have the killing power it needed to penetrate that much bone.

The jaws snapped shut early and the huge head withdrew, taking my snap-rifle with it. I was hauled up into a standing position by the strap, which was still wrapped around my arm.

I got a close look at the monster that had me. The scales were bright red—almost a crimson—and there was a long, old, ridged scar of gray skin running up its gut. At some point in this monster's past, it had been badly injured.

I was inches from the jugger's deadly maw. Dangling and cursing, I managed to slip free and fall back into shelter before the monsters could dismember me. I jeered at the lizard, which was still trying desperately to eat me.

"Retreat!" shouted Weaponeer Lund.

He hadn't been firing his belcher, and I'd been too busy to wonder why. Now, I didn't bother. Like the rest of them, I slithered down into the drilled holes and fell into the tunnels below. The juggers caught one more recruit by the foot and took him apart before we could make it to safety.

The weaponeer was on his com-link, reporting in. "We lost Twelve. Repeat, Bunker Twelve is gone. We've retreated underground."

I thought "bunker" was an extravagant name for the burnt, twisted pile of wreckage that we'd been crouching in for the last few hours. They'd once been real bunkers, with a roof and a door. Now, they all looked like blasted craters. The roof was gone; the walls were stubby and blackened. The interior was a mass of debris shoved into piles. Still, they worked like small forts scattered around the compound, and they were the best protection we had.

"My weapon overheated," the weaponeer reported.

I nodded as I climbed to my feet and dusted myself off. That would explain a lot. The black tube he still carried was emitting tendrils of steam and nothing else. I guess that the heat of the environment and the frequent firefights had overloaded the weapon. I hoped it wasn't permanently damaged.

Lund disconnected from the command channel by touching his tapper. He looked at us. "We're to report to central. They're hoping the techs can fix my unit. If they can, we're going back up there."

We looked at him grimly, and there were a few groans, but we didn't complain much. What was there to say? We had to fight them up there or wait for them to come down here. I preferred the open field of fire and the protection of the walls to these slimy tunnels. We all did.

We made it to the techs who looked over Weaponeer Lund's unit, and, after a few adjustments, declared it serviceable. We were trotting back down the tunnel to our former position when the next attack came.

"I can't believe it," Lund said as we followed him up into our bloody nest. "Why don't they all come at once? They keep coming in waves about a half-hour apart. That last wave would have finished us if they'd brought a hundred more sets of teeth to the party."

We had no answers for him. We were bone-tired, so we didn't even crack any jokes.

I checked the time. Lund was right, they'd been hitting us rhythmically every half-hour. In this last attack we'd lost

292

dozens of troops. I suspected there were only a few hundred of us left in all.

We set up again in the nest and tried to push the dead out of our positions. When the other bunkers had gotten our report, they'd unloaded on this location, killing one of our attackers in the center of the nest.

The body of a dead jugger is hard to dislodge. The weight was too much to move for only four people. We didn't have the strength to make it do more than flop and shift. We finally got it to the edge of our nest, but no farther. We decided to use the body as a shield and fire over it.

I had a new snap-rifle by this time, borrowed from a dead comrade. My own had been chewed into uselessness.

Once the big body was gone, we had the blasted bits to contend with. As I strained to shovel mounds of charred bone to make a new spot for myself at the edge of the crater, I reflected on my choices in life. Video games hadn't led me to expect this sort of experience. I found myself fantasizing about a quick death during the next go-round. I shook my head to clear it of such defeatist thoughts.

We all had a bad feeling about the fourth wave. The only good news was that the twin suns were beginning to go down. On Cancri-9, fighting in the dark was a blessing.

The fourth attack began like most of them did. But again, their tactics had changed. This time, when they all rushed in, they concentrated on just a few of the bunkers. Instead of sending three or four at each target, they clustered around the same spots where they'd had success before.

Ours was one of the lucky bunkers, naturally. Since they'd killed two recruits here and chased the rest of us underground, they decided to try their luck at the same spot again.

Weaponeer Lund did his best. He laid out heavy fire, melting two juggers before they even reached us. But our snap-rifles only brought down one more, and then we were overrun again.

"Retreat! Get down into—"

That was all we heard from Lund. We'd all been slithering backward, feeling with our boots for the holes that would allow us to drop back into the tunnel under this position and into relative safety. The weaponeer didn't make it. His head popped off in the jaws of the first saurian to reach the spot, the one that seemed to be leading the charge.

As I fell back into gloom of the tunnel below, I gazed up at the bloody, triumphant monster that had taken Lund's head. I realized with a jolt of recognition that I knew this monster. It had scales of crimson and a belly gouge along its gut. The mouth was painted red with Lund's blood. It looked proud of itself.

I fired a stream of pellets up out of the tunnel and into its face until it shied away.

Trotting toward the central gathering point where we were supposed to rally if we were pushed back, I began wondering: how had that same lizard returned to that same spot? When Leeson stepped into the rally point, I tried to get his attention. Leeson's face was white. He'd lost a hand and plenty of blood. I decided it was best to wait to bring up my thoughts. He might not live to see the next wave.

Specialist Matis came to work on him next. He soaked the stump of Leeson's wrist in orange fluid and I could tell it burned. Leeson was in agony. A needle appeared and plunged into his arm. After stiffening, Leeson's pain eased quickly.

"I could give you another, Adjunct," Matis said quietly.

Leeson looked up but shook his head. "That would be toxic."

Matis nodded his head. "Sometimes, a man has to know when he's beaten. Your hand is missing, sir. You can't keep fighting like this."

"Bullshit," slurred Leeson. "I'm a commander. I'm one of the last. I can give orders with one hand. Stop pumping happy-drugs into me."

"Yes sir," murmured Matis, as if he thought the adjunct was crazy.

My estimation of Leeson rose at that moment. He was going to stay here, fighting to beat the enemy. He was committed. It was hard not to admire that in an officer.

"What are you gawking at, Recruit? Never seen a man with one hand before?"

294

As a matter of fact, I had seen several during my short service in Legion Varus, but I decided not to bring it up. "Sir, I noticed something that I thought I should report. That is, if you are in good enough shape to listen."

"Talk all you want. I'm feeling fine."

To demonstrate, he waved his stump at me. Disinfectant fluids dribbled. I figured he was at least partially high from whatever Matis had shot into him. I wasn't sure if that was better than pain or not when it came to giving commands, but that wasn't my decision to make.

"I saw a red jugger up topside," I told him, "during the last attack. Then I saw him again just now."

Leeson frowned at me, concentrating on my words.

"So the hell what?" he asked. "They come in all kinds of colors. Saw three lime green bastards recently, running together like they were brothers."

"Right, sir. But bright red ones are rare. And this one had a scar, a belly-scar I recognized. He came at us twice, once this attack and once the last one. And he knew enough to kill our weaponeer right away this time."

"Yeah, so what? If you don't have a point, stop bothering me. I—"

"Sorry sir," I said quickly. "The point is that the report said all the lizards from the last wave were destroyed. All of them. If that's true, how can this one red bastard be back?"

Leeson stared at me for several seconds. I could tell he was trying to concentrate. "You're saying that we didn't get all of them. That at least one ran off."

"That's a possible answer, Adjunct."

"What the hell else could it be?" he snarled at me suddenly.

I suspected the initial euphoria of the drug Matis had injected was fading. He was wincing in pain again, as if he was being repeatedly stung. Leaning to his right side, he cradled his damaged limb.

"I'm sorry sir. I'll head back to my post."

"No point," he snapped. "We're abandoning Twelve. You have no weaponeer. I'm reassigning survivors to man other positions."

"Right. Who should pick up the weaponeer's tube, Adjunct?"

"Huh? Oh…nobody. Leave it down here. Has a bad actuator anyway, according to the techs."

I nodded disappointedly.

He laughed at me. "You wanted a chance to fire a heavy weapon, didn't you? Well, you don't have the kit or the training. You have to wear a heavy generator, and you have to know what you're doing. There's backwash, you know. You can't see it, but it's there. If you don't have training you're as likely to take out your own team with that thing as the enemy."

I didn't think it was all that difficult, but I nodded. "I'll be going, sir."

I turned to leave, but his good hand lashed out and gripped the fabric of my sleeve.

"McGill?" he asked, giving me an odd look. "If you see that red lizard of yours again—tell me about it."

I smiled. "Will do, sir."

As I walked across the rally point, Specialist Matis flagged me down.

"Good news, Recruit," he said.

"About the latest wave of lizards?" I asked. "Don't worry, they'll never kill us all."

He paused. "I don't know about that," he said, "but I've been in communication with Corvus. I've talked to the orderlies. They've dropped the charges. You're in the clear."

"That is good news. How did that happen?"

He shrugged and gave me a thin smile. "Sometimes people change their minds. At least now you know you can die down here in peace."

"Doesn't have to happen," I said. "We'll win."

"That's the spirit!" Matis said half-heartedly.

I could tell he didn't think we were going to win this one. I could easily see why. Each attack took out at least a dozen men—more each time. At this rate, we'd be down to a handful huddling underground by morning. Then, the smaller saurians would infiltrate the tunnels and finish us off.

"Hold on a second," he called out to me as I turned to go back to my post.

"Specialist?"

He gave me a strange look. "I could take care of it now, you know," he said quietly. "One injection and it will all be over. You're fighting on a bad grow anyway. Let me fix the mistake."

I opened my mouth, then closed it again. I saw he had a needle in his hand. The syringe was a large one and it dribbled amber liquid.

"I'm fine," I said.

"Hey!" roared a voice.

We startled and looked toward Leeson, who wandered closer. He glared at Matis. "What are you, some kind of ghoul?" he demanded.

"I'm sorry sir, but I'm sure I don't know—"

"Yeah, yeah," Leeson grumbled. "Leave my man alone. I need every hand topside. If you offer another soldier a free trip into space, I'll put you on report."

Matis made a prim face. He looked as if he smelled something putrid. "That won't be necessary, Adjunct."

"Make sure it isn't."

I left quickly after that. What was it with bios and killing people? They seemed to want to offer up death as some kind of benefit. I supposed that to them it looked like a good thing. This battle was hopeless and vicious. Wasn't a needle and a quick, heart-stopping injection better than getting torn apart by hungry monsters?

But, as I reached my new post, I began to wonder. Matis' expression hadn't been kind, it had been devious. He'd been hiding something. Why tell me I was in the clear then offer me a quick death? Could it be he'd lied about me being in the clear?

I wasn't sure what his motives were, but I decided I didn't want to die just now.

I reached my new post and slithered up into position. There were a number of dead juggers and troops around, and I didn't like the look of things. This bunker had been overrun more than once, just as my last one had. The only difference was this position still had an active weaponeer.

"Weaponeer Borges?" I asked. "Can I do a quick patrol? I want to check my firing ranges and entry points."

"Out there?" he asked, his voice indicating he thought I was crazy. He was a beefy guy with eyebrows that came together into one big, black caterpillar when he frowned, which he was doing now. "You're nuts. That pee-shooter of yours isn't going to do anything but piss them off, anyway."

"Still, Specialist," I said, "I'd like to see what's nearby before the next wave. They aren't due for ten minutes."

Borges huffed at that. "Enemies don't keep appointments, Recruit. But okay, if you want to be first on the buffet this time, I'll let you. Keep in mind, if I see you jump into a lizard's mouth just to get out of here, you're going on report."

"Right, sir," I said, and walked away across the compound.

I heard Borges and the others laughing behind me. I didn't care. At some point, every soldier caught up in a long battle stops caring about the small stuff.

It took me a few minutes, and I was beginning to get antsy by the time I found what I was looking for. A different corpse, one I recognized, was near one of the entrances on a pile of juggers stacked three high.

It was a crimson lizard. I shined my belt light on it to be sure, and took several snaps. The ridged belly-scar was precisely the same as the last two times I'd seen this exact enemy.

What the hell was going on?

-31-

I was still out eyeballing the mysterious red jugger when the next attack came. I wasn't sure, but it seemed early to me. Maybe the lizards were losing patience.

The first clue came with the sound of scrabbling along the walls outside. We didn't have scouts out there anymore because there weren't enough troops left alive for that. We didn't have cameras on the walls either, as they'd all been knocked out. Since our techs weren't even allowed to fly spy drones, we were blind.

When I heard the stealthy sounds of saurians on the move, I didn't bother waiting around. I sprinted for the crater-like shelter we'd been assigned.

"Incoming!" I shouted on the squad channel.

Ahead of me, the guys in the bunker scrambled into position.

"Are you sure, McGill?" demanded Specialist Borges.

I didn't bother to answer. The enemy was proving me right. They were pouring in through the damaged walls, and this time they weren't fooling around.

Right before they hit, the sky lit up overhead. Artillery—it couldn't be anything else.

When this long battle had begun days earlier, both sides had held off on using big guns because we couldn't risk killing the Nairbs. Now that they were absent, we still hadn't deployed so much as a mortar. I knew that, in our case, it was because we hadn't been issued any since the heavy troops had withdrawn. For the saurians, I suspected they didn't want to be seen using a weapon we didn't have. They wanted to prove they could beat us without superior arms.

So far, they were pulling it off. I was definitely feeling the burn. We were losing this fight, one death at a time.

I dove into the bunker and small arms fire splattered the burnt walls all around me. I didn't know juggers could carry guns...

"Raptors!" Borges shouted. "Hundreds of them! This is it!"

He was right. The enemy force wasn't made up of all juggers this time. They were coming in with regular saurian troops. At least they weren't armored, but that didn't make me feel much better. The smaller ones were smart and just as deadly. What they didn't have in sheer size and power they made up for with cunning and, in this case, weaponry.

Of the two types of lizards I'd met up with on this godforsaken hole of a planet, I think I preferred to fight with the juggers. I felt less paranoid when I fought them—I think that's why. They came in charging hard, and they either died or you did. They'd terrified me at first—but the fear had lessened as I grew accustomed to fighting with them. You didn't have to worry about getting taken out by a sniper or an infiltrator who'd snuck in behind your lines.

Wriggling like a frightened snake into my position right over the legs of my comrades, I put my snap-rifle up and sought a target. The others were rattling away, providing suppressing fire. This seemed to be slowing the enemy down. They were working their way toward us, dashing from one broken scrap of puff-crete to the next.

Using the night scope, I could see they weren't heavily armored. They were light troops, like our own. I thought about that for a second—and it made sense. They'd been watching us for years, copying our techniques and apparently some of our organization, as well. I'd seen both unarmored light saurians and heavily armored pros. These definitely fell into the former category. That was a relief because I knew my gun could kill them.

The second I saw a snout, I opened up. Firing short bursts, I forced the raptor to jerk back—but then he made a sprint for another, closer piece of cover. Around him, a group of his comrades began to fire back at us. They sprayed our bunker with rounds. The bullets sparked green against our sheltering walls when seen through my scope. Lizards weren't great marksmen, but I realized they were covering the one that was on the move.

I took a chance. I lifted my head up and held the trigger down. The recoil was jumpy on my weapon as it went into full-auto mode. Fighting to control it, I swept it after the saurian who was exposed. How that bastard could run!

Fortunately, not even a sprinting three hundred pound lizard can outrun a sliver from a snap-rifle. I hit him a dozen times, and he fell in a tumbling heap. It took ten times as much fire to bring down a jugger because there was so much more meat and bone on them.

This seemed to piss off the others behind him. They lashed our position with fire, and we were forced to duck and wait it out.

"Hold, hold, NOW!" shouted Borges, timing the enemy tactics. He called it perfectly. The moment he said "NOW", we wriggled back up into our firing positions and found them advancing, firing sporadically into our bunker. They'd gotten brave when we hadn't returned fire for a while.

We mowed them. The weaponeer finally unleashed the power of his big tube, shortening up the focus and sweeping the beam laterally. At least ten of them went down, their bodies seared with huge stripes of blackened flesh. They thrashed and made strange, croaking sounds.

I ignored the ones he nailed with the plasma sweep and poured rounds into those that were still on their feet. It was over in fifteen seconds, I'd say. Broken, the enemy fled for cover in every direction.

We cheered and high-fived one another in the bunker. Borges slapped me on the helmet twice, roaring: "Did you see that? Did you see that?"

I assured him that I did. But I wasn't in any mood for celebrating. I used my scope to scan the other bunkers to our sides and rear.

"Specialist!" I shouted. "Left flank, I think they breached Five!"

Everyone shut up, slithered back into their spots and swung their weapons to the west. The sounds of slaughter came in over our headsets as Borges connected to command chat and piped it to our helmets.

I wasn't happy he'd decided to share the input. Men and women screamed and hyperventilated into their microphones as they died. A few times, I thought I heard crunching sounds. We all did, and it was making us wince.

"Let's engage," he said.

I couldn't argue with him. Bunker Five was pretty much gone, and the odds of us hitting a living human target were low. It looked like a feeding frenzy over there. We reloaded as quickly as we could, shifted on our bellies, and waited for the signal.

Borges announced our entry into the fight with a direct beam into the pack of them. It punched a hole through the mass of bodies which came out the other side. We supported his big gun with our sprays of bullets. Caught from behind and exposed, the enemy melted. They broke off the attack and scattered for cover.

A few of them, however, dove into the mess in the bunker and returned fire. I was shocked to see our own snap-rifles used against us. Not every saurian was armed, but they were resourceful. They figured out the mechanism and forced us to respect the incoming hail of metal. It wasn't well-aimed, but it was accurate enough to make us hunker down.

"I wish our rifles had friend-or-foe recognition on them," Borges said. "If we built them, they would!"

I hugged the ground and found I agreed with him. But I knew we couldn't build our own accelerator rifles. Advanced weaponry was to be produced by the manufacturing planet that held the patent, which, in this case, was a world called "Coventry" by humanity—and some unpronounceable series of clicks by the native population of insects. Unless a competing race could prove they had a better product, no one in this sector of the galaxy was allowed to sell even a knock-off. Earth would have liked to copy and steal the tech, but we weren't allowed to make or distribute anything similar.

Since they had to accommodate a variety of races, snap-rifles were made to fit an average-build humanoid—or just about anything with hands or claws. They were a bit too small for us, and even smaller in the claws of a saurian, but I supposed that gave them the broadest possible market. They were fine weapons, that much I had to admit.

While we exchanged fire with the enemy that had taken Bunker Two, disaster struck. We'd all focused on the breach in our lines, wanting to repel it. Borges was on the command line talking to Leeson and following orders. The officers wanted the enemy out of that bunker and pushed back. Apparently, we'd lost about a quarter of our entrenched positions.

Unfortunately, the enemy had other ideas. The juggers we'd been expecting in the first place finally made their appearance. Somehow, we'd all thought the enemy had shifted tactics, using armed saurians instead of the regularly timed waves of juggers. That turned out not to be the case. The juggers showed up right when it looked like we were going to win.

The sound of their pounding feet, each step slamming down with around two thousand pounds of force, alerted us. I was the second guy to notice the enemy charge, squirming around to face the new unexpected threat. The first guy who saw them fired about a dozen rounds, then simply screamed and died a moment later, chomped by jaws as big as a bulldozer's.

I didn't even know his name. That made me feel bad as I watched him die. I thought, in a strange, accelerated-time-sense sort of way, that a man *should* know who is fighting and dying next to him. Sure, I'd only been assigned to this squad a few hours ago, but I still felt I should know the guy's name.

The jugger was a midnight blue female as big as a truck. Probably, her vast size had gotten her here faster, ahead of the pack. In triumph, she ate the nameless trooper next to me, taking the upper torso and the head into her mouth and crunching down. Legs dangled and blood ran. I heard a triumphant, burbling sound of pleasure coming from the vast throat.

Then the jugger was blasted apart. Borges had gotten his big tube around and aligned. Hit point-blank, the blue giant died on her feet. The beam was so violent at this close range, part of the lizard's skull was missing.

Before the jugger's body hit the ground, however, more of them came charging in after her. They seemed endless. Behind them, like excited cattle dogs, came the smaller lizards we'd routed earlier. They hid behind their bigger cousins. At least I knew that they respected our firepower.

The battle went from bad to worse. I'd been overrun before, and I can say a man fights differently in the final moments, when he knows he's going to die. Intellectually, you might know that you're going to be revived later, that you're going to come back live another day. Even in my case, where my odds were iffy after having personally pissed off every bio aboard *Corvus*, I still had that possible ace in the hole.

But when you're about to be eaten, it just doesn't matter. The basic, more primitive mind inside all of us takes hold. You scream, you roar at the top of your lungs and curse and possibly wet yourself. But you don't even know it's happening because you're too busy laying out every ounce of firepower into every soft alien belly you see in front of you.

That's what I did. I would like to say I did some kind of genius move, something no one had foreseen. Something I didn't think of until this final, fateful moment. But I didn't. I was on my knees, my weapon in my hands, chattering out every sliver of metal it could until the magazine ran dry. After it was empty, I kept the trigger down and the cylinder kept obediently whirling around, never jamming but firing dry. I was spraying nothing but spit which ran down my chin inside my helmet.

I could barely see when I finally figured out I was empty. My helmet had fogged up a little on the inside. Had my AC quit again? It didn't matter.

Three of the big lizards were down, as were most of my squaddies. Only Borges and I were still in one piece, and the world was full of giant lizards.

For a few seconds, the battle broke around us and the lizards frenzied on other bunkers. Maybe we'd been too hard of a nut to crack. Or maybe, they'd seen another one overwhelmed and were anxious to get in on the finish. I looked right and left. Bunker Five was ancient history. Seven and Nine were nothing but a churning mass of scaly flesh. Raised tails whipped excitedly over the defeated team strongholds like victorious flags.

I watched the lizards run around in circles looking for a way into the press to feed. The way their legs pumped, casting up dust and blood behind them, was amazing to see. They came at you with such singularity of purpose, with a berserker rage in their hearts and eyes. I knew it was different for them—they only had one life to live. If I'd had more time to think, I might have admired them for their perfect savagery. They weren't animals—they knew what they were doing. They were going to kill us or die trying.

Then, I saw *the one*. The crimson jugger. I'd seen a few red ones before him, and I'd reflexively checked, but I'd never seen the telltale scar on the belly.

This one had the color, and the scar. He was nearby, trying to get a spot to eat at the smorgasbord that had once been Bunker Nine.

I had the clarity of mind to turn on my suit recorder and aim it at the big red bastard, but I only got a glimpse of him before he disappeared in the pack.

"Only…one…chance," Borges said. He stood next to me, panting and in pain. He held his right arm oddly, and I surmised he'd been injured.

I'd expected him to call a retreat. I fully expected to be ordered to slither down into the tunnels.

"Down the chute?" I asked hopefully.

He shook his head. "No good. Officers said…it's no good down there."

I felt a chill, despite the blistering heat. If the enemy was down in the tunnels—well, this was over. We'd lost the battle.

"I've got to shorten up the focus on my projector, McGill," he said, pausing to gulp air. "You have to help me."

305

It took me a second to figure out what he was trying to do. He wanted to dial the tube to a shorter burst range. Up close the belcher would be like a cannon loaded with grapeshot. Turned upon rioters it didn't do as much damage, but it couldn't miss and it could hit everything at once.

Then I saw why he needed my help. His right arm wasn't just injured—it was missing. At some point, one of the monsters had run off with it as a trophy. His suit had automatically sealed the wound so he wouldn't bleed out, but he wasn't able to adjust his weapon.

I wriggled close to him and let go of my rifle. I began turning the big circular ring on the outside of the tube. It was hard to move, and I was surprised at the grunting strength I had to apply.

"Hurry up," Borges said, "they're running out of food over there."

I worked harder, and soon it clicked.

"That's as far as it goes," I said.

He nodded, moving stiffly and slowly. He was in shock, probably, but still in the game.

"Going to aim high. Can't kill them on this setting, but I can blind them."

I liked the idea of that. It sounded like an excellent last-ditch tactic.

We didn't have to wait long to try it out. As if a signal had been sounded—and perhaps it had—the team milling around Bunker Nine turned as a group and charged our way.

I fired my rifle, having reloaded in the meantime, but it had no noticeable effect. The enemy was soon swarming around us, and Borges got to his feet and let loose. He lifted that heavy tube with one arm, and I was impressed.

"Down, McGill!" he screamed.

I flattened myself in the darkest gouge I could find in the bunker while Borges burned them. He aimed high, just like he said he would, and the monsters were caught in a flare of wide-angled radiation.

They howled and raged, thundering around us in instant confusion. Some fell and thrashed, eyes welded shut. Others went mad, snapping and biting their fellows in their agony.

Borges was howling too—with laughter. He spun around, spraying out heat and pain toward any lizard who dared to come close enough.

The attack broke. They staggered away, tripping and falling. Borges still laughed and coughed, then laughed again.

But suddenly, he stiffened. I saw it in his eyes, even before I registered the spray of pellets that had ripped through his body. He'd been standing all this time, exposed. At least ten rounds had torn through his body and come out the far side. They'd finally taken him down.

He fell with his eyes open in disbelief, but a grin was still frozen on his face.

I realized I was alone. Everyone else was dead.

So much for being a bad grow, I thought to myself. *I've outlived them all.*

-32-

When Borges dropped his weapon, it had rolled out into the open. I grabbed at the tube, snagging the strap and reeling it back into the bunker. I fumbled with it. My snap-rifle was ineffective anyway and almost out of ammo. Borges' tube was all I had left.

Clamping the tube between my knees, I used both hands to wrench at the focusing dial. It was stiff and would barely move. Something in the mechanism was broken, or the designers hadn't wanted operators to fool with the range settings unless they really wanted to.

Outside, I could see the lizards milling, taking cover. Some had fled, but I could tell a few were rallying. I couldn't see any more tails or hear the chatter of human weapons. Only a few places were actively firing, and that was sporadic. I tried to talk to whoever might be in charge, but I didn't get any response on my com link. That was a very, very bad sign.

I tried not to think about the rest of the cohort. This was about me and the last double-wave of angry reptiles. I told myself that if I killed them all or drove them off, I'd worry about the rest of my unit afterward.

I considered slipping down into the tunnels—but I knew that wasn't going to work. I'd already seen them down there, flittering by in the dark. They were trotting to and fro probably looking for holdouts and survivors.

No, I didn't want to die in the trenches. Out here, I had a clear field of fire, and at least I'd meet my end under an open sky. I wasn't sure if the bio specialists up on *Corvus* would revive me, anyway. If they got another chance to correct the error many thought my continued existence to be, I figured they might take it.

I cranked on the tube, getting the focusing dial to move, but slowly. I cursed and growled in frustration. Maybe on the world where this damned weapon was made, everyone had three hundred pounds of torque in their hands or claws. I had no idea why it was so hard to move, but I was impressed by the weaponeers that used them. No wonder they were mostly big guys with powerful arms.

I heard the telltale click as it snapped into position at last. Configured for longer range, I immediately employed the tube by heaving it onto my shoulder and sighting in the direction of the surviving juggers. I saw a tail sticking out from behind a broken column, and I depressed the firing stud.

The results shocked me. The tube rocked in my hands. I hadn't expected recoil. But I knew that the most powerful of lasers and particle beam weapons gave a small kick. Anything that hurled mass and energy out of one end pushed in the opposite direction.

The tail was only scorched, but it was withdrawn quickly. I smiled and went hunting for the sniper who had killed Borges.

He found me first, spraying a shower of bullets my way. I ducked and waited, counting to three. Then I popped up again and sighted quickly.

Just as I'd hoped, the saurian had risen up, coming out of cover to get a better shot. Maybe he'd thought he'd hit me. Whatever the case, I caught him full in the chest with a focused beam of energy. He did a backflip and came down in three smoking pieces.

I was ready for the recoil this time, and I had my arms wrapped around the unwieldy tube. The weapon felt like it wasn't built for humans to operate, and I understood that more clearly every time I tried to use it.

Once I had control of the tube again, I looked up and my jaw dropped. A shape loomed over me. A jugger had come up

309

out of nowhere—probably from behind me while I was firing toward the sniper.

I knew right off I was screwed. I was lying in a shallow scratch in the pockmarked courtyard, totally exposed to the teeth of the giant that closed in for the kill. Compounding my sense of shock and dismay, I saw that this jugger was special— the ridged scar on his belly was unmistakable. This was my mystery lizard, back to fight me once again.

My first instinct was to attempt to wriggle down a hole. I got my boots in—but I could tell right away I wasn't moving fast enough.

I lifted the heavy tube and interposed it between me and the jugger. This didn't impress him. He lunged and those huge jaws came down. I saw the wet flesh inside. The mouth was so huge! I was about to be swallowed.

But the jugger's snapping jaws came up short. The tube had hit the back of his throat. Instinctively, he shut those massive jaws. My hands were almost chomped along with the tube.

I had no idea what the tube was made of, but it didn't buckle. It didn't even dent. Instead, a dozen four-inch fangs snapped and blood gushed over me—the jugger's blood.

My fingers sought the firing stud, but I couldn't find it. I realized in horror that the trigger mechanism was inside the jugger's mouth, enclosed with countless snaggled teeth. A roar washed over me, and I knew the big lizard wasn't happy.

Then he jerked up his head and I felt the tube being torn from my hands. I scrambled to hold on. It was hard, because there was a hot slurry of spit and blood all over that tube and nothing much to hold onto. But somehow I managed to get one hand wrapped up in the strap and the other hooked on the adjustment knobs.

The jugger reared up, lifting the tube high, and I went with it. I found myself dangling about fifteen feet up and looking down at a beast which was eager to finish its meal.

I knew what was going to happen next, and it did: the jugger opened its mouth. I felt myself sliding into the teeth, following the tube which was two thirds of the way down into that gaping maw.

I only had one split-second chance, and I took it: I reached my hands farther along the tube and touched the firing stud.

Fortunately, the weapon had been primed and charged. At my touch, it shot a gout of energy directly down the throat of the jugger.

He'd gotten more than he'd bargained for, I suspected. Dead on his feet, the monster swayed and toppled. His guts were a steaming mess on the ground.

When he went down, he thrashed for a moment. I found myself pinned under him. Something hit my head, and my helmet dented and the faceplate shattered.

I laid there on my back, under a thousand pounds of shivering reptile. My breath came in ragged gasps. The jugger had stopped breathing altogether.

I tried to move. I tried to free myself, but I couldn't. My com-link was either broken or there wasn't anyone listening.

After a period of struggling, I paused and listened.

The battlefield was quiet now. I couldn't hear a thing, even with my visor gone and the open wet heat of Steel World's night air rolling into my face.

I don't know how long I laid there. It might have been an hour or ten minutes. When you're trapped under a mass of flesh, it warps your perspective.

Finally, however, I saw something new. Lights glimmered and played over the ground around Bunker Five. I blinked and recognized the vehicle. It was an air car—a nice shiny one that reminded me of rich, snotty aliens.

Could it be the Galactics? Or maybe the Nairbs? It made sense either way. They were inspecting the damage, tallying the count. Who had left more bodies on this bloody field, now that it was over, them or us?

I felt an urge to do something. Not so much to get rescued—I didn't really expect them to care about me one way or another. But I wanted them to know my side wasn't out of this yet.

I reached down and drew my sidearm. It wasn't much, sort of like a snap-rifle with less power, range or accuracy. But it did fire pellets when you needed a last-ditch weapon.

Very carefully, I sighted on the air car. I squeezed the trigger four times—maybe five.

Orange sparks pinged off the bottom of the ship. I knew I'd hit it at least. It wasn't enough to damage the vehicle, just to get their attention.

The response came about a second later. The air car wobbled then lifted rapidly. I smiled. Maybe it had been the Galactics after all. They'd been shot down before, and quite possibly they were gun-shy today.

I relaxed and considered passing out. But I wanted to see what was going to happen, so I held on to consciousness with an effort of will. The weight of what amounted to a dead dinosaur lying over a third of my body made every breath a struggle. Already, my feet were numb. I knew I wasn't going to last the night.

Stealthily, the air car returned. I opened one eye and wondered if I'd been dozing. Was I dreaming now?

No. The air car played a quiet light over my part of the courtyard. Everything was still. A few bodies twitched now and again, a testament to the raw vigor of these reptiles. They often moved and tremored hours after their apparent deaths.

I could see the light only because a scrap of my shattered night vision visor was still operating. It caught the gleam of their lights, showing them as a soft green glow. I wasn't sure if they were using infrared or what, but it was catching the attention of my dying suit.

I lifted the pistol again. So as not to frighten the weasels, I shot a few bullets in the air when their light touched me. They had to be able to detect that.

They did. The light stopped drifting and focused upon me. I wondered if it was burning my retinas like any infrared laser—but I was too tired and injured to care.

I dropped my pistol to my side and lifted my gloved hand to wave at them. Then, I gave them the finger. Vigorously.

The beam seemed to study me for a full minute. I grew tired of shaking my middle finger at them, so I let my hand fall to my side. I was getting sleepy again, but I didn't want to miss whatever happened next so I struggled to stay awake.

Slowly, cautiously, the air car drifted closer. I watched with vague interest, feeling a little light-headed.

Finally, the ship landed nearby, and the hatch opened. A familiar shape emerged.

It was a Nairb. It had to be—either that, or someone had taught a terrestrial seal to fly and painted it a globular green.

I considered shooting the alien, I really did. I wasn't in my best of moods. These guys had a lot of gall, floating around counting bodies. They never died for their planet. They sat in posh offices and made snooty judgments about other people they barely understood.

But, sadly, my own better judgment kicked in. I simply waited as the creature approached.

A translator box clicked and rasped.

"You are a human combatant?"

"Yes," I said. My voice sounded weak, so I cleared my throat and tried again. "Yes! I'm Recruit McGill, of Legion Varus. Please be careful, there is a battle in progress."

The Nairb cocked its head and looked around for a moment. "The battle has ended."

"For the moment," I said, "but although the saurians have been defeated time and again, they always seem to come back."

The Nairb studied me. Another of its kind slithered out of the air car. They spoke together. I gathered they were debating the situation. I lay quietly on my back under the crushing weight of the lizard. I figured that whether I was about to die or not, I'd at least managed to upset the meticulous plans of the Nairbs one more time. That was worth a lot to me.

"I'm sorry," I said loudly. "I can't guarantee your safety if you stay here any longer. As I said, this is a dangerous region."

"There must be some mistake," said the second Nairb, speaking to me for the first time. "Your challengers claimed victory some time ago. They left the field victorious."

"Ha!" I said. "Indeed, there has been a mistake. We've beaten them time and again. It is a common tactic with losers who wish to save face: retreat and claim victory."

More chatter went back and forth between the two. I tried to shift into a more comfortable position but was unable to do so. Finally, they returned their attention to me.

313

"You are not a legal combatant. You are disabled."

"Not so. I'm pinned under a fallen enemy, that's true, but I'm not dead. I'm still dangerous. I shot your air car, didn't I?"

"Demonstrate your status. Mobility is required to be considered able-bodied."

He had me there, and I knew it. My mind was foggy, but it managed to come up with a card to play.

"Remove this corpse from my person," I said, "and I'll show you what I'm capable of."

They chatted about that for a time, then returned to their ship. I called after them, and as their air car floated upward, I drew my pistol again. I cursed them for leaving me for dead.

Just as I was about to fire again, aiming for the windows this time—something happened. I felt a tug at the mass of dead flesh that held me down.

A few more seconds passed, and the tug grew stronger. I felt myself being pulled with it. I howled with pain. The jugger lifted into the air. How were they doing this? Some kind of focused force field? Some of our troops had shields, but this was something different. The Nairbs were a rich folk indeed.

Just as quickly as the field had grown and gripped me, it let go. The body of the dead jugger slipped away from me. I fell on my face. My feet wouldn't hold me. I was on my knees, panting, freed but in agony. My pulse pounded in my head and purple splotches darkened my vision. I was close to passing out, I could feel it.

I gasped like a fish in a boat. I tried to control my breathing and gently rolled myself into a sitting position.

I found the two Nairbs staring at me. They studied me with interest.

"It's moving."

"That proves nothing," the translator rasped, interpreting their speech.

I put my hands under me and lifted myself onto my knees again. The Nairbs shuffled backwards on their flippers.

"I'm fine," I lied. "Now do you believe me? Score me as alive. Legion Varus wins."

"Wins? No, not at all. There is no chance your people have won the challenge. That has already been determined. Your

314

losses are greater by several hundred corpses. We are only trying to decide if you should be counted as dead, wounded or able. Our accounting must be complete, and accurate."

I sighed. *Body count.* Wasn't that what they'd said it was all about?

Still, I'm a stubborn man. Just ask anyone. I decided I would have to prove myself able.

I tried to stand up. The Nairbs backed up further. I stumbled, went to one knee, and stood again, hissing between my teeth.

"There," I said. "I'm mobile. Thanks for the help. Now, I'm afraid I'm going to have to ask you to leave. I'm going to have to kill a large number of saurians to reverse the score."

They made an odd sound. Maybe they were laughing—I really wasn't sure.

"Impossible. The odds of success are infinitesimal. Our ruling stands, and there will be no time extension."

"I didn't want to believe it, but the doubters were right," I said. "The corruption runs deep here on Steel World!"

"Your references are confusing to the point of being rendered meaningless."

"What I'm saying is, you Nairbs don't like my kind, and your judgment is slanted against us."

"Corruption! Yes, now I understand the accusation. Do you have any proof of your claims?"

"You have awarded victory to the defeated. I'm here, I'm able-bodied, and the enemy has withdrawn. Therefore, they are the losers."

"Insignificant. The accounting has been precise. No human survives here other than you. During the conflict, you were badly beaten."

I picked up my pistol painfully. The Nairbs watched me but did not retreat. I don't think they knew how very, very close I was to shooting them both dead. With difficulty, I controlled myself and kept the weapon at my side.

"All right," I said, shuffling toward the dead jugger. I pointed to his red scales and the ridged scar on his belly. "Take a look at this. This same exact lizard has attacked this

315

compound over and over. He nearly got me the last time, but I killed him yet again."

The Nairbs looked but didn't seem too impressed. "All of these life forms resemble one another."

"Take a DNA sample then. It's the same damned jugger."

"DNA sample? Unnecessary. We'll simply check the molecular manufacturing imprint on the cells. Much simpler and more accurate."

"Molecular...?" I began, and trailed off. "Are you saying the revival machines leave an imprint inside each body they produce?"

"Absolutely. Omitting the imprint would be a violation of Galactic Law."

"Huh," I said, thinking about my own body. Were my cells *stamped* inside with some tiny, sub-microscopic mark? Somehow, that idea made me feel a little sick. I shook it off and pressed my case.

"What are you going to do about this injustice?" I asked. "I demand to know."

"Are you lodging a formal grievance?"

"Yes," I said quickly. "Yes, I'm lodging a formal grievance."

They both made unhappy gargling sounds. I got the feeling that was extra work for them. I smiled tightly at the thought.

Although it hurt, I managed to locate and show them another of the bodies with the same scar. Then I transmitted images I'd taken with my suit, all showing the same saurian dead with the same scar. For the first time, they seemed interested and paid close attention.

When I was finished, I went in for the kill.

"There you have it, then," I said. "The enemy has been cheating. They used advanced revival technology to lower their body count. Surely, you see they must be disqualified."

One of the two Nairbs made a sniffing sound. "By no means. This will go into our report, but it is by no means grounds for disqualification. Your forces use the exact same technology to an abusive degree. Did you really believe we were unaware of that fact?"

316

I paused, mouth open. I had naturally assumed they didn't know we were doing it. In fact, we'd made a living out of abusing revival machines.

"A loophole in an accounting system must rightfully apply to all sides," said the Nairb. "At least until the loophole is closed."

I didn't like the sound of that. Could the Nairbs be advocating banning revival machines? That would mean every death Legion Varus suffered would be a permanent one. The mere thought was chilling.

I wanted to say a thousand things to those two Nairbs. I wanted to shoot them and pound them with my fists. I wanted to find out if their guts were as green as their exterior membranes.

But I did nothing. I stood there, swaying slightly on my feet like a drunk. Overhead, the sky was beginning to lighten. I was vaguely surprised—I *had* made it to see the dawn. I turned and looked up at the sky. Soon, the blazing twin eyes of Cancri would rise in what we called the east.

"Why, then, did you act like you cared?" I demanded. "Why'd you have me show you pictures and bodies?"

I turned painfully back around to face them—but they were gone. I watched in shock as the second one's green tail vanished into the air car. A moment later, it lifted off into the sky.

The suns rose as they always did, painfully bright. I squinted and lifted my pistol—but I lowered it again. Shooting at their ship a few more times wasn't going to gain me anything. We'd lost the challenge. It was over.

I heaved a sigh, and began hobbling around the stinking, corpse-littered battlefield. I finally found a body I recognized: the nameplate identified him as Adjunct Leeson.

I took off my helmet and replaced it with the officer's gear. The fit was a little snug, but it worked. I quickly found the command channel and beamed it up into the sky.

After a few minutes I managed to get none other than Centurion Graves on the channel.

"Sir?" I said. "This is Recruit McGill reporting in from the spaceport. I'm alive and requesting extraction."

317

"McGill? It figures. What are you doing alive down there?"

"Defending the spaceport sir, as ordered."

"We lost that battle, McGill. Didn't anyone tell you?"

"The Nairbs tried to. I couldn't talk them out of it, even at the point of a gun."

Graves was silent for several seconds. I thought he might start screaming at me, but he didn't. He chuckled instead. I could not recall ever having heard him laugh before.

"You're some piece of work, McGill. I'm getting something over the exec channel about the Nairbs. Something about a formal charge. Would that be your doing?"

"I did my best, sir."

"You've got a brass pair, kid. All right, I'm recalling you right now."

"When is the lifter due?"

"What lifter? I haven't got the time or resources for a lifter."

"Well then what—" I began, but trailed off. The channel was dead. I couldn't raise him again.

I stood around after that, watching the suns rise. I figured maybe Graves had an air car of his own or some other conveyance.

I was wrong.

The missile caught the corner of my eye. I barely had time to turn my head and face it. Streaking right down from orbit, it must have been riding my signal all the way from space. I had only a second or two to even realize what it was. The contrail, the tiny glimmer of fire…

They blew me up. One second, I was standing there on the rugged surface of Steel World, soaking up the harsh rays of the Cancri dawn—and the next I was broken down into my component atoms.

I hadn't even tried to run, or seek shelter. What would have been the point?

I'd been recalled to *Corvus*—the hard way.

318

-33-

I emerged from the revival unit dizzy and confused. In my mind, the missile was still coming down. That moment in which I'd realized what Graves had done was still fresh in my head.

"That prick," I mumbled, struggling to open my eyes.

"What have we got?" asked a voice. The voice was female and I thought I recognized it, but I wasn't completely sure...

"Stats are good. No toxins. No warping. I think we have a good grow this time."

"We'd better."

A good grow. Such strange words. They echoed through my mind bringing waves of relief. For the last few days I'd been haunted by the specter of a damaged body. It had been like being told you had a fatal dose of radiation or cancer—or both.

My elation slowly shifted back into anger. I'd worked so hard to stay alive. What was the point of all that desperate effort if Graves was just going to blow me up at the end?

With a growl of animal intensity, I tried to get off the tray they had me on. The tray was like a tongue sticking out of the mouth-like opening of the revival unit. When I tried to get up, I bumped my head on the upper manifold.

"What was that?" asked an orderly. "Was that a muscle spasm?"

"Sort of, he's trying to get up," said the female. I recognized her now: Anne Grant. The last time, she had revived me illegally.

"Remarkable," said the orderly.

"McGill always has ideas of his own."

I found a strap around my waist, holding me onto the tray. Fumbling blindly, I managed to get the buckle off and half-fell, half-rolled onto the ground. For the first time my eyes fluttered open. I struggled to speak.

"Specialist Grant," I said, slurring my words. "Anne—is that you?"

"Yes James, I'm here."

"Help me up. I've got to get up and move out."

"Where are you headed? The battle is over, Recruit."

"Not for me," I said, finally getting to my feet with help from both of them. They had my elbows on either side. "I'm on a mission. I'm going to kill Centurion Graves."

That caused them both to chuckle. "You're not the first to awaken with that thought firmly in mind, you know."

"Let go of me!" I demanded.

They did it, and I was immediately sorry. I fell to my knees without their support to steady me.

Dying and coming back to life is a strange experience. I can say with certainty I've never gotten used to the process. It's kind of like awakening from a week-long coma. You're disoriented, weak, and usually pissed-off, in my case.

Specialist Grant knelt beside me. I was on all fours, panting.

"Would it help if I told you Graves is pretty happy with you? He's talking about awarding you a silver nova."

I looked at her with bleary eyes. She was pretty, but it was as if I was looking at her underwater.

"A medal? Why?"

"Valor. Success. The usual thing."

"Huh," I said and tried to get to my feet again. I cursed and raved and pushed their hands away. Struggling to stand, I did it on my own this time. I was getting stronger, more coordinated.

I sucked in a gust of air. My chest felt tight and my new lungs burned. I guess it was their very first deep breath.

I endured a coughing fit, then looked at both of them. "I need a uniform."

After a few minutes, I was dressed and able to stand unaided without looking like a Saturday night drunk.

"Can I talk to you privately for a second?" I asked Anne. She nodded at the orderly, who disappeared.

"Is this regrow legit?" I asked her when he was gone. "No half-rotted brew of plasma? No bad grows?"

"That's right. You're as good as you've ever been."

"Do they really stamp a number in your cells?" I asked her. "What?"

"A counter—you know, to identify you and indicate how many times you've been regrown."

"Oh…" she said. Her face looked troubled. "How did you hear about that? We're not supposed to talk about it."

"The Nairbs told me."

Anne shook her head and laughed. "How do you get into these things, Recruit?"

"I have a gift. What about your people? The bio-squad. Are you guys going to leave me alone now?"

"I heard you had a little trouble with some of my colleagues after you managed to lose and then destroy a revival machine. Do you know how much those things cost? I think they want to forget about you."

"No charges, then?"

She shook her head. "Prosecution wouldn't be wise for the Legion. You're a hero now."

I pushed off the wall I'd been leaning against. I could stand comfortably now. In an hour or two, I knew, I'd be as good as new—literally. I adjusted my kit in a streaked mirror hung near the door. The door sensed I was thinking about leaving and intelligently swished open.

"McGill?" Anne called as I turned to leave.

I looked back at her. "Try not to make any new enemies, okay? I put in some good words for you. But you will always need us. When you are at your worst, your weakest we'll be there. That's not when you want to see the face of an enemy."

321

I nodded. "Thanks for the warning," I said. "Tell your colleagues that when the lizards break in and start eating everyone in the bunker—that's when you need my people."

It wasn't my most diplomatic speech, but she didn't seem to be offended by it. In fact, she seemed to like my new, uncompromising attitude. She smiled faintly as I left.

Putting one boot in front of the other as I walked down the long, long corridors of *Corvus* felt like a journey of countless miles, but it only took a few minutes. When I reached Centurion Graves' office, I put my hand on the key-plate and it opened immediately. Graves must have set it to recognize me and let me in.

"Ah, there you are McGill!" he said. He wore a twist of the lips I didn't recognize at first. He was smiling with half his mouth. I couldn't recall ever having seen him smile before.

I stepped into the office and had a look around. Almost everything was steel, but there were skins on the walls—big ones. I couldn't make out a single species. They were mostly gray or mottled brown, but there was a black one as shiny and curved as a beetle's back. In fact, that's what I thought it was: the shell of a huge insect. I wondered where Graves had gotten them all.

"Admiring my collection?" the Centurion asked. "You'll have one of your own someday if you keep up the good work."

I rotated my neck slowly, taking it all in.

"I don't know why you're happy with my performance, sir," I said.

"Because you did what no one else could do. You won the day."

"That's not what the Nairbs told me. They said we'd lost the challenge. The saurians won—unless they changed their minds."

He shook his head vigorously. "That never, *ever* happens. Once a Nairb makes up his mind and makes a judgment call, they don't reverse it."

I frowned. "Then we've been kicked off the planet? We lost the contract here and the neighboring worlds?"

"Not at all. Sure, we lost the battle. But we won where it counts—in fact, *you* won for us."

322

"I understand you're happy with my performance, even if you have a strange way of demonstrating it. But I have no idea what you're talking about."

"The revival units, of course. The Nairbs checked the imprints, and you were right. It's all in their report."

"But sir, if we lost the battle…"

He lifted up a single finger and held it near his face.

"Yes. We lost the key battle. But we won Steel World by forfeit. Sheer genius on your part. Surely, you can't stand there and tell me you have no idea what you've done?"

I was baffled. But it's in my nature to bluff it through in situations like this. Just ask my parents and professors.

"Of course I know what I did: I gave them the evidence. I showed them that the lizards were using revival technology. But the Nairbs said it didn't matter, since we were using it too."

"Ah, I see," said Graves. "At that point, you felt you must have failed. Well, you didn't. You see, the Nairbs don't just do body counts. They check into every detail, every nook and cranny. They found a violation that disqualified the saurians."

"A violation? You mean they cheated?"

"Worse," Graves said excitedly. "They violated patent laws! The Nairbs investigated and demanded to see their revival units *and* the receipts for their purchase. There was no paperwork, no licensing—nothing. The saurians pirated the tech. They probably got hold of one of the units and copied it as best they could. We now suspect that they wanted our revival unit not only to deprive us of its use but to study it and copy its advanced design."

I was finally beginning to get it. We'd lost—but the saurians had been declared cheaters. They'd broken Galactic Law and been disqualified. We'd won by forfeit. But I was still mad about being blown up arbitrarily.

"I still fail to see why you had to kill me after my victory. If I'm a hero, didn't I warrant a pick-up?"

Graves twisted his face into a look of disgust. "Such whining… I hadn't expected to hear this from you, McGill. We're grown-ups in this legion. We fight, we die—and then we fight again. It's no big deal. Besides, I was told you were operating on a bad grow. You should be happy to have a fully functional body again."

"I still don't see why—"

"Suck it up, McGill! We won the war, and you helped materially in achieving that goal. That's the job of every soldier in this legion. What do you want? A parade? Flowers?"

"Flowers would be nice, yes."

Graves snorted and shook his head. I could tell there weren't going to be any flowers.

Somehow however, his attitude made me less upset. In his eyes, I was being a baby. Right or wrong, it helped to understand that. I had to wonder how many times he'd died, how many years he'd fought for Legion Varus—and how many hard decisions he'd had to make.

For the first time since I'd been revived, a ghostly smile appeared on my lips. I realized I should be basking in the light of victory, and I felt better.

"So it wasn't all for nothing," I said, musing.

"Certainly not. We still hold the contract to this world and all its neighbors. The work of Legion Varus is never easy, but we always get the job done."

I looked at him and frowned again. "But sir, did you *really* have to launch a missile and blow me up?"

Graves huffed and shook his head. "You sound like Harris. Really, McGill, as a heavily equipped legionnaire on our next campaign, you shouldn't be so sentimentally attached to the corpse you happen to be residing in at the moment. It's unseemly."

"Heavily equipped? I'm going to be a heavy trooper, with armor?"

"Not just that. Every recruit is considered for advancement to heavy equipment after their first campaign. No, I'm recommending you for training as a weaponeer. I've reviewed the reports, and I was impressed by your improvisation with the equipment."

I stared at him for a moment. Internally, I was thinking that it hadn't been all that impressive. All I'd done was use the plasma tube as a reptile tongue-depressor. But when you're being promoted, it's best not to downplay your accomplishments.

"Nothing to say, McGill?" Graves asked stiffly. "You've been honored, man. Congratulations."

I really didn't know what to say for a moment, but then I had it: "Thank you, sir."

Those words didn't come easily for me. I could still see that missile arcing down to obliterate my body, and I still felt a twinge of that sick feeling left over from knowing I was about to die—again.

-34-

When I finally reached my quarters on Deck Nine, I was attacked from behind. Hands grabbed my elbow. Whoever my assailant was, I considered this opening move to be a mistake.

I stopped, planted my right foot and threw myself backward into him. I felt him fall back. Before we even hit the deck, I drove my elbow into a hard gut. It was unarmored, but muscular enough.

My attacker grunted and wheezed. The hands released me. I rolled to my feet, ready to fight. In my mind, I suspected the bio people, trying to finish their work before too many officers got used to seeing me around the ship again.

But when I looked down, I saw Carlos rolling around and groaning. He had his hands over his belly.

"Great way to greet a comrade," he said.

"You should know better than to grab a soldier from behind. Don't you know I was fighting for my life with an army of lizards an hour ago?"

"Yeah…a bad call, I admit."

I helped him up, and he recovered quickly. "I wanted to surprise you," he said.

"You achieved your goal."

He laughed, and we walked into our quarters. I was surprised to see no one was there—no one except Natasha. I smiled when I saw her. She'd put on a little make-up or done her hair, or something. I wasn't sure what it was, but she no longer looked like one more grunt in the squad.

"Where is everyone?"

"Special request from above," Carlos said, grinning. "You've got the place to yourselves."

He closed the door behind us, and I looked around in surprise. The barracks were usually pretty crowded. We kept it dark at night, as per regulations, but there was rarely much in the way of privacy. If two people wanted to be intimate, finding a spot for it was always a challenge.

Natasha was still smiling at me. She looked down shyly when I returned her stare. I walked forward and took her hand.

"Is this your idea?" I asked her.

"Yeah, sort of. It was everyone's idea."

"What's the occasion?"

"You know what you did. You beat the saurians—single-handedly, if you listen to Carlos."

"Hardly," I said. "I was just in the right place at the right time—or the wrong place at the wrong time, depending on how you look at it."

"But that's not why I'm here," she said. "I'm here because they tell me I would have been permed if it wasn't for you. You went down that tunnel and found those lizards and got my data back. I've got a new body because of you."

I smiled. That part was true, and I didn't try to deny it.

"I like this kind of gratitude much better than the variety Graves dishes out," I said.

We talked quietly for a time, and I told her she didn't have to do anything she didn't want to, but we got around to it in the end. When I was drifting off to sleep, the rest of the squad returned to the barracks and filed in. They made jokes and tossed pillows at us, but I barely cared.

* * *

At roll-call the next day, I was ordered out of line. Veteran Harris trotted away, and I followed him, double-time.

327

I wondered what this was all about. Foolishly, I thought perhaps I was in line for another accolade of some kind. The last two surprises had been good ones—what was next?

I was disappointed when he turned and headed for Blue Deck. I called for him to halt and talk. He ignored me and didn't stop until we were left waiting for a lift.

"Veteran? I don't think it's a good idea for me to get close to the bio people right now."

"Pissed them off bad, didn't you, kid?"

"Yes sir. I really did."

He chuckled. "Serves them right, those self-important ghouls. But this is out of my hands now. The brass is up there, waiting for you—including the primus. They've lodged some kind of complaint."

"What should I do, vet?"

He shrugged. "I don't know. Maybe you could ram a big gun into her face, like you did with the lizard down planet-side."

Harris laughed then, and I failed to join in his amusement. I decided to play it cool and dumb. I'd see how far that got me, then I'd go for evasiveness.

As I thought over these moves in the elevator, I felt my heart sink. This wasn't going to be an easy crowd to fool.

I stepped past the guards, orderlies and bio specialists. As I passed by, everyone who saw me stopped talking and stared. They didn't grind their teeth, but there was a certain cold curiosity in their eyes. I was a patient who'd stepped beyond the accepted boundaries. I was not one of them—and somehow, I knew I never would be.

I was led into a quiet conference room with muted light and a very high ceiling. I realized I didn't have any weapons with me. I glanced over to Veteran Harris, checking out his sidearm.

He noticed this with that extrasensory perception of his and coughed. When his hand came down from his mouth, it came to rest on the butt of his pistol. To me, the message was clear even though our eyes did not meet: I wasn't going to get his weapon away from him.

Primus Turov herself stared at me coldly. Her hands were steepled, and she had the same look on her face she'd had

328

when she'd ordered me to be permed before. Somehow, I knew she'd never liked me since that day. I was an aberration. A walking, talking dead man. She'd passed judgment upon me, and I'd somehow evaded it. I could tell by her cold, dead eyes that she intended to fix that error.

To her right sat Centurion Graves. He didn't look happy or upset. His face was stone. But I was happy to see him there, as I thought he had to be in my corner. He'd argued on my behalf before, and right now, I really needed a friend among the officers.

The last face present was the least pleasant of the bunch. It was none other than Bio Centurion Thompson, the queen of all James McGill haters. I wondered if she'd somehow begun to remember the details of her murder, or if others had put it together for her. She was my real enemy in this room—I was sure of that much.

"This conference is now in session," the primus announced.

I stood at attention at the end of the oval conference table. No one had invited me or Harris to take a seat. I stared at the wall above the officers' heads, tried to look cool, and hoped for the best.

"James McGill," she said officiously. "You stand charged of murder—again. But this time your victim was human and an officer. How do you plead?"

"I'm sorry Primus," I said. "Who am I accused of murdering?"

With a nod, she indicated Centurion Thompson who was doing her best to burn me to ash with her eyes.

"I'm sorry—but I must plead not guilty."

"On what grounds?" the Centurion interjected, earning herself a frown from the primus, which she seemed to miss entirely.

"Grounds, sir? You're sitting right here, clearly alive and well."

Graves cleared his throat. "Murder is still possible, despite the revival of the victim. If the act was performed, justice must be served."

I was beginning to feel heat rising in a ring around my neck. I wanted to open my shirt, but I remained stock-still.

"May I receive counsel?" I asked.

Graves and the primus exchanged glances.

"This is a military proceeding," Graves said. "We're following Hegemony Law, subservient to Galactic Law. I'm acting as your counsel, and the primus is the final arbiter."

This didn't fill me with confidence. I quickly glanced from one of them to the other. None of their faces had an ounce of sympathy in them. With Graves, I knew that didn't mean he wasn't pulling for me. He was as expressionless as a lizard most of the time.

"Is self-defense permissible as a defense?" I asked.

"It is," Graves answered.

"Then I claim self-defense," I said as calmly as I could. "The Centurion attempted to use deadly force on me, and I responded in kind."

"You don't have any evidence!" complained the bio.

I finally looked at her. "I have two witnesses. The orderlies. I looked up their names and contacted them last night. They know what was in that syringe. They know who had the skill to prepare such a dose of poison and who didn't."

This took her by surprise. She opened her mouth then closed it again. "I don't know what you're talking about."

I was, of course, bluffing. I hadn't contacted anyone. I'd been lying low, hoping this would all be swept under the rug. But she didn't know that.

Graves leaned in for the kill, staring coldly at the bio Centurion. "A syringe? You claimed you were strangled. We'll have to have an inquest."

"No," she said suddenly, dropping her eyes. "I—that won't be necessary. I'll drop the charges if he does."

Graves nodded approvingly. "Very adult of you. Under battlefield conditions, I've found many people lose their sense of judgment and proportion."

She looked pissed but nodded.

Graves now seemed slightly pleased, but not the primus. She was annoyed. That's when I knew Turov was still gunning for me.

"There is another issue," she said. "You, James McGill, are supposed to be dead."

"Everyone in Legion Varus dies now and again," I said, quoting Graves. "It's part of the job."

"That may very well be, but they aren't often executed for violating Galactic Law."

Our eyes met, and I knew there was no love lost in this woman. She was still upset that Graves had revived me.

"What's done is done," Graves said calmly. "Let's move forward. We have a capable soldier here, and we can go home and apply his unusual talents to a new campaign. I hear there's a newly colonized world in the Cerberus system and the locals can't agree who owns it. New contracts are our lifeblood. If we—"

"I can't let this go, Centurion," the primus said, cutting him off. "We're exposed, here. Not just you and I. Not just Legion Varus. All of Earth is threatened by what McGill did. He's undisciplined and a danger to everyone. Most importantly, the Galactics think we executed him—permanently. If they or the Nairbs figure out that didn't really happen—"

"I understand, Primus," Graves said. "But they won't. The Galactic didn't forward a formal complaint up the chain. He conferred with us, and witnessed his will being carried out. The event can be forgotten by all now."

The primus shook her head slowly. Graves was frowning, and the bio was smirking.

I could see the problem as it grew. I had two enemies and one friend on a committee of three. Those were not good odds.

"I'm afraid we'll have to err on the side of caution," the primus said. She looked at me coldly. "We appreciate your fighting skills, Recruit. But you must be put down as initially ordered. Surely, everyone here can see that. The risk for the Legion is too great otherwise. And, may I say, speaking for all of Varus, that you have our condolences. Now, let's put the matter to a vote."

"I vote nay," said Graves immediately.

The primus turned to Centurion Thompson. She managed not to grin.

"The situation is unfortunate, but I must agree with the primus on this occasion. I vote yea."

"I also vote yea," said the primus. "A verdict has been reached. The accused shall be—"

"I want to appeal the verdict," I said quickly.

"Appeal?" asked the primus. She seemed amused. "We're lightyears out into space. We're no longer orbiting Cancri-9. Every Hegemony Law states we have full jurisdiction—'we' meaning the officers of Legion Varus. There is no higher body to appeal to."

I was sweating now but determined. "I wish to appeal to the tribune," I said.

Graves gave me a slight nod of approval. He lowered his head and quietly worked his tapper.

The faces of the two women darkened. The primus paused, seemingly to consider my appeal. She took a deep breath, heaved a sigh, and said: "No. I'm sorry. There is merit in your request, however—"

"Excuse me, Primus," said Graves. "I'm sorry as well—but I've already relayed the request to the tribune."

"You did *what*?"

"I assumed, since this is a capital case, an appeal would be automatically honored. I'm sorry if I overstepped my authority. I simply wanted to get the case concluded quickly. Should I message the tribune and rebuff him? He has expressed interest in the matter."

"He wants to join us? When?"

"Immediately."

The primus stared at Graves, and he stared back at her. Although she didn't glare at him, I could tell she was highly displeased.

"All right then," she said. "We'll do it your way. We'll wait for the tribune."

We didn't have to wait long. The tribune showed up within a few minutes. I was impressed. Graves had to have a lot of pull to get the man down here from the command deck so fast. After all, the tribune had several primus-level subordinates and over fifty centurions to worry about. As a recruit—I was almost beneath notice.

The tribune looked small compared to Graves and I, but he carried himself with quiet confidence. You could tell he was in charge of the situation the moment he stepped into the room.

He didn't answer the chorus of greetings from the officers. Instead, he looked at me, Graves, then the primus. He nodded, as if confirming a suspicion.

"Don't let me stop you," he said, taking a seat at the side of the oval table. "Carry on."

There was a moment of uncomfortable silence as Primus Turov cleared her throat, worked on her tapper and shuffled a computer scroll that was stretched out on the table in front of her. "Well, we've been discussing the fate of Recruit James McGill. Really, it's an embarrassing situation."

"Embarrassing for whom?" asked the tribune.

"For Legion Varus at large, I would say. This man killed a Galactic—one of a species we'd never encountered. What a grim first-contact that was for all involved. He was subsequently sentenced to be executed for his crimes. The Galactic involved witnessed the proceedings and left, satisfied. No further charges have been filed in the matter by the Galactic, fortunately."

The tribune had begun to frown, and now his frown had deepened. "Let me see if I understand you: a Galactic was murdered by one of our troops?"

"Yes."

"And why was I not informed of this diplomatic breach?"

The primus cleared her throat. "We handled it as quickly and quietly as we could. It was an accident, after all, and the Galactic in question was not permed. He was offended but mollified by my quick action."

"I repeat: why was I not informed?"

"The matter is complex and not easy to—"

"Enough," said the tribune. The primus looked shocked at being shut down, and her voice trailed off.

The tribune turned to Graves. "Explain what happened, Centurion."

"The situation played out essentially as Primus Turov explained."

"Why was I not informed?"

333

"I assumed the primus was operating with your approval. I had no idea she had not informed you, sir."

If looks could kill, the centurion would have been struck dead by the primus' eyes. But he seemed to take no notice of her and feigned great interest in his tapper.

"I have a recording of the proceedings involving the Galactic here, sir," Graves said. "Should I transfer the video to your account?"

"By all means."

Primus Turov, who'd been angry, now looked alarmed. "You recorded the interchange?"

"All trials are recorded. It is standard procedure."

"This wasn't a formal trial—it was a very delicate matter! One which I handled to the satisfaction of everyone."

The tribune looked annoyed. Already, his tapper was receiving the video. He reviewed it while the rest of us sat in stony silence.

"Hmm," he said, nodding his head. He turned to me. "I see you weren't satisfied by the verdict, Recruit. You attacked your superiors in the final moments."

I was still standing at attention. "I was taken by surprise, sir. I felt I was the one under attack and threat of death. I took what I saw as appropriate action."

The tribune nodded again. "Appropriate action... Just as you did when you met up with the Galactic, eh? Also, another thing occurs to me. Why are you standing here talking to me if you were executed days ago?"

The primus leaned forward, seeing an opportunity. "That's why we are here, sir. Centurion Graves took it upon himself to revive this murderer, defying my orders."

"Murderer?" asked the Tribune. "I've heard that term tossed about liberally today. What makes this man a murderer?"

"First, he killed the Galactic," she said, ticking off her fingers. "Then he attempted to kill me when I ordered him executed. Finally, he murdered this centurion from the bio unit."

"Centurion Thompson? Ah, now I see why you're present. He murdered you?"

334

"Yes," she said angrily.

I was becoming angry myself. In my mind, I hadn't murdered anyone. I opened my mouth and began to make a retort, but Centurion Graves jumped into the conversation.

"If I may, sir," he said. He held his hand up toward me, and I shut up. It wasn't easy, but he had been my superior for some time now, and I managed to control myself. "This committee has already ruled the demise of Centurion Thompson to be a case of self-defense as she was threatening him with deadly force."

"Is that true?" the tribune asked Thompson.

She looked defensive. "I don't actually recall. My mind wasn't backed up. But the fact is, I died at his hands."

"And so you want him permed?"

"I want justice to be done. This man is dangerous."

The tribune eyed me seriously. "You know what I see here? I see a natural born killer. A man who takes action without hesitation. A man who defeats his enemies, and defeats death, with regularity."

He held up his hand to stop the protests that had begun.

"We need people like James McGill. Don't you two see that? Legion Varus is a rough outfit. Many have tried to tame this legion and all have failed. I'm displeased with all of you—except for the recruit. It is your job to guide and nurture the natural attributes of the recruits Earth sends us, not to perm anyone who annoys you. Let me remind you that we need people who think outside the box—people who win against the odds."

Everyone was silent for a moment. The tribune stood up and began to pace. He put his hands behind his back and walked around the room, passing behind the other officers. Even Graves looked uncomfortable.

"I'm overturning your ruling, Primus. But against my better judgment, I will not demote you. Not this time."

"What? Demote me? What possible—"

"Not for perming a promising recruit, that's bad, but insignificant compared to your other violations of legion policy. You did not inform me of the incident with the

Galactic. That kind of matter is beyond your office—hell, it's beyond mine, as well. I should really inform Hegemony."

Primus Turov met his eyes. She nodded as if in sudden understanding.

"But you won't inform Hegemony, will you?"

"No," he said. "And that's why I'm letting you off. The shit-storm would be tremendous. I feel the same reluctance you must have felt to kick it upstairs. I'm going to bury it, and you will all swear to bury it with me."

"Consider it done, sir," Graves said.

The other officers agreed quickly. But then their eyes all fell together upon me.

I shrugged. "What Galactic? I don't remember any such thing."

I'd meant it as a joke, but they all nodded seriously.

"Keep in mind," the tribune continued, "despite our silence, this might not be the end of it. The Galactics often pause for a long time—even years—before deciding to proceed on an issue. The Empire is unbelievably vast. There are more layers of bureaucracy than we can even imagine. Our best scholars and contact-specialists tell us their decision-making process is slow and ponderous—but it is also very thorough. Just because they haven't raised the issue yet doesn't mean we're in the clear."

"Perhaps we should carry out the original sentence properly," the primus said, seeing an opportunity.

I felt my gut twist. The woman wanted to see me dead at all costs.

The tribune shook his head. "It won't matter. Galactic Law doesn't work that way—no legal system does. You can't shoot someone and then throw away the gun, hoping that simple act will absolve you of your crime. The Galactics think of humanity as a single entity. Anything done by any member of our species inflicts guilt upon all the rest. The charges will be against all Earth, not an individual, if they come."

The meeting adjourned on that troubling note, and we each went our separate ways.

336

* * *

We exited the ship months later, riding lifters down into the atmosphere. Coming home on leave was strange. We carried our rucks to the terminal where we were surprised by a waiting throng of relatives and friends.

My parents hugged me, and my mom cried. It was strange to see them again. I'd been out in space nearly a year. How could I go back to sleeping on their couch after I'd been killed over and over again on another world?

I decided in the end that I'd just do it. That was how you returned home: you just did it. Thinking too much was never a good idea when dramatic changes were thrown at you.

None of the old friends I'd left behind had ever heard of Legion Varus, but they were impressed anyway. They were even more impressed when I told them stories of battling lizards, dying in combat, and breathing canned air for a year. Everyone knew about Cancri-9. They'd all played the game *Steel World*, and they couldn't believe I'd fought there for real.

After a few days, squaddies from my unit began to contact me. We all had similar problems: we felt a disconnect with our families and old friends.

Carlos put it best, I thought: "They're all a bunch of wannabes and lamers."

Yeah, that was about right. I met him at a bar in Philly, and we drank like we were still aboard ship. A few others joined us, including Natasha, and for a time it was like we'd never been apart.

"How long do you think we have?" I asked finally, breaking the jovial mood for everyone.

They stopped laughing and stared into their beer mugs.

"I heard they have a new contract already," Natasha said. "They're just dickering about the price."

I nodded, having heard the same thing. Legion Varus always had a job to do out in space. There was always another mess to be cleaned up, another rival to be put down.

337

I wondered where I would be next year. Since the question was impossible to answer, I up-ended my brew and guzzled it all down.

Books by B. V. Larson:

UNDYING MERCENARIES
Steel World
Dust World
Tech World
Machine World
Death World
Home World
Rogue World
Blood World
Dark World
Storm World
Armor World
Clone World
Glass World
Edge World

REBEL FLEET SERIES
Rebel Fleet
Orion Fleet
Alpha Fleet
Earth Fleet

Visit BVLarson.com for more information.

Made in the USA
Coppell, TX
09 October 2023

22629155R00190